PASSIONATE

Imagany! Charismatic. Beautiful. Fiery. Strong. She's inundated with raw passion and sex appeal. Men are drawn to her sensuality and her erotic ways. **Imagan**y temper the hungry, raging fires that dw to love. Passion and pleasure have their perfect place in her life.

Driven to success, Imagany must learn one of life's hardest lessons: True love exacts a price and all the accolades in the world cannot take the place of a deep burning love.

POWERFUL

Elliott! The dynamic, gorgeous "strong black man" who enters Imagany's life. With his character, his intelligence, his strength, and his love, he surpasses all stereotypes. **Elliott!** He leaves an indelible mark upon a woman's life that cannot be erased. Imagany quickly learns that a woman has never been loved until she's been loved by a man like Elliott Renfroe.

PROVOCATIVE

Imagany and Elliott! Their hearts match and their wills clash in an explosion of fireworks and canonry. Life for the two of them will never be the same. Together, they must discover that true love and happiness can only be attained when they forego their Preconceived Notions about life, love, passion, and one another.

**Experience ecstasy! Experience passion!
Experience...Preconceived Notions!**

Preconceived

Notions

by

Robyn Williams

Lushena Books, Inc.
1804 West Irving Park Road
Chicago, IL 60613
(773) 975-9945
E-mail: Lushena@aol.com

Printed in the United States of America.

ISBN 1-930097-01-8: $12.95

Library of Congress Catalog Card Number: 99-073775

Fourth Printing: 1999

Dedication

This book is lovingly dedicated to all those who dare to follow their dreams.

Special thanks is extended to my mother, Shirley Williams, for her indomitable strength and faith; to Chanette Beasley, my lifelong best friend, for believing in me every time I failed to believe in myself; to the wonderful Monnie E. Morris, for her unfailing ability to uplift and encourage; to my New York buddies Robin Frazier-Teele and Sheryl Geiger, for challenging me to dream bigger dreams; to Judy Gentry, a powerful beacon of light at Tennessee State University; to my godmother, E. Christine Sherard, for teaching me that it truly is better to give than to receive. To Prophetesses Juanita Bynum and Cecillia Love, thanks for undergirding me while in the trenches of faith. Together, these women are the strongest sisters I know.

Lastly, a huge note of gratitude to a wonderful friend whom I'll miss dearly: the incomparable Ms. Phyllis Hyman; to Les Brown, The Motivator; to renown musician Najee for his "Day by Day" album; to Terry McMillan for her *Disappearing Acts*. And finally, to Pastor Tom Bynum and Bishop Arthur M. Brazier, two special and true Men of God. All of you inspired me to relentlessly pursue my dreams.

Acknowledgment

It is with exceeding joy that I acknowledge my Lord and Savior, Jesus Christ, without Whom none of this would have been possible. It is truly Him who gives us the faith as well as the ability to triumph over every adversity in life.

I thank You for making my dream, *Preconceived Notions* (the book and the movie), come true.

Prologue

hyllis Hyman appeared on stage. Her very presence spoke volumes; her beauty was enough in itself. The small crowd waited expectantly, their faces flushed with excitement. And then it came. At first a flutter, maybe a sigh, but suddenly a melody full of soft whispers and strong husky undertones was faintly heard. The first note sent shivers down every spine. The audience was hypnotized. She made love to them as she whispered, crooned, touched and caressed them with her voice. Rich, deep, throaty, velvety to the ear, her voice was a web of brown sugar and honey molasses.

She sang of the pain and heartbreak every woman feels with the loss of her man. A deep sorrow emanated from her voice. Every woman present identified with the emotions her song evoked, every man present wanted to comfort and assure her that he would be the one whose love would never fade or die. There wasn't a man amidst the crowd who could have resisted her, and Phyllis knew it. Her hips were well rounded as she sat on the stool. The long sleeved, silver-sequined dress had a deep "V" neckline which cupped and emphasized her large breasts. A shapely leg protruded from a thigh-high slit in her dress.

Her skin was light cocoa brown, her nose finely chiseled, and her cheek bones strong and prominent. Her lips were full and sensuous. Glittering highlights showed in her thick shoulder-length black hair, which was crimped and parted on the far right side. Phyllis Hyman could only be defined as beautiful. As she hit a deep note, she gripped the microphone with both hands and dipped her upper body toward the floor. Her hair fell forward to frame the right side of her face, only to fall back into place as she lifted upright again. She was graceful as her body swayed softly from side to side. Her right hand gripped the microphone as her left hand rose slowly above her head. With her fingers pointing straight out, her hand wavered slowly from left to right, only to ball into a slow fist as a new wave of emotions hit her. And all the while, the melody continued to flow from her body.

Her head was thrown back now. Her neck craned to accompany the strong notes which she belted out. As she dipped backwards on her seat, she kicked her leg out and arched her body in unison. The audience was in sync with her every move. Slowly, an inch at a time, she circled on the stool, making eye contact and giving everyone a full view of herself. She eased off the stool and placed the microphone in its stand. With her feet spaced wide apart, she stood tall in her matching silver three-inch heels, putting her curvesome body on full display. The men strained to get a better look.

She lifted her hands to the audience, as if pushing them away. With her eyes closed and her head turned to the side, she started moving her hands in slow circular motions as her body rocked to the rhythm of her song.

The crowd was mesmerized as her entire body swayed sensuously with the music. Phyllis Hyman was a woman who knew how to captivate her audience. She cradled the microphone between her hands and crooned into it. As the tempo slowed, they knew she was nearing the end of her song and the crowd groaned with regret. Her voice fluttered and wavered on the last note, stretching it for as long as possible. The people, not wanting the song to end, spurred her on.

Holding the note for as long as she could, Phyllis finally released it to a whisper. The song ended and the crowd sighed audibly, tension leaving their bodies. So entranced and enamored were they that they needed a few seconds to gather their thoughts. And then they erupted into a round of applause, showing their appreciation with a standing ovation.

For many in the crowd, tickets had been hard to come by. But Phyllis had captivated them with her performance. The money spent had been well worth it.

One man in the crowd had another reason for coming. He had come to even an old score and to reclaim what was rightfully his. As the cheers and rounds of applause for Phyllis Hyman subsided, the man spotted the person he was looking for and deftly made his move across the crowded floor . . . .

Part One

Chapter One

magany Jenkins was a sophomore in college when she first met Elliott Renfroe. A student at Fisk University with a double major in business and journalism, she was the kind of girl who took her studies seriously.

Imagany was perceived by many as standoffish. But the few who knew her well simply thought of her as a solitary person who valued her privacy. Preferring to keep to herself, she avoided all the parties and pledging hoopla that was typical of most college campuses. She had done so much partying during her high school days that she developed a severe case of burn out. She was quite cynical about attending functions where the primary purpose was to preen and be seen.

She was also one of the few students who elected to live off campus as opposed to sharing a dormitory room. Many of her peers recognized her because she drove a candy apple red convertible BMW, a luxury most students could not afford.

But Imagany would have been noticed anywhere she went. She had an exotic look that caused people to do a double-take. She was five feet eight inches tall and walked with a confident stride. Her skin color was a tawny gold. Her thick, shoulder-length hair was the color of mahogany. Her eyes were brown and her facial features were strong with thick eyebrows, long eyelashes, a pointed nose, lips that were full and sensuous, and a cleft in her chin. Together, the impact was startling. Her body was shapely. Long and lean. Muscular, yet feminine. Her breasts were full, her waistline small, her hips flared sensuously and her long and shapely legs were perhaps her best asset.

Imagany was charismatic and possessed a heightened sense of sensuality. Her calm demeanor was a plus and she appeared mature well beyond her years.

The day she met Elliott, she was on her way to see Caprice McKnight, her lifelong friend who was studying to become a gynecologist at Meharry Medical College. Imagany smiled as she recalled some of the scrapes the two of them had gotten into as children growing up on the south side of Chicago. Who would have guessed that some twenty years later they would still be best of friends?

Imagany parked her car in the visitor's parking lot and headed for Meharry's co-ed dormitory. Passing through the double doors, she went straight to the visitor's counter. All guests were required to sign in while the receptionist called to inform the person that a visitor was waiting in the lobby.

Two students were sitting behind the counter. Sheena Dixon talked on the phone while Kerby Menard studied from a medical book.

"Can you ring Caprice McKnight in room 402?" Imagany asked her.

"Sure," Sheena replied.

Imagany walked to a nearby bulletin board, well aware of the appreciative look that the guy was giving her. He was cute, she thought, but he wasn't her type.

She was studying the flyers pinned to the board when she heard the entrance doors open and close. She watched as a tall man walked through the door and headed toward the counter. The guy behind rose from his chair and the two greeted each other by placing fists together.

The man was not aware of Imagany as she stood off to the side, but she was very much aware of him. He was dressed in faded denim jeans with a white sweat shirt that had Chicago Bulls written in red across the back. Studying his physique as he leaned over the counter, she definitely liked what she saw. The girl behind the counter gestured to her.

As she drew closer, Imagany eyed the man's rear and thighs. She appreciated how nicely built he was, but wondered if his facial features matched his overall image. As she moved closer, she saw that he was even taller than she first thought. He was a good six-four. She walked up to the counter trying to get a better look, when Mr. Chicago Bulls himself, turned in her direction. She looked into his face feeling as though someone had knocked the wind out of her. In slow motion Imagany thought, *"Somebody, please! Hold my hand! Does this man look good or what?"* She knew she was staring rudely and could only imagine how odd she must appear. The only thought registering in her brain was how fine the man truly, truly was.

He was ruggedly handsome. His skin was a dusky paper-bag brown. His jawline was covered with a light stubble, just the way she liked it. He had broad shoulders, a wide chest, and muscles that wouldn't quit. Imagany stared at him like a hungry dog eyeing a morsel of food. The only thing missing was saliva dripping from her mouth. His jeans fit him so well that she had to force herself to banish the thoughts that were suddenly running through her mind. The man even had eyes she could get lost in. Staring at him in a daze, she was powerless to stop the stupid kool-aid grin that spread across her face. Somewhere in the recesses of her mind, Imagany thought she heard someone clearing their throat.

"Your friend in 402 says for you to come on up," Sheena said sarcastically. Out of jealousy she wanted to tell Imagany to close her mouth before a bug flew in it. She, too, had been eyeing the man. She had even gotten off the telephone to give him her undivided attention. Sheena had to repeat her words three times and was about to get catty.

Unconsciously, Imagany reached over the counter to take the pass from the girl's hand. But her eyes never left the man's face. She didn't know why she was acting so foolishly. It was not like her to get excited about a man in this manner. She was used to men getting excited about her. She took a deep breath and mentally tried to gather her wits. She realized her hand had been groping in the air when Mr. Chicago Bulls took the pass out of the other girl's hand and placed it in hers.

"Thank you," Imagany told him in a voice that surprisingly sounded clear even to her own ears. The man had completely taken her by surprise! Imagany was embarrassed by her silliness and tried hard not to let it show. She knew that she was acting like a typical love-struck kid and wondered where her cool demeanor had disappeared to.

"You're welcome," the man replied with a twist to his lips. He had watched her approach out of the corner of his eye. The way she walked, how could he not? When he turned to get a full look at her, his only thought to himself was that God must have been smiling when He created her. She was gorgeous and the effect she had on him was swift. He stared into her brown eyes and finally realized what people meant when they said that the eyes were windows to the soul. He had to physically restrain himself from caressing the cleft in her chin. Placing the pass in her hand was only a means to keep himself from boldly touching her.

The smile on her face was catching as he extended his hand to shake hers.

Mechanically, Imagany placed her hand in his. His skin was as warm as his handshake was firm. As his hand closed over hers, the calluses on his palm caressed her skin. Big hands and long fingers. *My goodness! Every woman knows what they say about men like this!* Imagany felt her knees go weak.

"Hi, I'm Elliott Renfroe," the man said in a deeply amused voice.

Nothing could have snapped Imagany out of her trance-like state. Nothing except hearing the amusement in his voice. Imagany felt even more ridiculous as she tried to pull herself together. Because she was embarrassed, she suddenly decided to wipe the smile off the man's face. Snatching her hand from his before she melted, Imagany inclined her head in his direction. In a voice full of cutting sarcasm she said, "Good for you."

Instead of telling him her own name as he expected, she stepped to the side and walked past him to the bank of elevators down the hall. Imagany snickered to herself as she imagined the surprised looks that must be on all their faces. She didn't dare look back. The man probably had women throwing themselves at his feet all day long. She berated herself for drooling over him in the first place.

Inside the elevator, Imagany's hand was still warm where his had caressed hers. She flexed her fingers, enjoying the tingling sensations that lingered. She admitted to herself that she would have liked to have gotten to know him better. That face, that voice, that body, those hands! *Whatta man!* As Imagany stepped off the elevator, she shook her head regretfully and tried to console herself with the thought that Elliott Renfroe was probably just another conceited, brainless hunk.

Elliott had admired the way the girl's hips moved as she walked away. When she left without introducing herself, his expression had been one of curiosity. He could only wonder what had ticked her off. He turned and asked the girl behind the counter, "Was she a friend of yours?"

Sheena shook her head. She would have given anything to have him show a similar interest in herself. Maybe if she lost weight, got a weave, fixed her crooked teeth, ditched her coke-bottle glasses and got some hazel contacts, she could . . . .

"Have you ever seen her before, Kerby?"

"No. Not at all." Kerby knew that if he had seen her, he definitely would have remembered her. "She sure didn't look at me the way she looked at you. Who knows, maybe you'll run into her again." Kerby reached into his wallet to return the money he owed Elliott.

"Maybe so. I've got to run so I'll catch you later." Elliott slipped the money into his pocket and headed for the doors.

Caprice McKnight was sitting at her desk reading from a stack of medical journals when Imagany entered the room. Tall and willowy, Caprice was dark-skinned and extremely attractive. With her long hair, deep-set dimples and large doe-like eyes, men found her sexy and alluring.

Her room was cluttered with clothing and books. Imagany set her own book bag on the floor and climbed to the top bunk bed that belonged to Caprice. She lay on her side with her head propped on her elbow, staring at all the pictures of Phyllis Hyman plastered to the walls.

"Caprice, do you know someone named Elliott Renfroe?"

"Uh, uh," Caprice murmured, still deep in thought.

Her noncommittal reply did not dissuade Imagany from speaking further. Soft and slowly, Imagany sang the words, "I'm talkin' 'bout a strong black man!" The phrase was sung in a lilting voice that deepened when she reached the words "strong black man." Caprice's head jerked and her attention was immediately captured at the mention of anybody who was such a specimen. She turned from the desk and faced the bed.

"Did I hear you say something about a 'strong black man'? " Caprice spoke with her hands on her hips and her neck stuck out for emphasis.

Imagany now had her full attention. She sat up and dangled her feet over the edge of the bed. She held her right hand in the air and waved it back and forth as if to testify. "Talkin' 'bout a strong black man!" Imagany's neck rocked back and forth while her body gyrated to emphasize her words. The phrase was a private joke shared between the two of them. They used it to describe brothers whom they considered handsome and sexy. In their minds, a "strong black man" was one who could satisfy a woman righteously.

Suddenly all ears, Caprice got up and stood directly in front of Imagany. With her hands on her hips, she said, "Child, tell the story!"

Imagany explained to Caprice what had taken place in the lobby, even telling her about the stupid leer she'd had on her face. She topped her story off with a description of how she walked away leaving Elliott standing at the counter looking stupid.

"Wait a minute," Caprice said, looking down at the floor with a puzzled frown on her face. She held her hand up in a stop-sign gesture and said in a very slow voice, "You mean to tell me you walked away and left the brother standing there without giving him your name and your digits?"

"Yes, Caprice, I had to. He . . ."

"Wait, wait, wait, hold it." Caprice raised her hand again and paced the room like a trial lawyer trying to get the facts from a reluctant witness. With slow emphasis, she turned to face Imagany. "You said the man was tall, didn't you?"

"Yes."

Waving her hands using dramatic motions, Caprice asked in a voice that clearly indicated her confusion, "And did you not say he was fine?"

"Yes." Imagany's exasperation was obvious.

"And didn't you say the man was loaded?" Caprice asked imploringly, using their terminology for any man who had a large penis.

"Yes," Imagany replied, feeling as though she would never get the chance to explain her side of the story.

"Correct me if I'm wrong, but you did say the brother was 'strong,' right?" With her left fist pressed close to her chest, Caprice slowly extended her right arm out in front of her with the fist balled. She quickly snapped it back level with her chest. This movement, similar to a quick salute, was their trademark for the term "strong black man."

"Yes," Imagany replied with exasperation.

As if speaking to a dunce, Caprice said loudly, "Then my sister, forget about introducing yourself," her voice rose to a hysterical shriek. "Why didn't you get the man's number for me?"

Imagany laughed. She had begun to feel as if she acted too hastily by not getting Elliott's number. She grabbed a pillow and threw it hard at Caprice. "Witch!"

Laughing as she dodged the pillow, Caprice said, "Seriously, I don't know him." She added mockingly, "But, dahlin', if I should run into him, I'll let you know!"

Needing to be on her way, Imagany jumped down from the bed and prepared to leave. Caprice put on her shoes to walk Imagany to her car. Even before they reached the ground floor, Imagany wondered if Elliott would still be standing at the counter. Her heartbeat quickened at the thought of seeing him again. When they entered the lobby, her eyes immediately sought the people at the counter. When she didn't see him, she experienced a rush of disappointment.

"Get over it, kiddo," Caprice said in a knowing voice. She could tell what Imagany was up to.

Imagany could only laugh at having been caught looking for Elliott. It was funny how well Caprice knew her.

When they reached her car, she unlocked the door and got in. She pressed the button and rolled down the window on the passenger side, but instead of leaning inside, Caprice unlocked the door and slid into the car seat. Imagany could tell that Caprice wanted to ask her something. "Spit it out. What is it?"

Deciding not to beat around the bush, Caprice looked Imagany in the face and said, "I want you to tell me the truth about Anthony."

With a deep sigh Imagany started the car and turned on the air conditioner. She didn't want to discuss Anthony. Nothing positive ever came out of their conversations about him. Anthony was her lover, and he had been for the past two years. He didn't like the fact that she chose to have her own apartment instead of living with him. Lately, he had been pressuring her to marry him. Imagany was grateful to Anthony. He was a generous man who had done a lot for her and she owed him much in return. But not marriage. She didn't love him. She cared about Anthony, but not enough to marry him. She didn't care how much money he had. She was young; she knew she had her whole life ahead of her and she wasn't about to settle down with someone just because they could pave the way for her.

Caprice objected to the relationship because Anthony was in his forties while Imagany was only twenty-one. To her, the fact that Anthony was old enough to be Imagany's father was a turnoff. Caprice felt that any man his age who stooped to dating someone so young must be screwed up in the head. She couldn't understand why he didn't just date someone in his own age group.

But Imagany didn't see it that way. To her, Anthony was just a means to an end. She simply thought of him as an older man who enjoyed being in the company of younger women. Anthony was kind and considerate and treated her better than anyone she had ever known. That he was a very unselfish person only stacked the cards in his favor. She figured that he still dated women his own age and it was not a problem for her. While it was true that he was the only man she was dating, she told herself that this was only because she had yet to meet someone her own age whom she was really interested in. In the meantime, she saw nothing wrong with being with Anthony. And if he wanted to buy her things, like a brand new BMW, then why should she object? Besides, if it wasn't her that Anthony was with, then it would damn sure be somebody else.

Imagany folded her arms behind her head and leaned back against the headrest. "Caprice, there's nothing to tell that you don't already know. I keep telling you your fears about Anthony are completely groundless. I can handle him."

"Imagany, I'm just worried. I mean, what if this guy decides that since you're not going to marry him, he'll take this car back. Forget about the car, what about everything else he's given you? What if he takes all that back? Then where will you be?"

Sitting up, Imagany faced her. "Reese, look, you know I'm here on a scholarship. Yes, Anthony does give me money. Yes, Anthony does buy me expensive things. But if the bottom dropped out today, I could still make it. And Anthony's not going to take this car back, no matter what happens. That's why he bought it in my name and gave me the title. Besides, if I'm forced to, I can always get a part-time job at UPS or someplace else." She turned and faced the dashboard, clasping her hands over the steering wheel.

Softly Imagany said, "I know you don't approve of my relationship with Anthony, but in this one instance, I'm not asking for your approval. I have to look out for numero uno, Reese, and no one's in a better position to do that than me. You don't have to worry, I'm not going to change my mind and suddenly decide to marry Anthony. It's just that I don't want to be with someone who can't do for me. Anybody I'm with has to be doing just as well as me, if not better."

Caprice interrupted her, "I just don't want to see you hurt."

Imagany raised her hand and turned her head to the side. "I know that." Turning to look at Caprice, she said, "But I also know that you feel I'm using Anthony, and maybe I am. What you don't understand is that," she paused, searching for the right words, "I don't want to be like multitudes of other women. I want a man who can do for me. What's wrong with that? I choose to be with someone who can inspire me, someone who can lift me up. I don't need someone leeching out of my pockets. I don't have much but whatever I do have, Anthony is more than welcome to it. I don't need Anthony to make it. That's why I'm here at Fisk getting an education. I'm ensuring my future so that I can make it on my own."

She turned and stared out the window. There was a long silence in the car. Finally Imagany spoke again. "All my life, I said I never wanted to be like my mother, dependent on some man to give her this or give her that, to take her here or take her there. Like it or not, she's tied to someone who's holding her hostage. Never again will I wake up in the middle of the night to the sounds of a man pounding on a woman. With God as my witness, that will never be my fate."

As flashbacks of her father assaulting her mother passed before her eyes, tears began to trickle down Imagany's face. She shook her head and said, "I want to be the one who's in control of my life. And the only way I can ever do that is by having my own." Imagany wiped her eyes. "So don't worry about me as far as Anthony is concerned. Believe me, things have a way of working themselves out."

Caprice stared straight ahead reflecting on her own memories of their childhood. She could remember many times when Imagany would come to school or to her house with marks all over her body. Caprice knew first hand what Imagany and her sister, Zabree, had gone through as children. She could recall once having spent the night over Imagany's house when Mr. Jenkins attacked Imagany's mother. As a child, Caprice had had nightmares for days after. She still shuddered when she remembered the sudden violence of it all and how, as children, they had called the police. Afterwards, her own parents had forbidden her from ever returning to Imagany's house. It wasn't until they had reached adulthood that Caprice could even get Imagany to talk about the incident.

Caprice was sorry she had even brought Anthony's name up. She hadn't meant for the conversation to take such a morbid turn. She reached out and grabbed Imagany's hand and they sat for awhile, just holding hands, neither one speaking.

Suddenly, Imagany laughed. She withdrew her hand from Caprice's to remind her of a happier time in their childhood. Caprice laughed along with her as she remembered, too. But Caprice knew that this was just Imagany's way of eluding all the hurt and pain which she had suffered as a child. Imagany's mood swings were not uncommon to Caprice. She recognized them for what they were: just a means of trying to escape a pain-filled past.

Chapter Two

n Nashville, an early morning fog sets in, bringing with it a lingering chill. But by mid-morning the sun is out, the sky is clear and the city is ablaze with heat. On one such sweltering day, Imagany was driving down White Bridge Road with her convertible top down and the wind whipping through her hair. She made quite a picture as she drove by and caused more than a few heads to turn. Imagany was accustomed to such looks and indifferent to the curious stares.

She was nearly late for dance practice at Tennessee State University where her dance group was rehearsing for an upcoming production. Imagany had been one of ten dancers selected to join the dance team. The selection process was long and grueling and the dance steps were rigorous. For Imagany, the competition had merely been a challenge. Dancing was her favorite pastime. She'd started dancing as a child and had continued when she discovered how quickly it became her primary focus. Dance was an artful way of expressing her emotions. She could forget herself when she danced and the high she experienced afterwards was better than any drug.

She parked her car in the rear lot behind Tennessee State's gymnasium and was about to dash inside to the waiting coolness, when she decided to close the roof of her car. As she closed the top, she noticed the TSU football team practicing downhill from where she stood. They were starting to disperse and some of the players were heading uphill in her direction. Imagany made a sucking noise with her teeth as she waited impatiently for the top to close. She didn't want to be around when any of the football players reached the area where she was. She was not in the mood for the catcalls and whistles she knew would be forthcoming. By the time she finished locking her car, several members of the team had already reached the parking lot.

TSU's gymnasium was located at the top of the hill and there were about sixty stairs leading to its entrance. Grabbing her bag, Imagany began a steady jog through the parking lot until she reached the steps. Swiftly, she took them three at a time. She enjoyed climbing stairs and often did it as a form of exercise.

The coolness of the gymnasium provided a welcome relief from the heat. She walked past the bleachers to the open space where the other dancers were limbering up. Quickly removing her sweats and sneakers, she stripped down to her white lycra spandex suit. The pants reached her waist level while the top, which was sleeveless with a square neckline, left her midriff bare. The outfit molded to her hourglass shape. Her hair was pulled back into a French braid down the middle of her head and her face was free of all make-up except a light shade of red lipstick. She made quite an imposing figure as she joined the other members in the circle, oblivious to the admiring stares of both males and females.

The dance instructor, Judy Geiger, was a formidable woman. She was a difficult taskmaster known to be exceedingly hard to please. One look at Ms. Geiger's lean, muscular body and people knew they were going to be in pain by the end of the day. Students who were not majoring in dance only took her classes if all other physical education classes were closed. Ms. Geiger was a stickler for perfection, but the shows she produced were grand performances. She stood now in the middle of the circle clapping her hands to bring the group together.

"Okay, people, practice is only going to be sixty minutes today, so let's use the time wisely." She snapped her fingers in her no-nonsense manner and shouted, "Positions everyone!"

The dancers formed two circles, one consisting of four people sitting closely together, and a larger one of six people surrounding the group of four. The inner group sat huddled together while the outer group kneeled in fetal positions with their feet tucked beneath them, their chests resting on their knees, their chins touching the floor and their arms at their sides.

A slow African medley sounded and the outer group of dancers slowly began to stir. As each outer dancer shifted from side to side, they raised their chests and arms only to lower them again, as if they were worshiping an idol. The inner group began to rise. Their heads fell forward on their chests and their arms were like dead weights. Suddenly, the music's tempo quickened and the wild beat of African drums filled the air. The inner dancers' heads snapped up and their arms shot outward. Next, the outer dancers rose in unison and together all dancers leaped and lunged creating an explosion of movement. Their bodies twisted and turned like flowers in the wind. Their arms flowed together and their chests touched teasingly only to quickly withdraw in broken movements. The melody was as wild as the beat was strong and the dancers stomped their feet and flapped their arms as they whirled and twirled in a flurry of motions.

Just as slowly as the dance had begun, the tempo slowed, and the inner circle drifted together to clasp hands while the outer dancers joined again to form their outer circle. One by one, the outer dancers began to drop into their fetal positions leaving the inner circle standing. The inner members huddled closely together with clasped hands and slowly lowered themselves to the ground in their original positions. The music dwindled to an eerie silence and all the dancers remained still.

When the dance ended, the bystanders began to applaud. Judy stepped forward, fingers snapping angrily as she called the dancers to her side. She was not entirely satisfied with the dance routine. They gathered around her as she fired out criticisms, instructions, praise and advice.

When the dance routine began, members of the football team were idly strolling by at a short distance from where the dancers were practicing. They knew better than to interrupt; Ms. Geiger was also known for her wrath. Many stopped to watch the entire dance session, but some looked for a while and then continued on their way. Those who could afford to stay were treated to an extravaganza.

Elliott Renfroe was among the members of the football team that stayed behind to watch the entire dance sequence. He had been one of the first to reach the top of the hill when he saw a flash of white jogging by. Something about the person's movements reminded him of the girl he had met at Meharry. He had quickened his step to catch up with her but slowed when he saw her take the stairs at such a quick pace. Elliott was tired from hours of football practice and didn't have the energy to catch her.

He entered the gym heading straight for the locker room when he spotted a group of girls in lycra suits. Thinking they were the TSU band dancers, he was about to keep walking when he saw Imagany stretching with the others.

Elliott stopped in his tracks. It was her, all right. His stomach muscles clenched as he watched her flow through a series of quick graceful movements. His mouth opened in a silent gasp as she leisurely lowered herself into a Chinese split. She bent her chest to the floor and slowly crawled forward. Her curving movements reminded him of a snake. It wasn't just the movement itself that was arousing, it was her. She made limberness seem natural. Her movements were so quick and effortless that he felt like he was watching a contortionist. In one flowing movement, she snapped her legs together and rolled over, only to come up on her knees and gently fold into a fetal position.

More members of the team joined him in his examination of the dancers. He heard his teammates comment that if this was just their warm up, they couldn't wait to see the dancers' actual routine. When several of the players singled out the girl he was watching, Elliott experienced a sense of possessiveness. Again he was struck by her. But this time he noticed that she had a way of drawing people to her. When the dance began he watched eagerly, feeling a wealth of emotions as the dancers went through their movements. When it ended, he clapped even louder than the rest of the people standing around. Afterwards, he wanted to draw her attention, but hesitated when he thought of how grungy he must appear. He headed for the locker room, intent on showering and freshening up. Although he was bone tired and had much studying to do, Elliott intended to return before the dancers left. Only this time, he'd be damned if he'd allow her to get away without telling him who she was.

***

Imagany was exhilarated after the dance was over. She was breathless, but far from tired. Her pulse raced, her senses were alive and her body felt pumped. She had been so involved in the dance, that it took her a moment to become aware of the applause and the curious stares of the people standing around. Noting that the majority of the onlookers were football players, Imagany paid them no mind.

As it turned out, she was not in the next sequence that Ms. Geiger wanted the dancers to rehearse. Imagany sat cross-legged with her back against the wooden bleachers. Larry Teele, the only male dancer in the group, came and sat down beside her.

"You were good," Larry said. Coming from him, it was a compliment. Imagany knew him to be a stickler for excellence.

"Thank you. So were you." Imagany was about to ask him a question when he said, "I wanted to ask you if you would like to do a solo with me." Then quickly, before she could interrupt, "I've already cleared it with Ms. Geiger."

Imagany stared at Larry and he turned away before he lost himself and wound up saying something stupid. He had selected her for the solo because he admired her gracefulness, liked the way she moved, and above all, because he felt that there was something special about her. As attractive as she was, she didn't come across as conceited.

Imagany's thoughts had drifted to when Ms. Geiger had asked her if she would like to perform a solo. The dance instructor had even given her permission to select her own dance steps. Imagany's heart had almost burst in her chest knowing this woman had that kind of confidence in her. It was as if she had received a rare gift.

After what seemed like a long pause Imagany said softly, "I'd be honored to dance with you, Larry. Thank you for asking me."

Feeling awkward, Larry jumped to his feet and held his hand out to her. "Come on, let me show you some of the moves I have in mind."

Back in the locker room, Elliott shed the rest of his gear and rushed into the first available shower stall. His intent was to quickly clean himself up and slip away from the locker area unnoticed. He wanted none of the usual locker room banter where teammates lolly-gagged and shot the breeze before eventually straggling off to their destinations. He toweled himself dry, quickly brushed his hair and hurriedly threw on his clothes.

Several teammates slapped him on the back as he made his way toward the exit.

"Good game, Froe. You should play like that every day." Elliott was quarterback for the team and they considered him the man with the golden arm.

"Man," another teammate addressed the one who had just spoken, "the day Froe plays like that on a daily basis will be the same day you go get them rotten, twisted up teeth of yours fixed." Laughter spread around the room as they continued their jocular bantering. However, Elliott moved steadily towards the exit, hi-fiving players along the way. All he wanted was to depart without any unnecessary delay. He had almost reached the safety of the doors when someone shouted his name.

"Hey Renfroe! I want to see you in my office before you leave!"

Oh, no! Not Coach Hadley! Please let it be anybody but Coach Hadley, Elliott thought dejectedly. He groaned out loud as he slumped against the wall. Whenever Coach Hadley wanted something, the person knew he was in trouble. Hadley was extremely long-winded and had a way of stretching out stories for hours.

Several players threw up their hands in a "what's up" gesture as they walked past Elliott. Others punched him in the shoulder, giving him a "better-you-than-me" smirk.

"See you next spring, Froe."

"Yeah, man, we'll tell the folks in the cafeteria not to close down 'til midnight, 'cause that's what time your black ass is gonna be here 'til." More laughter as they all passed by him.

"Damn, Froe! If it wasn't for bad luck, yo' ass wouldn't have no luck at all." Elliott's teammates shook their heads at him as they left the locker room.

Walking backwards, Elliott held up the middle finger on both of his hands, flipping them all the bird sign. He turned and walked back to Coach Hadley's office, trying to concoct some urgent excuse as to why he could only stay a short while.

"Close the door Renfroe, this won't take long." Coach Hadley's voice bellowed from behind his desk. Now Elliott really knew he was in for it. The old "this won't take long" routine usually meant that it would be at least an hour or two before Hadley tired of the sound of his own voice. Elliott pulled up a chair and sat in front of the coach's desk. Hadley proceeded to give him pointers on how to improve his game. He laced each suggestion with a different story of how, back in his day, things were different.

As Hadley droned on, Elliott began to tap his fingers against his thigh and constantly watch the clock. He tried several times to put an end to the coach's story but Hadley merely skipped over anything Elliott said by adding a new twist to his tale.

Just when Elliott thought he couldn't take any more, Coach Hadley wound down. "You see, Renfroe, I thought it best that I pull you inside to tell you how proud I am of you."

Proud? Elliott wondered what Hadley was talking about. He had long since tuned the coach out. Whatever Hadley was referring to now had gone in one ear and out the other.

Hadley continued. "The fact that your dad and I were college roommates at Grambling has nothing to do with it. It's just not often that we get a student who excels in the game the way you do and then doubles as an engineering student, and an honorary one at that. You're an exemplary student, Renfroe, and you're making this school look mighty fine."

Elliott didn't know what had brought all this on, but he decided to seize the moment. "Coach, you've always been a good mentor to me. And not just to me, but to the other guys as well. So, it means a great deal to know that you have such pride in my game. You have my word that I'll do my best not to let you or the school down."

Hadley's chest swelled as Elliott stood to shake his hand. Damned if the boy wasn't the spitting image of himself when he had been Elliott's age!

Elliott released the coach's hand, said he had something important to do, and quickly headed for the door before Hadley could think of another story to tell.

When Elliott reached the safety of the outer area, he breathed a sigh of relief. He had been in Hadley's office for well over an hour. He doubted if any of the dancers would still be practicing. Music drifted to his ears as he walked closer to the area where the dancers had been rehearsing. He drew closer and heard the unmistakable sounds of the renowned instrumentalist, Najee. Elliott recognized the title cut from Najee's "Day by Day" album. It was a slow jazz tune interlaced with occasional vocals. He saw two people dancing and had only to see the flash of white to know that one of the dancers was the girl he had met at Meharry. He walked closer to them and sat on a nearby bench, not wanting to interrupt but certainly wanting to be a spectator. Elliott leaned forward with his elbows on his knees, becoming totally entranced by the dance.

Her partner was the same male dancer Elliott remembered seeing earlier. He spun her around and she twirled in circles before stopping with her arms outstretched, her head lifted high. She seemed to be inviting a lover to come to her. In one swift move, her partner reached her side and lifted her up in the air. He held her there gazing up at her before letting her body slide down the length of his.

She seemed to melt into him. As the sound of Najee's clarinet filled the gym, she slid to his feet twisting her body around his legs before he spun away leaving her lying there. She rose gracefully and moved to stand in front of him turning her back to his chest. She leaned back into him, her head hanging to one side. He tilted her body toward the floor and she raised her leg as if doing a split in air. Her partner grabbed her extended leg and lifted her around him so that her legs were wrapped around his body. She sat on his chest and bent her body backwards with her arms trailing the floor. His hands encircled her waist and he spun her around several times before setting her on the floor. Again she spun away from him only to run back to him and slide on the floor between his legs. He reached down, gracefully pulling her up to meet him, twisting her around so that her body shaped itself completely to his. She lifted her arms to slowly entwine them around his neck and with his body fitted to hers, they spun in a series of circles. They moved together lightly, seeming to float on air.

When Najee's "Day by Day" ended, it was followed by "So Hard to Let Go," "Gina," "That's the Way of the World" and "Tonight I'm Yours." Their dancing continued nonstop. Each song flowed into the next before Elliott realized that they were dancing unrehearsed. They were creating their own litany of movements as they went along. They were so graceful together that Elliott envied the rapport they had with one another. He had never been a fan of ballet or modern dance, but in this one instance, he wished it was he whom she danced with. What Elliott didn't know was that though she wasn't dancing *with* him, she danced *for* him.

Imagany was conscious of Elliott from the moment he sat on the bench. Although she never made eye contact with him, she could feel how intensely he watched her. Unconsciously, her movements became more pronounced, more sensual, until she finally became aware that she was trying to express to him that it was he whom she danced for.

When the last song ended, Imagany was drenched in sweat. She and Larry both were out of breath as they stood facing each other with their hands on their hips. "Larry, I think we're going to be pretty explosive together."

"I think we're already pretty explosive." Larry's breath came in short gasps.

"I guess that means all we have to do is select which song we're going to dance to. Since it's your solo, you pick." Imagany tilted her head to the side.

"You're the mastermind who selected Najee, so you decide."

"Then let's make it either 'Day by Day' or 'That's the Way of the World,' " Imagany replied.

As they debated which song to use, Elliott rose to make his way out of the gym. From the way they danced and stood together arguing, anyone could tell they were lovers. Though disappointed, Elliott was glad he had stayed to watch the dance. At least now he could stop wondering if he would ever see her again. But he was not about to stick around and be the third man. Besides, he was tired and definitely had other things to do. Elliott quickly strolled away with an angry feeling inside him, realizing that his anger stemmed from disappointment. He had reached the exit and was pushing the door open when someone called out his name.

When Imagany finished talking with Larry, she turned only to find Elliott gone. She spun around looking for him and saw him heading towards the exit doors. Before she knew it, she'd called out his name. "Elliott!"

Imagany had thought about him constantly since that day in Caprice's dorm. She had even come to regret not introducing herself. Seeing him now was too much of a coincidence and Imagany knew she could not let him leave without saying hello.

As she approached him, her eyes took in all of him from head to toe. If he was a dream, surely she didn't want to wake up.

As she leisurely walked up to him she asked softly, "Did anyone ever tell you that it's bad manners not to speak to someone when they greet you?"

Elliott leaned against the door with his hands in his pockets. Finding it hard to believe that she was standing before him, he experienced a mixture of emotions. Anger, jealousy, and most notably, a curious sense of relief.

"No," he answered. "But I do know it's impolite not to return someone else's introduction." Elliott made a point of reminding her of how she had walked away from him before.

Imagany laughed as she extended her hand. "I apologize for that. I was having a bad day. I'm Imagany Jenkins. Don't tell me, you're Elliott Renfroe." They shook hands for the second time. But unlike before when she had nearly fainted, Imagany was prepared for his touch.

"Imagany." Elliott repeated her name. She had pronounced it similar to "mahogany" and he liked the way it sounded. "I see you have a good memory."

"Actually, it's a selective memory." Though she really wanted to ask him why he was leaving so suddenly, she realized that she would have asked him anything just to keep him from departing. "Did you enjoy the dance?"

"I thought it was very. . ." Elliott paused as he searched for the right word, "exciting. I didn't know dance could be so wonderful." Standing before him with the sweat beading on her body, she looked good enough for him to eat. Again, he found himself having to resist the impulse to touch the cleft in her chin.

"How come I've never seen you practice in here before?" Elliott ravished her with his eyes.

"We usually practice in the Hall Building but they're doing some renovating there so we had to come here instead." Deciding not to let him get away, Imagany said, "Will you come with me so I can get my things?" It was more a statement than a request.

Elliott would discover that directness was a typical trait of Imagany's. At that moment he would have gladly followed her to hell and back. But instead, found himself idly walking beside her as she went to collect her belongings. She rambled in the bag for her warm-up suit and slipped it on over her dance outfit.

As she stepped into her pants, Elliott tried unsuccessfully not to openly stare. "You must have just started here."

"Nope, I'm a Fiskite." She slid her arms through the sleeves of her jacket and zipped it up. "What about you? I would have thought you attended Meharry."

He shook his head. "TSU all the way."

Elliott's eyes fixed on some point behind Imagany and she turned to see what he was staring at. Larry was leaving the gym and was signaling good night. "See you," Imagany yelled as she waved up to him. When she turned back to Elliott, he had a curious look on his face.

"Is that the Mister?"

"Excuse me?" Now it was Imagany's turn to look curious.

"Your friend," Elliott nodded his head in Larry's direction. "Or should I say your boyfriend?" He stared at her intently.

Imagany's eyes widened and her hands flew to her hips as it suddenly dawned on her. "Is that why you left so abruptly?" Her voice was filled with disbelief. "Wait a minute, Elliott. You were going to walk right out of here without acknowledging me because you thought Larry and I were. . ." Imagany's voice trailed off as she waved her hand back and forth searching for an appropriate word. Finding none, she said, "Why, that's one of the silliest preconceived notions I've heard in a while."

Elliott laughed at the look on her face. "Okay, so I jumped to conclusions. But the way you two were standing there having a lover's tiff, I thought he was your man." Elliott was on the defensive as he shifted from side to side.

"Lover's tiff?" Her eyebrows raised as she shook her head. She told him in a playful voice, "I don't know if I can forgive you for this." She folded her hands across her chest and looked up at him mockingly as if debating whether or not to forgive him. "No, I don't think so. This has been too much of a shock for me." She put her hand over her heart to signal how much pain she was in. "I don't think I can recover from this, Elliott." She shook her head and turned her back to him as if she were under a great deal of emotional stress.

Elliott burst out laughing at her theatrics. She looked so cute to him as she pretended to be angry. Unable to help himself, he put his hands on her shoulders and turned her around to face him. They stood gazing at one another. Elliott put his hands in his front pockets and Imagany stood with her arms folded across her chest. They felt so comfortable together, as if they had known each other a long time.

Finally, Elliott said softly, "Okay, I was wrong and I apologize. How can I redeem myself?"

"My, but don't we apologize so very humbly," she told him in a teasing voice. "I'm not sure. I'll need some time to think this one over."

She shook her head with a sorrowful expression on her face. "Until then, it looks like you'll have to remain in my doghouse."

This was the first time in Elliott's life that he had ever been happy about being in someone's doghouse. He smiled as he said, "I see right now that I'm going to have to do everything humanly possible to stay in your good graces."

She picked up her things. "That's true. I should warn you though that it's not an easy task to accomplish. I've been known to be very hard to please."

Elliott grinned, "I look forward to the challenge. Can I start digging my way out of the doghouse by giving you a ride up to Fisk? My car is parked by my dorm."

"No, I'm driving. And besides, I'm not going to make it that easy for you. To get out of my doghouse, you're going to have to dig a lot harder than that."

"You're a tough lady, huh? Then may I walk you to your car?" He reached out and took her bag to carry it.

"Hmmmm, that's a start." Imagany smiled as she led the way to the parking lot.

"So who's the Najee fan?" Elliott asked as he held the gymnasium door for her to exit before him.

"I am. You like him too?" Imagany asked.

"Certainly, I used to play the clarinet myself."

"No way," she said unbelievingly. "A big guy like yourself with a little clarinet? Incredible," she told him jokingly.

"Hey, watch yourself," Elliott said as he pretended to be offended.

Outside, a soft, warm breeze stirred the air. Nighttime had arrived. The darkness was broken only by the occasional lamp posts which were placed around the area. Imagany lead the way down the stairs feeling as light as a feather.

When they reached the bottom of the stairs, the parking lot was deserted of all cars but for hers and two others. Walking backwards in front of him, she asked, "So which song did you like best?"

"On the Najee tape?"

"Yeah."

"Well, the entire tape is great. But 'Day by Day' and 'Gina' are my favorites." When they reached her BMW, Elliott stopped in his tracks.

"This is your car?" He looked at her with an expression of disbelief on his face.

Imagany got in and started the ignition. Elliott was still standing there looking surprised when she rolled down the window and said, "Excuse me, sir, but can I offer you a ride somewhere?"

Shaking his head, he kneeled down and looked into the car. "Did anyone ever tell you that car theft is a felony in the state of Tennessee?"

She unlocked his door with a smile on her face. "I knew my parole officer forgot to tell me something when I got out of jail."

Elliott looked at her with a doubtful expression on his face. "I'm not sure if I should get in this car with you, Imagany."

Imagany laughed outright at the look of uncertainty on his face. "Look, knuckle head, it's my car, so get in."

"Knuckle head?" As he climbed into the car, Elliott couldn't believe he had heard her right. This was one shock after another.

"No offense, it's simply a term of endearment," Imagany told him as she put the car in reverse and pulled off.

"You mean you call everybody 'knuckle head?' " Elliott had to get the facts straight.

"Only special people."

"I see." Elliott looked around, impressed with the car's interior. "The woman can even drive a stick-shift." He felt beneath his seat to find the lever that would allow him to adjust his seat.

"There's no lever," Imagany told him. "The button's on the arm rest."

"Now I'm really impressed."

"Don't be." Imagany smiled as she turned to look at him. With his handsome features and broad shoulders, he was definitely going to be a positive addition to her car. She removed the Najee tape from her portable radio and slipped it into the car's cassette player. The smooth sounds filled the car. "You'll have to show me how to get to where you live."

"No problem," Elliott said as he gave her directions to his dormitory. He was impressed despite her telling him not to be.

When they pulled up in front of his dorm, people passing by strained to get a look at who was in the BMW. Like it or not, Elliott knew that as soon as he got out of her car, the fellows were going to give him the third degree about whose car he had been in and who he had been with.

Imagany read the lettering on the doors. "Athletic Dorm? I guess I should have known. What sport do you play?"

"Football," Elliott told her proudly. "I'm the quarterback." He gave her a challenging look.

Imagany didn't have the nerve to tell him what she really thought. Her impression of most athletes was that, intellectually, they didn't quite have it all. From his speech, she could tell that Elliott was certainly no dunce, but she would have pegged him as anything but a jock. Imagany was disappointed.

Elliott didn't want to leave the confines of the car. And despite her new found reservations about him, Imagany was not ready for him to leave either.

"So tell me, Imagany, when I depart from this car will I ever see you again?"

Najee's "So Hard to Let Go" was playing now. The music flowed throughout the car. They had their own private barrier against the outside world. Imagany leaned her head against the seat and stared straight ahead. She mentally weighed the pros and cons of becoming involved with him, questioning whether she really needed the headache. She turned to stare at him only to find him watching her closely with an intense look upon his face. Their eyes held as she gazed back at him.

She thought it best to be honest with him. She would just tell him about Anthony and explain that she was not looking for someone else to get involved with.

She stared into his eyes. "Elliott," her voice trailed off when his hand reached out and his thumb gently caressed the cleft in her chin. The rush of heat that washed over her body was instantaneous. She felt it down to her very core. Her speech was caught in her throat and no words would come forth. Good God! The man had only touched her chin. What in the world would happen if. . .

"I've been wanting to do that from the first moment I saw you." Elliott's voice was so low Imagany could barely hear him.

Unconsciously, Imagany's hand tightened on the knob of her stick shift. She stared into his face as if memorizing every detail. She noted the thickness of his eyebrows, the length of his eyelashes, the way the tips of his nose flared and the fullness of his lips. She had a strong urge to run her palm across the stubble on his chin. It had been a long time since a man had ignited sparks in her like this. And even longer since she had met someone whom she felt could even begin to stoke her flames.

The pact was sealed. Without saying a word, Imagany reached into her glove compartment and handed Elliott a pencil and pad. Elliott jotted down his phone number and placed it into the palm of her outstretched hand.

"Don't lose it, Imagany." He opened the door and got out.

"I won't, Elliott. That's a promise from me to you." Imagany's voice was low and husky.

Elliott closed the car door and watched as Imagany drove off. He anxiously wondered how long it would take her to call him.

Chapter Three

he phone rang incessantly as Imagany wrestled with the key in the door. Damn! She had forgotten to turn on the answering machine. Dropping her bags on the living room table, she ran to snatch up the receiver.

"Hello," Imagany breathed heavily into the phone.

"Where the hell have you been? I've been calling you for the last three hours." An irate Caprice was on the other end.

"Caprice, sometimes you can be worse than Anthony. I had dance practice, knuckle head. Remember?"

"Jeez. I thought practice was only for an hour," Caprice said with a trace of annoyance in her voice.

"Yeah, well," Imagany paused as she bent down to remove her shoes. "Larry, one of the dancers, asked me to do a solo with him. So we stayed afterwards to practice. Plus, I stopped off to get some Chinese food. And now I'm ravenous. So listen, kiddo, let me jump in the tub and then call you back. Besides, I've got a story to tell you."

"Ooh, child! Tell me now before you go," Caprice begged.

"Can't. It would take too long." Overriding more pleas from Caprice, Imagany said, "See yaaaaaaa." She hung up before Caprice could keep her any longer and took the phone off the hook.

Inside the bathroom, Imagany drew her bath water and poured in a fair amount of Chloe bath gel. Tying her hair on top of her head, she smeared her face with moisturizer. The tub was filled with bubbles and her body thanked her as she stepped into the warm, scented water.

She raised the sponge over her body and squeezed it, letting the warm water slide down her chest. The water felt refreshing as she continued to let it trickle down her body. Elliott's image came to her mind and her hands froze in mid-air. Deciding not to fight it, Imagany let her imagination have free reign.

She pictured Elliott's strong neck and broad shoulders, his muscular arms and his big, long-fingered hands. Imagany's knees raised to her chest and her hands clasped themselves between them.

As a deep languor came over her body, Imagany closed her eyes, leaned her head back against the inflatable pillow and sank deeper into the tub. She pictured Elliott standing naked above her peering down at her in the tub. She stretched her hand out and ran her wet fingertips over the muscles of his calf. Her hand inched its way up his strong, muscular thighs and her lips opened invitingly as she reached out to grab him.

Imagany's eyes fluttered open and she shook her head to redirect her thoughts. It would be so easy to bring herself to an orgasm, right here and now. But she couldn't afford that tonight. Whenever she pleased herself in that manner, it drained her of too much energy. The only thing she could do afterwards was fall gently asleep. She had homework that had to be completed. An orgasm was a luxury she could not afford.

Stepping out of the tub to avoid further temptation, Imagany dried herself off and rubbed down with Chloe body lotion. She donned her favorite nightgown, a black satin teddy with laced edges. Imagany wasn't expecting anyone. This was just part of her normal routine, part of loving and caring for herself.

She was starving by the time she heated her Chinese food. She carried her food and water into the living room and set everything on the table. One last item was needed to put the final touches to her meal. She went to her stereo to find it. Rummaging through her collection of tape cassettes, she found her all-time favorite. She slipped it in and pressed the play button.

"There's a spark of magic in your eyes,
Candy land appears each time you smile . . ."

The soulful sounds of Phyllis Hyman cascaded around the room and Imagany sank blissfully to the floor singing "Betcha By Golly Wow." Once full, she reached over to set the phone down next to her. No sooner had she done this than the phone rang. It was Caprice, of course.

"Look, girlfriend, I want the goods, and I want them now."

"I was just about to call you," Imagany explained.

"Good for you. Just think of it as my having saved you some spare change. Spit it out."

Imagany took a deep breath. "Well, remember the guy I met in your dorm a few weeks ago? The one I drooled over?"

"Yeah. What about him?" Caprice asked impatiently.

"I saw him today."

"Get out of here. Where?" Caprice slurred her words together, saying "gedouddahere."

"He was up at Tennessee State while I was practicing. He stayed to watch the rest of the dance session and then I gave him a lift back to his dorm. That was it." Imagany shrugged her shoulder, ready to talk about something else.

"Wait, back up. He goes to TSU. He watched you dance. He jumped in your car. Then you took him home. No, excuse me, you drove him back to his dorm. Imagany, who the hell do you think you're talking to? I want the dirt. Like what happened in between him watching you dance and him jumping in your car."

"Caprice, nothing happened. There is no dirt. It was all very innocent. Really."

"Look, can you let me be the judge of that? Just tell me what happened."

Imagany was at a loss for words. Finally, as if speaking to a numbskull, Caprice said, "Okay. Let's start over. How old is he? What year is he in and what's his major?"

"Caprice, all I know is that he's a football player."

"What! A football player! You? Ye who swore that all athletes were born without brains? Well I'll be damned. The girl must be losing her mind. I have got to see this man."

"Will you listen? I only gave him a ride back to his dorm." At this point, Imagany was even trying to convince herself of this.

On the other end of the phone, Caprice was shaking her head. "All I know is that from day one, you've had this concept that all athletes were dodo birds. And now, suddenly, you're telling me that what you believed for years is simply a preconceived notion? Again, all I can say is I've got to meet this man. What's his name again?"

"Elliott."

"Right. So when do I get to meet Mr. Elliott?" Before Imagany could answer, Caprice said ponderingly, "You know, I've said it time and time again. All it takes is for a woman to meet a strong black man and the next thing you know, not only does she forget all the principles she's ever stood for, but she loses her mind! Child, again I ask, when do I get to meet this Elliott?"

"You know something, Caprice, you are totally corrupt. I can't introduce you. I don't even know him myself. The man only gave me his phone number."

"Tell me about it," Caprice dryly interrupted.

Imagany continued, "All we did was have a perfectly innocent conversation and then I left. That was it. Thank you very much."

"Uh, huh. Just wait 'til Anthony finds out about this innocent conversation."

Imagany admonished her threateningly, "You'd better not utter a word."

"Dahlin' my lips are sealed. Anyway, it's time you had some young, fresh stuff. After being with Mr. Geritol, at least this one will get your blood pumping again. I've just got one question."

"What?" Imagany asked warily.

"Was the brother still strong?"

Imagany answered without hesitation. "Awww Reese," she groaned. She lay on her back with her legs propped on the couch. Twisting her head from side to side, Imagany said, "Girl, the man was so strong, he could make a blind woman see."

"Wewww, child! Say it ain't so!"

"Girlfriend, I'm only telling it like it is." Imagany's voice deepened into a soft whisper. "Caprice, the man had it goin' on." Her voice trailed off as her mind drifted. Long minutes passed before Imagany sighed deeply and shook herself out of her daze. Imagany said reluctantly, "Anyway, we'll have to continue this conversation some other time. Right now, I've got three pages of calculus homework waiting for me."

"Mmmmm." Caprice, too, was reluctant to hang up. "Oh, Imagany?"

"What?"

"Call him."

Lost in her thoughts of Elliott, Imagany said, "I plan to." The phone went dead as Imagany continued to stare up at the ceiling.

***

The remainder of the week seemed to drag by for Imagany. The dance production was the next night and she had not heard from Anthony in over a week. Though he knew about the dance, she didn't know whether or not he would come.

Imagany assumed he was still steaming over their last argument about her refusal to further discuss his marriage proposal. It was mind-boggling to her that Anthony just assumed she would jump at the chance to marry him. She figured that soon he would start using his financial support of her as a means of barter. While she didn't think he would yank it away without warning her, she did believe that he would soon give her an ultimatum.

Though Imagany tried to deny it, it bothered her that she was at Anthony's whim. It only served to remind her of the patterns in her mother's life and how she had promised herself that she wouldn't repeat them. Imagany admitted to herself that as far as Anthony was concerned it was time to move on. She had allowed herself to become complacent. She'd grown accustomed to the lifestyle and manner in which Anthony could afford to keep her. She would now have to sit and figure out how far her savings would last until she could get a job. Though jobs were reportedly scarce, she would simply have to find one. Imposing on her parents for financial assistance was out of the question. In the meantime she would enjoy the solitude, mulling over her thoughts of Elliott in private.

Imagany had nearly called Elliott every night of the week. But whenever she went to pick up the phone, the butterflies in her stomach grew too intense. On this day she was sitting at her kitchen table studying for her economics class with thoughts of Elliott running through her mind. Periodically, she would find herself glancing at the phone, thinking about calling him. But each time she decided against it. It was late afternoon and he would probably be at football practice anyway. Before she knew it, she was standing in front of the telephone. Just when she was about to pick it up, the phone rang, startling her. She laughed at her own foolishness.

"Hi." It was her sister Zabree.

"Well, well, well, and to what do I owe the unexpected pleasure of this call?" Zabree, who was six years younger than Imagany, almost never called unless their parents put her up to it.

"Just the usual. Mom and Pops haven't heard from you in awhile so they thought it best that I give you a call to make sure you were still among the living. But you know them. They would rather die before they admitted it."

"Yeah, I know," Imagany replied flatly. "So how are you, kiddo?" Imagany and Zabree were the only children in their family and though they were not that far apart in age, they were close in some ways and distant in so many others. Imagany was considered the rebel in the family, the one who never went along complacently with the program, while Zabree was the more pliable one. It was Zabree who, sometimes along with their mother, was forced to play the role of family mediator.

"When are you coming home, Mog?" Zabree asked her in a quiet voice that was filled with longing to see her. Imagany could tell immediately that something was wrong.

She sat on the couch and closed her eyes as she heard the reflection in Zabree's voice. Zabree only reverted to calling her that childhood name when she was feeling some kind of pain. Imagany held her forehead in her hand, "I can't come home, Bree. You know that. It would cause too many problems for all of us. Where is he, Bree? Can you talk right now? He's not in one of his moods, is he?" Imagany never addressed her father by any name. She would always refer to him as "him" or "he." If their father was feeling particularly violent or abusive, they would just say he was in one of his moods. Imagany had grown tired of making excuses for him and as a result, she had chosen to go away to school as opposed to staying in Chicago.

Zabree was quiet on the other end, not answering her. Finally she whispered, "Mog, I'm thinking about running away from home."

Imagany knew this must mean that their father was assaulting Zabree again. Her heart clenched and tears began to trickle down Imagany's face. All the old horrible memories came flooding back, anger, helplessness. . . . Their father had started doing the same thing to Imagany when she had only been a child. The assaults had continued until Imagany had grown older and had learned to fight back. But she had gained that knowledge at a high price. Imagany struggled with feelings of worthlessness and low self esteem. She came to realize long ago that outer beauty had no bearings on the way a person felt inside. Though Imagany's spirit was bruised, her will was strong, thus enabling her to find the strength within herself to regroup and rebuild.

Zabree was not so fortunate. She may have had Imagany to shield her while Imagany was there with her, but now that Imagany was in college, there was no one to fight the battle for her. Zabree just was not strong enough to fend for herself. Imagany's anger toward her mother, who pretended that the problem did not exist, deepened. How any woman could stand by and watch her own children be assaulted by someone, let alone their own father, was a mystery to her. She had come to the conclusion that her mother loved her father so much that she was willing to turn a blind eye to anything he did. But Imagany didn't understand it. To her, there was no amount of love in the world that could justify a woman turning away from the pain and suffering of her own children.

Imagany shook her head and through her tears said, "Zabree you can't. There's no place for you to go. It's too dangerous out there on the streets. If anything, you must go to a shelter." Imagany didn't know what else to say to her. How could she tell Zabree to find the strength within herself to break the cycle when those around her wouldn't even acknowledge that a pattern existed?

Finally, Zabree said, "Don't worry, Mog, before I do anything I'll let you know what I decide." Imagany could hear the silent tears in Zabree's voice and she felt all her own old wounds come to the surface. She didn't want Zabree to know she was crying, she wanted her to think she was strong. Imagany wanted Zabree to be able to draw strength from her.

"Bree, promise me you'll talk to me before you do anything, okay?"

"Yeah, I promise." Zabree sounded distant now, as if she wanted to end the conversation. "You want to speak to Mom and Pops?"

"No." Imagany hesitated. "Just tell them I'm doing fine."

They hung up the phone and Imagany sat on the floor and wrapped her arms around her knees. She needed desperately to erase the feelings of unworthiness, anger, hurt, emptiness and sorrow that were weighing her down. She suddenly remembered word for word an old poem she had written many years ago to help her sort through what she was dealing with at the time.

What can I do
with all this pain I feel inside

where can I put the anger
when it eats me alive
who can I turn to when all else fails
who can I talk to, to help me prevail
Oh, Lord up above,
up yonder in the sky,
can you explain
or at least tell me why
How in the world,
in this land of good and plenty
where people think there are few
but in reality so many
children who are being
assaulted on a daily basis
all creeds, and all colors,
all ages and all races
Once again, Dear Lord
can you at least tell me why
no one will acknowledge
our screams with a reply

Imagany lay on the floor curled up in a ball wondering how she could help her sister, Zabree, when she couldn't even help herself.

Chapter Four

T he day of the dance dawned bright and early. Imagany flew through the day in a blaze of energy, smiling at everyone as she strolled along the campus on her way to class. People smiled back appreciatively, wishing that they had some of whatever it was that was making her appear so lively.

She finished her last class of the day and drove back to her apartment to prepare for the evening's performance. There was still no message from Anthony on the answering machine and she was starting to worry. True to form, whenever he was angry or annoyed with her, he would punish her with silence and withdrawal. But what Anthony didn't understand was that Imagany had been raised in the same type of environment that he was subjecting her to. It didn't work because Imagany was a master at blocking people and their deeds from her mind. It only worried her now because he had never stayed away this long. On impulse she picked up the phone and dialed Elliott's number.

The phone rang once when a deep voice on the other end said, "Hello."

Imagany almost hung up but at the last second said, "Hi." With all the butterflies in her stomach, she imagined she sounded quite stupid.

"Yesss," the voice on the other end asked encouragingly.

"May I speak with Elliott?" Was her voice husky?

"I'm afraid Elliott's not in right now. Care to leave a message?"

There is a God! "Sure. Can you tell him Imagany called?"

"Certainly." The way he said it implied that he knew all about her. Or was it just her imagination? Suddenly, Imagany said before he could hang up, "Can you also let him know there's going to be a modern dance show held in the Administration Building at 7:30 tonight?" Breathlessly she added, "Tell him I'm going to be dancing in it and that I'd really appreciate it if he could come."

"I'm sure he'll be there," the voice said knowingly. "Anything else?"

"Yes," she paused. "There is just one other thing."

"Okay, and that is?"

"Tell the brother that he's still in my doghouse."

Laughing, the voice on the other end said, "Will do."

When Imagany picked Caprice up on her way to the dance, she was a bundle of nerves.

"Imagany, why are you so keyed up? I've seen you dance hundreds of times and I've never known you to be so jittery. Is it Anthony that's bothering you? What gives?" Caprice stared at her piercingly.

They were at a stop sign and Imagany was cracking her knuckles. She didn't perform this gesture often because it was just one of a number of things that her mother had instilled in her not to do. Rule number one: Always be ladylike. Shifting in her seat, she said, "No, Anthony is the furthest thing from my mind." She glanced at Caprice and said, "I called Elliott and invited him to the dance."

"You're kidding." Caprice said dryly as if she had known all along.

"No, I'm not. I'm just shaky at the prospect of him not showing up."

"Oh, I'm sure he'll be there. No wonder you're in la-la land. I couldn't figure it out. I thought maybe you were worried because that bastard Anthony hadn't called. So, I'm finally going to meet Mr. Elliott."

"Reese, if you embarrass me, I swear to you right here and now that our friendship will be over. So behave yourself. Capeesh?" Imagany's voice held a warning note.

"You have my word of honor that I'll be on my best behavior," Caprice said with a gleam in her eye.

"Your word of honor, all right. That's what troubles me."

"Just relax, kiddo, and do your thing. I'll take care of the rest."

Imagany groaned. "Reese, if you embarrass me tonight, I promise you, you'll be walking from now until your *grandchildren* can afford to buy you a car."

A crowd had begun to gather and form a line as they pulled into the Administration parking lot. Imagany had her pass to go backstage while Caprice waited in line with some students from TSU whom she knew.

People were being seated in the audience and Ms. Geiger was doing last minute checks to ensure that all the props were in place. The stage had been set to resemble an African jungle with pictures of trees and bushes and wild animals hanging in the background. Thick vines hung from the ceiling all around the stage.

All ten dancers would take part in the first sequence. They would be costumed in short grass skirts with round plates of green straw covering their breasts while Larry would wear nothing but a grass bikini that left hardly anything to the imagination. The women in the audience were guaranteed to ooh and aah when they saw him. Probably some of the men would too. All would wear necklaces and bracelets of teeth and bones around their necks, arms, and ankles.

There would be a total of seven dance sequences. Five would contain all ten dancers, one would showcase Larry and Imagany and one would be Imagany's solo. In between dances, members of the TSU band had been invited to accompany several singers who would perform solos. There would even be a comedian. The evening's lineup of events promised to be a good one.

Imagany knew she had no cause to be nervous. Just as Caprice had said, she had danced through many a performance like this one. Yet she felt this time would be different. For once, she was not dancing to forget or escape anything. She would be dancing to please not just an entire audience, but mainly one person in particular. She gritted her teeth at the thought. Listening to the sounds of the people in the audience, she could tell the place was packed. She willed herself to be calm. The show was about to begin.

Ms. Geiger was on stage thanking everyone for coming and promising all that if they didn't enjoy the show, they could have their money refunded. The premise of TSU refunding money to anybody was a grand joke and the audience laughed as she knew they would. As the lights dimmed and the people quieted, Ms. Geiger knew she had done her part. The rest was left to the dancers.

And what a performance it turned out to be. As the curtain rose the dancers were hidden amid a tide of twisted vines. African music vibrated throughout the building and the vines lifted to reveal the dancers in their fetal positions. The audience watched in fascination.

Elliott Renfroe sat in the first row, spellbound just like everyone else. As he watched each performance, his eyes automatically focused on

Imagany. He had thought of her often during the week, wondering whether or not she would really call him. But with football practice and classes consuming so much of his time, Elliott was lucky to find the time to eat and sleep. When his roommate told him earlier that she had called, he felt a rush of adrenaline shoot through him. He wouldn't have missed the dance for all the world. Just the thought of seeing her again was enough to whet his appetite.

The evening progressed rapidly. Elliott even enjoyed the solo with Larry and Imagany. When the women saw Larry in another pair of his now infamous bikinis with his muscles bulging, they went wild. Elliott could only shake his head as he heard women comment lewdly about what they would do to Larry if they could only get their hands on him.

Ms. Geiger had outdone herself with the choreography. Even the stage had been creatively set. Elliott looked at the program unable to believe that the next dance was the last dance of the evening. As the comedian departed from the stage, the audience hushed once more as the curtains prepared to rise.

This time the stage was bathed in blue lights and clouded in a haze of smoke. Music drifted out to the audience. Suddenly, as the mist began to clear, a figure emerged. Elliott gasped as he recognized Imagany. She was wrapped in a wispy gauze-like fabric. She stretched her arms to the heavens and slowly twirled. The material teasingly unwound itself from her body, revealing her attire. Imagany wore a skimpy two-piece bikini the color of fuscia. She began her dance with a series of slow movements holding the gauze material above her head and letting it trail onto the floor. Gusts of air blew from somewhere in the background causing the fabric and her hair to waver in the wind.

Imagany danced along in harmony with the words of the song. This time, Elliott recognized Phyllis Hyman singing "The Answer Is You."

"I was just a rider on the storm,
I needed love to keep me feeling warm . . ."

Imagany twirled and balanced on one leg, the muscles in her body clearly defined. She circled the stage, her hair and scarf flowing in the wind behind her, leaving the entire audience breathless.

Imagany leapt around the stage, her body twisting and turning. She was poetry in motion as she glided to and fro. With her arms stretched over her head, her rib cage was outlined for all to see. In the next breath she slid her body to the floor of the stage into a Chinese split causing those who were seated closest to the stage to gasp. People who were not seated up close suddenly wished they had binoculars.

Imagany twirled faster and faster as Phyllis Hyman's voice drew to a close. On the last note, she danced off into the shadows of the stage with the sheer gauze material flowing behind her.

The curtains closed and the audience burst into thunderous applause. The essence of her dance had been conveyed to everyone. She had captured the spirit of the song, and had brought its message to life. As she danced, people could literally envision what the song meant. If they weren't familiar with the tune, it made them yearn to know it, and if they were familiar with it, then they wanted to hear it over and over again.

The audience was still applauding as all the dancers along with Ms. Geiger appeared on stage holding hands, taking bow after bow. Ms. Geiger had truly outdone herself and the dancers had made her proud.

Elliott was one of the last to leave the auditorium. Maybe the final dance routine had affected him much more deeply than it did others.

On impulse, he took the exit door that led to the backstage entrance. He found himself among the chaotic chatter of the dancers and their friends. They were elated from the dynamic performance they had just given. Elliott lounged against a nearby column watching the dancers as they huddled together, celebrating their performance.

The dancers were dressed in their street garb and those who weren't were behind makeshift curtains getting dressed. Elliott searched the crowded area for Imagany. Not finding her, he assumed she was still dressing. He saw Larry, who was dressed in his street clothes, come out from behind one of the curtains. Elliott approached him as Larry started talking to one of the other dancers.

"That was some performance."

"Thanks, glad you enjoyed it." Larry recognized Elliott as the guy who had ousted him earlier in the week when he had been practicing with Imagany.

"Have you seen Imagany?" Elliott asked.

"Yeah, she should be here somewhere." Larry looked around in search of Imagany. He bore Elliott no grudge, realizing that Imagany had just chosen Elliott over himself.

As the two of them stood talking, others were sizing Elliott up. A group of girls had taken note of him the moment he stepped away from the column he had been leaning against.

They stood together across the room when one of the dancers nudged another one with her elbow. She pointed in Elliott's direction and they continued to nudge one another until the conversation came to a lull and all eyes were focused on Elliott.

"Tell me my eyes ain't deceivin' me! Who is the brotha ova' *theya?*" Cynthia Sanders was a personal friend of one of the dancers. She was a bodacious woman who was obviously used to getting whatever she wanted. She had one hand on her hip and the other on the rim of her designer glasses as she pulled them down over the tip of her nose to scope out Elliott.

"Girlfriends, that specimen is none other than Elliott Renfroe. You know, he plays quarterback for the TSU football team."

"Baby, the man can play on my team any damn day! Just say the word!" She made crisscross motions across her chest as she snapped her fingers in quick motions.

"*Yayse.*" They all agreed in harmony as they high-fived each other and laughed.

Cynthia was still peering at Elliott over the top of her glasses. "That brother is *foine!* Look at the way he's wearing them *jines.* Does anybody know whether the man is taken?" Without waiting for a reply Cynthia said, "Let me rephrase that, my sistahs. The brotha is about to be taken!"

"Well, girlfriend, don't waste no time, now," another girl said. "Cause that stuff is hot off the press! If you ain't goin', let me just go and introduce myself."

Cynthia grabbed the girl's arm hard and gave her one of her "don't even try it" looks.

Knowing how easily Cynthia could be pushed into a fight, the girl was quick to apologize. "Oh, I'm sorry Cynt. What I meant to say was let me introduce *you.*"

"That's right baby, cause I spotted the brotha first. Don't let me have to kick no tail up in this joint," Cynthia told her menacingly as she led the group over in Elliott's direction.

Imagany had just come from behind one of the makeshift dressing rooms. She was dressed in a white cotton, sleeveless turtleneck tank-top and a pair of 501 jeans. She was putting her flats on when she spotted Elliott surrounded by a group of about six girls. One of the girls had her arm wrapped possessively around his elbow and Elliott looked for all the world like the only thing he wanted to do was escape. A red light went off inside Imagany's head and the next thing she knew she was striding swiftly and purposefully toward Elliott and all of his fawning bimbos.

Imagany parted the group and made her way up front to where Elliott was standing. "Excuse me ladies. Is there a problem here?" Imagany did not believe in putting people in their places. She just believed in letting others know what *her* place was. She had a look in her eye and a tone in her voice that immediately let the other girls know that she had an attitude. When the girls took note of Imagany's stance, none of them could look her in the eye. All except Cynthia, that is.

Cynthia stepped away from Elliott's side and said to Imagany, "We didn't think there was no problem here. At least there wasn't before you came along. So, Ms. Thing, that must mean *you* are the problem."

Calmly, Imagany turned to address Cynthia. "Dahlin', let me help you. If I'm the problem, I can quickly be the solution." Imagany let her duffel bag fall to the floor with a loud thud. She had years of pent-up anger and frustration inside her just waiting to explode. Woe unto the person who was unfortunate enough to pull the straw that would break the camel's back.

Cynthia bristled visibly, her neck jerking to the side. One of the girls from Cynthia's clique said loudly, "Uuh uhn, Cynt! No she didn't go there! You gon' take that?" Someone else shouted, "Who the hell does this girl think she is? Bunk that!" Finally, "Go 'head, Cynt! We got 'cho back. Kick her ass!" With her girls spurring her on, Cynthia was suddenly ready for a fight.

Dear God! *Women!* For the life of him, Elliott would never understand them. How did all this mess get started? Firmly, Elliott stepped forward between Imagany and Cynthia and said to the group, "Forgive me for interrupting, ladies, but it is rather late and my woman and I must be going." He turned to Cynthia and said, "Cynthia, it was a pleasure to have met you. Have a nice evening, all of you." Elliott grabbed Imagany's bag, gripped her by the arm, and led her toward the exit door.

"He better take that bitch and go," Cynthia said sulkingly, still angry over the fact that Imagany had just disrupted the serious rap that she had been about to put on the brother.

Elliott and Imagany had almost reached the exit door when Imagany overheard the comment. When she stopped in her tracks, Elliott pulled her along. "Imagany please, don't do this to me." He could tell that Imagany wanted to go back to finish what she had started. "Let's just go peacefully. How about we go some place where we can talk? Just you and me."

They went through the side exit and ended up behind the building where only a few stragglers were passing by. Imagany angrily pulled away from him and leaned against the building with her knee raised and her foot resting on the wall behind her. She folded her arms across her chest and tried to blow off her steam. Suddenly, she started to laugh.

Elliott, on the other hand, didn't know whether to be angry or not. He had heard guys talk and laugh about how women fought over them. But to him, this was no laughing matter. One of them could have wound up being hurt or seriously injured. Disregarding her laughter, he stood in front of her with a serious look on his face.

Finally, Imagany took a deep breath and said, "I'm sorry, Elliott, I owe you an apology." She lifted her arms and ran her hands through her hair. "Umph, umph, umph," shaking her head she said, "I can't believe I did that."

Unexpectedly Elliott smiled, "So how come you didn't tell me you had a violent streak inside you?"

"I don't know. Maybe you didn't give me the chance. No. I really am sorry, though. I didn't mean to embarrass you. I don't normally do things like that. It's just that when I saw the way . . ." Imagany stopped. She knew what she was about to say would sound silly even to her own ears. Instead she said, "It seems that whenever I'm around you, I do something crazy. What are you trying to do to me?" Imagany casually shifted the blame to Elliott.

Elliott stepped closer to her and put one arm on either side of the wall where she was leaning, trapping her between his arms. "You don't get off the hook that easily. As a matter of fact, I believe this exonerates me and puts you in my doghouse."

Imagany stared up at him thinking that he had the prettiest teeth. Her eyes drifted hungrily to his lips. There was nothing that she wanted more than to kiss them and taste the sweetness of his mouth. Realizing that they were still out in public, Imagany ducked under his arms and twisted away from him.

"Did anyone ever tell you that two wrongs don't make a right? I mean, I'm not trying to get out of being in your doghouse or anything like that. But I just think that we should let bygones be bygones." Imagany had her hands clasped behind her back as she faced him.

"You know, you're good. You're very good. But I'm afraid I can't let you off just like that. If I don't reprimand you now, you'll be pulling stunts like that for the rest of our lives." Elliott reached down and lifted her face so he could run his thumb across the cleft in her chin.

"Does that mean we're going to be together for the rest of our lives?" Imagany asked flirtatiously.

"Until we're old and gray," Elliott replied, looking at her with an earnest expression on his face.

"Elliott Renfroe." Imagany said his name tenderly, as if testing it to see how sweet it would sound. "I think I like you." She spoke the last part so soft and slowly that Elliott had to strain to hear her. She took his hand from her chin and enfolded her hand in his. She stepped backwards, pulling him with her, dragging him along.

"Wait," Elliott told her, using his strength to reel her back toward him until she stood directly in front of him. Looking down at her as if to take in every detail of her face, he slid both his hands along either side of her chin, lifting her face up to his. He stared deeply into her eyes before bending down to kiss her.

Imagany knew it was coming. From the moment his semi-roughened hands gently clasped themselves around her chin, she knew he would kiss her. Her face lifted willingly to meet his. Her eyes closed and her lips parted expectantly. For the longest time she waited and finally when his mouth touched hers, his lips were warm and tender. He kissed her softly but passionately. Just the way she liked it; just the way she needed it.

On their own volition, her arms wound themselves around his neck and her hands cupped the back of his head. When his hands slid to her hips, instinctively, Imagany tightened her grip on his shoulders and lifted herself around his waist so that her legs were wrapped tightly around him. Elliott was left holding her in his arms.

Elliott smiled as he looked into Imagany's eyes thinking they were the most beautiful eyes he had ever seen.

"Did anyone ever tell you that you're no lightweight?"

"No, but do you always encourage women to jump into your arms at the drop of a hat?" Imagany must have thought she was still dancing on stage. She had wrapped herself around him before she was even aware of what she was doing.

"Only the ones that fight over me," he reminded her teasingly.

"Oh, Elliott," Imagany buried her face in his neck. "Promise me you won't ever mention that again." When he said nothing, she looked him dead in the eye. "Promise me, Elliott."

A couple was strolling by at a distance. Elliott and Imagany heard one of them say, "Damn! They need to go get a hotel room. Wit' they cheap selves."

They laughed as they became aware of what a spectacle they must be making of themselves with him holding her in his arms. Reluctantly, Elliott set her down. "You were wonderful tonight, Imagany. I thought the last dance was brilliant. You seem to have a knack for picking the perfect song to dance to."

All the applause in the world couldn't equal the praise Elliott had just given her. Imagany instantly forgot about what she had asked him to promise her as she told him humbly, "Thank you. Some people have a way of inspiring and encouraging others to reach greater heights." She knew he incorrectly assumed that she was referring to Ms. Geiger and not him. But she didn't correct him.

Though happy, Imagany was somewhat uncomfortable with Elliott's compliment. She linked her arm through his and changed the subject to divert attention away from herself. "Come on," she said, "I have someone I want you to meet."

They reached the front of the building and were heading toward the parking lot when someone called out Elliott's name.

"Yo, El!"

Elliott stopped and looked back as a friend of his approached them.

"Hey, Carl. How come you didn't call me back last night? Did you figure the problem out?" Elliott and Carl were fellow electrical engineering students. They had been up late on the phone with each other the night before, trying to work out a problem from their thermodynamics class when Carl had said he needed to take a break. When Elliott didn't hear back from him, he, too, had fallen asleep.

Though lighter in weight and bulk, Carl was just as tall and broad as Elliott. He had dark chocolate-brown skin and his wavy hair was cropped close to his head. He had a hawk-like nose and wore small round wire-framed glasses. Imagany immediately appreciated his stature and knew Caprice would surely drool if she saw him.

"Man, I crashed. I must have been out of it." His eyes flitted curiously from Imagany to Elliott.

"*You* were out of it? Then what should I have been?" Elliott saw the way Imagany and Carl were looking at each other and remembered to introduce them.

"Imagany, this is Carl Beasley, my partner in crime. Carl, this is Imagany Jenkins." Elliott grinned as he introduced them.

"So you're the elusive Imagany that I've been hearing so much about."

Smiling, Imagany shook Carl's hand. "I'm not sure if I like how that sounds."

"Oh, don't worry, I've only heard good things," Carl reassured her.

Imagany could contain her curiosity no longer. "Are you on the football team, too?" She assumed that with his size, he must be.

Shaking his head, Carl said, "No, I'm one of the people who chooses to watch sports and leave the actual playing to guys like Elliott." Carl raised his hand to slap Elliott on the shoulder but Elliott stepped away and dodged him.

With his hands in the front pockets of his jeans, Elliott moved back close to Imagany. "Imagany's trying to pry, Carl. She wants to know how we came to know each other."

"Elliott, I was not. Carl looks like he could be a football player so I wanted to know if he was." Imagany smiled because Elliott had read her mind.

Carl came to her defense. "You're probably just wondering how someone of my caliber could wind up hanging out with someone like him, right?"

"Exactly." Imagany gave Carl a silent stamp of approval.

"Elliott and I met about two years ago when we were freshmen first studying to be electrical engineers. What can I tell you?" Carl shrugged his shoulders. "He's been following me around ever since."

Elliott laughed. "Man, don't even try it." He turned to Imagany, "The way the story really goes is that this bucket head boy would have flunked out of school long ago if it weren't for me."

"Don't believe him, Imagany. The only way he's able to play on the football team and retain his engineering scholarship is through my good graces. I can't even count the number of times I've had to do his homework and take tests for him."

Imagany looked from one to the other as they traded baits, not knowing whom to believe. So in addition to playing on the football team, Elliott was an electrical engineer. Well I'll be damned, Imagany thought. One should never judge a book by its cover. A smile broke out on her face as she stared at Elliott with a new appreciation.

Out of the corner of her eye, Imagany spotted Caprice standing outside the entrance of the building. She stepped forward and waved her arms wildly in the air. "Reese! Over here!" Turning back to Elliott, Imagany put her hand on his arm. "Elliott, Caprice is the person I was talking about earlier when I said I wanted you to meet someone." When Imagany touched Elliott, she instantly became aware of the muscles in his arm. She also liked the way her nails glistened against his skin. She wanted him to be aware of it too, so she subtly turned her touch into a light caress. "And you can meet her, too, Carl." Imagany intended to detain Carl in case he was thinking about leaving before she could introduce him to Caprice.

When she introduced Caprice, Imagany smirked when she noticed Carl holding Caprice's hand longer than was necessary. Before she could introduce her to Elliott, Caprice turned to him and held out her hand. "And you must be Elliott."

"In the flesh," Elliott said as they shook hands.

Imagany could read Caprice's mind just by looking at the expression on her face. She braced herself because she knew Caprice was about to say something brazen. Surprisingly, Caprice said, "Imagany, let me speak to you for a moment. Excuse us guys, we'll be right back." Caprice stared at Carl as she grabbed Imagany's hand and whisked her off to the side.

When they reached a safe enough distance, Caprice turned to Imagany and let her mouth drop open. She pointed her finger inside of it as she pantomimed the words, "Can I close my mouth?" But the only sounds that were emitted were "huh, huh, huh, huh, huh." Caprice waited for Imagany to give her the signal to stop gawking.

Imagany reached over and lifted Caprice's chin upward in a gesture that closed her mouth. Feeling like someone who had just hit the lottery, Imagany told Caprice, "Pick your tongue up off the ground and close your mouth, dahlin'. I warned you that the man was fine."

"*That's* Elliott? Hold my hand!" Caprice whispered reverentially when she finally closed her mouth. Her hand slowly drifted toward the sky as if to testify and Imagany quickly reached out to grab it. "You mean to tell me that hunk of a man was in my dorm and I didn't know about it? Girlfriend, I must be losing my touch." Disbelief was apparent in Caprice's voice. "Who's his friend? He's not bad looking either." Caprice peered over Imagany's shoulder at Elliott and Carl.

"They're classmates. I mean, they're good friends. I knew Elliott was not a typical athlete. Caprice, he's an electrical engineer." Imagany's excitement was evident in her voice and she spoke in a rush of words, aware that she wasn't making much sense. Imagany preened for Caprice as she gave herself a mental pat on the back. "Do I know how to pick 'em or what?"

"Imagany, get a grip, girl. Knuckle head is here looking for you." Caprice knew this would bring her back to reality.

"What?" Imagany's heart hit the ground.

"Girl, you heard me. Now close *your* mouth. Anthony is here. As a matter of fact, he's waiting for you by your car. I told him I knew where you were and that I'd go get you. I figured I'd catch you before he did."

Imagany groaned. "I wanted all of us to do something together. I'm going to have to think of some way to get rid of him." Imagany shook her head beginning to feel angry. "I haven't heard from Anthony in weeks and now all of a sudden he just shows up out of the blue. No way. I'll just tell him I'm busy tonight."

"You want me to come with you?" Caprice relished the thought of seeing Anthony get dissed.

"No. Go back and entertain Elliott and Carl. Ask them if they want to go get something to eat."

"All right. Maybe we can go to the Po' Folk's Restaurant on White Bridge Road. If my cousin, Lavon, is there, we can get a discount." As Imagany walked away, Caprice said, "Just tell him you'll talk to him later, Imagany."

"I will."

***

Elliott and Carl watched inquisitively as Caprice dragged Imagany away. Elliott turned to find Carl staring at him with a sly smile on his face.

"So that's Imagany, huh?" Carl shook his head appreciatively. "The woman is stacked better than a full deck of cards." He gave Elliott his full attention. "So what's up?"

Elliott threw up his hands. "Hey, I'm still trying to figure it out myself."

Another slow grin spread across Carl's face. "Well, one thing's for damn sure. You and I both know what your track record is like when it comes to lovin' 'em and leavin' 'em. Somehow, this girl just doesn't fit the mode, though. She's too sophisticated. What's the deal with her? Is she going to be another hit-'n-run or what?"

Although Elliott was not serious with any one person, he did have quite a few to pick from. In a reflective voice, Elliott said, "I don't think so, Carl. She seems different from all the others to me, too."

"Yeah. She just doesn't look like the type you can bang and leave without ever wanting to see again. Don't think I'm trying to talk you out of anything. She just doesn't seem like she can be strung along like all the rest. Personally, I think you need another woman hanging on your jock string about as much as I need to screw a giraffe." Elliott laughed. "It's true, man. Just don't make me have to clean up behind you when it's over. Since you already know you're not interested in anything long term, let her know right off the bat. That way, if she chooses to file in line with the rest of the crowd, then, hey," Carl threw up his hands, "so be it. At least she can't say you didn't warn her." Carl held his hand out and Elliott slammed his into it in agreement. "Besides," Carl folded his arms across his chest and pulled at his chin with one hand. "Her friend, dimples, looks like she could be my type. Should anything go wrong between you and Imagany, I wouldn't want her to be troubled with thoughts of how my friend just so happened to diss hers. Something simple like that can be the difference between me getting some good lovin' and getting the door slammed in my face."

"Word."

***

Imagany walked to her car and sure enough, Anthony was leaning against the door with his arms folded across his chest. He was a distinguished looking gentleman. He had handsome features, was 6'2", and kept his body in good condition. He was dressed in an expensive two-piece double-breasted black suit.

"Hi." Imagany spoke flatly, unable to evoke enthusiasm at the sight of him.

Anthony noted her distant attitude but attributed it to the fact that he had been away so long without calling her. He had expected her to be angry. "How are you?"

Imagany merely shrugged her shoulder as she faced him, leaning her hip against the door of the car. She said nothing as she let him direct the conversation. Anyone passing by would have thought they were strangers who had just been introduced.

"The performance was beautiful and your solo was exquisite."

"Thank you. I'm glad you could come." Imagany knew he was trying to soften her up, but she was not in the mood to be pacified.

"Are you going home now?"

"Nope." Imagany stuck her thumbs in the waistband of her jeans. "Caprice and I were going to hang out for a while."

"So what time will you be home?"

"I'm not sure." She certainly didn't want him to wait for her.

Imagany wore a gold necklace with a diamond heart pendant that Anthony had given her sometime ago and his eyes wandered to it. As he reached out to hold the pendant part of the necklace, his hand rested heavily between the cups of her breasts.

"I want to see you tonight, Imagany."

She could tell by the possessive look in Anthony's eyes and the deceptive softness in his voice that he wanted to make love to her. How typical of him to think that lovemaking would wipe away all of their problems. She covered his hand decisively with hers. "I don't know about tonight, Anthony. Caprice might stay over."

Anthony smiled knowingly as he released her necklace. "I had planned on taking you out to dinner to celebrate your performance tonight, but since you've made other plans, go ahead and enjoy yourself. Just make sure your friend doesn't mind being at your place alone tonight. I want *you* to spend the night at mine."

"Then you may have a long wait."

He glanced at his watch. "I'll take my chances. It's after nine now. Be back by midnight." He straightened up, preparing to walk away. "Did you miss me?"

"Not at all," she told him challengingly, with a slight smile on her face.

Anthony smiled. "I'll see you later," he told her as he walked off to his car.

Imagany looked after him with a calculating smile on her face. He may not know it, but she had him wrapped around her finger.

Imagany apologized as she rejoined the group.

"Imagany, I was trying to persuade them to come with us to eat." Caprice was standing between Carl and Elliott with one hand on each of their arms. She looked like a cat who had just caught a mouse.

"And what did you guys decide?" Imagany stood next to Elliott.

"Can you believe they're still debating? I even told them that if we go to Po' Folk's my cousin Lavon would let us eat for little or nothing."

"Okay. Then what is it? How come you guys are stalling?" Imagany looked at Elliott as she spoke.

"We're not stalling. We just wanted to make sure everybody was in agreement," Elliott said.

"So where do you two want to go?" Imagany directed her question to both him and Carl.

"Po' Folk's sounds good to us. So who's going to drive, Elliott? You or me?" Carl asked.

"I think we should let Imagany drive. At least then we'll ride in style." Elliott glanced at his watch. "Carl and I need to go back to our dorm rooms to get some money, so why don't you two meet us back at my dorm in fifteen minutes?"

"Okay. Want a lift?" Imagany asked.

"No. It'll be faster if we walk from here."

Caprice said saucily, "Fifteen minutes guys. Don't be late."

"We won't be." Carl turned and called back to her.

Imagany and Caprice went to the car and got in.

"So, what did Anthony have to say?" Caprice was curious.

Imagany shrugged, "He wanted to take me out for dinner. But I told him that you and I were hanging out for a while and that you might be spending the night over."

"Hah! I know he didn't want to hear that." Since their dislike for one another was mutual, Caprice could only imagine what Anthony had to say about the two of them hanging out together.

Imagany never repeated to either one of them everything that they said about each other. It would only cause them to dislike each other even more. Instead she said, "He's going to wait up for me. I might go to his place later just so he won't have to come to mine."

Caprice shook her head, confused. "Imagany, I'll never understand your relationship with Anthony."

"Let's not even discuss him. So what did you think of Elliott? And what about Carl? I noticed the way you were buttering up to him."

"Wewwwwww weeee!" Caprice raised both of her arms and pushed her hands against the roof of the car as she stomped her feet on the floor. Anybody would have thought she was having a temper tantrum. When she finally got a grip on herself, she lowered her hands slowly and rested them in her lap as if nothing had happened. "Girl, Elliott is too fine." Caprice crossed her arms and legs as she turned in her seat to look at Imagany. In a deep voice, Caprice sang, "I'm talkin' 'bout a strong black man!" By the time she finished, Imagany had joined in. Laughing, they held their hands up and hi-fived.

"Girlfriend, what can I say?" Imagany started the car and they fell in line behind all the other cars exiting the parking lot. "He just seems so nice and strong and . . . oh, Lord! Hold my hand!" In slow motion, Imagany extended her hand to Caprice who took it and gripped it hard.

"Handle it, girlfriend! Handle it!" Caprice told her encouragingly. When they released each other's hand, they clutched their hearts and shook their heads. Both of them were at a loss for words.

Imagany told her about how she had almost gotten into a fight with another girl whom she felt had disrespected her.

Caprice looked dismayed. She said, "Imagany, are you mad? You are going to have to take a serious chill pill where Elliott's concerned. The man is gorgeous. Don't think you're the only woman who can see it. There will always be women who'll throw themselves at his feet in the blink of an eye. If you think you can fight off every woman who casts herself in his path, dahlin', you're going to be old before your time." Caprice shook her head. "You know, suddenly, I'm grateful that you met him first. He seems like he's a wonderful person and all. Very down to earth. I just don't think I could handle the competition. And, baby, believe me. There will always be competition over someone like him. What you have to decide is whether you want to enter the race." Caprice reached over and playfully squeezed Imagany's chin. She mockingly imitated the same gesture Elliott had made earlier. In a sassy imitation of a southern belle, Caprice said, "I think I'll happily stick with Carl."

"Caprice, I really like him though. So I guess that means I'm entering the race for the long haul." Imagany took a deep breath and yelled at the top of her lungs. "Let the games begin, people!" Heaving a deep sigh to calm herself down, she said, "Now let's talk about Carl."

Caprice folded her arms. "He looks like something I can work with."

"Well get on it then, girlfriend."

Caprice snapped her fingers, "Correction, my sistah. I'm already on it."

Hers was a two-door car so Elliott and Carl got in first since they would sit in the back. When she and Caprice got in, they moved their seats forward to accommodate the long legs of both the guys.

Imagany searched through her cassette compartment for another Najee tape. She found Najee's "Theme" and slid it into the player. As she drove off, Carl complimented her on her car.

"Imagany, how is it that you get to drive a BMW when folks like me and Elliott have to drive chug-a-lug 1969 'get-out-and-push-'ems?'"

Who do you know that we don't know?" Carl asked the same question that Elliott had wanted to ask her.

Imagany laughed as she said, "Well, for starters, I know my mom and pops." She left the statement at that, preferring to let them believe the car was a gift from her parents.

Caprice turned around in her seat and asked Carl, "Where are you from, Carl?"

"Queens, New York. Have you ever been there?"

"Never. But I've heard it said that New York is a pretty tough place. So I suppose the people who come from there must be pretty tough too, huh?"

"It's possible," Carl said without giving her a definite answer. "It depends on what borough and what part of the neighborhood you're from."

"And what about you Elliott?" Imagany asked him. "Where are you from?"

"A little town called McDonough, Georgia. If you blink when you drive by, you've already missed it."

"Well, well, so we have a southern gentleman among us," Caprice teased him. "Tell us what life was like growing up in Georgia, Elliott."

As Elliott gave his interpretation of a Southern lifestyle, there was never a lull in the conversation. Everybody had something to say. When they pulled into the restaurant's parking lot, they were surprised at how fast they had gotten there.

They entered the place and, sure enough, Lavon was there. She noticed them and came right over before anyone else could seat them.

Though the place was crowded, Lavon was able to seat them at a booth next to a window. Imagany and Elliott sat side by side across from Caprice and Carl. Lavon brought them menus and they took a moment to look them over before ordering. Po' Folk's was a down home Southern restaurant that served home cooked meals in huge proportions. They were famous for their smothered pork chops and their Southern fried chicken and biscuits.

As they waited for their food to come, Elliott and Carl wanted to know how long Imagany and Caprice had known each other and what life had been like for them growing up in Chicago.

"Good ol' Chi-Town," Caprice said fondly as she gave them her rendition of what city life was to her. "Imagany and I have known each other ever since nineteen . . ." Her brow wrinkled as she searched for the approximate year.

"Kindergarten," Imagany supplied helpfully.

"Get out of here," Carl interjected disbelievingly.

"No, it's true. We went to grammar school, high school and almost college together. Boy! Can you believe it, Imagany? Where did all the time go?" Without waiting for her to answer, Caprice explained that they only went to different schools now because of varying goals and majors.

Imagany was content to listen. She had her elbows on the table and her hands clasped and raised so that her chin rested on her hands. She was deriving pleasure just from sitting next to Elliott. Their shoulders occasionally brushed against each other and whenever Imagany spoke, she would make a point of touching his hand or arm to capture his attention.

When their food arrived it came in great heaping portions.

Elliott said as he tasted his food, "Okay ladies, don't be shy. Just go right ahead and dig in."

"Don't worry. Caprice and I have healthy appetites. Right Reese?"

"I think we can show them better than we can tell them."

"We shall see," Carl said. He didn't believe they would finish all the food on their plates either.

Between bites of his own, Elliott said, "Imagany, tell us about your childhood on those south side streets of Chicago."

"It was all about growing up in the hood, Elliott. I'm sure it was no different from growing up in . . ." Imagany asked Carl, "What part of Queens did you say, Carl?"

"East Elmhurst," Carl replied.

"There you go. Nothing more to tell." Imagany wasn't about to discuss her childhood.

When Lavon brought them their discounted bill, it only came to $10. They left Lavon a $10 tip and split everything down the middle. They were all stuffed as they filed out of the restaurant.

It was beautiful outside. The night was complete with full moon and matching stars. Imagany decided to lower the roof of her car. The seating arrangements were different this time. Elliott sat up front with her, while Carl sat in back with Caprice. Imagany slid one of Luther Vandross' cassettes into the player. They drove off to Luther's "Since I Lost My Baby."

"Where to?" she asked Elliott.

"You're the driver. Take us wherever you want." Elliott put the ball in her court.

The two couples began having separate conversations and Imagany asked Elliott about his family.

"I have two sisters, both younger than me."

"No boys other than yourself?" Imagany's tone was shaded with disappointment.

"No, there's just me. What about you?"

"Well, there's just me and my sister, Zabree, who's fifteen and incredibly intelligent." Imagany paused in her description of Zabree before continuing to expound her sister's qualities. She gave Elliott a portrayal of how precocious Zabree was and how knowledgeable she was in math. She described for him Zabree's many accolades and trophies. Imagany was rattling on and on about their occasional sibling rivalries when she became aware that she was monopolizing the conversation.

"Don't let me take up the whole conversation, Elliott. Tell me more about yourself."

"That's okay. It just sounds like you're crazy about your sister and that the two of you are really close."

Imagany nodded her head, saying, "Yes, we are. So tell me about your family." Imagany liked the sound of his voice and wanted to hear him talk. Elliott talked about his father and told her of some of the antics of his sisters, especially how they vied for his attention whenever he went home. From the way he talked, Imagany could tell that Elliott emulated his father and adored his mother. He was a very family-oriented person and it was obvious he missed them.

It was midnight when Imagany pulled into Elliott's dormitory driveway. Neither he nor Carl was ready to depart so they all sat talking a while longer.

Imagany turned around to face Caprice and said, "Why don't I invite everyone over for dinner next Saturday?"

Caprice looked at Imagany, whom she knew couldn't cook, and had to stop herself from bursting out laughing. "Yeah, why don't you?"

"Okay, then it's a done deal. How does 7:30 sound? That is, if you guys can find time in your busy schedules?"

"Sounds like a plan to me," Carl said.

"And you, Elliott?" Imagany prodded him when he gave her no answer.

"Hmmmm." Elliott rubbed his chin as he said, "I think I can make time to fit you in. What shall we bring?"

"Just yourselves," Caprice replied. She wanted to warn them that they had better bring bags to throw up in if Imagany was going to cook.

"Then 7:30 it is," Carl said.

Elliott got out and went to the driver's side of the car. Imagany watched him as he came around, admiring again how sexy he looked in his jeans and plain tee-shirt.

Elliott bent down and leaned inside the car. His face was just a short distance from hers as his eyes took in her face and body. "So how long do I have to wait before you call me again?" He wasn't going to ask her for her phone number but instead chose to wait until she offered it to him.

"Until tomorrow night." Her voice was low and husky.

"Are you sure about that?" Elliott recalled that it had taken her a whole week to call him before.

"I'm certain," Imagany said. She meant it too. Just looking at him was enough to arouse her.

"Maybe we can go to the movies tomorrow night." Elliott's eyes flitted over her and lingered on her lips.

"I'd like that," she told him. "Shall we invite Caprice and Carl?" Imagany ran her own eyes all over his face as she spoke. She was having a hard time following his words. The sexiness of his lips was throwing her off, merely reminding her of the way he had kissed her earlier. She had the urge to caress his chin but knew that if she did, she would only be starting something she couldn't finish.

"Why not, but we'll drive in separate cars next time." Elliott reached out to caress her cleft. She was used to his touch now, and she lifted her chin, inviting the feel of his hand anywhere on her body. As his hand brushed her face, a silent message of intense arousal passed between them. He could sense her willingness as she yielded to his touch. Elliott ran his hand over Imagany's hair until he lightly gripped the braid at the back of her head. He applied a light pressure and gently pulled it downward, causing her head to lift upward. Her throat was arched, begging to be kissed. He held her braid in a viselike grip as he stared into her limpid eyes. He had no intention of kissing her. He just wanted to look into her eyes to see if he was having the same effect upon her as she was having on him.

Imagany's neck craned as she stared back at him, reading his silent directive for what it was. An alluring smile lit her face as she twisted her head free of his grasp. She lifted herself up on her knees and posed sexily before him. She leaned forward and whispered in his ear. "Your horns are showing, Elliott." Her voice was husky as she brushed her lips against his earlobe.

Elliott laughed as he pulled himself away from the tantalizing web she was weaving around him. Her body language, the way she touched him when she wanted to emphasize a point whenever she spoke and the way she smiled at him all combined to have a teasing effect upon his nerves and emotions. Imagany had a way of ravaging his feelings, making him feel as though he were the only man in her world and he believed she knew what she was doing. Elliott observed the seductive smile she had on her face as she watched him. He noted the length of her long eyelashes as her eyes fluttered up and down, and he viewed the fullness of her lips. Elliott felt himself throb as his eyes drifted lazily down to her breasts.

Trying to break the spell, Elliott tore his gaze away from her and stared straight ahead at the dormitory doors in an effort to regain his senses. When he turned his face back to her he said, "You're not being nice, Imagany." Elliott spoke so softly that only she could hear him.

Imagany had her elbow on the seat rest as she leaned the side of her face against the palm of her hand. She merely smiled as she stared mercilessly at Elliott, wanting to arouse him and wanting him to take note of her own arousal. She needed to make him aware that she had many things in store for him.

Leisurely, Imagany turned back to Caprice and Carl to ask them if they were interested in coming to the movies with her and Elliott. They consented and Carl agreed to pick Caprice up in his car so they could meet them there. Carl got out and Caprice climbed into the front seat.

Elliott went around to where Carl was standing and told Caprice, "Make sure speed racer here," he pointed to Imagany, "gets you home in one piece."

"Don't worry, I'll make sure she gets home in one piece too." Caprice gave Elliott a knowing look. "So we'll see you guys tomorrow?"

"Be there or be square," Carl said.

They lingered a bit longer before saying goodbye, waving as they sped off.

Caprice turned to Imagany with a smile on her face that immediately turned into a leer. She was waiting for Imagany to give her the lowdown. But Imagany was not forthcoming.

"Have you noticed that it's awfully hot inside this car?" Caprice asked facetiously.

"No, I haven't."

"Well I have. And if it gets any hotter something is guaranteed to catch on fire."

"Okay, Caprice. What are you talking about?"

"Girlfriend, come off it. It's obvious, isn't it?" Imagany continued to play the dumb role and Caprice said, "You and Elliott, my dahlin'. I mean, the sparks were flying so heavily between you two that Carl and I felt we were intruding. Are you sure there's nothing more you have to tell me?"

Without giving Imagany a chance to answer, Caprice said, "Wew child. I can't get over the way that man looked at you. I felt shivers run up my own spine." Caprice shook her head. "Imagany, I'm scared of that brother. The man looks like he definitely knows how to whip it on a woman." Caprice slapped her knee for the sound effects.

Imagany tried to deflect Caprice's comments. "I noticed that you and Carl hit it off pretty well too. I saw the way the two of you were snuggled up."

"Uh, uh. Don't even try it. Sure, we got along great. But we were hardly snuggled up. If anyone was snuggled up, it was you and Elliott. My goodness! You two were in your own little world. Imagany, between you, me and the bedpost, I think Mr. Anthony is about to be history."

"Why do you say that?"

"Because, girlfriend, there's no way you can handle Elliott and Anthony at the same time. Someone's got to be X'd from the picture."

Caprice started snapping her fingers as she sang a song from *Sesame Street*. "Which one of these don't belong with the other . . ."

"I get your point." Imagany cut her off abruptly. It was as if Caprice had struck a nerve.

Caprice said wonderingly, "You know if it were someone other than Elliott, I think you might be able to juggle them. But with a brother like him, honey, you're going to have your hands full just trying to deal with him alone." Caprice had a malicious gleam in her eye. "I just want to be there when you tell Anthony to get lost."

Imagany tried to reason with Caprice. "Slow down a minute, Caprice. There's nothing concrete between Elliott and myself. For all we know, the man could have a slew of women. I think it's illogical to believe he doesn't already have someone else as it is."

"Concrete? Baby, the man's body language is concrete. Anybody looking at the two of you together can tell something's there. Sure, it's possible that he has someone else. But you don't know that. All I'm saying is give him a chance. I just don't think you'll be able to do that sufficiently with Anthony in the picture, that's all."

Not committing to anything, Imagany simply said, "We shall see." They reached Caprice's dorm and Caprice got out of the car. She slammed the door saying, "I'll call you in the morning."

Shaking her head, Imagany pulled off and headed for Anthony's home in Antioch.

Chapter Five

magany awakened in her own bed with the feeling that the day was not going to turn out right. She was tired after the previous night's activities. She peered at the bedside clock. It was nearly twelve o'clock in the afternoon. Though it was Saturday, she had plenty of things that had to be done, like spending time at the library, especially if she intended to go to the movies with Elliott later on.

She searched painstakingly for her car keys, retracing her every step when the phone rang. When the answering machine picked up, she heard Anthony's voice on the line.

"Imagany, I wanted to know what time you would be free tonight so I could make good on the dinner date I offered you. Call me and let me know what time you'll be ready." Click.

Imagany sucked her teeth out of irritation. It was just like Anthony to assume she would want to go with him in the first place. More and more she was starting to notice little things like that about him. And they were beginning to get on her nerves. Imagany was on her knees looking underneath the couch when she found her keys. How the hell did they get under there? She sat back and rubbed the right side of her temple. She could feel a splitting headache coming on. She knew whenever her head started pounding like it was, she was suffering from stress, or some other kind of tension.

Dressed and ready to go, Imagany threw her bookbag over her shoulder and was turning the key in the lock when the doorbell rang. "Shoot," she muttered to herself. She would meet whoever the person was downstairs on her way out. She couldn't imagine who it could be anyway since she insisted that anyone visiting her have the courtesy to call first. Anybody who violated this policy ran the risk of being left out on the doorstep. Imagany reached the lobby area and was curious when the only person she saw standing there was a woman dressed in a double-breasted mauve pants suit. She was attractive and had a regal appearance. From the lines and cut of the material, Imagany recognized the suit as one of Givenchy's. She loved clothes and knew an expensive suit when she saw one. The woman wore stylish alligator pumps and had a matching Chanel bag. Whoever she was, she was well groomed from head to toe with not a hair out of place. Imagany clocked her somewhere in her early thirties.

She approached the woman and said, "I think you must have rang my bell by mistake."

The woman stepped closer to Imagany and surveyed her from head to foot. "Imagany Jenkins?"

Imagany was offended by the woman's haughtiness. She didn't appreciate the demeaning look the woman had just given her either. Throwing her bookbag over her other shoulder, Imagany said belligerently, "Who wants to know?"

"I do. I'm Leslie Lowe." Her voice was meant to intimidate as she held out her hand in greeting.

Leslie Lowe? Why did that name sound so familiar? Drawing a blank, Imagany reluctantly shook the woman's hand. "How may I help you?"

"Actually, I was hoping that the two of us might sit and have a nice long chat."

"About what?"

"A mutual acquaintance."

Imagany quickly placed the name and person. Leslie Lowe was Anthony's ex-girlfriend. The way Anthony told the story, Leslie had been disappointed when he had not offered to marry her and had broken off the relationship. Imagany could understand Leslie's disappointment. Anthony was wealthy and was a good catch by any woman's standards. She recalled being at Anthony's place a couple of times when Leslie had called. Each time, Imagany vaguely remembered him giving Leslie the brush off. But it would come as no surprise to Imagany if Anthony were still seeing the woman.

Even though Imagany did not find Leslie threatening, she came to her guard. Not knowing what to expect, she wanted to be prepared for anything that was thrown her way.

Imagany said, "Now is not a good time."

Imagany started walking away, leaving Leslie no choice but to follow her. She was curious even though she could very well guess what the woman wanted to discuss. When Imagany reached her car, instead of getting in, she unlocked the door and hit the button that would lower the convertible roof.

"Nice car."

Imagany accepted the compliment without comment. She suspected that Leslie had a tendency to be cunning and conniving and was only trying to butter her up. Imagany's composure was commendable and she was sure that Leslie was a little taken aback. Maybe Leslie had expected to find an air head or some silly twit, but Imagany was willing to bet that Leslie had not expected to find someone of her own stature.

Though Leslie looked as if she had just stepped from the pages of a magazine, Imagany's first impression of her diminished. She felt that the woman had to be insecure since she'd stooped to seeking her out. They stood face to face alongside the car. Imagany stared at Leslie impassively, choosing to let her speak first.

"You're not exactly what I expected. But at least I can see why Anthony's infatuated with you."

"So you came all the way here just to discuss Anthony and to tell me that I look good?"

"Let's just say I came to discuss Anthony."

In a haughty voice of her own, Imagany said, "And what, may I ask, did you expect to find?"

Leslie gave Imagany an appraising look. "When Anthony told me he was seeing someone younger, much younger, I might add, I assumed it would be a quick fling. Men being men, I was quite willing to turn a blind eye to the entire affair. But two years is a long time to wait for someone to crawl back into the hole that they've come out of." She spoke in such a way that Imagany had no doubt that Leslie was referring to her.

At the mention of crawling in and out of some kind of hole, Imagany threw her book bag inside the car and was prepared to throw down. Maybe wherever Leslie came from, they did things like this in a civilized manner. But where Imagany grew up, on the mean south side streets of Chicago, if a person pulled a stunt like this, they had better come prepared to back it up.

Leslie held up both her hands appeasingly. "Please, just let me finish."

Imagany leaned back against the car, clasping her hands into fists. She stared at Leslie in a manner that conveyed her irritation.

Leslie continued her story. "I've known Anthony Barrington since we were small children. As a young girl, Anthony was my first love and I knew then that I wanted to be his wife. But Anthony is a hard man to pin down and he's kept me waiting a long time. I'm forty-one years old and damned proud of it because I know I don't look a day over thirty." When Leslie volunteered her age, she accepted Imagany's surprised look as a compliment. "But as you can see, I'm not getting any younger. Though I've seen Anthony stray with women of all kinds, I never lost my composure because I always knew that eventually, he would come back home. None of his women were ever a threat to me. That is, until you came along." Leslie fumbled in her Chanel bag and pulled out a picture. She looked at it before passing it to Imagany.

"You're prettier in person than you are in this snapshot." Leslie's tone of voice clearly showed that she was not attempting to flatter her. "Maybe you should keep your clothes on."

Imagany took the picture and gasped when she saw that it was one that Anthony had taken of her a year ago at his home while she was in his Jacuzzi. Taken from the side view, the picture was a body shot of her stepping out of the water. Her head was thrown back and her wet hair streamed down past her shoulders. Imagany wore a flimsy two piece bikini that Anthony had insisted she wear. It emphasized her ribcage and large breasts and showed off her hips to perfection. The swim suit actually left very little to the imagination. Imagany hadn't wanted Anthony to take the picture. When she had made a big fuss about it, he had promised her he would let her have it. Imagany had forgotten all about the picture until she had found it among some things of his weeks later. She had taken it, thinking at the time that it was the only copy.

"Keep it," Leslie said snidely when Imagany made no move to return it. "You see, Imagany," Leslie paused, "may I call you Imagany?"

Imagany didn't answer. She was humiliated by the fact that Anthony had deceived her about the picture. She had no doubt that Leslie had taken it from among Anthony's things, but that didn't matter. It angered her that Anthony had duplicated the picture and had even allowed a copy of it out of his possession. She immediately vowed never again to let a man photograph her in another uncompromising position.

Leslie carried on as if the two of them were old friends. "There's really very little that I don't know about Anthony. From his head right down to the Giorgio Armani underwear that he insists upon wearing. I know his likes, his dislikes, his uneven temperament. I even know the way he prefers to make love." Leslie watched Imagany closely. She shifted and came to lean up against the car next to Imagany. In a quiet voice, she continued, "I especially know about you, Imagany. In the last two years, I've more or less made it my business to find out everything I could. Yes, this is a very nice car." Leslie ran her finger along the rim of the door. "I can tell you how much your monthly car note is. Or maybe you'd prefer that I tell you how much rent Anthony pays for your little apartment every month. And since you're such a nicely dressed little girl, maybe you're curious to know if I can tell you how much your monthly shopping sprees cost him, or are you more interested in your weekly allowance?"

Each dart was delivered with precision. Though Imagany's face was impassive, Leslie knew her digs were getting through.

"Have I made my point clear?" Leslie stared into Imagany's face. "How do I know all these things? Well, my dear, I know them because I keep Anthony's financial records. You look at Anthony and you wouldn't know that behind him is a very successful black woman. That woman happens to be me, Imagany. So anytime you read an article about him or see his picture somewhere, just know that I helped Anthony build Barrington Industries from the ground up to the conglomerate it is today. If you thought he had broken off his relationship with me, as I'm sure he told you, then you're sadly mistaken. You did know that he was seeing me, did you not?"

Imagany had suspected that Anthony saw other women, but it was another thing to have it confirmed. If Leslie were such a major factor in his life, why hadn't Anthony at least mentioned her? Imagany's silence spoke for itself.

"Let me show you something." This time, Leslie left Imagany to follow her.

Imagany followed on wooden legs. When they reached Leslie's car, Imagany was not surprised to discover that she drove a brand new midnight blue Jaguar. Leslie unlocked the doors and motioned Imagany to get in.

Though no words were spoken, Leslie knew Imagany was impressed. She was in familiar territory now as she ran her hand possessively over the steering wheel. "When Anthony purchased my car, I made sure he bought me something of quality. I would never, ever accept anything less than the best." Leslie's words clearly implied that she would never drive anything as lowly as a mere BMW.

Imagany took Leslie's jabs with a grain of salt. She was tiring of Leslie's subtle putdowns and would soon put a stop to it if it continued.

Apparently Leslie was just warming up. She reached into the glove compartment to take out several sheets of paper and handed them to Imagany.

"Do these look familiar to you?"

Imagany took the papers. They were copies of her recent American Express, Citibank, Chemical and Chase Manhattan visa bills, all paid for by Anthony.

"You're a very expensive girl, Imagany, and you're obviously no dummy. I'm sure those are only two more reasons why Anthony is attracted to you. Nevertheless, I've said all of that to say this: About two months ago, Anthony came to me and told me that he was finally thinking about getting married. You can imagine my joy at believing that my lifelong dream was about to be fulfilled. But no. The joke was on me. You see, he was talking about marrying you, Imagany. Imagine that. A man of his age being foolish enough to want to marry someone of your age. My first thought was that you had tricked him by getting pregnant." Leslie paused when Imagany snickered loudly. "When he denied that was the case, I pleaded with him to think it over. Two weeks went by and I didn't hear a word from Anthony. So I thought that maybe he was staying at your place just to spite me. I've since discovered otherwise."

Imagany knew the period in question must have been the time when she, too, hadn't heard from Anthony.

Leslie tapped her fingers on the dashboard before turning to Imagany with a reckless expression on her face. "I don't know what the hell it is you do to Anthony, and to be honest, I don't even want to know. But I will tell you this. Don't believe for one moment that I'd allow you to even think about marrying him. I would make your life a living hell." Leslie delivered her last statement with a parting blow.

Imagany may have been sitting like a puppy with her tail between her legs. Her pride may even have been hurt, but her brain was still in good working order. At Leslie's direct attack, Imagany bounced back with a confidence that surprised Leslie. "You may be older than I am, Leslie, but I hesitate to add wiser. It amazes me that a woman of your caliber has to stoop to using threats as a form of intimidation. Don't you know that if I truly wanted to marry Anthony Barrington, I would already be his wife? There would be nothing you or anybody else could do to stop me." Imagany spat fire. If Leslie wanted to engage in a verbal war, then she would find that she had met her match. But the prospect of a physical battle was what Imagany wanted.

Imagany continued her assault. "Since you seem to know everything else, did you know that Anthony has already set the date?" By Leslie's look of surprise, Imagany could tell that she didn't. "Then I guess you also didn't know that the only thing that's holding up the program is my unwillingness to say I do." When Leslie's eyes widened, Imagany said, "Believe me, it's true. If I said yes today, Anthony would marry me tomorrow. Maybe he would even be doing it to spite you." Imagany shrugged her shoulders indifferently. "I don't know; nor do I care. But what I do know, Leslie, is this: You may very well have been the one to help Anthony build his enterprise. But as his wife, I'll be the one entitled to the profits, while you on the other hand, will only be his secretary or whatever the hell it is you are. Should I agree to marry Anthony tomorrow, I'll be the one who gets everything since not once has Anthony ever mentioned anything to me about signing a prenuptial agreement. In the event that we get a divorce, I'll still be set for life." Imagany gave Leslie a moment to let all of this sink in as she sat back with a satisfied smirk on her face. She knew she had hit Leslie where it hurt the most.

The thought of Imagany having even partial ownership to what was rightfully hers was too much for Leslie to bear. Bristling, she said, "Why you . . ." Leslie's anger was nearly tangible as Imagany goaded her. Leslie could easily sense through Imagany's body language and hostile manner that the girl was spoiling for a fight. Not being of that frame of mind, Leslie put a reign on her own temper. She had expected to find some gooey-eyed, love struck kid who was naive and simple. But this cold-blooded calculatedness was too much for her to take. Leslie stared at Imagany with loathing as if Imagany were a snake. She shook her head in dismay as she spoke in a voice that was filled with total disbelief. "You don't even love him, do you?"

"What do you think?" Imagany answered in a voice that still seethed with amused anger.

"I think you're a greedy, self-serving little witch who's out for everything she can get." To think that Anthony was being manipulated and pussy-whipped by someone of Imagany's age was all too fitting and ironic. It served him right. *Men.* Suddenly, Leslie broke out in laughter.

Leslie's laughter surprised Imagany and served to relieve the tension. Imagany shrugged her shoulders. She wasn't offended by what Leslie had said. She had been called worse. Right or wrong, it didn't matter to her in the least what Leslie thought of her.

Leslie now viewed Imagany in a totally different light. She could certainly say that she no longer envisioned her as a child. Leslie was now ready to deal with Imagany on her own level and she decided to try a different tactic. "I think Anthony and I both underestimated you, Imagany. Since you obviously have no desire to be married to Anthony, how much would it take to make you continue to tell him no?"

Imagany knew that Leslie was willing to pay her off. Not being one to beat around the bush, she pulled her calculator out of her purse and started tallying up her bills. Imagany estimated how much her rent, utilities, and basic necessities would cost her over the next two years. She added in money for her personal use, too. She simply wanted to ensure that if Anthony dropped her like a hot potato tomorrow, she wouldn't have to worry about making it. In light of all the new found information, Imagany no longer trusted Anthony to have her best interest at heart. This opportunity was as good as having money in the bank. With that done, Imagany put her things away and looked Leslie dead in the eye. "Sixty thousand should do the trick nicely."

Leslie never batted an eye. She pulled out a cigarette from a gold cigarette case and lit it, blowing the smoke toward the roof of the car. She flicked her ashes into the ashtray and said calmly, "That's a lot of money for a college student."

"Not when you consider how long it's got to last me. But if that's your final answer then I don't think we have anything further to discuss. I can't say it was nice meeting you." Imagany opened the door of the car and made a move to get out.

"Wait." Leslie quickly calculated how she could maneuver the money from Anthony's funds without having to use her own.

Imagany closed the door and sat back in the seat while Leslie continued to smoke her cigarette and ponder her thoughts.

"Once I give you the money, you're to emphatically tell Anthony the answer is unequivocally no."

"Gladly."

"Then I'll have the money next week."

"Fine. Make it cash. If, between now and next week, you should change your mind, don't even worry about it. Just think of me as Mrs. Imagany Barrington because I'll be getting the money from my new husband." Imagany got out of the car, but before she closed the door, she leaned in and said, "Leslie, it's been a pleasure doing business with you. I really would love to stay and chat a while longer, but unfortunately, I must be on my way to the library. Call me sometime, we'll do lunch." Imagany was merely being facetious. She had barely slammed the car door when Leslie drove off at a pace that left skid marks on the pavement.

Imagany shook her head, thinking that there was no limit to the things some women would do, even resorting to selling their souls, just to have and keep a man. Imagany thought to herself: May God never let that be me.

Chapter Six

magany whistled under her breath as she searched the library shelves for the books she needed. She was in high spirits as she breezed through the aisles. She rounded a corner heading back to her table when a male figure cut in front of her, causing her to crash into him. Imagany glared at him as his hands reached out to steady her.

"Helloooo, Imagany." Crenshaw was a member of the Que Psi Phi fraternity. He was a typical frat boy. They tended to think their membership gave them carte blanche to any woman on campus. Many of the guys found Imagany's air of unapproachableness intimidating and they accepted her firm denials to their advancements. But there were always a few, like Crenshaw, who found her "hard-to-get" attitude all the more appealing.

Imagany rolled her eyes as she stepped to the side to go around him. Crenshaw stepped to the side in unison with her, blocking her path.

Imagany sighed audibly as she placed one of her hands on her hip. "Do you have a personal problem, Crenshaw?"

"Yes, I do. As a matter of fact, I've had it since the first day I met you." Crenshaw glanced at his groin area. "It seems I only get this particular problem whenever I run into you. I wonder if there's anything you can do to help me?" Crenshaw spoke loud enough so his partners sitting at a nearby table could hear him. They snickered loudly at Crenshaw's comments.

Imagany shook her head as she exhaled her breath. On a normal day, she would have ignored Crenshaw and continued on her way. But he had overstepped his bounds and it was time for her to let him know where she came from. She clasped her books to her chest and wrapped her arms around them. "You know, Crenshaw, you should save the drama for your mama. See, even on a bad day there would be nothing that I could do for you. Understand that I was never the kind of person who doled out charity screws. You do know what a charity screw is, do you not?"

When Imagany spoke loud enough for all of his friends to hear, Crenshaw had no choice but to say, "No, enlighten me."

Imagany was only too happy to oblige him. She spoke loudly as she broke it down to his level. "It's when a man with a weak and limp-needled dick is so hard up, the only way he can get any kind of pussy is by tricking a woman into screwing him. But since most of the women already know that he only has a stub of a penis to offer them, the only ones he's likely to find are those he can dupe or those who don't mind contributing to his charitable cause. The word around campus on you, Crenshaw, is they call you the 'three-second bandit.' That's your nickname, Crenshaw. In on the first count. Out on the third. It seems that all the women agree that you're in need of a serious penile implant. So, my dickless brotha, there's absolutely nothing that I can or ever will do for you in this lifetime. But cheer up, Crenshaw. With modern technology as it is today, they're bound to have institutions for people with problems like yours."

When Imagany finished cutting Crenshaw down, he barely had a stub of a leg left to stand on. With his ego crushed, the next time Imagany stepped to the side, Crenshaw made no move to stop her. His boys at the nearby table were all laughing loudly, covering their faces with paper or burying their heads in their arms while they slapped the table with their hands. Imagany continued to whistle as she walked away leaving Crenshaw standing with a look of definite shame on his face. She heard one of his boys say, "Daaaaammmmnn! Man, that woman is cold as ice! I told 'cho monkey ass not to say anything to her in the first place!"

When Imagany reached her home, it was exactly five-thirty. Caprice had a key to her apartment and had let herself in. They weren't expecting Elliott and Carl for at least another hour and a half so they had time to shoot the breeze.

Imagany kept plenty of food in her refrigerator. Caprice, as always, was only too willing to whip up something quick. Cooking was one of Caprice's fortes and she enjoyed doing it. As Caprice cooked, she talked nonstop. She could tell something was on Imagany's mind and that, whatever it was, Imagany wasn't ready to talk about it. It was at times like this, when Imagany was in such a reflective mood, that Caprice kept up a constant stream of chatter.

Caprice had given Carl instructions to Imagany's place as they had all agreed it would be best if everyone met there. At exactly seven-thirty the doorbell rang and Imagany ran downstairs to meet them.

The apartment complex which Imagany lived in was a very elegant one. It catered mostly to upper-middle-class working adults and had very few college students as residents. It had an outdoor swimming pool, tennis court, and a built-in sauna for all the tenants to share. The grounds were nicely kept and all the lawn hedges were cut in decorative swirls.

As Imagany let Elliott and Carl in, she was suddenly proud of where she lived. She touched cheeks with both of them as she said hello. They were wearing jeans and Imagany was grateful that she, too, had changed into hers. "You found the place with no problem?"

"None at all. Caprice gave very explicit instructions."

Imagany closed the door behind them as they stepped inside her apartment.

"This is a very beautiful place you have," Elliott said as he looked around in appreciation.

Imagany took pride in the artful way in which her apartment was decorated. She had done the decorating herself. Her place was furnished in a flourish of warm colors that were mostly of a light gray and a pinkish-mauve. Her living room furniture consisted of a light gray three-piece leather group while the end tables and center piece were glass with brass trimmings. Mauve lacquer and cream granite ornaments adorned the end tables and a large floral arrangement garnished the center one. Huge oversized paintings hung on two of the walls while a large diamond-shaped brass etagere filled with brass and crystal knickknacks rested against a third wall. In front of the last wall sat a 60" screen TV and a Pioneer stereo system that looked as if one needed to be an engineer to operate it. Behind the large leather sofa was a potpourri of large potted plants that seemed to vie with each other for space. Gold vertical blinds encased the floor-to-ceiling picture window and a huge chandelier with crystal glass panels hung from the ceiling to bathe the room with a soft glow.

Imagany showed them the kitchen, bed and bathroom areas. Everything was modern, high-tech, and contemporary. Imagany enjoyed their looks of surprised approval.

"This is something right out of a Better Homes & Gardens magazine, Imagany. Did you do this yourself?" Though Elliott asked the question, Carl was curious too.

"Yes," Imagany answered, pleased with herself. "What can I tell you other than that I love to decorate?"

"Then you'll have to do our home someday," Elliott said.

Carl nudged him in the side. "Just don't expect it to be any time soon, Imagany. It'll be fifty years before this bucket head boy will be able to afford any of this stuff. What's in the fridge?" Carl wasted no time as he walked back into the kitchen and went directly to the refrigerator. He opened the door and stared inside.

"Man, get out of there!" Don't you have any kind of home training? You don't just come inside someone's house for the first time and go into their refrigerator." Elliott playfully kicked Carl in the rear end as he bent head first in the fridge.

Imagany was not in the least offended. She admired Carl's boldness. "It's okay, Elliott. Carl and I go a long way back. Right, Carl?"

"Ever since kindergarten." Carl jokingly made reference to the length of time Imagany and Caprice had known each other. He pulled out an apple and bit into it. "This woman has more food than a grocery store. So I know you can throw down in the kitchen." Without waiting for a reply, Carl closed the refrigerator to look inquisitively in all the kitchen cabinets. Imagany laughed as she watched him.

Elliott put his hand to his head as if he were ashamed of Carl. "Man, will you stop? I can't take you anywhere." Elliott turned to Imagany and Caprice, who were both watching Carl humorously, and held up his hands. "You have to forgive him. He doesn't get out much. His parents found him in a garbage can when he was a little baby and he's been eating them out of house and home ever since. They had to get rid of him so that's why they shipped him down here to TSU. His poor mother and father are in an insane asylum now because he drove them crazy."

"Hey, watch it. Don't talk about my folks." Carl leaned against the kitchen counter and finished the last bite of his apple. "Elliott you now have my stamp of approval. I now pronounce Imagany rightfully yours." While Carl appeared to be doing his own version of matchmaking, what he really was doing was stalling for time. He felt awkward around Caprice. Having thought of her all day, now that she was standing here before him, for some unknown reason, he suddenly felt shy.

"You know, Carl, just because a person has a house full of food does not necessarily mean they know how to cook. Caprice is the one who does all the cooking around here. Whenever Caprice cooks, the food tastes so good, you'd think she put her foot in it." Imagany played up Caprice's culinary skills for what they were.

"Uh, oh. Anytime a person sticks their foot in the food, it's guaranteed to be good. Does this mean you'll be doing the cooking next Saturday?" This was the first opportunity Carl had to address Caprice directly.

Caprice had started to wonder if she had bad breath or something. As far as she was concerned, Carl had played her to the extreme far left. She was thrown off guard, wondering if she had done something to offend him. Now she only nodded her head in reply to his question.

"In that case, woman, come with me and let me whisper in your ear what I would like to eat." Carl took Caprice's hand and led her into the living room.

Imagany and Elliott were left standing alone in the kitchen. Elliott had his hands in his pockets as he leaned up against the refrigerator door. He seemed to always be at a loss for words whenever he was with her.

The moment Caprice and Carl left the kitchen, Imagany watched Elliott with a giddy smile on her face. Without even thinking about it, she stepped directly in front of him and rested her chin on his chest. Elliott's arms quickly wrapped around her, pulling the full weight of her body against his.

Elliott had been consumed with thoughts of Imagany. Throughout the day, her image had plagued him, and he reveled in the feel of her now. He brushed his nose lightly along Imagany's widow-peak, breathing in the smell of her, memorizing her scent. "I missed you." There was a husky quality to Elliott's voice when he spoke.

"Since yesterday?" Though Imagany teased him playfully, she knew exactly what he meant. Standing in his arms, she knew this was where she was truly meant to be. She realized that she had gotten through the entire day in anticipation of being with him. Elliott's sweater was tucked into his jeans and Imagany stared him straight in the eye as she pulled it from his pants. Her hands moved underneath it to seek the flesh of his chest. When she felt how hard and warm he was, her eyes closed and her head fell backwards. Her nipples hardened as a warm fire spread over her.

When Elliott pulled her head back to his chest, she nipped him softly with her teeth and lightly dug her nails into his chest. She yearned to drag him into the bedroom and teach him all the techniques to the art of seduction.

Elliott could barely stand the way Imagany was making him feel. No matter where he went or what he did, the smell and feel of her was with him. He plunged his hands into her hair and gripped her head possessively. He lowered his head and pried her lips apart with his tongue and kissed her demandingly. When her arms encircled his neck, he could feel her body yield to him so he picked her up and placed her on top of the kitchen counter, planting himself firmly between her legs.

Imagany rested her fingertips behind his ears as she stared longingly into his eyes. Before his hand could reach up to caress the cleft in her chin, she purposely locked him between her legs by crossing her ankles behind him. She pulled his head back to hers and lightly traced the outline of his lips with her tongue.

Elliott's eyes closed as her tender touch washed over him. He was willing to be her slave for as long as she wanted him and he was as pliable in her arms as a tender reed. She felt so right to him, as if she were made just for him. He opened his mouth and suckled her lips, pulling her tighter against him.

Behind them, someone cleared their throat. Elliott didn't care to turn around, nor did Imagany look up.

Carl loudly clapped his hands. "Okay, kids, let's not have any of that now. It's time to hit the road."

A moment passed before Imagany asked Elliott in a dazed voice, "Where are we going?"

Caprice said exasperatedly, "Excuse me people, but we were going to the movies, remember? You know, the place people go to watch a picture?" Caprice spoke in a "let me break it down for you" manner that was meant to bring Imagany back to reality. Watching the two of them cuddled up was like watching an erotic film.

Elliott turned around and said to Carl, "Give us a few minutes, Carl. We'll be right there." He watched them file out of the kitchen. Elliott turned back to Imagany and tried to decipher the expression on her face. Her lips were bare of all lipstick and they had that bruised, just-kissed quality to them. Elliott's eyes glided possessively over Imagany's face. Her eyes were downcast and he leaned down to catch her gaze. When she wouldn't meet his gaze, he lifted her chin and made her look at him. "What's wrong, baby?"

At the softness of his tone and the caring note in his voice, Imagany's heart melted. Unable to look at him, she buried her face in his neck. When she finally lifted her face and stared at Elliott, she decided to be honest with him. "I don't think I've ever felt this way before, Elliott, and it scares me. I've never been obsessed with a person in my life. The emotions that I'm feeling now are all so new to me." Imagany paused to take a deep breath before saying slowly, "I think I might be falling in love."

Imagany spoke in a voice that was so sad that Elliott thought she was going to cry. To him, it felt like the luckiest day of his life. He wanted her to feel the same way, too. He lifted her down from the counter and raised her chin to force her to look at him. Imagany continued to cast her eyes downward and Elliott said tenderly, "Look at me, Imagany." When Imagany still could not meet his gaze, Elliott continued. "There's nothing wrong with the way you feel, and if it helps any, I feel the very same way." Elliott placed Imagany's hand over his heart. "If you could only know how fast my heart is beating right now, you'd be laughing at me. So come on, look at me."

When Imagany finally met his gaze, she stared into his eyes and knew at that moment that she had fallen in love with this beautiful black man. The smile that lit her face was so radiant that Elliott was immediately affected by its glow.

He reached down and clasped his hands behind her neck and affectionately touched his forehead to hers. "We've got years and years to work on this, Imagany. And we'll keep working on it until we get it right. Do you hear me?"

Imagany was not sure if Elliott was referring to her emotions or their feelings for one another. Either one was fine with her. She asked him playfully, "Until we're old and gray?"

"You got it, kid. So come on, let's go. Carl and Caprice are getting anxious." Elliott tucked his sweater back into his jeans before taking her hand to lead her out of the room.

They had all reached the lobby when Imagany noticed she had forgotten her purse. She told them she would meet them by the car and ran back upstairs to get it. As soon as she entered the apartment, the phone started ringing. She knew it could only be Anthony and she debated whether she should answer it. Deciding against it, Imagany quickly unplugged the power cord from the machine so that, regardless of how many times the phone rang, the answering machine would not pick it up. As she grabbed her purse and locked the door behind her, she thought maliciously, ring, baby, ring.

As promised, the guys drove this time, and the two couples rode in separate cars. Elliott warned Imagany before hand, "My car is not the lap of luxury that you're accustomed to Imagany, but it'll get us wherever we need to go."

His car was the least of her concerns. She felt wonderfully lightheaded as the two of them held hands. Imagany kept up a lively stream of conversation all the way to the movie theater.

Carl and Caprice beat them there and were already in line as Elliott parked his car next to Carl's. As they joined them in line, Elliott pulled Imagany in front of him and clasped his arms around her waist. Together, they looked as if they were the perfect couple and they appeared to be in their own little world.

The four of them ran into many people whom they knew. But the majority of them were people who knew Elliott and Carl. They were standing in line for popcorn when several guys, most of them football players, came over to greet Elliott. Elliott introduced Imagany but his possessiveness was clearly in his voice.

They moved from the refreshment stand and selected their seats when Imagany and Caprice decided to go to the ladies' room before the movie began. Once inside, Imagany hummed as she applied lip gloss to her mouth.

"Earth to Imagany. Earth to Imagany." Caprice sang as she tried to attract Imagany's attention.

Imagany was feeling benevolent and her voice reflected it. "My ear drums were still working the last time I checked. What is it, dahlin'?"

As Caprice combed her own hair, she said, "Your ears may be working, but what about your eyes? Don't you see those girls over there checking you out?"

Imagany glanced in the direction Caprice indicated. Sure enough, there were three girls staring daggers at her. She stared back at them and noted that she didn't know any of them when one of the girls broke from the group to approach her.

Imagany turned to face the girl before she could reach her. As they stood face to face the other girl said, "You don't know me but my name is Giovanni. Since I couldn't help but notice the way you and Elliott Renfroe were snuggled up, I just had to come over and tell you a little bit about him. Elliott is nothing but a dog, honey, and you need to know it."

"Oh, really." Though Imagany spoke condescendingly, the sarcasm was lost on Giovanni.

"Yes, really. I know because I dated him for a while. Elliott never lasts longer than a few weeks with any girl and you're only fooling yourself if you think you'll be any different. You're only one out of maybe a hundred. But if you don't believe me, ask any woman on the yard up at State. Or better yet, ask Elliott about 'Gio' and see if he remembers who I am. But then he sleeps around so much, he probably won't remember me anyway. Time will only tell how long you'll last." Giovanni went back to her friends and they all walked out of the restroom.

There were about four other girls standing around looking curiously at Imagany to see what her reaction would be. She turned back to the mirror to fluff her hair and tried to play it off. She said jokingly to Caprice, "I know I said I wanted to be in the race, but I didn't realize there were going to be a million other contestants."

Caprice was staring at her with raised eyebrows. "Do you believe her, though?"

Imagany stuffed her comb in her purse. She wanted to downplay the seriousness of the incident. She didn't want to ruin the way she was feeling.

"I believe there was some truth to what she said. Even though women do a lot of things out of spite, she was too bitter and angry to have just made it all up. Hers is just one side of the story, Caprice, and before I jump to any conclusions, I'd like to hear Elliott's side, too."

"That's true. But, you know," Caprice shook her head as she zipped up her own purse, "I told you before, the competition over Elliott is going to be stiff. Something tells me that the fun is just beginning."

When they returned to their seats, Imagany was determined not to let the incident spoil the rest of the evening. When Elliott threw his arm over the back of her chair, she forced it out of her mind. The movie, Waiting To Exhale, turned out to be an enjoyable one and they agreed it was worth the money they had spent.

They filed out of the theater behind everyone else and walked to their cars. They leaned against them discussing the movie.

"I think they portrayed the men as wimps and dogs. We're not all like that. Society makes it seem like all the good men are either on drugs, in jail, or dead."

Caprice disagreed. "No, Elliott. I thought the movie was about women bonding together. If anything, they just let you see the macho side of men. But we women expect men to have a sensitive side, too. We want to see that same macho man be tender, loving, caring, and gentle." Caprice looked at Carl as she spoke. "That's the man for me. Someone who knows there's a time for a man to be a man but also a time when he has to be warm and compassionate." She gave Carl a challenging look.

"That sounds like the kind of man for me, too, Caprice. I wonder where I might find such a two-legged creature?" Imagany put her hand to her forehead and cast her eyes over the entire parking lot as if looking for something she had lost.

Elliott loudly cleared his throat. "Excuse me, miss, but I do believe you're looking at him. One kind, warm, and considerate gentleman at your service." Elliott took a bow. "How may I be of help?"

"Well, first of all, you can start by . . ."

"Hey, Elliott!"

At the sound of such a raucous voice, they all turned to see who was calling Elliott's name. Imagany saw some girls standing by the curb outside the theater entrance. Though she recognized Giovanni and the two other girls from the ladies' room, she didn't know the girl who was coming toward them with such a purposeful stride. Before the girl could reach them, Elliott excused himself and walked toward her.

When Elliott left the group, Carl opened the door of his car and gestured for Imagany and Caprice to get in. Caprice got in on the passenger's side but Imagany wasn't about to budge. When Carl got in on the driver's side, he left the door open and sat sideways with his legs out of the car.

Imagany stood looking after Elliott before turning to ask Carl point blank, "Who is she, Carl?"

Looking and feeling extremely uncomfortable, Carl said, "Imagany, you'll have to ask Elliott."

"Thank you very much, Carl. I'll do that." Imagany turned away from Carl with an attitude and went to prop herself on the hood of Elliott's car. Though she could not make out what they were saying, from where she was sitting she could see that Elliott and the girl were having words. Whoever the girl was, she was gesturing wildly with her hands, waving them and snapping her fingers in Elliott's face. Imagany could not see Elliott's face, as his back was turned to her, but he appeared to be trying to reason with her. She glanced to the side and saw Giovanni and her girls watching, too.

When the girl stepped away from Elliott to walk in Imagany's direction, that was all Imagany needed. Before Carl could even think of stopping her, she jumped down off the hood of the car and walked toward Elliott and his friend. Elliott had stepped in front of the girl and didn't know that Imagany was walking toward them. But his friend knew.

As Imagany came upon them, she heard the girl say, "So, what am I, Elliott? Just some whore for you to play with? You throw me away," the girl snapped her fingers loudly and pointed to Imagany, "and then bring the next one in? Just what do you take me for?"

When Elliott turned and saw Imagany standing behind him, Imagany could see that he was both frustrated and embarrassed. The girl had tears streaming down her face and she made no move to wipe them away. She clearly wanted an answer to her questions.

"Imagany, let me speak to Sheldon in private please." Elliott's tone was sharp.

"Why in private, Elliott? Because you don't want her to know what a dog you are? Or are you afraid she might find out that you sleep with anything that's got a hole between its legs?" As the tears continued to stream down Sheldon's face, Imagany couldn't tell if her tears were from anger or if she was just feeling wounded.

With both Imagany and Sheldon staring at him, Elliott had to offer an explanation. When he spoke, there was a quiet anger in his voice and his tone was filled with firmness. "Sheldon, I told you from day one that I wasn't interested in a relationship with you. So don't try to act like I deceived you in some kind of way. If it's the truth you want told here then tell it like it really happened. I never dogged you. You knew what the terms were and you accepted them. And since that was the case back then, why is there a problem now?"

"Elliott, I don't want there to be a problem." Sheldon was whining now. "I just want us to be the way we used to be."

Elliott sucked his teeth impatiently. "What in the world are you talking about, Sheldon? We never . . ."

As Elliott's voice trailed on, Imagany tuned him out. She had been stung by Elliott's sharp words to her about giving him and Sheldon privacy. She had even been about to walk away. But something in the way Sheldon stood there crying rooted her to the spot. Imagany pitied Sheldon, but her sympathy was laced with contempt. She suddenly had a flashback of the scene with her and Leslie and then she remembered how the other girl, Giovanni, had approached her in the ladies' room. All of this, coupled with how she had almost fought the girl Cynthia, made Imagany feel ashamed of herself. She felt as if she had degraded herself where Elliott was concerned, thereby compromising the very principles she had vowed not to break. That Sheldon could stand pleading with him in front of all these people with no pride only made Imagany determined not to end up as one of the many dozens of women who would crawl, beg, or do anything just to be with Elliott Renfroe.

Imagany didn't want to hear anymore. She turned to walk away and bumped smack dead into Carl who was standing right behind her. She had been so wrapped up in what was taking place in front of her that she hadn't even heard Carl approach. Imagany sidestepped Carl and made her way back to the car. What she didn't see was Elliott turning to come after her but he stopped after Sheldon put both her hands on his arm to detain him.

As Imagany leaned against the car door with her hands in her pockets, Caprice got out of the car and came to stand next to her, hooking her arm through hers. So impassive was she that Caprice knew she was dealing with feelings of hurt and anger.

"Kiddo, are you okay?"

Imagany didn't look at Caprice right away. She continued to stare straight ahead. Finally she looked down at the ground and said, "Caprice, I feel so stupid. It's like a gigantic boulder was sitting right in front of me and instead of going around it, I ran right into it." Imagany laughed humorlessly. "I feel like a little kid who had to touch the hot stove despite being warned not to."

At the bitter sound in Imagany's voice, Caprice smiled. She jerked Imagany's arm. "Do you remember Kenny Thornton?"

Imagany smiled as she looked up. How could she forget? Kenny was one of the guys that Caprice had fallen madly in love with back in high school. When the two of them had broken up, Caprice had cried on Imagany's shoulder every day for three months straight. Imagany had eventually tired of the whole affair and told Caprice to snap out of it and get over him. Ever since that time, Caprice had always warned Imagany that the day would come when the roles would be reversed and it would be her turn to cry on Caprice's shoulder.

Imagany pulled her hands out of her pockets and threw her arm around Caprice's shoulder. "Yeah, I remember ol' fine, bowlegged Kenny. But I can guarantee you that I'm a long way from where you were at. God, you were sickening." Imagany laughed and leaned her head on Caprice's shoulder. "Where would I be without you, Reese?" They got into Carl's car and continued to watch Elliott as he spoke with Sheldon and Carl.

Elliott watched Imagany walk away, leaving him standing with Carl and Sheldon. At this moment, Elliott wished he could shake some sense into Sheldon and he regretted having slept with her. Sheldon had hounded him for months on end and because she was an attractive girl, he admitted that his ego had been stroked. Elliott had finally decided to sleep with Sheldon after she had made it known that she was only too willing to make herself available to him in any way. Since that time, Sheldon continued to call and come around him despite his telling her that he was seeing other women and that he was not interested in anything serious with her. That Sheldon could stand here now acting as if he had deliberately set about to use her, angered Elliott and prompted him to set the record straight once and for all. Elliott glanced at Carl to indicate that he wanted to speak with Sheldon alone.

When Carl left, Elliott removed Sheldon's hands from his arm and brought them down to her sides. "Sheldon, listen to me. Make damned sure you hear me well the first time, because I don't expect to have to repeat myself, understand? I never told you or led you to believe that we had anything more than what we did. You made me feel good for one night and I'd like to believe that I did the same for you. You knew I saw other women and I know damned well you've been seeing other guys on the campus." At Sheldon's firm denials, Elliott held up his hands. "Whether you are is irrelevant, Sheldon. A monogamous relationship is something I've never been interested in with you. Don't make me out to be some monster that I'm not. So let's get the facts straight. From this point forward, I don't want you lurking outside my dorm room, I don't want you waiting for me outside any of my classes and I damned sure don't want you calling me. Do we understand each other?"

"Is that why you don't return any of my calls anymore Elliott?"

Elliott's irritation was obvious as he interrupted her. "That's beside the point, Sheldon."

"Then what is the point, Elliott? That it's like that now? Wham, bam, thank you ma'am? I thought you loved me, Elliott." When Elliott rolled his eyes heavenward in an exasperated manner, Sheldon said, "But I guess I was wrong. The one thing I do know I wasn't wrong about, Elliott, is when it came time for you to get some pussy, I don't remember hearing you talk all this crap about there being no relationship between us. Now that you're ready to screw someone else, all I'm suddenly hearing is 'I never told you this and I never told you that.' Well, go on, Mr. 'I'm God's gift to every woman on the planet.' Have your fun with Ms. Thing over there. But you mark my words, Elliott Renfroe, one day you're going to reap what you sow. I may be the one crying today. But the shoe will be on the other foot sooner than you think. I just hope when that day comes, I'm around to see it when it happens." With that, Sheldon turned and walked away.

Elliott looked after Sheldon trying, unsuccessfully, to justify his reasons for having slept with her. He felt that just maybe it had been wrong of him to sleep with Sheldon in the first place.

When Elliott made his way back to where they were, Imagany was sitting in the driver's seat of Carl's car while Carl stood outside. She must have been telling them something funny because both Carl and Caprice were laughing.

Elliott leaned into the car as if nothing out of the ordinary had occurred. "Ready?"

Imagany got out of the car and stretched. "Yep. I've got an early day of it tomorrow, so it's best we get a move on." If Elliott wanted to act as if all was well, then so be it. Turning back to Caprice, she said, "Call me later, Reese."

As Elliott unlocked the car doors, Imagany heard Carl say, "Is Caprice the only person you see?"

Imagany faced Carl and addressed him with irony in her voice, "As always, Carl, it's been a thrill. We must get together and do this again sometime." As she spoke, she held up her middle finger and flipped him the bird sign.

Carl laughed. "I love you too, Imagany." When Elliott and Caprice looked at them inquiringly, Carl smiled as he shook his head. He knew it was Imagany's response to him for not answering her question about Sheldon.

Imagany climbed into the car and stared out the window as they drove off in silence.

"Imagany, I owe you an explanation."

From nowhere, sketches of her conversation with Caprice came back to her. *And believe me, baby, there will always be competition over someone like him.* Imagany sighed deeply. "Elliott, you don't owe me anything, so please, there's no need to justify what happened tonight."

"I wasn't attempting to justify anything, Imagany. I only wanted to explain to you about Sheldon."

"Elliott, I don't even want to know about Sheldon. Common sense told me from day one that there were other women in your life. Now that it's been confirmed, it's no big deal. I expected it in advance. What I don't expect is to be accosted everywhere I go by women who want to either warn me or advise me about the 'great' Elliott Renfroe."

"Don't exaggerate. I doubt very seriously if you'll be accosted by anyone."

"Oh, do you now?" Imagany used the same sharp tone that Elliott had used on her when he had wanted to be alone with Sheldon. "For your information, Elliott, three girls approached me as soon as I walked into the ladies' room back at the theater. And do you know why,

Elliott? Because they, no excuse me, Giovanni was her name, wanted me to know that your reputation preceded you. If what she had to say is true, then I wonder, if the situation was reversed, would you be as receptive and understanding as you seem to expect me to be?" When Imagany looked at Elliott piercingly, he remained quiet. "I can't help but wonder if you would still feel the same way about me if even one of those guys back at the movie theater had been able to say that they had slept with me. Would you honestly be able to sit here and just shrug it off as if it's just one of those things?"

Elliott appeared to give it some thought. After a while he said, "I would never accept someone else's word without forming my own opinion about the person. But in reference to Giovanni and Sheldon, I can think of a thousand and one reasons as to why they did what they did."

Imagany interrupted him. "Don't bother telling me about the thousand reasons, Elliott. It's the one reason that comes after the thousand that worries me."

Elliott smirked. "I'm not going to make excuses, Imagany. Whatever I did before I met you, cannot be changed. I think it's only fair that you judge me on not just how I treated the women in my life before you, but more importantly, on how I treat you. I can't change the past. I can only be honest with you and tell you that there have been many women in my life but there hasn't been anyone serious. I just don't want what happened tonight to spoil things for us before we've even had a chance to know if there really is something between us. If two women can influence you to drop everything without even trying to find out for yourself if the relationship is worth pursuing, then maybe you should think about it, because there have been many more than two women."

"That many, huh?" Imagany was sarcastic.

"Not as many as some would have you believe, but there have been a few. The point is, Imagany, if you asked any of them to step forward that could say that I mistreated them, that I deceived them or even that I lied to them, not one of them could honestly say that I did any of those things. I don't make promises that I have no intentions of keeping, nor do I leave mistakes behind me." Elliott looked at Imagany. "And by mistakes, I mean babies. So no, Imagany, I'm not seeing anyone seriously." A challenging note crept into Elliott's voice. "But I'd like that to change now and it can only happen if you're willing to give it a chance. I have no idea what Giovanni said to you, but I can just imagine. People are strange in that they don't like to see other people happy, especially if the happy one has something that the other person doesn't. So get to know me before you jump to conclusions. And unless someone has something legitimate to say, don't ever let someone else's word come between us."

Imagany slipped off her shoes and lifted her legs up to sit cross-legged in the seat. She leaned her head back and said, "Sweet talking Elliott."

"Don't say that. You make me sound like some fast talking pimp." Elliott was offended. He was not vain and he had never considered himself 'God's gift to every woman.'

"That's not what I meant."

"Then I accept your apology."

"Wait a minute. You'll accept my apology? Who's the one that really needs to be apologizing here, Elliott?"

"You know what? Are we having our first argument?"

Imagany laughed. "I guess we are. And it's going to continue until we reach an agreement on who owes who an apology."

"If I thought an apology would make all of this go away, then I'd be the first to say 'I'm sorry,' but since I don't think I have anything to apologize to you about, I won't say anything."

They rode in silence for a while before Imagany said, "Don't misunderstand me, Elliott. I'm not interested in grilling you about the women in your life. I guess I just wanted to know about the people you're involved with in order to understand you better. I think you can tell a lot about a person just by the company they keep. That especially includes the kind of men or women they date. When Giovanni ran through her spiel in the ladies' room, the only conclusion that I jumped to was that she was a person who had a lot of hurt inside her and she was lashing out in the only way she knew how. The same was true for Sheldon. Imagany shook her head. "What I saw tonight, Elliott, were two very attractive and angry women who were both trying to come to grips with what has happened between you and them. You may have moved on to the next person, Elliott. But mentally, those two women have not. They're still holding on to whatever it is they think you shared with them in the past. I guess because I'm a woman, I can identify with them, even if it is in a minimal way. Whatever's happened tonight, Elliott, has not made me want to give up knowing you better, it's only made me determined not to end up in the same boat as those other women."

Elliott listened intently to Imagany's words.

"There are different sides to every story. That's why I wanted to give you the chance to explain yours. Contrary to what you might think, I'm not sitting here judging you. I've had my own share of men and failed relationships. If you're involved with a ton of women, I'm not condemning you. I just know to remove myself from the picture simply because I can't allow you to waste my time. I refuse to ever be strung out like the women we encountered tonight. The bottom line, Elliott, is that you can be open with me about anything. Especially things like this. I think it's when people feel that they cannot tell another person something for fear of their reaction that they start to hide things. If there is going to be anything between us, I agree that we have to get off on a good note."

They exited the highway and as they drew nearer to Imagany's complex, Elliott wanted to lay the subject to rest. "Imagany, I am sorry that you had to go through what you did tonight. It was uncalled for. So yes, I can and do apologize."

Imagany smiled. She realized it had taken a lot for him to agree to this concession. "No problem, Elliott. I've already put it behind me."

As they pulled into her parking lot, she reached down to retrieve her purse from the floor of the car. They had almost reached her apartment complex when she caught a glimpse of a silver Bentley. Her eyebrows wrinkled as she thought about how familiar the Rolls Royce looked to her. "What the . . . !"

Imagany panicked when she finally recognized Anthony's car and realized that it was he who was sitting in it. She almost choked for lack of breath as she managed to sputter out, "Elliott, stop!"

Elliott swerved into a nearby parking slot. "What's wrong?" His voice was full of concern at the note of hysteria in hers.

Imagany was flustered as she quickly rambled through her purse. "I just remembered. Caprice has my house keys so I'm locked out. Can you drive me back to her dorm to get them?"

Elliott looked at Imagany curiously. "Sure. Calm down. You scared the hell out of me."

As Elliott turned the car around, Imagany lowered herself by bending over, using her hand to feel along the bottom of the car's surface as if she were searching for her keys on the floor. She was certain that Anthony was waiting in the car and she damned sure couldn't afford for him to see her.

As she lifted back up, she noted Elliott's look of curiosity and said, "I, I wanted to be certain that my keys didn't fall out of my purse." As Imagany peered into the rear view mirror, her heart didn't return to its regular beat until they had driven a safe distance. What the hell was Anthony doing coming to her apartment without calling her first? Her head began to pound when she thought of what might have transpired if she had not spotted him in time. She didn't know what Anthony's reaction would have been but she could guarantee that it would not have been pleasant. Imagany shook her head at having escaped such a close call. She regretted having to be deceitful, especially after the way she had just lectured Elliott, but self-preservation must always come first. Imagany rubbed her temple with the new found knowledge that she was not into the "I spy" business. She became aware that Elliott was calling her name and she turned to look at him.

"What's wrong? Is your head hurting you?"

"I've developed a terrible headache. I'll just take some aspirin when I get to Caprice's room." Imagany felt guilty at the concern in Elliott's voice. How could she tell him that she'd just had the living daylights scared out of her? She couldn't, of course.

"I was asking you what you'd do if Caprice hadn't made it back to her room yet. She and Carl may have decided to go somewhere else."

If Elliott had asked her all of that, Imagany certainly hadn't heard a word of it. She answered him in a preoccupied voice. "I don't know. I guess I'll just have to wait for her."

Since Elliott intended to wait on her to drive her back home, he parked the car and came inside the dormitory with her. They approached the visitor's desk and the same guy who was there when Imagany had first met Elliott was there now. He and Elliott clasped hands in greeting before Elliott introduced him to Imagany.

"Imagany, this is Kerby." Elliott pulled Imagany to him possessively as he made introductions.

"Hi, Kerby. We didn't exactly get a chance to meet the last time."

"No, I guess we didn't." Kerby silently wondered how Elliott always managed to get the gorgeous ones.

As he and Elliott started discussing football, Imagany gave Kerby the name and room number of the person she wanted him to call. When Kerby tried Caprice's line and got a busy signal, Imagany was relieved. She told Elliott that she would be right back and indicated to Kerby that she was going upstairs. Not bothering to wait for the elevator, she went to the stairwell and flew up the stairs in a flash.

Caprice was on the telephone when she answered the door and her eyes widened in surprise when she saw Imagany standing there. She held the phone away from her ear and lifted her hand in a "what's up" gesture. Imagany closed the door behind her and leaned against it. When she mouthed the words, "Who are you talking to," Caprice put her hand over the receiver to whisper, "Carl." Imagany rolled her eyes as she plopped down on the bed and motioned for Caprice to get off the phone.

Caprice could tell from Imagany's agitation that she had a story to tell. Unable to contain her own curiosity, she told Carl that she would call him back later and hung up. "What happened?"

Taking a deep breath, she said, "Elliott was pulling into the parking lot of my complex when I spotted Anthony sitting in his Bentley right outside my apartment building. Caprice, I panicked!" Imagany threw her hands in the air. "I *saw* Anthony's car parked there, but it didn't even register!" Imagany knocked herself on the head. "I mean, how many people in my complex drive Rolls Royces? We were almost upon him before I even thought to tell Elliott to stop!" Imagany still had a sick feeling inside her stomach as she bounced on the bed and pushed her hands through her hair, pulling it away from her face.

"Get the hell out of here!" Caprice jumped up and came to sit on the bed next to Imagany. She had a look of amazement on her face. "Did he see you?"

Imagany spoke breathlessly as she shook her head. "No, I don't think so. But Caprice, I felt like someone had punched me in the stomach. Girl, my head started pounding and the only thing I could think of to tell Elliott was that you had my house keys." Imagany lowered her head into her folded hands. "The only thing I knew was that I had to get the hell out of there before Anthony saw me."

Caprice expelled her breath loudly as if she had been holding it. "I'll be damned." She shook her head to think for a moment. "So where's Elliott now?"

"He's downstairs waiting for me to get the keys from you so he can take me home. If this hadn't happened, I would have invited him to spend the night. I'm just going to tell him that I decided to stay over here. One thing's for damned sure, I can't let him take me back home. There's no telling how long Anthony will wait for me." Imagany lifted her head angrily. "Anthony knows I never permit anyone to come by without telling me first."

"That's very nice, Imagany, but since he pays your rent, I really don't think the rule applies to him."

Imagany threw herself back on the bed shaking her head from side to side. "Caprice, I am not cut out to lead a double life."

"Yeah, well, you appear to be doing pretty well to me." When Caprice looked at Imagany speculatively, Imagany flipped her the bird.

Caprice pulled her knees to her chest and said, "I wonder if he suspects that you might be seeing someone else?"

"Please, Reese, don't even say that! My nerves can't take it."

"Then what do you plan to do about it?"

"I don't plan to do anything but go downstairs and tell Elliott that I'll see him later. Preferably sometime in the distant future."

Caprice looked dumbfounded. "I thought you liked Elliott?"

"I do like him, Caprice. But I refuse to start sneaking and creeping around afraid that Anthony is going to be watching my every move. I don't know. I just need some time to think this whole thing over."

"Damn, Imagany! What is there to think over? Do I have to tell you everything? Just dump Anthony and be done with it." Caprice spoke exasperatedly.

Imagany laughed ironically. "If only it were that simple." Imagany nervously ran her hands through her hair. She stretched and let out a loud groan. "Let me just go tell Elliott that I'll talk to him later. I'll be right back."

Elliott and Kerby were still talking when Imagany got downstairs. Elliott was leaning on the desk and Imagany came and slid her arm around his waist.

Elliott stood up. "Ready?"

Imagany grabbed Elliott's hand and pulled him away from the desk. When they were standing off to the side, she said, "I've decided to stay here tonight."

Elliott looked surprised. "You're sure?"

When Imagany nodded her head, Elliott asked her, "How will you get back home?"

"Caprice's roommate has a car. She'll give me a lift."

Elliott's disappointment was obvious. "Okay. If you get stranded, just give me a call."

"Thanks, Elliott. You're a sweetheart." Imagany reached up and gave him a quick kiss on the chin. "Call me tomorrow?"

"Sure. I have football practice in the morning and afternoon, but I'll try to call you sometime in the evening."

Elliott threw his arm over her shoulders and she walked him out to his car. After he got in, he rolled down the window and Imagany leaned in. "I just want to make sure you understand one thing."

"And what's that?"

Imagany grabbed Elliott's nose. "That you're to go straight back to the dorm and don't make any detours along the way. Capeesh?"

Elliott laughed. "Since I can't be with you, I have no choice but to go straight back to my room."

Imagany looked at Elliott skeptically. "Just keep that in mind as you drive down the road." Imagany glanced at her watch. "You should be back in your room half an hour from now. So I'm giving you exactly that long before I call you."

"So you're timing me now, huh? Before I know it, I'll even have a leash and a curfew."

"That's right, baby. I'm clocking you." Imagany looked at her watch again. "So get a move on, dahlin', the clock is ticking." Imagany leaned in and lightly kissed Elliott on the forehead. She pulled away from him before he could grab her and waved as she walked back to the dorm.

Back in Caprice's room, Imagany decided that she had better call Anthony. She left a message on the answering machine at his home and then called him on his car phone.

Anthony's voice was gruff and abrupt when he answered his phone. "Barrington speaking."

"How are you?" Imagany's voice was soft and neutral because she intended to keep the conversation short.

Anthony's tone softened when he recognized Imagany on the other end of the line. "I've been trying to get in touch with you all day. Where have you been?"

"Well, let's see. I was at the library for the better part of the day. And then this evening, Caprice and I went to the movies." Imagany sat on Caprice's roommate's bed as she continued to talk. "After that, we came back here to Caprice's room and this is where I've been ever since."

"No wonder I wasn't able to reach you. How did you get around today without your car?"

"Caprice's roommate, Myra, played chauffeur. And how did you know I wasn't driving my car?" Imagany was on her P's and Q's.

"Because I can see your car from where I'm sitting."

"Anthony, my car is parked in front of my apartment. If you can see it from where you're sitting, that can only mean one thing."

"Very perceptive of you. When I couldn't reach you on the phone, I thought I'd just pop over and surprise you." With his own brand of humor, Anthony added, "And check up on you at the same time."

"Oh, did you now." Imagany was once again grateful for the fact that Anthony had no keys to her apartment. "How long have you been waiting?"

"Not too long."

Imagany wasn't sure if Anthony was being evasive or not. And not knowing what his motive was for showing up at her place, she kept her tone light, making sure there were no undertones of anger in her voice. "Well, however long it is, it serves you right. What do you mean, 'check up on me?' If I didn't know any better, Anthony Barrington, I'd think you were jealous of something."

"Not at all. I came by simply because I had a surprise for you."

Imagany remembered the scare she had just had and she was not impressed. "It must be some gift to make you drive all the way to my apartment. I wonder what it could be?"

"If I told you, it wouldn't be a surprise, now would it?"

Imagany could not muster the usual excitement that she normally felt whenever Anthony told her he had something for her. Several weeks ago, Anthony had promised her a diamond Rolex watch and she guessed this was the surprise.

"What time are you going to be home?"

"I don't know. Myra went somewhere and it's no telling what time she'll be back."

"I'll come get you. What's the address?"

"No, Anthony. But thank you anyway. I'll probably end up staying the night over here." Imagany was in no mood to see Anthony. She still had plenty of unresolved anger toward him because of her earlier conversation with Leslie.

"I'm leaving tomorrow afternoon for Atlanta and I probably won't be returning for about eight days or so. That means you'll have to wait until I return to claim your surprise."

Imagany knew Anthony had offices in Atlanta. If she didn't get the chance to see him before he traveled tomorrow, then so be it. She recognized the psychology behind Anthony's words and knew that his intentions were merely to convince her to see him.

Imagany glanced up and saw Caprice giving her the cue to get off the phone. "All right then, Anthony. You have a safe trip and just call me when you come back, okay?"

When Anthony gave a noncommittal reply, Imagany took it as some form of assent and said her good-byes. She stood by the phone chewing her lip, lost in her own thoughts.

When Caprice picked up the phone to dial Carl's number, she nudged Imagany with her foot, breaking her train of thought. Because it was a Saturday night, Myra, Caprice's roommate, was with her boyfriend and would not be returning to the room. As Caprice continued her flirtatious conversation with Carl, Imagany removed her clothes and put on one of Caprice's nightgowns. She climbed into Myra's bed to think everything over but was asleep before she even knew it. She never even remembered to call Elliott.

Anthony Barrington's eyes narrowed pensively as he replaced his car phone in its cradle. He leaned back into the most expensive leather seats that money could buy and tapped his fingers against the coolness of the material. Anthony considered himself perceptive enough to know when a woman's interest was waning, and especially when she was seeing another man. Though he doubted that she was, he could not be certain. Normally when he informed her he had a gift for her, she jumped for joy and afterwards gave him the "royal" treatment. This time she was different. Colder, somehow more remote. A slow anger burned through him at the thought of another man even touching what he considered his. Anthony had spent two years grooming Imagany. He was not about to let all the time, money and energy he had invested in her go to waste.

He pulled out the gift that he had brought back with him from his recent trip to New York City. A woman's diamond-studded Rolex watch glittered and shimmered inside the case. Anthony removed the watch from its velvet jacket and held it in the palm of his hand. His fist balled tightly around it and he knew that with the amount of anger inside him, he could easily crush it. Anthony dropped the Rolex back into its case and threw it on the passenger seat. He ran his finger over the thickness of his mustache and contemplated what he would do to Imagany if he ever discovered she was seeing someone else.

Chapter Seven

magany awoke to a flood of lights. She covered her head with the pillow to block out the brightness of the room. She could hear Caprice humming to herself as she busily flew around the room.

In a groggy voice, Imagany said, "My, aren't we the busy little bee this morning."

"That's right, dahlin'. If it's the early bird that catches the worm, then I've got to get a move on."

Imagany propped her head on her hand as she watched Caprice apply moisturizer to her face. "And where are you going this morning?"

"Carl's taking me out to breakfast and then we'll probably go to the museum." Caprice spun around. "Do you want to come with us?"

"No, sweetie. I just want to go home, fix myself something to eat and relax. Since Carl is coming to pick you up, maybe he can give me a lift home."

"I'm sure he wouldn't mind." Caprice approached the bed, scrubbing her face. "Are you feeling better, kiddo?"

"Yes. Why?"

"Because you tossed and turned all night." Caprice was watching her closely.

Imagany shrugged it off. "Probably because I'm in a different bed. And speaking of different beds, I'll bet Myra is having the time of her life. That girl is somewhere as we speak, taking care of serious business."

Caprice stopped scrubbing her face and tossed the wash cloth in the basin. She clapped her hands together and bent over touching her hands to the floor. Raising her rear end in circular motions, she sang the song. "I'm talkin' 'bout a strong black man!"

Imagany burst out laughing as Caprice continued to swing her rear end in gyrating motions. She swung her own legs over the side of the bed and started gyrating her upper body as they both sang the song.

Caprice raised herself and came over to the bed to high five Imagany. "Girlfriend, ain't nobody ever lied when they said Myra had herself a strong black man!"

"Yeah, baby! That man's got a body like BAM!" Imagany raised herself on her knees. Lifting her arms, she balled her fists as she positioned herself in a muscle man pose. "Girl, one day I was driving and that man came jogging down the street. Well, honey, the next thing I knew, I was out of my car and was about to run after him when it dawned on me that the man was already taken. Wew, child!" In a hysterical fit, Imagany threw herself upon the bed. "That man has a body on him that's just begging to be fondled and touched!"

"Tell me about it. And from the looks of things, ol' Myra is doing plenty much touching. When that girl comes back in the room tonight, you mark my words, Imagany, that child will be limping for the next few days. I wish you could be here to see her when she comes in tonight. Every weekend Myra is out of here like clock work. And on Sunday evenings when she comes back to the room, the girl is walking like a penguin. Now you try to tell me that the brother isn't puttin' a hurtin' on her."

Imagany shook her head, laughing. "All right now! Don't start no mess."

Caprice took a deep breath and said, "But you know, there's just one problem."

Imagany shook her head as she held up her hand in a stop sign gesture. "Dahlin', I know what you're about to say. Don't even go there."

"Imagany, girl, I've got to say it." Caprice placed her hands on her hips and leaned forward.

"Naw, Reese, don't say it, girl! Please. Please, don't say it!" Imagany pleaded with Caprice not to say what she knew she was about to say.

Caprice couldn't help herself. "Girlfriend, that boy is uglier than a mug! I mean, the man is hurtin' for certain! *To' up from the flo' up!*"

Imagany was rolling on the bed clutching her stomach as she laughed in loud guffaws.

Caprice was far from finished. "Baby boy's so ugly, he looks like he crawled out of somebody's sewer! Only the good Lawd can help that po' child. And girl, you don't wanna run into his black butt at night.

No way! We're talking about something that would scare the crap outta you for sure!"

Imagany rolled over on her back and coughed as she tried to sit up. "Caprice stop. Don't talk about that man like that. He's nice. Besides, Myra loves him. Girl, if Myra knew we were talking about her man like this, she'd be ready to fight."

"Yeah, I guess you're right. I'm glad somebody loves him, though. I guess there really is someone for everybody. But I'll tell you this, I know quite a few women around here, who, if they could only put a paper bag over his head, would snap him up just like that." Caprice snapped her fingers loudly.

Imagany jumped down off the bed and eyed Caprice slyly. "Speaking of strong black men, Mr. Carl Beasley falls in that category, too."

Caprice leaned against the wall and crossed her legs. She folded her hands over her chest and pulled at her chin with one hand. "Yeah, some folk's just got it like that. And he does seem to have it goin' on, doesn't he?" A sexy smile curled Caprice's lips as she thought of Carl. Caprice grabbed a chair and straddled it as she faced Imagany with a dreamy expression on her face. "I like his thighs. So big and muscular." Caprice lifted her hands in the air as if forming the shape of Carl's thighs.

At the look on Caprice's face, Imagany had to sit down. "Go on, girl. Talk about it!" She leaned forward in anticipation of what Caprice was about to say.

Caprice spoke soft and sexily as she opened her mouth and sucked air through her teeth. "Hands as strong as you'd want 'em. Skin and lips as smooth as you could expect. And a love tool as big as any woman could want it to be."

Imagany whispered reverentially, "Preach, girlfriend, preach!"

Caprice grabbed the back of the chair to bring herself back to reality as she got a grip on her emotions. "Yes, child. That man does things to me."

Imagany took a deep breath as she stood and went to the basin to wash her face. "One thing's for certain."

"What's that?" Caprice asked.

"It's just a matter of time before ol' Myra and I are sitting in this very room saying the same things about you that you and I are saying about her. With the exception of Carl being ugly."

"If Carl can make me walk like Myra's boyfriend makes her walk, then honey, I can hardly wait."

It was nearly eleven-thirty when Carl dropped Imagany back at her apartment. She fixed herself something to eat and shortly afterwards, worked up a sweat by performing a Tai Kwon Do routine. Imagany enjoyed the positions which were required to perform the movements. They helped tone and build muscular strength throughout her entire body. The routine was good for her mentally too because it always helped to reduce her stress. Imagany lowered into a Chinese split and touched her chest and forehead to the floor. She relaxed in this manner before curling into her favorite fetal position. She laid like this for a good fifteen minutes before the phone rang. Imagany sat up and crossed her legs as she let the machine answer.

"It's me. I just called to hear your voice and say hello. I'll try back again another time. Bye."

Imagany recognized Zabree's voice on the line as she raced to snatch up the phone. "Bree!"

"I was just about to hang up."

"I could tell." Imagany settled down on the couch. "I've been meaning to call you but things have been so hectic around here that I haven't had the chance. How are you?"

"Hey, things are just lovely."

"Lovely? You have to explain that one. What are you doing?" Imagany thought she could detect a note of drowsiness in Zabree's voice, as if she were slurring her words together.

"I'm just laying here enjoying the cool breeze of the fan. It's so hot here in Chicago, Mog. So I'm just doing my best to stay away from the fire."

Imagany's antennas went up when Zabree called her "Mog." "Bree, are you sure everything's okay? You don't sound like yourself. And what do you mean 'stay away from the fire?' " Imagany became worried when she noticed the dull and slow quality of Zabree's voice.

"Oh that's because I've had a touch of the flu. Can you believe it? Here it is 103 degrees outside and I had to get the flu. The doctor gave me some pills to take so that's why I sound so doped up." It was obvious as Zabree's voice trailed off that she was falling asleep.

Imagany immediately felt better. "So listen, nut, you called long distance just to fall asleep on the other end of the line? I don't know whether to be flattered or insulted."

"Mog, I'm getting ready to fall off now. It's so much simpler in the darkness. I'll talk to you once the drugs have worn off, okay?" Zabree hung up the phone before Imagany could say goodbye.

Imagany sat cross-legged on the sofa and stared at the receiver in her hand. After awhile, she replaced it in its cradle. It bothered her that Zabree had sounded as listless as she had. But if she had taken medication as she said she had, then that would explain it.

Imagany cupped her chin in her hand, unable to shake her feelings of unease. On impulse, she picked up the phone and dialed the number to her parent's house in Chicago. As the phone continued to ring unanswered, she glanced at the clock on her etagere. It was nearly two o'clock in the afternoon. She figured her parents must be out somewhere and that Zabree was knocked out from the medication she had taken. Imagany hung up and sat back on the sofa to ponder her thoughts.

Chapter Eight

The room was encased in darkness. No sunlight filtered through the heavily drawn curtains because the Venetian blinds were closed tightly behind them. Books and magazines cluttered the area and clothes were thrown haphazardly over two dressers. A chair was placed in front of the door as if to warn the occupant of anyone trying to enter. A large canopy bed covered with frilly white lace coverings took up most of the space in an otherwise large room. Sheer gauze netting hung from the ceiling, draping the entire bed, its hems trailing the floor.

The girl lay naked across the bed. She was sprawled diagonally on top of the covers and her hands overlapped the sides of the bed. Somewhere deep inside the hazy recesses of her mind she thought she heard a phone ring, or maybe it could have been a doorbell. It could also have been her mind playing tricks on her as it sometimes did when her body absorbed the drugs. In her special world, she was surrounded by blackness and was safe from the harsh realities of life. Veiled in darkness, she no longer had to deal with the empty void that threatened to consume her. And most of all, there was nothing to forget. No shame to bear and no secrets to hide from the world. Wrapped in the cocoon which the heroin provided, she could forget whose face loomed above hers on a nightly basis. Zabree heard an insistent noise that kept trying to intrude on her privacy and she begged it to go away. Didn't they know no one was allowed to trouble her whenever she was down in the hole? Was somebody opening the door to her room? No, that couldn't be, because hadn't she pushed the chair under the door? Yes, she must have. She never forgot to do that whenever she used the drugs. Zabree felt someone tug at her naked body. Through the deep fog of her mind, she recognized her lover and her arms stretched out to welcome him as he removed his robe from his body. Zabree spread her legs and waited for her lover to come to her in silence. As his body enfolded itself to hers, she wondered for the umpteenth time why her lover always kissed so roughly and why he never told her he loved her. She felt her lover's hands crawl all over her body and knew that the pounding would soon *begin. When her lover began pounding himself between her legs, she wondered also why she felt no stirrings of pleasure. She let her mind float elsewhere as she focused on the effects of the drugs, knowing that her lover would not last much longer. When it was over, she knew the familiar sense of relief as her lover departed. Tears flooded her eyes and she wondered why she always cried when it was over. Somehow though, none of it mattered. The drugs would soon remove all the hurt and make everything right. Mog had once made things right for her, too. But that was before Mog had gone away and deserted her, leaving her to deal with her lover alone. Why was it that the ones she loved and trusted the most either hurt her or deserted her? The drugs would never harm her though, for they were her truest friend. As long as she continued to do whatever she had to do to get them, she was certain the drugs would never abandon her. The drugs were the one sure thing that would never let her down.*

Chapter Nine

magany went through the week feeling drained. When the little red man paid her a visit, she became extremely short tempered with anyone who rubbed her the wrong way. She had turned her answering machine on that same day and had not taken a call from anyone since, including Caprice.

On Friday morning, Imagany awakened to the sound of Caprice's voice on the line.

"Look, wench, I know you're there, and I'm tired of you playing me off. So pick up the damned phone."

Imagany sucked her teeth as she picked up the phone. "Why are you annoying me at six in the morning? Is there a problem? Can't a person have some peace and solitude?"

Caprice climbed back into her bed with the phone cradled to her ear. "Oh, so you're back among the living again, huh? How special." Caprice's voice dripped with sarcasm.

Imagany stretched as she yawned. "Look, people, why are you troubling me at this early hour of the morning? Don't you sleep?"

"Imagany, girl, you are so lowdown. You know I've been calling you ever since Sunday. But did you bother returning any of my calls? No, you didn't. And furthermore, apparently you haven't been returning any of Elliott's calls either because Carl asked me several times how you were doing."

"I'm sure you told him that I was faring well. How do you know he wasn't just asking out of genuine curiosity?"

"Because, dahlin', he mentioned that Elliott had not spoken with you for some time. They wanted to know, too, if we were still on for dinner Saturday evening. I told them not to worry because whenever you get your monthly visit, you turn into a witch and have a tendency to go into hibernation. Oh, and I also told them that, of course, we were on for dinner tomorrow. Did I cover for you or what?" Caprice blew on her fingertips and rubbed them across her chest.

"That was covering for me? Caprice, you didn't tell them all that crap about the hibernation stuff?"

"Yes I did. Serves your black butt right. That's what you get for playing off your phone all the time. But here's the punch, Wednesday was 99¢ night at the movie theater so Carl and I went." Caprice loudly cleared her throat. "Along with Mr. Elliott, of course." Caprice yawned in Imagany's ear. "Close your mouth dahlin'. I knew you'd be shocked. You simply missed out on a helluva good time."

"Wench! You didn't call me at all on Wednesday."

"I know. But I told them I did. I wanted to punish you for ignoring me. I guess I did a good job, didn't I?" Caprice was proud of her handiwork.

Imagany laughed. "And you called *me* lowdown?"

"Hey, a girl's got to do what she must. But even though we all had a nice time, I could tell Elliott wished you were with us. He even asked me when I had spoken with you last. I think he probably assumed that you were still upset about the incident with Sheldon. That's why I told him what I did about the PMS stuff. So what are you doing after classes tonight?"

"I'm not sure. With Anthony gone, all of this peace and quiet has been good for me. But to be honest, I have thought about Elliott quite a bit. I even started to call him several times, but then I said, what the hell, why bother." Imagany paused as thoughts of Elliott passed through her mind. Slowly she said, "Yes, I miss him, Caprice. Now that I've admitted it, it doesn't seem so bad." Imagany wound the cord around her finger as she said, "I think the time has come for me to indulge in a little bit of mischief."

"Hmmmmmm, I'll bet the kind of mischief you're referring to can only mean Elliott Renfroe."

"You guessed it! But we'll just have to see what the day brings. So on that note, my sistah, I shall speak to you sometime this evening."

"See yaaaa."

Fridays were light days for Imagany. On these days she only had three classes. After her classes were completed, she went to the library to put in a couple of hours of studying. Afterwards, Imagany decided to catch one of Ms. Geiger's dance classes before she went home.

As she parked her car behind the gym, she noticed that TSU's football team was still in practice. She smiled as she pictured Elliott among the members on the field. She grabbed her bag and headed for the stairs.

Imagany reached the top and was heading for the entrance doors when several football players came out of the building. She smiled at them as they stepped aside to let her pass through the doors. One of the guys remembered her from the movie theater and he spoke with much familiarity in his voice.

Imagany had no intentions of stopping to hold a conversation with any of them. She threw up her hands in a "nothing much" gesture as she continued on her way. Imagany arrived at Ms. Geiger's class just as one class was ending and another one was about to begin.

"Well hello Ms. Jenkins. What do I owe to the pleasure of this visit?" Ms. Geiger looked surprised to see her.

Imagany hadn't seen Ms. Geiger since the night of the performance and it was a pleasure to see her now. "Let's just say that I couldn't stay away. Can I join in on the next session?"

Ms. Geiger smiled. "I'll go one step further than that. You may instruct the next session."

Imagany was pleasantly surprised and it showed in her laughter. "Ms. G., I don't think anybody could follow in your footsteps. How about if we do it together?"

"Sounds like a winner."

All the students who filed in were females and most of them were in their senior year of college. They obviously needed the credit toward graduating, because they looked as if they would not be there otherwise.

Imagany changed into her dance gear and put on a Stephanie Mills' tape. Ms. Geiger was still in her office and she motioned Imagany to go ahead and instruct the class without her.

The way the girls were lined up reminded Imagany of lambs being lead to the slaughter. Almost all of them looked as if they had no desire to be there. Before the class was over, Imagany intended to change that. She wanted to impart to them her love of dance and wanted them to see that moving the body was an art in itself, one that everyone should learn to develop. Imagany snapped her fingers and brought everyone together. Already, her body was rocking from side to side as she moved to the rhythm of Stephanie Mills' song.

"All right, ladies! We're going to have some fun in this house today. So loosen up and get prepared to have a ball! Ms. Geiger just gave me permission to teach the class so let's enjoy it while we can because I can guarantee you the next time you come to class, the woman is going to go off on all of you." Imagany lifted her hands over her head and spun in a 360-degree turn. She clapped her hands and told them to line up in three rows. Realizing that they really were going to have some fun for a change, the girls were starting to enjoy themselves. Imagany ran to the stereo system and blasted the volume.

She instructed the class as if she were giving them aerobic lessons interspersed with dance steps. Twenty-five minutes later, the girls were still keeping up with her and were shouting out their approval.

Imagany had the whole class in an uproar when she changed records and let them do their own thing as she encouraged them by shouting, "Go ladies, go ladies, go ladies, go!" The girls were shouting right along with her. With all the commotion they were keeping up, Ms. Geiger soon came out of her office to watch them.

With fifteen minutes left in the class, Ms. Geiger stepped to the stereo system and halted the music. She stepped forward and addressed the group. "Since today has become a 'do what you feel' day," she glanced at Imagany, "I'm going to show you girls a thing or two. Imagany go get a pair of those tap shoes out of the room and put them on. You might as well join me."

Sensing that Ms. Geiger was about to give one of her rare performances, the girls became excited. Somebody in the class shouted loudly, "All right, Ms. Geiger. Don't hurt 'em, now." Laughter spread around the room as Imagany came back with the tap dancing shoes. Ms. Geiger went to the stereo and put on George Benson's "Give Me The Night."

Judy Geiger went to the center of the floor and all the girls stepped back to give her room. In sync with the music, she started out in a light patter before taking off like a butterfly in flight. Imagany stood to the side, content to watch. She knew she couldn't hold a candle to the dance instructor and she would join in only if Judy indicated for her to do so.

The music was in full swing now, and Ms. Geiger was rockin' as she tapped along to the beat of the music. Her movements reminded all the girls of the great legends such as Sammy Davis Jr., Honi Coles, Sandman Simms, Bunny Briggs and even Gregory Hines. Ms. Geiger was obviously enjoying herself as she glided across the floor. All the girls were clapping their hands and stomping their feet as they took in the moves that the dance instructor was putting on them. When Ms. Geiger motioned for Imagany to join her, Imagany did so reluctantly, laughing as she fell right in step with her. The two of them wrapped elbows together as they twisted and spun their feet lightly over the surface of the floor creating a smooth symphony of sounds that were right in step with the music.

When George Benson's song came to an end, both of them were breathless. Amidst the shouts and applause, Imagany bent forward with her hands on her knees to catch her breath. She turned her head in Ms. Geiger's direction and said, "God, you're good."

"When you get as much practice as I do, honey, you'd better be good." Ms. Geiger turned to address the class. "Don't think I don't realize that you people got away with murder today. I can only promise you that we'll make up for it the next time."

All the ladies groaned as they made their way out of the class. As Imagany went with them to change back into her street clothes, Ms. Geiger called her name.

"Imagany, thanks for stopping by. Don't be a stranger from now on. You're welcome to come by anytime you please."

"Thanks, Ms. G. I'll remember that."

She was walking down the hall after the dance class when someone softly called out her name.

"Imagany."

Imagany's eyes closed and her heart skipped a beat as she stopped in her tracks. She would know that voice anywhere and she turned to see Elliott slowly coming toward her. A smile broke out on her face as she walked toward him. Though many people were walking through the hallway, as far as Imagany was concerned, the area may as well have been empty. She didn't see anyone other than Elliott.

Imagany stood in front of him, her eyes hungrily taking him in. Elliott still had on his football gear and what a fine figure he made.

Imagany smiled and grabbed her bag tightly to keep from throwing herself in his arms.

Elliott stared down at Imagany and watched the smile on her lips. Just the sight of her made him realize how much he had missed her. He had been on the field, finishing for the day, when one of the guys told him that he'd just seen the fine fox who was with him the other night at the theater and that she had been headed in the direction of the dance classes. Regardless of how dirty he was, Elliott had nearly broken his neck trying to get here before Imagany had a chance to leave. As she stood in front of him, he took in the length of her hair and noted how her body still shined from the sweat of her exertion.

Imagany leaned her head to the side and said huskily, "Hi, baby."

At the sound of her voice, Elliott knew he would have to keep a tight reign on his emotions. He reached out to touch the cleft in her chin and said, "Hello, clefto." What he really longed to do was sweep her into his arms.

Imagany laughed as she reached up to kiss him on the chin. "I've missed you, Elliott."

Elliott shifted his gear to his other arm and grabbed Imagany's hand. "That's right, tell me all about it. You missed me so much that you couldn't return any of my phone calls. You even missed me so much that you couldn't at least call me to say hello." Elliott looked down at her. "Damn, baby, I love it when you miss me."

Imagany felt as miserable as Elliott intended for her to feel. She stopped in her tracks and pulled him to the side. "Elliott, I was wrong not to call you, but I needed time to think. Seeing you now just makes me know that you are the only reason I even came here today. All week long I thought I was miserable because I was suffering from PMS. But I wasn't, Elliott. I was miserable because I didn't see or talk to you for all of that time. I'm really sorry that I didn't call you. I see now that the loss was all mine." Imagany looked at Elliott with her heart in her eyes.

Neither Elliott nor Imagany was aware of the casual glances that were being thrown their way by both male and female passersby. Their body chemistry was so compatible that it was obvious to all who looked their way. And as they stood gazing into each other's eyes, their passion for one another was visible.

For Elliott, the entire week had gone by all too slowly. Never in his life had he been consumed with thoughts of one woman as he was with Imagany. Sure, he had been in love before, had even had his heart broken a time or two. But this confusion and desire just to see and be with another human being was too much for him to bear. When Imagany had not returned any of his calls, he had tried to block out all thoughts of her from his mind. He had even tried pushing himself to the limits of his physical capabilities, but neither had worked. Elliott had awakened in the middle of the night, unable to sleep, to search his heart and soul for the reasons he was so captivated by Imagany. He came to the conclusion that it wasn't just her physical beauty that attracted him, but that it was something indefinable that he could not lay reason to. He also realized that he would not be able to give anything around him the concentration required of him until he had the opportunity to find out just where she was coming from. To think that after all the soul-searching he had gone through, she was telling him that she felt the same way about him, only made Elliott know that sometimes the ironies in life were too much for an individual to bear.

Elliott cupped his hand around the back of Imagany's neck and drew her closer to him. He bent his head down to hers and said softly for her ears alone, "I'm going to go back to my room to take a shower and get cleaned up. After that, I'm going to go downstairs and get in my car and come straight to your place. I'm going to be in so much of a hurry to get there, Imagany, that I may not even bother to ring your bell. And the only thing that I ask of you is that you be ready for me when I get there."

Imagany smiled in anticipation as she reached her hand up to caress his jaw. "Oh, I'll be ready all right. But more importantly Elliott, I'll be willing, ready and waiting. The only thing that I ask of you in return, baby, is that you don't make any detours along the way."

Imagany wrapped her arm around his waist and walked him to the door of his locker room before continuing on her way.

Imagany hummed merrily to herself as she came through the door of her apartment with an arm full of bags, kicking the door shut behind her. Knowing that she wouldn't have time to cook even had she wanted to, she'd stopped at Mama Leone's, a famous soul-food restaurant that specialized in serious home-cooked meals. She ordered the Southern fried chicken, corn bread, green beans and mashed potatoes with gravy.

Imagany came into the kitchen and transferred all the food to her china and put everything in the oven to keep it warm. After setting the table for two, she removed the floral display and replaced it with two crystal candle holders with white scented candles set in them. She also gave her apartment a quick dust over. She went into the bathroom to draw her bath water and laced it with Chanel bath gel. Coming back into the living room, she went to the stereo system and put on some Anita Baker. She stepped into the bath tub in tune with Anita singing "Angel" followed by "You're The Best Thing Yet" and "Feel The Need." As Anita Baker poured her heart out, Imagany sat back and luxuriated in the tub. She mentally planned a special treat just for Elliott Renfroe, one he wasn't likely to forget any time soon.

Imagany climbed out of the tub and rubbed herself down with Chanel body lotion. As she styled her hair, fluffing it and pulling it forward in her face, she reveled in the thickness and coarseness of it. She decided to limit her make up to eye shadow and lipstick, figuring that, by the time the evening was over, all traces of any make up would be gone from her face anyway. After choosing a pair of dangling spear-shaped gold earrings, Imagany went to her walk-in closet and debated what to wear. She didn't want to appear over dressed, but she did want to look classy. She eventually settled on a two-piece black crepe wraparound outfit. The top portion of the outfit consisted merely of a long, thin scarf-like material that crisscrossed over her shoulders and breasts. It left her midriff bare and wrapped around to fasten in the back. The skirt was long and came to about six inches above her ankles. It wrapped around her hips snugly and fastened on the side. A pair of black pumps completed the outfit. For her underwear, Imagany had chosen a black strapless silk bra with matching bikini panties. Deciding against wearing pantyhose and jewelry, Imagany dabbled a little bit of Chanel perfume behind her ears, between her breasts, on her wrists, and on the inside of her navel. She was ready.

Back in the living room, she stood in front of her stereo system trying to decide what they should listen to. Since she was already in an Anita Baker frame of mind, she chose Anita's Rapture album. No sooner had she put it on than her doorbell rang. Suddenly, Imagany became a bundle of nerves. Electing to buzz Elliott in as opposed to going downstairs to meet him, she cracked her door and stood in the doorway as she waited for him to reach the landing.

Elliott came up the three flights of stairs in a bound and Imagany's heart skipped a beat when he turned the corner. As he approached her, he watched as an alluring smile covered the edges of her lips. He took in the adorable picture she made as she framed the entrance of the door. With her hair down, Imagany reminded him of a goddess dressed in black.

Elliott was dressed in black pants with a stark white shirt and he wore leather dress shoes. Though Imagany admired the way Elliott looked in his jeans, it pleased her that he had taken the time to come dressed the way he had. He had one hand behind his back and when he reached her, he pulled from behind him a bouquet of red roses and handed them to her.

"Oh, thank you, Elliott. They're lovely," Imagany whispered softly.

Elliott kissed her lightly on her neck before murmuring in her ear, "You're welcome, and so are you."

Imagany had been given many things in her lifetime, all of them more expensive than roses. But something as simple as flowers touched her deeply because she knew they came from Elliott's heart. She didn't know what his financial situation was, but knowing he was a college student like herself, she could imagine that he had better things to do with his money than waste it on flowers. Imagany felt touched as she invited him inside and closed the door behind him.

"Something smells delicious." Elliott eyed her with a smile on his face.

"I hope you're hungry. I picked some things up from Mama Leone's. Come, let me put these in some water." As they walked toward the kitchen, Anita Baker's "Sweet Love" played softly.

Imagany put the roses inside a crystal vase and placed it in the center of the table between the candles. She took the food from the oven and set everything onto the table. She handed Elliott a book of matches to light the candles and gestured for him to sit as she filled both their glasses with sparkling grape juice.

When everything they needed was placed on the table, Imagany joined him and handed Elliott the platter of chicken.

"It's been a long time since I've eaten from Mama Leone's. I didn't even realize she had takeout service."

Imagany smiled as she added mashed potatoes to her plate. With raised eyebrows, she said, "Ahh, but when one doesn't cook, one must learn where to go in times of need."

Elliott said teasingly, "I'll have to remember that." As he bit into the chicken, he rolled his eyes.

Imagany laughed at the faces Elliott made to show how much he was enjoying the food. She was still on her first round when she offered seconds to him, and he didn't resist. When she finished her meal, she was full and she folded her hands and placed her chin upon them as she watched Elliott continue to eat.

Satisfied, he sat back to rub his stomach, thoroughly satiated.

Imagany smiled as she tilted her head to the side. "There's plenty left. Would you like some more?"

Elliott shook his head. "No. Even if I wanted to, I'd have nowhere to put it."

As Imagany got up and began to remove the dishes from the table, Elliott rose to help her. At the surprised look that Imagany gave him, he said, "I told you I came from a house full of women. So bussin' suds is nothing new to me. Here, let me help." Elliott rolled up his sleeves before grabbing the rest of the dishes.

Imagany was delighted that he wanted to help. "I'll tell you what. I'll wash and you dry. Fair enough?"

"Deal."

The two of them washed and dried dishes in a companionable silence. When they were done, Imagany handed Elliott a towel to dry off his hands.

"You know, you're pretty good at this. A girl could get used to having someone like you around."

"That could only happen if a girl like you invites me back."

"Hmmmm, I guess that's something else we'll have to work on. Come, let's go up front."

Anita Baker's Rapture album had played in its entirety by the time they made their way up front and Imagany put on her old faithful Najee tape. As "Sweet Sensation" poured out of the speakers, Imagany led Elliott to the sofa to sit down.

He sat in the middle of the sofa and Imagany curled up on the other end. She removed her shoes and was about to tuck her feet up underneath her when Elliott grabbed her feet and lifted them on top of his legs.

Imagany smiled at him as she slid against the sofa and propped her head against her hand. When Elliott started rubbing her feet caressingly, she enjoyed the sensations he was arousing inside her. In a soft voice that reflected her mellowness, Imagany said invitingly, "Tell me about Elliott Renfroe."

Elliott enjoyed the feel of her feet in his hand as he answered her. "Now, that's a tough one to answer, considering that you already know most of what there is to know about him."

Imagany lifted her foot and ran her toes along the buttons of his shirt. His touch on her feet was sending shivers down her spine and she found herself speaking just to keep herself focused. "Oh, no. There's plenty that I don't know about him, and the little that I do know has only made me want to know more. So talk to me."

"Tell me what you'd like to know and I'll try to fill you in." Looking at her as he spoke, Elliott admired the smoothness of her shoulders and he liked the muscle tone she had acquired to her arms. She was by no means a little woman and he appreciated the fullness of her body. He watched her play in her hair and knew that it wouldn't be much longer before it was his own fingers that played in it. He looked down at her feet as he caressed her toes, running his fingers along the pink polish that covered her toenails. He felt her foot flex in his hand as her other foot played upon his chest. He reached up to take hold of the foot that was slowly making its way up to his chin. As he gripped the ball of her feet, he brought both together and wrapped his hands around her ankles. He began to slowly massage them.

"Tell me what pleases Elliott." Imagany's voice was low.

At the soft, husky quality in Imagany's voice, Elliott looked up and stared into her brown eyes. As he gazed at her to take in the statuesque picture she presented, he could feel his own nature rising. He looked down at her feet as he shifted on the sofa and quietly cleared his throat. There were many ways he could take her question, and he had the distinct feeling that she had intended it to be this way. He smiled at her as he looked up. "In what way are you referring?" Elliott slightly parted her feet and ran his hands under the hem of her skirt. His hands were between her ankles and he slowly moved them up the calves of her legs.

At the touch of his hands on her calves, Imagany felt her nipples harden. It was becoming increasingly harder to concentrate and she wanted to make sure that Elliott did most of the talking. If she started talking, there was no telling what might come out of her mouth. Through half-closed eyes Imagany said, "Tell me what Elliott likes in a woman." This should definitely keep him talking for a while.

Raising her skirt above her knees, Elliott put an end to the third person scenario which they had been using. "I like a sweet-natured woman who has a strong character, one who knows her mind, knows what she wants out of life and is not afraid to go after it. I like a woman who's not sitting around waiting for a man to walk into her life just to make her happy. A woman who's just as ambitious as I am. Someone I can respect as well as admire." As he spoke, Elliott caressed the entire area from her ankles to her calves. "And just as importantly, I like a woman who knows how to be soft. My kind of woman knows how to please as well as be pleased." Elliott stayed his hands on Imagany's ankles and reached out to take hold of her hand, spreading his fingers and interlacing them between hers. He deliberately pulled her toward him until her knees overlapped his legs. When he used the strength in his hands to lift Imagany on top of his lap, she was more than willing to come to him.

Imagany's skirt was bunched around her thighs. She fitted her body to his and wound her arms around his neck. She clasped her hands behind his head and pressed her nose to his. Before Elliott could kiss her, Imagany lifted her head, inviting him to nuzzle her neck. As Elliott bit gently into her collar bone, Imagany felt her body go limp. He cupped the side of her face and lifted her head for his kiss. His mouth was insistent upon hers as his tongue played with her lips and her teeth. Imagany pulled her head back and felt Elliott caress the side of her face. She nuzzled her face deeper into his hand, welcoming the feel of his touch. When Imagany found the strength that she needed, she pulled herself up and straddled Elliott after lifting both of his legs onto the sofa.

She sat astride him and looked down at him, her look one of total possession. She felt like the huntress who had just slain the giant beast. Without removing her eyes from his, Imagany lifted her skirt higher around her thighs to allow her legs to spread as far as they wanted to go. Elliott's neck rested on the back of the sofa and Imagany removed a pillow to stuff it gently behind his head. She placed her hands on either side of him, looking down at him as if he were at her mercy.

Elliott placed his hands on Imagany's hips as he returned her never-ending gaze. The seductive smile that curled her lips hinted that she had many good things in store for him and he couldn't wait to sample her pleasures. Elliott's hands caressed her body as he slid them down her hips to her thighs, softly kneading her skin along the way. He slid his hands up her thighs, until he reached the area where her skirt was gathered around her hips. He fit his hands beneath it to allow the tips of his thumbs to caress the softness of her inner thighs. His hands massaged her harder now as, little by little, he pulled her down deeper on top of him.

When Elliott's fingers touched the softness of her groin area, her back arched to accommodate the gnawing hunger that grew within her loins. It made her reassess just who was the hunter in this game. Spreading her legs just a little bit further, she could feel the hardness and largeness of him underneath her. Imagany lowered her torso so that her face was right above his. She clasped her hands around his neck again and heard him whisper something in her ear.

"Tell me what pleases Imagany." Elliott brushed his lips and tongue against her ear as he spoke.

At the feel of his tongue in her ear, Imagany tightened her grip around his neck and rested her head on top of his. She slid her lips down along his neck and back up until she again reached his ear. Imagany took his earlobe between her teeth and nipped it gently. She ran her lips lightly along his jawline, enjoying the feel of his stubble. Caressing the back of his head, she looked into his eyes as she whispered, "You please me, Elliott." Imagany's insides turned to liquid gold as her emotions became a burning fever. Oh, yes, this man pleased her in very mysterious ways. It was her turn now to run her tongue lightly over his lips and when she pried his lips apart, his hands rose to entwine themselves in her hair as he cupped her head and fastened his lips to hers. Imagany kissed him with all the passion she had inside of her as she slid her body down the full length of his, molding herself to him.

Elliott ran his hands caressingly over her body as she lay atop him, reveling in the smooth softness of her skin. As he shifted his hands to her hips to pull the material completely over them, he brought his hands to her buttocks and gripped them assertively. She was soft but firm, round and full, and Elliott longed to plant himself inside her. He kneaded her buttocks as he slowly spread her apart and pulled her deeper onto him. Unable to stand the unnecessary barrier that their clothing provided, Elliott wanted only to plunge himself into the sweet depths of her womanhood. He shifted to rest part of his weight on top of her.

Imagany welcomed the feel of his body against hers. When she bent her knee and lifted her leg to slide it over his, Elliott took the opportunity to fit himself snugly between her legs. Imagany's body was alive with sensation after sensation as Elliott's hands played over her. She loved the way his callused hands made her feel. As she relaxed against him, it seemed as if his hands and lips were everywhere, covering every inch of her body. She cradled his head as his lips and tongue nuzzled her neck.

She became aware of the music playing softly in the background and knew that she must have blocked it out of her consciousness because she didn't even remember hearing it before. Najee's "That's The Way of The World" was coming to an end and Imagany knew the time was right for her little surprise. She raised herself on top of Elliott and put her finger to his lips, indicating that she would be right back. Imagany lifted herself off the sofa and went toward the bedroom. She went to her linen closet and pulled out a black satin comforter along with two pillows and a small wicker basket and carried everything back up front with her.

By the time Imagany came back into the room, Elliott had removed his shoes and socks. She set everything on the floor, pushed the center table to the far corner of the room, spread the blanket in the middle of the floor, and placed the two pillows upon it. She walked back to the sofa where Elliott sat and stood directly in front of him. Imagany straddled his knees and sat on top of them. Wrapping her arms around his neck, she pulled his head to hers. "There's something that I want to do for you," she whispered into his ear.

Elliott pulled his head back and turned to kiss her lips. Biting them and sucking on them, Elliott asked, "And what might that be?"

Gazing directly into his eyes, Imagany loosened his belt buckle. She heard him suck in his breath as she unfastened the button of his trousers to unzip his zipper. Sticking her hands inside of his pants, she dug her nails deeply into him as she pulled his shirt out of his pants. Unbuttoning every button of his shirt, Imagany firmly snapped it open to reveal the burgeoning depths of his chest. Looking down upon the muscles of his body, she felt as if she had found a treasure chest of gold. She felt her inner self moisten as she ran her hands searchingly over the muscles of his chest. Imagany lifted herself from his knees and pried them apart with her legs. She spread his knees further apart and sat on the floor between them. Before Elliott could suspect anything, Imagany plunged her head into his groin area and gripped his zipper with her teeth, tugging it all the way down. She took Elliott totally by surprise as she grasped his thighs with her hands, feeling his muscles underneath. As Imagany wiggled her head inside his pants, she opened her mouth and through the material of his underwear, traced the outline of his manhood with her teeth and tongue. Feeling him tense under her hands she lifted her head unhastily to run her tongue along the flesh of his taut stomach and chest. When Imagany reached his shoulder area, she veered to the right as her lips sought the nipple of his chest. Elliott's head flopped back on the sofa as she hungrily sucked one of his nipples into her mouth, teasing it with both her tongue and her teeth. Imagany leaned her body over him and lifted her head to his neck. With her tongue fully inside his ear, she finally whispered, "It's a surprise created especially for you, so just sit back, relax, watch, and enjoy."

As she stepped away from him, she turned off all the lights and turned on two lamps that had red light bulbs inside them. Najee's "Tonight I'm Yours" played softly in the background and Imagany went to the stereo to turn it up just a bit. She came back to the center of the blanket and stood directly in front of Elliott's view. As Najee blew into his clarinet, so did Imagany play on Elliott's nerves and emotions. She began to slowly swing her hips as she unhurriedly lifted her hands above her head in the air to sway softly. She brought her hands to her neck and up through her hair. Imagany lifted it away from her neck and shoulders and pulled it on top of her head. Lifting it out to the side between her fingers, she let it fall back down to her shoulders, sensuously moving her hips in small circles from side to side. Molding her hands along the sides of her body, she dipped to the floor only to raise up again as she covered her breasts with her hands, squeezing them firmly. As Imagany spread her fingers and rubbed them along her waist, she turned sideways and bent forward at the waist, extending her rear. She dipped her chest down toward the floor and slowly shifted from leg to leg. Running her hands from her breasts to her hips, she turned her back to Elliott and ran her hands teasingly over her buttocks as she undulated her hips. Turning to face him again, she unfastened the skirt and very slowly unwound it from around her hips. She teased him by running her tongue suggestively over her lips as she finally removed the garment, tossing it to the side. Imagany reached up to unfasten the top portion of her garment and gyrated her body windingly as she did so. She teasingly unfastened a portion of the material at a time, turning from him only to face him again when she was ready to completely take it off. Clothed in nothing but her brief underwear now, Imagany then took the scarf and pulled it lovingly along her body. Her movements were meant to tease and seduce as she performed her erotic dance of seduction. Imagany lowered herself sensuously to the floor on her knees. She pretended the scarf was Elliott's hands, pulling it over her head, around her neck, down past her waist, and finally between her legs. With each movement she made with the scarf, Imagany lifted herself up and down as if plunging on top of him. She lay back on the floor and in one fluid motion lifted her legs in the air, using her elbows and hands to hold herself up. She flexed her feet in the air, one foot after the other, enjoying the feel and mastery of the muscles in her body. She extended her legs as far as they would go before spreading them in a wide "V" only to quickly snap them together again. She moved her arms from her sides and lowered her legs to the floor, rising to sit on top of them. While still sitting upon her spread knees, Imagany bent backwards and rested her back on the floor. Her body had become totally aroused now, turning itself into a live wire of throbbing sensations. A light sheen of sweat covered her, and her muscles were thoroughly stretched. When Imagany raised herself, she tossed the scarf away from her as she laid onto her side with her head propped against her hand and stared directly into Elliott's eyes.

Elliott had never been entertained so sensuously in all his life. He had watched the dance unfold in front of him with nothing less than total fascination. She had played upon his senses, arousing every bone and nerve in his body, and it seemed to him as if he were always her willing spectator. As she lay before him now, spread upon the blanket as she was, Elliott knew the true meaning of the word desire. When he slowly stood up and removed the shirt from his body, letting it drop to the floor, he had but one thought in his mind and that was to arouse and satisfy her as she had just aroused him. Elliott stepped to the edges of the blanket and began to lower the pants from his hips. When they fell to the floor, he used his leg to kick them aside.

As Imagany watched him stand above her, she knew what was coming. She saw the determined look on his face and it was as if she could read his mind. Her eyes floated over the entire length of his body before coming to rest on the bulging area of his underwear. As she took in the full view of him, she felt herself grow even wetter and she could feel her moistness seeping between her legs. As Elliott lay down beside her, so weak was Imagany at the thought of what he was about to do to her, that she could only smile at him invitingly. As they interlaced their fingers together, they smiled at one another. They knew that the night was young. They both knew, too, that they would use the time wisely by loving each other in slow, unhurried motions.

Elliott pulled her closer to him. Using his knee, he gently pried her legs apart. He barely had to touch her because Imagany parted her legs willingly. With her legs slightly parted, Elliott slowly removed the last vestiges of his underwear from his body. Completely naked, he came to rest on top of her body.

At the feel of him pressing his hardness against her, Imagany's limbs turned to molten lava. As he moved against her, he felt so big and thick and strong and firm! Rapture washed over. She closed her eyes and knew she couldn't have moved had her life depended upon it. Imagany knew, too, that the tides had been turned. No longer was she the orchestrator of this sensuous melody. Elliott had taken over this overwhelmingly seductive show. So weak from pleasure was her body, it became an effort just for her to lift up her head. She felt as if every one of her muscles had deserted her. When she felt his hands unclasp her bra and remove her panties, she had no strength left to help him. With both of them now naked, Elliott positioned the full weight of his body on hers and began a slow assault of his own. Imagany murmured incoherently as she twisted her head without really moving it. With one hand, Elliott cupped the side of her head and brought his lips down to hers, covering her mouth with his own. This was the moment that Elliott realized her surrender was complete. As her body languished under him, he knew that she was now his willing slave. He slid his free hand down to her hips and lifted her right leg across his back, bending her knee over him.

As Elliott plunged his tongue into her mouth, the slow fire that had spread over Imagany's entire body now became a raging inferno. He lifted her left leg in the air and playfully bit the inside of her knee. Elliott positioned her leg over his left shoulder as he forced the limberness of her body to come into full play, stretching her to the limits as he lifted himself up to kiss her again. Removing her leg from his shoulder, Elliott watched in fascination as he extended her leg out to the side, marveling at her ability to stretch herself in so many wonderful ways. He brought her leg back and pulled her legs together as he straddled her for a change. Sitting on his own knees, Elliott raised himself above her. He took a moment to just stare down at her and admire her beauty. As he shifted himself to the side, he sat back and traced his fingers softly over her face, trailing them down the bridge of her nose and down to the cleft in her chin. Elliott's hands strayed to finally cup her breasts. He bent down beside her again as he fondled the fullness of each breast, playing gently with her nipples, covering them with the roughness of his hand. So darkened and hardened had her nipples become, when he finally touched them, a pleasing pain shot through her, causing a soft hiss to escape from her lips. He stretched along side the length of her body as he took one of her nipples into his mouth. Though he wanted to bite into her hungrily, he heard her soft whimper and settled for sucking them gently between his teeth while his hands firmly massaged her buttocks. For the longest time, Elliott wrought havoc over Imagany. His tongue played with her and he refused to let up even after he felt her dig her nails sharply into his back. Again, Elliott raised himself up to greedily suck Imagany's lips. Grabbing her gently by the waist, he pulled her closer to him, molding her body to his. He pushed her onto her back and once more plunged his tongue demandingly into her mouth. He spread both of her legs as he parted them to place himself firmly where he rightfully belonged. As he covered her body with his, Elliott felt his manhood pulse as it dug probingly into her, as if searching for the place where it knew it belonged. Positioned between her legs as he was, Elliott reached down between them and caressed the insides of her thighs.

When he tantalized her by sliding his hand through the silky bush of her hair, Imagany felt her toes curl while her hands dug themselves dangerously into the blanket. The pressure in her aching loins was building to the point of explosion. When one of Elliott's fingers plunged into the creamy core of her being, Imagany nearly screamed out loud. A loud audible gasp escaped her and Elliott cut it off by covering her mouth with his own.

As soon as he removed his mouth from hers, another sigh of ecstasy immediately escaped Imagany's lips as Elliott's fingers continued to examine the moistness of her loins. Her legs parted wide on their own accord when Elliott lowered his head down to the center of her being. She felt him suck greedily at her inner thighs before nuzzling his face in the thickness of her pubic hairs. Unable to stand it any longer, Imagany found the strength within herself to lift her legs and plant them around Elliott's neck, locking him in a steadfast grip. Imagany used the muscles in her legs to pull his face up to her chest. She unwound her legs from around his neck and wrapped them tightly around his waist. With her arms around his neck, she kissed him and whispered pleadingly into his mouth, "Please me, Elliott."

At the begging note in her voice, Elliott had no choice but to make her wish his command. With his hands on her buttocks, he spread them apart and lifted her up to meet him as he unhurriedly found her core and slowly plunged himself inside her, little by little, deeper and deeper. Elliott felt the smoothness and silkiness of her being wrap itself around him, enveloping him in all her glory. He groaned into her ear when he felt her inner muscles contract around him, and he firmly gripped her hips. When Elliott caught his breath, he performed a teasing dance of his own as he moved slowly in and out of her only to plunge back inside her each time after he withdrew.

As ecstasy washed over Imagany in sensation after sensation, she felt as if she were about to lose her mind. Needing desperately to grab onto something, she loosened the grip that she had on Elliott in order to dig her nails deeply into the carpeting on the floor. She released her legs from around his waist to slowly spread them in every direction that would allow Elliott better and easier access to her. Every time he pulled away from her, she would moan until he came back to refill her emptiness again. She moved under him in wild abandonment and the room was filled with her sweet whispered sighs of pleasure.

Elliott was lost inside her. The feel of her body moving under him caused him to lower his chest to hers and pull them both onto their sides. Again, Elliott found himself lifting her leg over his shoulder. This time when he moved his hand under her leg, locking it into place, he brought his hand up to once again cup the side of her face. He pulled her mouth to his as he plunged himself deeper inside her inner depths. Elliott felt her inner muscles contract around him and he found himself gently pushing Imagany once more onto her back. Lifting himself on his arms above her, he set about pleasing her in a manner that she would not soon forget. As the sensations washed over him too, he knew that he could not last for much longer. Elliott lowered his torso down to her chest. Raising his hands, he gently pushed them into the thickness of her hair and whispered her name demandingly into her ear. When the only response he received was a mumble of jargon, Elliott tried again.

"Imagany," Elliott whispered huskily into her ear as he held himself away from her in order to capture her attention. As he gazed down at her, he noted the look of love about her. He took in the sweat from her glistening body, her tangled hair and the swollenness of her kissed lips. When Imagany realized he was not about to return himself to her, she panicked and clawed insistently at his back. Elliott grabbed her wrists and gently lifted them above her head. When her eyes finally fluttered open, Elliott saw in them the incoherent look of desire. But for him that look was not enough. All along, Imagany had been softly whispering and moaning into his ear, but he wanted to hear clearly from her own lips the sweet words of passion that especially turned him on. "Talk to me, baby," he whispered passionately. "Tell me what you want."

Though it was agony for Elliott to hold himself back, he would continue to do so until she told him exactly what he wanted to hear.

Elliott heard Imagany whisper something unintelligible that he could not make out. He put his ear to her lips and again whispered demandingly for her to talk to him.

Understanding that her needs would not be met until she did so, Imagany poured forth all the love words she knew. Pulling her arms from his grip, she wrapped them tightly around his neck and begged him to please her. She placed her tongue inside his ear as she encouraged him to give her what she needed. She whispered his name over and over as she told him how sweet it was to her, how much she was enjoying what he was doing to her, how good he was making her feel, how much she really needed him, and how she would never ever let him stop doing what he was doing.

In an entanglement of arms and legs, the two of them satisfied each other, thrashing upon the floor as they stoked the flames of one another's fire. They filled the room with their sweet muted cries of passion and when the two of them finally exploded in ecstasy, they both shook with powerful convulsions, holding on to each other for dear life. And afterwards, as their bodies tingled with the aftermath of their lovemaking, Elliott lay beside Imagany as the two of them shone with the sweat of their desire, lost together in the land of love.

Chapter Ten

glimmer of sunlight along with the chirping of birds outside her window penetrated Imagany's consciousness. When she finally came to, she found herself nestled snugly in Elliott's arms, amidst a twist of blanket and pillows. A warm smile curled the corner of her lips at the knowledge that she and Elliott never did make it to the bedroom.

Imagany savored the feel of Elliott's body as it rested partially over hers. She was unwilling to disturb their equilibrium so she buried her head further into the crook of his arm. She became aware of a deep throbbing soreness that persisted between her legs and she closed her eyes as a contented languor stole over her body. As she willed sleep to reclaim her, Imagany felt Elliott's hand cover and softly squeeze her breast. At his tender prodding, the nipple hardened and rose beneath his fingers.

"Good morning." Elliott spoke in a deep, gruff voice. He leaned over Imagany and grazed her temple lightly with his lips.

"Mmmmm." Imagany opened her eyes and attempted to twist her head around to meet his gaze. Part of her hair was trapped underneath his arm and she was unable to completely turn her head in his direction. As Imagany moved to shift on her back, needles of pain shot through her. Her eyes widened in surprise and a gasp shot forth from her lips.

Elliott peered down at Imagany with concern in his gaze. "What's the matter?"

Imagany slowly lifted her right arm around Elliott's neck. When Elliott pulled his leg from between hers, Imagany groaned as she grabbed his neck tighter, pulling on it for support, in an attempt to halt his movements. "Wait, wait, wait," she whispered hoarsely. Imagany felt as if every muscle in her body had tightened itself into a knot. Wrapping her arm tighter around Elliott's neck, Imagany pulled his head down to hers to whimper into his ear, "Elliott?"

Realizing the nature of her dilemma, Elliott asked sympathetically, "What is it, baby?"

Imagany shook with laughter as she whispered, "I think you broke my body."

Elliott leaned on his elbow and propped his head upon his hand. Staring down at her, he gently laced his fingers through the fingers of her free hand. He asked humorously, "I broke your body?"

As Elliott kissed her hand, Imagany accused him with her eyes. "Yes, sweetie, you did. I feel as if my whole body has whiplash and it's all your fault."

Elliott laughed as he kissed the inside of her wrist. "I wasn't the one who told you to try to be Ms. Acrobat last night. Had I contorted my body into all the positions that you did, I'm sure I would feel the same way."

Imagany answered him tenderly, "How come you didn't tell me this last night when I was doing it instead of waiting 'til now?"

Elliott held her wrist to the floor as he nuzzled the nape of her neck. "Because I was too busy enjoying myself."

"Elliott, that's terrible. I thought you were concerned about my welfare."

He moved his lips and tongue to a spot behind her ear as Imagany's hand curled itself behind his head. "I am."

As Elliott's lips moved to the sides of her mouth, she whispered, "I thought you had my best interests at heart."

Elliott lightly traced the outline of her lips with his tongue. "I do."

Imagany weakened as she felt Elliott's maleness grow firm and hard against her leg. She twisted her head to breathe huskily into Elliott's ear, "Then why are you trying to kill me?"

Elliott laughed. "What are you talking about?"

"Sweetheart, I think you already know." Imagany could feel a warm glow seeping through her body. A deep huskiness pervaded her voice as she said, "You know I love your body, don't you?"

Elliott went back to nuzzling her neck before he answered her. "Keep calling me 'sweetheart,' baby." He looked at her teasingly, "And how much do you love my body?"

Imagany smiled back at him as she lightly kneaded the back of his head. "So much so, that I'd love to do luscious things to you."

Elliott shifted his body and lifted himself to straddle her, positioning her between his legs. He was conscious of the stiffness of her body. Trying not to cause her any more pain, he took care to ensure that all of his weight rested on his knees. Unable to help himself, his male hardness rose to press against her. He cupped the sides of her head and with laughter in his voice, whispered into her ear, "I love it when you talk dirty to me. When do we start?"

Laughing, Imagany wound her arms around his neck. Feeling him ready above her, she knew she had to quickly put a rein on Mr. Elliott Renfroe. "We can start whenever you want to. Except for right now. You see, dahlin'," Imagany nipped him lightly on his chin, "unfortunately, I'm only human. And since you have already worn me out, that means we'll have to continue this the next time."

Elliott kissed her earlobe before raising himself to gaze down at her. "Promise?"

"Yes, baby, I do. Now, help me up."

Elliott grabbed hold of both her hands and slowly pulled her forward. Imagany groaned as he gently lifted her up. Elliott laughed out loud. He found it hard to believe that this sore woman was the very same one who had wrapped her legs so passionately around his neck just a few short hours ago.

When he had her fully upright, Imagany gingerly lifted herself to sit on her knees. Paying Elliott no mind as he laughed at her, she lifted her hands above her head as she slowly parted her knees and lowered herself to the floor, as if paying homage to some god. A pleasurable sigh came from her lips as she lay stretching her muscles.

Elliott couldn't prevent his manhood from becoming overjoyed as he sat there and watched her stretch herself. He took immense pleasure in just observing the lushness and sinewy muscles of her body. Before Elliott knew it, he had positioned himself behind her, tucking his knees underneath her rear. He had no intentions of descending upon her, he merely wanted to sit behind her as he watched her stretch.

When Imagany came out of her brief meditation, she became aware of Elliott sitting directly behind her, his body touching hers. She lifted herself upright and immediately felt Elliott's arms wrap themselves around her. With the front of his body pressed tightly to her backside, Imagany cuddled her head in the curve of his arms. Once more, she was able to appreciate the muscles of his body.

When she finally lifted her head, she became aware of the mess they had made around them. Kleenex tissues bearing the remains of Elliott's used condoms were balled up and scattered across the floor. Noting that there were at least five or six of them strewn everywhere, Imagany was now able to identify the reason why her body ached so.

"Elliott, look at us." She motioned for him to look across the floor.

Elliott shifted with her in his arms as he looked about him. Shaking his head, he said, "Wow, I was really something, wasn't I?"

Imagany broke out in laughter as she fell to the floor and rolled on her back. "You conceited thing." She crawled forward between his legs and rose on her own knees in front of him. As each of them sat on their knees facing one another, Imagany leaned forward and wrapped her arms around his neck. With the side of her face pressed against his chest, for the first time she became aware that there was no self-consciousness between them. She felt as if they were two kindred spirits who had miraculously found each other in a cold, lonely world.

Without raising her head, she said, "Know what I would like to do?"

With his eyes closed, Elliott shook his head and said, "Mphm, mphm. Tell me."

"I'd like to go into the kitchen and fix some beef bacon, eggs, toast, grits and pancakes."

"Oooooooh, baby. When?" Elliott's mouth watered at the prospect.

"But I'm not."

"You're not?" Elliott found it hard to believe she would build him up like that just to let him drop back down. "Why, baby?"

"Because." Imagany spoke as if that explained it all.

Elliott lifted her chin to stare at her. "Talk to me, I'm listening," Elliott's voice was encouraging.

Imagany pulled her chin out of his hand and wrapped her arms around his massive muscles, pressing her face back to his chest. "Because my muscles are too sore for me to move right now." Imagany was whining now.

Elliott wrapped his arms around her and placed his head on top of hers. "You lazy thing. That's a lame excuse and you know it."

"I know. I can't even cook. Does that mean I'm a sorry excuse for a woman?"

Elliott's lips brushed her hair. "No, baby, you could never be that. We'll learn how to cook together, okay?"

Imagany was impressed. "Promise?"

"Sure I do." Elliott glanced at the clock on her stereo system. "But as of right now, I've got to get a move on. I've got to be at practice shortly so I'll give you a rain check."

Imagany looked over and saw that it was nearly eleven-thirty. She shifted to her side and ran her hands through her tangled hair. "Sheese, where did the time go?"

Elliott reached for his underwear as he lifted himself up to go inside the bathroom. "It flew because we were having so much fun."

As he left the room, Imagany told him where he would find the towels and wash cloths. Picking herself up, she gathered what she thought were all the used condoms and went into the kitchen to throw them away. As she folded the blanket and picked up the pillows to take everything back to the bedroom, her eyes fell on the small wicker basket that was sitting off to the side. Imagany smiled as she bent down to pick it up. In it were the remaining unused condoms that she had brought out with her when she had carried in the pillows and blanket. Taking everything back into the bedroom, she put everything back in its place. Undetected was one lone used condom left underneath the sofa. By the time Imagany finished straightening up the living room, Elliott was out of the shower.

She was lying down on the sofa when he walked back into the room. She raised herself up to look at him as he reached for his pants and socks. She put her fingertips together and raised her hands to her mouth as if she were saying a prayer.

With her head tilted to the side, she had to once again admire the muscular contours of his body. So defined was his chest, his waist and his thighs that she thanked God for sending him her way.

"Elliott?" Imagany's voice was a soft, quiet whisper and Elliott turned to face her as he stepped into his pants.

"Hmmmm."

"Do you remember what we're supposed to be doing tonight?"

Tucking his shirt into his pants, he came to sit on the sofa next to her as he put on his socks. "Yes I do. We're supposed to continue where we left off this morning."

Imagany laughed softly as she shook her head. She moved to sit behind him so that he was sitting between her legs. Wrapping her arms around his waist, she pushed her chin into his back. "Yes, darling, that too. But more specifically, tonight's the night we're to have dinner with Caprice and Carl. Remember now?"

Elliott had a preoccupied look on his face as he put on his shoes. "Yep, seven-thirty sharp. And Caprice is going to do all the cooking."

Imagany came from behind his back to rest on the floor on her knees between his thighs. "And what are you going to bring me?"

Elliott smiled as he lifted her face for his kiss. He lightly brushed his lips across hers. "I'm going to bring you myself."

Imagany sighed pleasurably. "That's right, baby. Just bring yourself. And make sure you're not a minute late."

The husky quality in her voice made Elliott's insides contract again. He stood up and pulled her up with him. He wrapped his arms about her as he gripped her buttocks and pulled her up against him. Lifting her chin with his hand, Elliott dabbed his thumb into her cleft. "I can barely wait for seven thirty. You're sure we don't have time?"

Imagany put her fingers to his lips. "No, Boo. We don't."

"Boo, huh?" Elliott liked the sound of it. "I think I could learn to like that name."

"I think you should learn to like it. Because from now on that's going to be your nickname."

Elliott placed his hands on her hips. "Okay, Ms. Demanding. Whatever you say."

Imagany walked Elliott to the door. She stood on her tiptoes and kissed him on his nose. As he stepped into the hallway, she called after him. "Seven-thirty sharp, Mr. Renfroe." When Elliott turned to look back at her, she blew him a kiss and closed the door.

Imagany leaned against the door with her head thrown back and inhaled deeply. A satisfied smile donned her face as she walked into the bathroom to wash out the tub and take a long leisurely bath. As Imagany enjoyed the satiny feel of the water around her skin, she listened to the melodious sounds of Nancy Wilson and Jeane Carne.

Indulging herself among the thickness of the bubbles, she tenderly stroked the soreness between her legs. While her entire body continued to tingle all over, she welcomed each sweet sensation. As Imagany sang softly in tune with "This Is Your Life," her doorbell suddenly rang. She swore loudly at the interruption. As she lifted herself out of the comfort of the tub, rivulets of soap and water cascaded down her body. Imagany wondered what person would dare to intrude on her privacy without calling first. She knew Anthony was still out of town so it couldn't be him. At the thought that it might be Elliott returning for something, she quickened her step to the door.

Wrapped in nothing but a large bath towel, Imagany depressed her intercom button. "Who is it?"

"It's Leslie Lowe."

Imagany gasped and a small current of shock ran through her. The only reason Leslie would have for returning to her apartment would be to bring her the money. She buzzed Leslie up and willed herself to remain calm as she ran to throw on her silk peignoir. She was putting her arms through its matching robe when Leslie rang the bell to her door.

When Imagany opened the door, Leslie stepped through it, leaving a plume of Opium perfume trailing behind her as she walked in. Just as before, Leslie was dressed elegantly and expensively. Imagany invited her to sit down.

Looking around her, Leslie walked to the love seat and sat down. She lifted her brief case to rest it upon the center table, snapping it open. Leslie wasted no time as she brusquely pulled out a sheath of documents before turning the brief case around and pushing it in Imagany's direction. "It's all there. Count it."

Imagany wasted no time as she did exactly that. Tremors of excitement coursed through her as she counted the stacks of one hundred dollar bills, laying each one on the table. When she reached sixty thousand, Imagany looked up with a crazed, ecstatic gleam in her eye to find Leslie watching her contemptuously with unveiled hostility. Imagany paid Leslie no mind as she willed her consciousness to stay in the present. What she really longed to do was kick Leslie the hell out of her apartment and throw all the money on the floor and romp naked all over it. She thought to herself: 'Leslie, I don't give a damn where you go, my sistah, but you've got to get the hell up outta here!'

Leslie interrupted Imagany's thoughts by thrusting some papers and an ink pen at her. "Here. Sign these."

With all the money sitting upon the table as it was, Imagany would have gladly signed her life away. But common sense told her to get a grip on her nerves. Imagany took the papers and began to read over them. Seeing all the legalese, Imagany skimmed the papers cursorily. What she got out of reading them was that Leslie wanted her to agree to no longer accept any more monies or gifts from Anthony Barrington, that he would no longer pay the rent on her apartment, and neither would he continue to pay for her car. Imagany's brow raised as she quickly glanced up at Leslie before returning to read the papers. Leslie had to be misinformed because Imagany's car was already paid for and Imagany had the title to prove it. Her rent was also paid up for the next seven months and she had the receipts to prove that, too. If Leslie assumed otherwise, then Imagany would continue to let her do so.

Imagany picked up the pen and asked, "What is the point here, Leslie?"

"The point is exactly what the papers say. That you'll agree not to marry Anthony Barrington in exchange for the said amount. That you will agree to no longer accept financial support from him and neither will you continue to see him. As of today you are to break off all contact with him."

In answer to Leslie's little speech, Imagany signed on the dotted line. Now that everything had been finalized, if Leslie's elegantly clad behind was not out of her apartment within the next few seconds, then Imagany would make sure Leslie's butt was out of her place via the window. Imagany handed Leslie the signed papers. She generously closed Leslie's now empty brief case for her and stood to go open the door.

Leslie followed Imagany to the door, full of disdain. As Imagany held the door open for her, she said to Leslie, "I got what I wanted out of the deal, Leslie. I only hope after everything's said and done, you'll be able to say the same." Imagany didn't give Leslie a chance to reply. She slammed the door hard in her face before the woman could even think about changing her mind!

Imagany turned and walked calmly to the table and stood looking down at all the money. Although sixty thousand dollars was not a lot of money, for a person with only a few hundred dollars in their personal bank account, it would do. Imagany threw her head back and let out a loud, exuberant scream. In one fell swoop, she swept the money off the table, scattering it onto the floor, and dived into it head first.

Back in her car, a chilling smile covered Leslie Lowe's face as, once again, she looked at Imagany's signature on the documents. She had maneuvered and used funds from one of Anthony's many accounts, so this little feat had not cost her one red cent. Leslie felt a self-satisfied glow steal over her. Knowing first-hand what a volatile man Anthony Barrington was, Leslie could hardly wait for his return just to show him the papers that the so-called love of his life had willingly and so nonchalantly agreed to sign. Above all else, Leslie would make it a point to give Anthony the colorful used condom she had stealthily removed from Imagany's living room floor. She would taunt Anthony mercilessly by telling him that he obviously wasn't the only man in his little girlfriend's life and that the least he could do was teach his mistress to cover her tracks by learning the art of discretion. A cruel laugh escaped Leslie's throat as she considered how, in the end, *she* would have the last laugh!

Chapter Eleven

magany had several errands to run before her dinner date that evening. There was homework to be completed, house cleaning to be done, books to be returned to the library, and groceries that had to be bought from the store. Caprice had designed the menu; all that was required of Imagany was that she purchase the necessary ingredients.

She had finished her errands and was lying on her bed daydreaming about Elliott, when Caprice called her from a pay phone.

"Hey. Were you able to get everything from the store?"

"Yes, darling. I did."

"Darling?" Caprice was taken aback. They never used the full expression of the word "darling." The two of them always shortened it to "dahlin'." "Excuse me, people, but this is Reese on the line, not someone else. Stop trippin' and get a grip, please." Caprice sucked her teeth and shook her head wondering what was on Imagany's mind. "Have you called Elliott to make sure he's still coming? With the way you've been playing him, it wouldn't surprise me if he didn't even bother showing up."

Imagany had drifted off into another world when she heard Caprice banging the receiver against something metal.

"Helloooo! People? Is anybody there?"

"Yes, I'm here. What is the problem?"

"Imagany, what is with you? I asked you if Elliott is still coming?" Caprice had the distinct feeling that Imagany was trying to play her.

Imagany's chest heaved as she breathed rapturously into the phone, "Oh, he'll be here all right." Her subtle hint was not lost on Caprice.

"Imagany, what do you mean? Is there something you're not telling me?" Caprice's voice was laced with both irritation and curiosity.

"Mmmmm." Imagany's eyes closed as she recalled all that had transpired between her and Elliott.

"Oh, no!" Caprice's eyes widened as she clutched the phone. It suddenly dawned on her why Imagany was acting the way she was.

"Reese . . ." Imagany's voice trailed off as she started daydreaming again.

Caprice could now tell from Imagany's tone that something serious had gone down. She began to shake with excitement. The image of Imagany and Elliott in bed together caused lewd thoughts to run through her mind. She could only imagine the things Imagany had done to the man.

"Imagany?" Caprice was shouting her name now. "Girl, what happened?" Her own heart had begun to pump faster.

"Reese, I . . ." Imagany couldn't get the words out of her mouth. Even fantasies weren't supposed to be this good.

Caprice figured it out. Before she knew it, a loud ecstatic scream tore from her throat and hit the air, causing several passersby to run in her direction to ask her if everything was all right. They must have thought she had just escaped from the Bellevue Insane Asylum. Caprice cupped her hand over the phone as she told them everything was fine and that she was okay, she had just heard some extremely good news. "Thanks, folks. Yes. I'm sure I'm all right. Thank you. Thank you very much."

She came back to the phone and said, "Imagany, don't do me like this. Tell me what the hell happened? Did he . . . Did you two . . . Oh my God! What am I saying?" Caprice slapped her hand to her forehead. "Of course you two made love. What am I talking about?" Caprice clutched at her heart as she locked her knees together. "Just tell me how it was. That's all I want to know." Caprice was chanting into the phone now like a junkie begging her drug dealer for a fix. She shifted the phone from hand to hand and gestured wildly, throwing her hand in the air, as she turned around in circles. Passersby shook their heads, probably thinking that it was an awful shame that such a pretty girl was so messed up in the head.

"Well, go on, tell me, how was it?"

Imagany took a deep breath and gripped the bed sheets before she said, "Reese, it was the best lovin' I've ever had in my life! Do you hear me?" By the time Imagany finished the sentence, she, too, was yelling into the phone. She flipped over in the bed on her stomach before rolling up in a ball as she held the phone tightly to her ear.

Caprice must have dropped the phone from her ear, because Imagany heard another loud scream tear through the air. All any passerby saw was a girl clutching the phone to her ear with one hand while waving the other one frantically in the air. When Caprice finally came back to the phone, she was nearly hoarse. In a voice that pulsed with excitement, Caprice shouted, "I knew it! I told you the brother had it goin' on. I could tell he was loaded from the moment I laid my eyes on him." Imagany heard Caprice pound her fist against something. "Imagany, just tell me how good it was, girl. No, second thought, don't tell me. I can't take it. Not out here in public." Caprice lifted her head to look around frenziedly. "Look, girlfriend, hold that thought. I'm on my way over." Caprice tried to hang up the phone, but when she couldn't quite get it on its hook, she dropped the receiver and left it to swing in the wind. She ran frantically into the street to search desperately for a cab.

There couldn't have been more than twenty minutes that elapsed from the time Caprice hung up 'til she was ringing Imagany's bell. Imagany buzzed her up and peeped from the doorway as she waited for Caprice to reach her level.

When Caprice turned the corner, she was huffing and puffing from having just run up the stairs three at a time. She leaned her hand on the wall for support as she crawled down the hallway, dragging her bookbag behind her. Thin as she was, exercise was not one of Caprice's better habits and she looked now like a straggler in a race trying to make it to the finish line.

Clad only in a silk nightgown, Imagany didn't want to come all the way out into the hallway to help her, but she laughed hard at the picture that Caprice presented as she struggled to her door. Caprice entered and dropped to the floor in exertion, resting her head upon her arms.

Imagany locked the door and walked past Caprice to go back into the bedroom. "I hate to do this to you, kid, but you have to come in here so I can get back in my bed."

Caprice groaned as she wrestled her body from the floor to crawl inside the bedroom.

On her knees, Caprice made it to the edge of the bed and lifted her chest to rest it upon the bed. In a voice full of breathless impatience, she said, "Now tell the story!"

"Girl, come get up here with me." Imagany was already nestled comfortably in the king-sized bed as she gestured for Caprice to come lay on the bed too.

Caprice shook her head. "I'm not getting up there. This bed is probably so hot from last night, I'm scared it might set me on fire!"

Imagany sucked her teeth. "Reese, please. We were in the living room on the floor. We never made it to the bed."

Caprice fell backwards on the floor spread eagled. Her voice shook with tremors as she said dramatically, "Oh, no! They never even made it to the bedroom! What is the world coming to?"

When Imagany saw that Caprice had no intentions of climbing up on the bed with her, she turned around to lie on the other end. She lay on her stomach with her elbows underneath her, pressing her chin into the bed. Imagany took a moment to shake her head and gather her thoughts. She turned over on her back, raised both her knees and stretched her arms over the edge of the bed. In a voice filled with wonder, she said, "Caprice, it was like an incredible dream come true. As if I pulled a fantasy right out of a magician's hat."

Caprice turned on her side and propped her head on her arm. Though she was listening carefully to Imagany's every word, it was taking far too long for Imagany to get to the juicy part. She gave Imagany a push as she said, "First off, tell me how it started."

Knowing that she would not be able to keep things in chronological order, Imagany simply said, "Well, we were on the couch and I was sitting on his lap with my arms around his neck and at first we were just talking. Before I knew it, we were kissing and hugging and then the man had his hands and lips all over the place. Sucking my breasts, grabbing my thighs, between my legs, and . . . Oh, my goodness! Caprice, the man's lovin' was so good I nearly went out of my mind!" Imagany cut herself short as she jumped to her knees with her hands outstretched and her fists rolled up in a tight ball. She threw back her head and bent her body backwards to scream out at the top of her lungs. With her hair standing all over her head, Imagany's resemblance to a madwoman was startling.

Caprice rolled over onto her side with her knees curled up as she pounded the floor with her fists, hollering out, "Dear Lawd, somebody please, pretty please, just hold my hand!"

After the two of them stopped babbling incoherently, they managed to grab hold of each other's hands and sing in unison at a thundering volume, "Talkin' 'bout a strong black man!"

Afterwards, Imagany sat up on the bed with her legs touching the floor. With her elbows on her knees, she looked down at Caprice and said quietly, "Reese, the man was so strong, so firm, so solid and so good." Imagany shook her head to think and gather her thoughts. Unable to find the right words to describe what had taken place between her and Elliott, she said, "The only thing I can tell you, Reese, is I've never had any lovin' like that in all my life. And you know I've sampled a few. If I could bottle and sell what Elliott did to me last night, baby, every black woman in America would wake up every morning screaming, 'I am somebody!' "

"Umph!" Caprice lifted her hand in the air as if to testify. "All right now! Tell me what a strong black man can't do for a woman. Girlfriend, can I get a witness?" Caprice reached her hand out to Imagany and once again they locked their hands together in a strong grip.

After they managed to release each other's grasp, Imagany laid back on the bed and tread her fingers through her tangled hair. She laced her fingers behind her head and said, "You know, Reese, even though I enjoyed having sex with Anthony, it was nothing compared to this. With Anthony, the sex was good but there were times when my body just wouldn't respond unless he went down on me. And even then, he'd have to work extra hard just to satisfy me."

"That's because his ass is old, girl!"

Imagany laughed. "No, that wasn't why. It was because my heart wasn't in it, Reese. My body may have responded to him physically, but inside, I was cold. Last night with Elliott, for the first time in my life, I gave of myself. There was no need to wrench anything out of me. I wanted to give everything to him willingly. It's like I can see the difference so clearly now. With Anthony, it was all about reciprocity. 'You do for me and I'll do for you.' I'm not downing Anthony because he's been good to me. But we both knew up front what we wanted from each other and we knew how to get it. We also knew where the other was trying to go. But things are going to be different now." Imagany thought about the money that Leslie Lowe had just given her. "I'm tired of being with men who are like father figures to me. All they want to do is to mold me into something I'm not. I'm ready to experience what it's like to be with someone like Elliott. Someone I can grow with for a change. Not someone who's already at the point where they're so set in their ways that all they want to do is change you. I want to be with Elliott." Her eyes closed as she thought of what he did to her. With her eyes still closed, Imagany whispered, "And it's not just the sex, Reese. I like Elliott." She thought about it and then repeated it stronger. "I like him a lot."

"And what about Anthony?"

"Anthony who?" Imagany stared down at the floor before looking up and staring into space. "I think it's time for me to tell Anthony goodbye."

"Yes!" Caprice pounded her fist on the floor and jumped up to throw her arms around Imagany as they hugged each other and laughed. Caprice said, "Imagany, I'm so proud of you. I didn't think I'd ever see the day when you'd actually tell that creep to get lost. You go, girl! I always knew you had it in you." Caprice sat back and stared at her. "At one point, I even thought you were going to marry him, and that's why I was so worried about you. He may be filthy rich, Imagany, but he could never have made you happy. When I look at you and Elliott, I see sparks there, girl. The two of you just look so happy together. I know we've never agreed about Anthony, but I think life is too short to waste it on someone like him. I don't know where or how you found the strength to let him go. I'm just happy that it happened. Thank God for Elliott!"

Suddenly, Imagany felt guilty. She couldn't bring herself to tell Caprice the true reason why she was now so willing to dump Anthony. Chances were that Caprice wouldn't feel the same if she knew the truth, so Imagany decided to remain quiet about Leslie Lowe.

Caprice sat back on the floor and leaned her back against the wall as she contemplated her thoughts. She lifted one of her knees and rested her elbow upon it and said, "If I know you, Imagany, right now you're probably thinking about how you'll be able to maintain this apartment and everything else. The only thing I can say to encourage you, girlfriend, is that somehow, I believe God will provide."

Biting the tip of her finger guiltily, Imagany said, "You're right. Even when we find ways to bungle things up, He always manages to provide." No longer wishing to dwell upon the topic, Imagany changed the subject by reminding Caprice that she still had to cook for the evening. As Imagany led the way into the kitchen, Caprice teased her by singing Stephanie Mills' song, "I Feel Good All Over." Imagany watched as Caprice started preparing the meal, but after Caprice pulled out a maze of pots and pans, Imagany quickly lost interest and went back to bed.

Caprice laughed. She knew Imagany wouldn't last long in the kitchen. As Imagany departed, Caprice called after her, "Imagany, if you're planning on wearing anything other than jeans, I'm going to have to borrow something to wear."

"Help yourself, dahlin'. I'm going back to sleep."

When Imagany pronounced the word "darling" as the two of them normally did, she didn't hear Caprice's mumbled reply. "Now that's more like it!"

It was a quarter to seven when Imagany awoke. She raised herself from the bed and went up front to see what Caprice was doing. As she passed through the kitchen, tempting aromas floated past her nose. Caprice was in the living room studying when Imagany entered the room. She was sitting on the floor with her papers spread around her as Imagany came and laid down near her feet.

With her hands behind her head, Imagany said, "That food smells so good, I could go dive in it right now."

Without looking up, Caprice took her pencil out of her mouth and said, "Greedy thing. I made a platter of chips, dips, cheese and crackers as appetizers. I knew you would want to eat before everyone got here."

Imagany wrinkled her nose. "I'll just eat some fruit. It's time for us to start getting ready anyway. Did you decide what to wear?"

"Unh, unh. You pick out something for me. And bring me an apple, too."

With her apple clamped between her teeth, she shifted through her vast selection of clothes. She enjoyed having so many clothes, but Anthony was the reason she had them.

For Caprice, Imagany selected a black minidress. For herself, she chose an orange mini skirt with a wide belt along with a matching orange silk blouse.

She selected their accessories with the notion that less was better. Earrings, bracelets and necklaces would do the trick. Both of them would wear low-heeled pumps.

Imagany was laying everything out on the bed when Caprice walked into the bedroom and admired the clothes.

"We have Anthony to thank for most of these outfits."

"I knew the old bird was good for something."

Imagany sat on the bed smiling. "Reese, will you stop calling the man old? He is not!"

"When I reach seventy, I'm sure I'll be saying I'm not old either."

Imagany laughed. "Get out. Hurry up and take your shower so I can take my bath."

"Yep. Let me hurry up. As long as you linger in the tub, you'll be in there until tomorrow." Caprice laughed as she went to turn on the water. She called from the bathroom, "When we were younger, Imagany, it seemed like every time I called your house, I had to wait for you to get out of the tub. I've never met anybody who stayed in the bathroom as long as you do. I'm just surprised you're not wrinkled up like a prune."

"Don't start with me, Reese. Go ahead and do what you've got to do and stay out of grown folk's business." Caprice's words conjured up an image in Imagany's mind, one she could never forget. She remembered all too well why, even as a child, she had lived in the tub. It had been her way of attempting to wash away her feelings of uncleanliness. Imagany's eyes closed and her head turned to the side as unwanted childhood memories came flooding back to her.

It was hot outside. She had been jumping rope and playing in her front yard by herself. She even remembered the words she sang as she jumped faster and faster, her braids flopping in the wind. Suddenly, she had to use the bathroom badly. She threw her rope to the ground and entered her house via the back door. She remembered passing her mother in the living room. She was reading from her book and never looked up as Imagany skipped past her up the stairs. Imagany raced up the stairs and was on the last stair when she saw that the bathroom door was ajar. She pushed the door open and closed it behind her. Quickly pulling down her panties, she sat on the toilet seat and let the urine flow from her body. Suddenly the shower doors opened causing the steam from the shower to immerse the room. When the man stepped naked from behind the fogged-up glass doors, Imagany froze and her eyes rounded like saucers. As he stepped toward her, her mouth opened in a silent gasp. He stood in front of her now, his penis fully erect, holding himself in his hand. Imagany turned her head away because she knew this to be wrong. He whispered for her to touch him, that he knew she wanted to and that it wasn't wrong for her to do so. He took hold of her small hands and placed them around him, clamping his hands over hers, sliding them back and forth, slowly and then much faster. As she tried to pull her hands away it seemed to go on forever. She tried to lift herself off the toilet seat but it was too late. The jerking motions continued and a stream of warm liquid shot onto her face and dribbled down to her chest. Tears of humiliation fell from her eyes as the man reached down to wipe himself with some tissue. Using the same tissue, he bent over and pushed his hands between her legs as he wiped the urine from underneath her. Imagany had squeezed her legs together to prevent him from touching her but he had forced her legs open, telling her that what was there belonged only to him. She cried as he turned away from her to pull on his robe. He lifted her head to wipe the tears away from her eyes and kissed her on her forehead, telling her not to cry because she would always be daddy's sweet little girl. After he left, Imagany sat on the stool with tears streaming down her face, her hands between her legs. Somehow she knew what had happened was wrong, and she couldn't stop the tears from falling from her eyes. She felt unclean as she got up to lock the bathroom door. She walked to the basin and used a wash cloth to scrub her face. Feeling as if the sticky, nasty stuff was still all over her, she ran water inside the tub. After removing her clothes, she'd stepped into the water to wash away all traces of the filthiness, trying desperately to also wash away the feeling of shame from her body.

Imagany lifted her head from her hands to stare at the ceiling, tears trickling down the sides of her face. She sucked in huge breaths of air to stop the flow of tears. Imagany remembered the shame and degradation of that moment, and others which had followed. She painfully searched her heart for the reason why anyone would destroy the innocence of a child's unworldly mind. She heard Caprice turn the water off in the bathroom and quickly wiped her hands across her face. Imagany willed herself to control her emotions as she erased all the tracks of her tears.

When Caprice walked into the bedroom with a towel wrapped around her, Imagany appeared to be deep in meditation as she sat cross-legged on the bed with her arms behind her for support. Caprice applied lotion and perfume to her body before turning to Imagany to say, "Imagany, girl, will you quit daydreaming and go get ready? You don't have time to take a long bath so just take a shower." Caprice turned back to the mirror as Imagany left the room. "What in the world am I going to do with my hair?"

Imagany sat on the stool and through self-discipline, mentally commanded a hardness to come over her body. She was determined not to let her memories depress her and ruin the entire evening. With resolve, Imagany got up and stepped into the shower to cleanse herself one more time.

Imagany pinned Caprice's hair into a ball at the back of her head and was tying a matching sheer black ribbon around it when the doorbell rang. She stepped alongside Caprice as they stared into the mirror and asked, "Do we look good or what?"

Caprice turned sideways while looking in the mirror to run her hands over the flatness of her stomach. "Too good. Now let's go find us a couple of loaded strong black men. And I don't mean loaded with money either."

Imagany left the bedroom smiling to buzz the guys in. "I'm game for that, although a little money never hurts the cause."

Elliott and Carl stepped through the door, smelling and looking all too fine. Both of them were dressed just alike in jeans with dark blue dress shoes, pin-striped shirts and dark blue suit jackets. Elliott was carrying two bottles of Asti Spumante Gancia and he handed them to Imagany as he walked through the door.

Imagany smiled radiantly at Elliott as she took the bottles from him, lifting her head for his kiss. "What time is it?"

Elliott threw his arm around her shoulders as he led her into the kitchen. "Seven-thirty, baby. And we're not a minute late. Right, Carl?"

"The man hasn't lied yet." Carl gave Caprice a bear hug before leading her into the kitchen.

Imagany was at the sink rinsing out four wine glasses as Carl stepped beside her to look in all the pots and pans.

"How are you, Imagany?" Carl asked.

She smiled at him brightly. "I couldn't be better, Carl. Forgive my manners. How are you?"

Carl stepped beside her and spoke quietly so that only she could hear him. "I'm a lot better now that you aren't flipping me the bird sign anymore."

"Yeah, that was kind of bad of me wasn't it?"

"It sure was. I'm still trying to get over the shock."

"In that case, next time just tell me what I want to know."

Carl wagged his finger in her face. "Hopefully, there won't be a next time."

As the two of them laughed, Elliott asked, "What kind of trouble are you two stirring up?"

"Were we stirring up trouble, Imagany?"

"None that I know of."

"Don't believe them, Elliott. They look too guilty," Caprice said as she started setting the table for them to eat.

Carl stepped toward Caprice with cheese and crackers in his hand and said, "I see the chef has outdone herself again."

Caprice smugly ran her fingers across her chest and blew on them. "Hey, when you're good, you're good. Sit down so we can eat, guys."

When everyone's plate was fixed, Caprice and Imagany sat down and joined them. Before they ate, Carl said grace, and afterwards, Elliott proposed a toast:

"Here's to the loveliest ladies I have the pleasure of knowing. May we all live long and prosperous lives and may there be many more fun-filled evenings such as this one."

As the four of them clicked glasses, Carl said, "I couldn't have said it better myself."

The dinner conversation covered a variety of topics. Everyone complimented Caprice on the meal. After they finished eating, the two of them washed the dishes while Elliott and Carl went into the living room. Elliott turned the television on and put the volume on mute as Carl searched through Imagany's large collection of records and tape cassettes. He settled on an old one by Cameo, playing one of their most famous tunes called "Sparkle." Imagany and Caprice sang along to the lyrics.

When they were finished, Caprice went to curl up on the love seat next to Carl. Imagany sat on the floor with her shoulder turned into Elliott's chest. She listened to him sing the lyrics to Sparkle. "Elliott, I do believe you can sing."

"Oh yeah. Carl and I can hum a few notes, now. Don't get us started. Tell 'em, Carl. We can blow a little bit."

Carl looked in their direction and said, "I don't think they could stand the pressure, El. We don't want to hurt 'em."

Imagany switched to her other side and said tauntingly, "Hurt us, baby! Don't hold back, show us what you've got. Right, Reese?"

"I say they should go for it. Especially now that they've built us up."

"Carl, man, I think they're challenging us. We can't let them get away with that. Let's do it." Elliott and Carl got up to move to the center of the room and were about to start singing when Imagany interrupted them.

"Hold it guys. Just one second. Let's put this on the loud speaker." Imagany went to the stereo cabinet and pulled out the microphone that had come along with a stand as an accessory to her stereo system. She hooked it up and blew into it to test it before setting it on its stand.

Caprice and Imagany went to the love seat and huddled together to watch them perform. The two of them snickered and laughed because they knew that Elliott and Carl were about to make fools of themselves.

The guys removed their suit jackets and Elliott laid them on the sofa. He stepped back to the mic and before he could say anything, Caprice started clapping while Imagany cupped her hands to the sides of her mouth and yelled, "Don't be ashamed! Just do what you gotta do."

Elliott was about to speak again when he laughed. He noticed Caprice scooping up some round marble pebbles that Imagany kept in her vases as decorations, as if she were about to throw the pebbles at the guys if they didn't perform up to par.

Carl noticed it, too, and he stepped up to the mic and said, "Please, ladies, let's not have any violence in the house. We are here solely for your entertainment and enjoyment. Let's try to keep it clean. Thank you very much."

Carl stepped back and again Elliott stepped to the microphone. "Yes, ladies, as I was saying before I was so crudely and rudely interrupted by members of the audience, my partner and I would like to perform for you a very special number. It's dedicated to all the special ladies in the house." Carl stepped up to the mic and added, "We would also like to thank the other members of the band who, for unknown reasons, could not be here with us tonight."

Imagany laughed as Caprice yelled, "Shut up and get on with the show."

Elliott and Carl stepped away from the mic and turned around to twirl before they both stepped to the mic in unison. They harmonized together for a moment and then broke out with Heat Wave's infamous "Always And Forever." They sang in conjunction with each other as they took turns singing different lines. Carl hit all the high notes while Elliott sang bass. Coming from both of them, the tune was so smooth and resonant that both Imagany and Caprice had to admit that they were impressed.

When they finished, Carl and Elliott stepped up to the mic and said, "Thank you for the applause. We'd like to take this opportunity to thank all the ladies in the house for coming out to support us tonight, you can catch our upcoming act at . . ."

Imagany quickly rose to the microphone, stepped between Carl and Elliott and pushed them both to the side as she said, "Yes, folks, that was a nice performance. So let's put our hands together and give it up for our very own special group called the 'Has Beens!' "

Caprice and Carl laughed as Elliott grabbed Imagany by the waist and swung her around. "Woman, what do you mean by calling us the 'Has Beens?' Don't you know how important we are?" Elliott dragged her along with him as he walked backwards toward the couch and when he sat down, he pulled Imagany on top of his knees.

Carl wrapped his arm around Caprice's shoulders, and said braggingly, "Now that we've put you girls to shame, it's time for you two to show us what you can do."

"That's right ladies. Entertain us for a change." As he spoke, Elliott tried to push Imagany off his knees.

Never one to be at a loss for words, Imagany said, "Wait a minute, now! Caprice can hum a few bars herself. Don't even try her. Reese, go on up there, girl, and sing Aretha Franklin's 'Giving Him Something He Can Feel'." Imagany knew Caprice could sing because Caprice had sung solo at church many times when they were growing up. She especially knew Caprice knew the words to Aretha's song because she had sung it so much when they were younger that Imagany had grown tired of hearing it. Whenever Imagany heard the song, to this day, she immediately associated it with Caprice.

"What? You mean to tell me my baby can sing as well as cook? Aw, come here and give daddy a big sloppy kiss." Caprice pulled laughingly away from Carl's eager grasp.

She turned to Imagany and said, "Hold it, Imagany. Remember whose side you're supposed to be on?"

"Okay, ladies, that settles it. Go on up there. Don't be shamed either." This time Elliott did manage to push Imagany off of him as he goaded her.

"Come on, Reese. Let's put these guys to shame. You sing and I'll dance." Imagany had Aretha's record in her collection so she went to search for it.

"Yo, El? Should we let them use the record? That's cheating, isn't it?"

"Yeah, it is. But they look pretty sorry up there, so we'll let 'em slide this time."

Imagany stood poised and ready with her backside to the audience as the music began to play. When Caprice started singing into the mic, doing her thing, Imagany started slowly working her hands down her body, winding her hips suggestively. All eyes were focused upon her. She dipped down to the floor on her knees and teasingly raised back up only to spin around and face the audience and stretch her hands out toward them. She spread her legs apart and slowly raised her skirt. She crouched slightly, gyrating her hips, pushing them back and forth in quick, jerking motions. Elliott and Carl continued to stare at Imagany rivetingly. After a while, Imagany's movements became wildly suggestive. Even Caprice had to stop singing and turned around to look at Imagany with raised eyebrows. Caprice stepped to the side with her hands on her hips and gave Imagany the floor.

Clearing his throat loudly, Elliott rose from his seat to stop the music and stepped in front of the mic. With his arm around Caprice's shoulder, he said, "Excuse me ladies and gentlemen, but due to the explicit nature and content of this show, unfortunately we are forced to disqualify one of the performers." With that, Elliott grabbed Imagany's arm and dragged her along with him back to the sofa. He sat her down on his knees and asked her scoldingly, "Imagany, how many times do I have to tell you not to act this way in front of the kids?" Elliott turned back to Carl, who was laughing along with Imagany and said, "Hit the music, my man."

This time when Caprice sang into the microphone, all eyes were focused on her and not on Imagany's rear end.

As the evening progressed, they played Pictionary and listened to more music and had begun to discuss the pros and cons of sororities and fraternities, when Caprice, who was a Delta, and Carl, who was an Alpha, gave their supporting views on why they thought such organizations were a necessity to schools and communities.

As Elliott excused himself to go into the bathroom, the telephone rang and Imagany caught Caprice's look as she rose to go answer the phone in her bedroom.

"Hello."

"Well, hello, Imagany. How are you?" Relief washed over her as she recognized Caprice's mother's voice on the line.

"I'm fine Mrs. McKnight. How are you feeling?" Caprice's mom always had been one of Imagany's favorite people.

Mrs. McKnight was telling her that she was just calling to say hello and see how they were doing since Caprice had told her she was spending the weekend over at her place. Imagany told her to hold on for a second and called out to Caprice to pick up the phone. When she looked up, she saw Elliott standing in the doorway watching her. Not knowing how long he had been standing there, Imagany put her finger to her lips and gestured for him to come to her.

Elliott came and lay on the bed behind her, sliding his arm around her waist. As his hand caressed the area just below her breasts, he was content to simply sit near her, touching her, enjoying having her body so close to his. Elliott propped his head on his elbow, watching Imagany. He used his other hand to pull her backwards, curling her even closer to him. As his hand continued to rub in circular motions, he leaned his head forward to gently nip her in the side. When her fingers reached out to slide through his hair, her nails dug into his scalp. Elliott felt his body tingle and he found himself rising on his knees behind her to pull the hair away from the nape of her neck. Bending her head forward, he began to plant soft kisses over the entire area of her neck while his hand weaved itself into her hair. An insatiable hunger rose within his body, and before Elliott knew it, he had pulled her down with him, partially covering her body with his. In slow motion, he moved the receiver part of the phone away from her mouth and covered her lips with his own. When his tongue slid deep into her mouth, to taste her, Imagany released her grip on the phone to wrap her own hands around the back of his head. Elliott slid his hands underneath her bottom to raise her skirt past the silkiness of her stockinged legs and over her rounded hips. When the two of them heard the phone hit the floor, Elliott leisurely pulled himself away from her and rose from the bed to return it to its hook. He walked to the door and closed it, turning the lock in its place. When he returned to the edge of the bed, without removing his eyes from hers, he slowly began to unfasten the buckle of his belt. The look on his face clearly expressed that his intent was to claim what she had promised him earlier.

Imagany lay on her back with her knees turned to the side. As she watched Elliott remove his clothing, she felt a familiar languor glide over her and thread itself throughout her body. When Elliott's now naked body straddled hers, she closed her eyes and turned her head to the side, letting his warmthness embrace her. Once again, inertia crept over her and she was unable to aid or assist him as he slowly removed all of her clothing.

Elliott's hands seemed to flit over her whisperingly as he removed her clothing piece by piece. Once she was completely naked, he sat on his haunches and stared down at her. The look in his eyes alone sent shivers down Imagany's spine as she sensed the things that he was about to do to her and make her want to do to him in return. Elliott entwined his fingers through hers and pulled her body up to meet him. He pressed himself against her, holding her body tightly to him with one arm. With her breasts crushed to his chest, his other arm locked her head in a grip as his mouth fastened itself to hers, their tongues engaging in an arduous battle. When he released her, her body slunk against him, as if it had no life of its own. Letting her fall back onto the bed, Elliott positioned Imagany by turning her body around, pushing her onto her knees. Planting his own knees fixedly between hers, he gently wrapped his arm around her neck and covered her body with his. With his chest completely covering her back, his manhood pricked her teasingly and he heard a soft, purring whimper slide from somewhere deep within her throat. Elliott had her right where he wanted her, and as he bent his head over hers, he thrust his tongue into her mouth as he simultaneously plunged himself into the core of her being.

As they rocked in slow motion with their mouths clasped together, Imagany's hands clung tightly to Elliott's thighs. And whenever she pulled her mouth away to emit a pleasurable gasp, Elliott would quickly cover it again with his own, causing both their sighs to rumble deep within their throats. Trapped inside their own magical world, time had no boundaries and desire knew no constraints. Locked in the grip of a deep, burning love, the two of them filled each other with a euphoric enchantment as they transported themselves to a higher plane where only blissfulness could be found awaiting them.

***

Outside the bedroom, Caprice and Carl sat curled up contentedly as they listened to one of Imagany's old Phyllis Hyman tapes. Much time had passed since Elliott had gone to the bathroom and Imagany had left them to answer the phone. But so involved had they been with each other, they hadn't even noticed. Carl brushed his lips against Caprice's temple as he spoke softly into her ear. "I think you and I are getting played once again, Reese. Something tells me they're not coming back."

Caprice glanced at her watch. "I think you're right. But we weren't waiting for them anyway." Caprice raised herself on her knees as she turned around to face him.

Carl wrapped his arms around Caprice and folded his legs behind her. "The night's still young, you know. Since it's only ten-thirty, we could go out and paint the town red." With those words, Carl put the ball in Caprice's court.

Caprice stared into Carl's eyes and knew that the only place she wanted to go with him was somewhere where they could be alone. She gazed at him and said, "I know of just the perfect place." Caprice raised herself and took his outstretched hand. When Carl lifted himself up, he bent down to retrieve his jacket. He wrapped it around Caprice's shoulders before she led the way out of the apartment. Caprice knew the front door would lock by itself. As an afterthought, she walked to the phone, lifted the receiver off its hook and laid it on the table. She walked back to Carl with a smile on her face, and as he threw his arm around her shoulders, she led the way to their intended destination.

Chapter Twelve

With his hands folded behind his head, Elliott experienced a sense of rightness which he had never known and the word "karma" kept running through his brain.

Imagany leaned her head against Elliott's chest. Feeling content and thoroughly satisfied, she listened to the steady beat of his heart. A smile crossed her face as thoughts about their relationship ran through her mind. Raising her head, she pressed her chin into his chest.

Imagany said, "Boo?"

Elliott liked the sound of his new nickname. "How may I help you?" He answered in a slightly amused voice.

"Do you realize that we finally made it to the bedroom?"

Elliott opened his eyes and stared down at her. "We would have made it here a lot sooner if you hadn't torn my clothes off every chance you got."

Imagany lifted herself up to straddle him. She placed her hands upon her hips and peered down the length of her nose at him. "Me? Tear your clothes off? Are we confused here, people, or what?"

With his hands still behind his head, Elliott stared at her admiringly. With her hair framing her face and her hands positioned on her hips, she reminded him of a huntress who was staking her claim. He enjoyed having her sit atop him and he closed his eyes contentedly once more before saying, "Yep, the way I see it, you just can't seem to keep your hands off me. Boy, do I love it! And I'm also going to have to teach you to be a better hostess, too. We're supposed to be out there entertaining but we're locked in here instead."

Imagany smiled at his version of the story. She placed her hands flat on his chest and gave him her own. "Caprice will understand why we locked ourselves in here. And so will Carl after I explain to both of them how you dragged me in here kicking and screaming." Imagany slid off of Elliott, intending to throw on some clothes and go back up front with Caprice and Carl.

Just as she reached the edge of the bed, in one swift movement, Elliott rose to wrestle her down into the softness of the sheets. Imagany squealed as he straddled her, holding her arms above her head, trapping her body between his thighs.

Imagany lay underneath him, watching the way his muscles rippled in his arms. She enjoyed the feel of him holding her captive and her struggles to escape were merely halfhearted.

"The only screaming and kicking I can recall, Ms. Jenkins, seems to have come after the fact. And speaking of facts, I want to know what you told Caprice to cause her to look at me so slyly all evening." Elliott's eyebrows arched as he waited for Imagany to respond.

Imagany's eyes widened innocently as she stopped struggling. She masked the smile on her face by playing the innocent role. "I don't have the slightest idea what you're talking about, Elliott. Caprice didn't look at you any differently from the way I looked at Carl. You must have imagined it." Though she would never admit it, Imagany had caught Caprice watching Elliott knowingly at times and she had to clamp her lips together to keep from laughing.

Elliott released his grip on her hands and slid his body along side hers, propping his head on his elbow. "No way did I imagine it. Every time I looked up, I caught her examining me like I was a bug or something. I swear! When I got up to go to the bathroom, I caught her staring at my crotch." Elliott paused to imitate the look Caprice had on her face. When he narrowed his eyes and leered at her, Imagany could no longer hold back her laughter. As her body shook with laughter, Elliott placed his hand on the curve of her hip, pulling her closer to him. "Uh, uh. Don't laugh. Just tell me what you told her."

Imagany turned on her own side to face him. "Don't be nosy, Boo." When he continued to look at her inquiringly, as if waiting for an answer, she said, "You really want to know, don't you?"

Elliott inclined his head, "Yes, I really do."

Imagany laced her arms behind his neck as she pondered what story to tell him. "First, I told her how you seduced me with flowers and sweet words of passion. And then I told her about how you enticed me to the floor before telling me that you had a terrible secret." She lifted one of her arms from around his neck to cup his manhood lovingly in her hand. "The secret was that your penis was so big that you had to tie it into a knot just to fit it inside your pants." Elliott flopped on his back and threw his arm over his face. Imagany sat up with a smirk on her face and stared down at him. "I told her that you also told me that no woman in her right mind would sleep with you because women always ended up having to get stitches after being intimate with you. And then I assured her that the only reason I gave you some was because you promised. . ." Imagany's voice was cut off when Elliott covered her mouth with his hand.

"Thank you very much, sweetheart, but I don't think I want to hear any more. I guess that's what I get for prying into private female affairs." Elliott tried unsuccessfully to keep a straight look on his face as he removed his hand from her mouth and continued to stare at her.

Imagany trailed her fingers down the length of his chest. "It's girl talk, Boo. It's against our code of ethics to reveal what we talk about. Okay?" Without giving him a chance to respond, she changed the subject. "Let's go see what Carl and Caprice are doing."

Elliott rose reluctantly from the bed to get dressed, still shaking his head at her overly active imagination. Imagany stood in front of the mirror running a comb through her tangled hair. Not wanting to dress in the same clothes which she had worn at dinner, she put on a silk gown with a matching robe and tied it in front. They joined hands together as they walked out of the bedroom.

The living room was unoccupied but it had been restored to its normal orderliness. Imagany smiled when she noticed the telephone receiver off the hook. 'My girl Reese is always on the ball,' Imagany thought to herself. She decided to leave the phone as it was.

Elliott stood behind her with his hands around her waist, resting his chin on top of her head. Imagany clasped her own hands over his and arched her neck to look up at him. With disappointment in her voice, she said, "They left, Boo."

"Yeah baby, I can see that. I told you I'm going to have to teach you to be a better hostess." Suddenly Elliott released Imagany.

At the look on his face, Imagany asked, "What is it?"

Elliott walked to the sofa and picked up his jacket, running his hands through its pockets. He found what he was looking for and gestured for Imagany to come to him. When she sat on the couch with her knees curled under her, he pulled from his pocket a small square package wrapped in newspaper. As Elliott handed it to her he said, "I meant to give this to you earlier this evening. Take a look." Imagany opened the package with curious fingers.

A gasp of shock escaped from Imagany's mouth as she stared at the package in her hand. She looked up at him, her fingers clutching her gift. "Elliott, where did you get this?" She examined it thoroughly. "I didn't even know she had a new album out." Awe was in her voice as she read with amazement the cover of Phyllis Hyman's newest release, "Living All Alone." "I heard the title cut one day and I immediately ran out to buy it, but they told me it wasn't out yet! How did you get this?" Her eyes lingered on the cover of the cassette tape. A statuesque Phyllis Hyman sat on what appeared to be a square object, her upper body leaned against a tall, square, marble-like column. Her fingers were spread against the column as she posed sexily with pouted lips. Her hair was piled flatteringly upon her head and, as always, Phyllis Hyman looked beautiful.

Imagany threw her arms around Elliott's neck and hugged him tightly. Grabbing the sides of his head, she gave him a juicy smack on his forehead, then ran to the stereo system and dropped the cassette into the player. When she hit the play button, the smooth soulful sounds of her favorite female entertainer flowed from the speakers. Imagany sat cross-legged on the floor slowly waving her arms and hands in the air and twisting her upper body in small circles. Elliott lay on the sofa with his hands behind his head. He smiled as he watched her. He could see in her all the passion and zest that music brought forth from within her. It wasn't just the music, though. The passion was inside her. He could see it in the way she walked, how she talked, the way she moved and even in the wild manner in which she laughed. Elliott admitted to himself that he had never met anybody like Imagany. He watched her as she lay on the floor upon her stomach, her feet flexing in the air behind her. She was in her own little world where only she and Phyllis Hyman existed.

Carl's brother, Vincent, worked for a record company. When Elliott overheard him mention to Carl that Phyllis Hyman had a jam album about to be released, Elliott had asked Vincent to send him an advance copy of it via next day air postal service. He knew Imagany would enjoy the tape since she was one of Phyllis Hyman's biggest fans.

Elliott rose from the sofa and went into the kitchen to reheat some of the leftover food. He brought his plate back into the living room with him and sat on the floor with his back to the sofa. When Imagany looked up at him, he held a fork full of the chicken parmigiana out to her. She smiled and shook her head as she continued listening to the music.

Elliott finished his food and washed his plate before coming back into the room. He laid down next to her with his head propped on his elbow. Imagany inched closer to him and turned to rest her back against his chest, using his body as her pillow.

It suddenly dawned on Elliott that since he had ridden to Imagany's place in Carl's car, he was now stranded. When he reminded Imagany that she was going to have to give him a lift back to his dorm, Imagany looked at him as if he were crazy. "No, stay here with me." Her tone indicated there was no room for argument.

Elliott smiled, noting that Imagany was not asking him to stay, but was telling him to. Her boldness amused him. "Are you inviting me to spend the night with you?"

Imagany changed her position by moving her body down to where his feet lay. "Yes, Mr. Renfroe, I'm asking you to be with me."

"In that case, how can I refuse?" In truth, Elliott was happy to spend the night with her. He was starting to feel drowsy from the food and their lovemaking, and he wanted only to sleep. He was also sore from his afternoon session of football practice. He could feel the day taking its toll upon him as he pulled away from her to stand and stretch.

With her knees tucked underneath her, Imagany stared at the bulging muscles in Elliott's chest. She tilted her head to the side and asked him, "Tired?"

Elliott put his hands on his hips. "Yes, and a little sore too. I think I'll hit the sack."

Imagany watched him leave the room. If his body was aching, she had just the right thing for him. She went into the bathroom and took out her Keri lotion and brought it back with her into the kitchen. Still listening to Phyllis Hyman, she removed the cap from the bottle and set the container in the microwave for forty-five seconds. If Elliott was even slightly sore, the heated lotion, when massaged into his body, would make him feel as good as new.

Before turning off all the lights in the apartment, Imagany removed the cassette from the stereo and took it with her into the bedroom. She entered quietly to find Elliott sprawled on top of the bed with nothing on except his underwear. She closed the door behind her and set everything down on the dresser. The only remaining light came from the floor-length fish tank which stood in the corner of the bedroom. The bottom and top halves of the aquarium were made of black lacquer while a huge bubble made of Plexiglas protruded from its middle. The neon lights inside the aquarium cast their glorious colors upon the room as large tropical fish existed in their own world. Imagany stuck the Phyllis Hyman tape into her small bedroom stereo and turned the volume down low.

Elliott was nearly asleep as Imagany shed her clothing and straddled him. She sat naked astride him, her weight resting upon her knees. After pouring a good amount of the hot lotion into one of her palms, she set the bottle on the nightstand and lathered it into both of her hands. As she gingerly rubbed it into his back, she enjoyed the feel of the hot, silky lotion.

A contented sigh escaped from Elliott. Imagany could feel his body relax deeper into the bed. She massaged the heated lotion into his skin, taking care to rub deeply all areas where she thought he might be sore. She used the lotion on his back, his neck, his shoulders, his arms and his sides before moving down to his buttocks. When Imagany shifted off of him to remove his underwear, Elliott lifted his hips to allow her to remove them. She spread his legs and continued her heavenly assault. She poured more of the lotion into her hands as she massaged his thighs, his calves, his ankles, his feet and back up to his buttocks. Imagany's hands lingered tenderly over every muscle of his body. When she gestured for Elliott to turn over onto his back, he did so all too willingly. Again she sat astride him, feeling his large maleness rise beneath her. With him laying on his back, she massaged more of the lotion into his chest, his arms and his waist. She spread his legs once more and kneeled between them to massage his thighs. Moving her hands to the inner area of his thighs, she rubbed lotion tenderly onto that part of his skin before sliding her hands through the hair of his groin area. Elliott's manhood stood straight in the air and Imagany lowered her head to nuzzle it fondly with both her chin and her neck.

Elliott felt his insides contract when Imagany took him into the silky confines of her mouth. He felt as though he was on a roller coaster that was being lifted higher and higher. As pleasurable waves washed over him, his hands gripped the sides of the bed as if to hold on.

Imagany's own passions were equally aroused. Unable to endure the gnawing desire that rose within her, she slid herself on top of him and rode him with a fierce passion, taking both of them to their highest pinnacle.

Afterwards, Imagany lay spent on top of Elliott, waiting for her heartbeat to return to its regular pace. She gradually became aware of the music that played softly in the background.

They were listening to the lyrics of Phyllis Hyman's "Old Friend" when Elliott clasped his arms around her. He spoke softly, surprising her with his words. "When I saw you talking on the phone earlier tonight, I thought you were talking to another man and my first reaction was jealousy. I told myself that I should have known it was too good to be true that someone like yourself could be single with no attachments. I assumed, without probable cause, that I was the only man in your life. I want to know everything there is to know about you, Imagany. So tell me now about the men in your life because if there's someone else, I would prefer to know about him now rather than later." He watched closely as Imagany slid off his chest to lie on her side facing him. She raised her leg to rest it over his thigh.

Imagany took a long time to answer him and when she spoke she knew she could only tell him part of the truth. Slowly she said, "There was someone in my life right before I met you. But we agreed to break things off because he wanted to see someone else. Someone whom he's known a lot longer than me. Someone whom he'll probably marry a short time from now." Imagany looked past Elliott to stare into the aquarium as she spoke.

Whoever the man was, Elliott couldn't tell from her voice whether or not she still cared for him. He needed to know. "Do you still love him?"

Imagany answered him. "No, I don't love him. Sometimes I wonder if I ever did. But I do know that before I met you, there were times when I needed him. I think that my inability to return his feelings was one of the reasons he went back to the other woman." Imagany believed firmly that this was why Anthony had never mentioned that he was continuing to see Leslie Lowe. "I just didn't feel the same way about him as he did about me." Imagany didn't want to discuss Anthony anymore and she smiled as she changed the subject. "And you? Tell me about how barren and empty your life was before you met me. Tell me about how you were wandering around lost and feeling forsaken until I walked into your life." Elliott watched her with raised eyebrows. She continued. "You were like a man without vision who suddenly was able to see. I brought you hope, renewed your dreams, gave your life joy and sustenance where once before there had only been despair. Wow! After all that, can you imagine where you would be without me in your life?"

Elliott had turned on his side to listen to her poetic reasoning. When she was done, he could only laugh and shake his head. "You make it sound as if I was a bum on the street when you first met me."

Imagany traced the amused smile on his face with her finger, enjoying her little charade. "Yes, baby, you were pretty down and out. But look at you now. Who would have guessed that just a few weeks later you would be enrolled in college and even become a member of the football team. It just goes to show that all you needed was a strong Black woman like me to show you the potential you had within yourself. Yes, dahlin', you may now kiss my hand."

Instead of kissing her hand, Elliott cupped his hand to the back of her head, pulling her head closer to tease her by examining the whites of her eyes.

Imagany laughed as she tried to pull away from him. "Elliott, what are you doing?"

"You were beginning to scare me a little bit, baby, so I'm just checking to make sure you're not on crack. Are you sure you don't use drugs?" Elliott playfully pulled her body back on top of him. He enjoyed having her this way.

Imagany laughed as she sprawled on top of him. "No, Boo. I don't do drugs."

"Glad to hear it. Now tell me about how your family had to win the lottery in order to keep you living in this place and driving your expensive car."

Imagany knew Elliott wanted to know how, as a college student with no job, she could afford her apartment and car. She evaded the question with ease by turning it around. "How did you know my family won the lottery?" She shrugged her shoulders. "Seriously though, my parents do okay for themselves. I guess you could say I'm just a spoiled child."

"And your old boyfriend? Do you still see him?"

Imagany shook her head. His questions were making her uncomfortable. "Boo, you have nothing to worry about where Anthony is concerned. He's a part of my past." Imagany lifted her chin to stare at him directly. "I wonder if you're to be my future."

He returned her persistent gaze. "Only if you're willing to work at it."

Imagany nodded her head. She, too, was now beginning to feel sleepy as she pressed her face back into his chest. She mumbled something to him about her willingness to work on their relationship. Minutes later she was fast asleep.

Elliott lay awake just holding her, envisioning in his own mind what the future might hold for them. As he lay deep in concentration, he considered how complete his life felt with Imagany in it. He fell asleep wondering what his mother would think of her when she finally met her.

***

Carl and Caprice lay entwined amidst the rumpled sheets of her bed. Both of them were exhausted but content after several gratifying rounds of lovemaking. As Carl held Caprice in his arms, they basked in the feel of each other's bodies. They had spent hours tenderly exploring the surface of each other's skin.

Carl appreciated the fact that there was no deceitfulness about Caprice. Because she was honest and forthright, he would always know where he stood with her. He understood, too, that there was a quiet shyness about her until one got to know her better. She had within her a gentle strength that ran as deep as still waters.

Caprice was on cloud one hundred and nine. If there had ever been a time in her life when she had been happier than she was now, she couldn't recall it. Being here wrapped in Carl's arms made her feel so warm, so protected, so special and so good. She admired everything there was about him and knew within her heart of hearts that she would be willing to work with any qualities that she didn't like. In the few weeks that they had come to know one another, Caprice felt that this was the man she would marry. This was the man whose children she would bear. She smiled because she could picture her mother giving her words of caution. She knew her mother would also tell her that it took time to know if a person was meant for her. Her brow wrinkled as she thought of

160

ways to explain to her mother, or to anyone else, that somehow she knew that Carl was the man for her.

The two of them consumed even more hours just talking and getting to know things about each other that they hadn't had time to find out before. They spoke of the things they both wanted and expected out of life. They spoke of their fears, their goals and aspirations, their dreams and their hopes for the future. Many hours passed as they revealed their inner thoughts and inner selves to one another. In the wee hours of the morning, they made love once more before enfolding each other in their arms and nodding off to never-never land.

***

Anthony Barrington sat in his Atlanta office with his legs atop his large cherry oak wood desk. He had been working all night and his appearance was slightly disheveled. He had long since removed the silk tie from around his neck and unbuttoned the top four buttons of his expensive dress shirt. His sleeves were rolled past his elbows.

It was sometime in the twilight hours of the morning. His office building was now empty of all personnel except himself. It was quiet and would continue to be so until Monday morning, the next official day of business. Weekend or not, Anthony was hard at work. There were business matters which had to be attended to, matters which only he could administer the final decisions.

He reached over to pick up the phone and quickly dialed a number. The phone rang once and when the other party picked up, he spoke softly into the phone.

"Yes, operator. I'm having difficulty reaching 867-5309 in Nashville, Tennessee. Please check it and tell me if there's conversation on the line or whether it's out of service."

"Yes, sir. Please hold the line."

Anthony ran his fingers down the length of his gold pen as he waited for the operator to return. He had tried numerous times to reach Imagany during the entire evening. After the first few times he had assumed she was home but was just on the phone with her girlfriend, whose name he could never seem to remember. He had made a note to himself to call Imagany later. So engrossed had he become in matters around him that he had forgotten to try her again until several hours later.

When he continued to get a busy signal, at first he was curious. He knew Imagany was not the type of person who liked to talk on the phone so he wondered whom she could be speaking to. Six or seven hours later, the line was still busy. Anthony then became suspicious.

"Sir, I'm sorry to keep you holding. There's no conversation on the line and the line itself is in working order. So we can assume the phone is probably just off its hook. Is there anything else I can help you with?"

Anthony noted with disinterest the flirtatious note in the operator's voice. "No. You've been of tremendous help as it is. Thank you." He reached over and softly replaced the phone in its cradle.

Anthony leaned back in the leather chair with his suspicions confirmed. His eyes narrowed in pensive thought as he continued to slowly press and depress the small lever on the top of his gold ink pen. He would have to quickly finish things in Atlanta in order to return home to deal with matters of a more personal and pressing concern.

Part Two

Chapter Thirteen

unday morning arrived with a deluge of heavy rain. As the rain beat against her windows, the day promised to be a dark and dismal one. Imagany snuggled deeper into her pillow when the aroma of beef sausage and eggs drifted to her nose. Inhaling deeply, Imagany sought to find the energy to rally herself from the bed. She was still struggling unsuccessfully when Elliott entered the room with a tray full of food.

Imagany sat up and opened her mouth in a silent gasp as Elliott carried in beef sausages, eggs, grits with cheese, biscuits, jelly, milk and orange juice. The tray was arranged so beautifully that Imagany could only be impressed. She laughed in pleased surprise when he put her breakfast tray in front of her. He went back into the kitchen to retrieve his own tray before climbing carefully into the bed beside her and reaching for his tray.

"Boo, this is beautiful! I'm so impressed that I'm at a loss for words!" She continued to stare at him in amazement.

Elliott began to feel slightly uncomfortable. To him, Imagany was blowing it out of proportion. It wasn't as if bringing her breakfast was a big deal or anything. He did this all the time for his sisters, just as his father sometimes did for his mom. To cover his self-consciousness, Elliott said, "Okay, nut. Cut out the theatrics and eat your food."

Imagany recognized his discomfort because it showed on his face. It only made her heart soften even more. Though she wanted to, she decided not to push the issue. She had just one more thing to say to him as she looked at him with adoring eyes. "My baby's so sweet to me. Come here and give mama a big kiss." She reached out to him, but Elliott laughingly pushed her hand away.

"Stop, woman, and eat your food before it gets cold. Haven't you ever had anybody bring you breakfast in bed before?" Elliott looked at her sheepishly.

Imagany's face was still covered with a loving smile. "No, Boo, I haven't. So if I'm making a big deal out of it, it's only because it means so much to me."

Imagany picked up her fork and began to eat. "But don't worry. From now on, I'll be serving you." As Imagany bit into her food, she rolled her eyes upward and raised her hand to her mouth to blow him a kiss.

"Oh yeah? Breakfast in bed from now on? You promise?"

"You can hold me to it."

Elliott was on a roll. The next words popped out of his mouth before he could even think about them. "Love me?"

Imagany paused with her fork near her mouth. She thought about it and said in a voice filled with wonder, "Yes, Elliott, I do."

What could have been a tense moment for both of them passed with ease as they continued to eat in contented silence. Afterwards, Imagany removed their trays and washed all the dishes, pots, and pans. She came back into the bedroom, turned off the light and lay beside Elliott who was snuggled deep into his pillow.

With the rain continuing to pour steadily down outside, it was the perfect day to stay in bed and just laze around. Though it was damp and dark outside, as Imagany snuggled closer to Elliott, her insides were filled with a sunny glow. Maybe it was too much of a glow because she was starting to feel slightly warm. She got up to turn on her oscillating fan which stood in a corner of the room and returned to the bed to nestle beside Elliott.

Elliott was nearly asleep when he felt her body snuggle against him. As she nestled even closer to him, he thought his body would be too tired from the previous night to make love to her, but again, he felt his manhood slowly begin to stir. Elliott lifted his arm to pull the thin black silk sheet over their heads, surrounding them in total darkness. He half covered her body with his, slowly pressing himself into her. He cupped her head in his hand and, taking his time, suckled her lips hungrily.

Neither did Imagany think that she had sufficient energy within her for another go-round, but when she felt the molten lava course through her veins, she knew otherwise. And when his hand trailed down her belly, she tightened her arms around his neck and parted her legs for him willingly.

Turning her completely on her back, Elliott slid his body fully over hers, slowly lifting her buttocks for his gentle, unhurried entry. Her arms surrounded his shoulders and her legs instinctively wrapped themselves around his waist in a viselike grip. Imagany hung on as

Elliott gave her one of the slowest, most agonizingly pleasurable rides of her life.

Afterwards, Elliott lay between the smooth creaminess of Imagany's thighs depleted of all energy. With barely enough strength to rouse himself from her, he felt drained and was grateful that there was nothing awaiting him but sleep.

Hours later, Imagany awoke to an empty bed. She got up to use the bathroom and found Elliott inside in front of the basin with a towel wrapped around him, brushing his teeth with one of her spare tooth brushes.

He turned to her and said, "I opened one of your packs of tooth brushes. You don't mind, do you?"

Imagany shook her head. "So where are you going?"

"I've got some studying to do. I need to go hit the books."

The soap from his freshly washed body smelled so fragrant that she stepped closer to him and trailed her nose across his chest.

Elliott laughed because she was tickling him. He gently grabbed the sides of her head to pull her to him.

"Don't leave, Elliott."

Imagany's whispered plea tugged at his heart. He kissed her earlobe and said, "I don't want to, baby, but I need to do some homework." He felt her inhale deeply. "I could bring my books back here." Elliott looked down at her and as she watched him with her big, pretty eyes, his heart melted.

A smile lit her face. "Please, Boo? And then you can spend the night."

Elliott laughed. "Well, I don't know about spending the night because I've got to wash, too."

Imagany knew from the tone of his voice that he was weakening. "So do I, Boo. Bring your clothes over here, and I'll wash them with mine. Please?"

Elliott knew he wouldn't refuse her because he wanted to be here with her. He lifted her head and touched her lips lightly with his. "Okay. Get dressed so you can take me back to my room."

Imagany hurried to get dressed, preferring to wait until she returned to take a long leisurely bath. She was stepping slowly and gingerly into a pair of jeans when Elliott came into the bedroom.

"What's wrong?" he asked.

"I'm sore, Boo." Imagany meant it, too. She could feel a tender soreness persisting between her legs. She held onto Elliott's arm as she put her foot tenderly into the other leg of the jeans.

"Poor baby." Elliott reached around her to fasten her jeans for her.

Imagany wrapped her arm around his neck and said, "Does this mean you're going to go easy on me the next time?" She played on his sympathy.

Elliott turned her around to face him. With his hands on her hips, he said, "Baby, I always go easy on you." When she stared at him with no reply, he asked uncertainly, "Don't I?"

Imagany smiled and wrapped her arms around his neck. "You do me just right, Elliott. Just keep doing it the way you do it." She gave him a lingering kiss before leading him out of the apartment.

The rain had slowed to a fine drizzle as the two of them entered her car. She drove quickly and reached Elliott's dorm in no time. About five minutes after he had gotten out of the car, Imagany spotted Carl going into another dorm down the street. She blew her horn but he didn't hear or see her so she got out of the car with her umbrella and walked quickly to catch him. She caught him just as he was about to walk away from the reception desk.

"Carl!" He turned at the sound of his name.

"Hey! What are you doing here?" At the sight of her, Carl didn't know whether to be alarmed or not. He had just left Caprice not too long ago and he immediately wondered if something was wrong.

Imagany noted the concerned look on his face as he threw his arm around her shoulders. Imagany laughed self-consciously because she was starting to feel stupid for having run after him, and she especially felt uncomfortable because she had never been inside a men's dormitory before.

"I was giving Elliott a lift back when I saw you and I just had the impulse to say hello. Don't look at me like that Carl. I feel silly enough as it is."

Carl noticed her discomfort and laughed. "This is my opportunity to get you back for flipping me the bird the other day."

"Are you ever going to let me forget that?"

"No, I'm not, because you never apologized." Guys going in and out of the dorm were staring at Imagany. "What are you and El up to?"

"Well, we're just going to go back to my place to study and that's about it." Imagany was impatient to leave now.

"What? You mean he's not going to be glued to the tube watching football? Do you know how hard it is to pry him away from the tube on a Sunday when there's a game on?"

"So that's why he wanted to leave so soon. Thanks for telling me."

Carl rolled his eyes. "Imagany, you're always getting me in trouble. Once again, I've put my foot in my mouth. When you light into him, just don't mention my name. Okay?"

Imagany poked him in the chest. "Gotcha. Why don't you and Caprice come over? There's plenty of food left and we can do some studying too."

"Hmmmm. Sounds like a plan. Maybe after I wash my clothes."

Imagany smirked at him and said, "You've got to wash too? Bring your clothes with you. Elliott's bringing his. I know Reese will want to come, so give her a call and ask her, okay?" Imagany backed away from him toward the exit.

"Will do. I'll see you in about a half hour then." Carl watched her as she left the dorm to run back to her car. He liked Imagany and thought she suited Elliott to the tee. She was just what Elliott needed to keep him in line. He also liked the fact that she wasn't hung up on her looks. He, too, could see the fireworks whenever she and Elliott were together and it just made him appreciate Caprice's calm and steady demeanor even more.

Elliott walked into his room to find his roommate, Tyrone, deep into his studies. Tyrone glanced up as Elliott came through the door.

"Well I'll be damned. The man lives! Where the hell have you been, Froe? Coach Hadley's been calling around everywhere looking for you." Tyrone continued to stare at him as if he expected an answer.

"I wonder what for. Did he say what he wanted?" Elliott started gathering his books. He wasn't concerned because he knew Hadley checked up on all the players from time to time in an attempt to keep track of their whereabouts.

"No. Just asked me if I knew why you've been so quiet and reserved lately." Elliott turned to look at Tyrone who was watching him closely.

"Go on." Elliott prompted him. "What else did he say?"

"Nothing. I just told him I hadn't noticed anything but that as soon as you came in I'd have you call him. Oh, and you had a couple of other calls, too."

As he gathered all of his socks, Elliott asked, "Who?"

"So many of 'em, I had to write 'em down. Women must think I'm your damn personal secretary or something." Tyrone picked up the list from Elliott's desk and read it out loud. "Chanette, Valarie, Ambi, Lavon, Nefreterie, Cynthia, Sheila Downer and Tina McFarland." Tyrone tossed the list into Elliott's book bag and shook his head. He would have been happy if only one of the women on the list had called him. Sometimes he felt as if Froe had all the luck in the world.

Elliott nearly bumped his head on the top bunk bed as he stood up. "Lavon? I don't know a Lavon."

"Yeah, well she sure knew you." She said she met you in a restaurant and got your number from a friend. Said to tell you that after all the trouble she went through to get it, the least you could do is call her back. And crazy Tina McFarland called at least ten times. Not to mention the usual number of hang-ups." Tyrone was irritated because the phone had rung at least thirty times last night and every call had been for Froe. Even now, he still couldn't believe that not one woman had called for him!

Elliott sucked his teeth irritably as he continued to stuff his clothes into his laundry bag.

Noticing that Elliott seemed to be packing for the night, Tyrone asked him, "Are you coming back to the room tonight?"

"Nope."

"Good. Just make sure you remember not to bring your black ass back until sometime tomorrow. I might as well invite someone up and use the time wisely." Tyrone was already on the phone going through his little black book before Elliott even had a chance to close the door behind him.

It seemed even muggier outside as Elliott entered the car and he was thankful that Imagany had turned on the air conditioner. The coolness of the car provided respite from the humidity outside.

"I ran into Carl while you were upstairs."

"Oh, yeah? What did he have to say?"

"Nothing much. I invited him and Caprice over to the apartment to watch the football game and to study. He said okay so I guess they'll arrive in about an hour." They reached a stop sign and Imagany turned to look at him. "Is that okay with you?" She was also about to tease him for telling her that his primary reason for wanting to leave was to study when all he really wanted to do was watch the game with the guys.

"Sure." As Elliott pulled out one of his books from his bag, he never saw the message slip that Tyrone had written all the names on fall out of his bag.

Before Imagany could tease him, she reached down to pick up the piece of paper.

"Froe, your women called? Chanette, Valarie, Ambi, Nefreterie, Lavon, Cynthia, Sheila Downer and Tina McFarland? What the hell is this, Elliott?"

Elliott nearly jumped out of his skin as Imagany read off the list of female names. That dumb ass Tyrone must have put the stupid list in his book bag. That son of a . . .

The car in back of them blew its horn and Imagany realized she was holding up traffic as she waited for Elliott to answer her. She was obviously angry as she drove on.

Elliott thought hard and quick about how he could get himself out of the mess he had unknowingly gotten himself into. Finally, he decided to just tell the truth. "Those are calls that were made to the room."

Imagany tried to remain calm. "I can see that Elliott, but who are they? And Lavon? That's Reese's cousin for God's sake!"

Elliott couldn't help but laugh at the look on her face. "Imagany, I don't know how Lavon got my number. I haven't seen or talked to her since we both saw her at the restaurant. Nor do I have any intentions of seeing her. As for the rest, Valarie and Chanette are both in my Physics class. Sheila, Tina, Ambi, Carolyn, Cynthia and Nefreterie are part of the past." Elliott noticed the look that she gave him and he tried to reassure her. "I'm not seeing them anymore, Imagany."

"That's wonderful, Elliott." Imagany's tone was dry. She was not amused. They drove in silence and when they reached her apartment, she pulled up into her parking lot and parked the car. Suddenly Imagany didn't want to be bothered with Elliott. She had the urge to be alone.

Elliott could feel her irritation. "You want to take me back to my room now, is that it?" Elliott felt she was making mountains out of molehills. He had no control over who called his room and he was beginning to become irritated himself.

Imagany thought about it and asked him, "Do you want to go back, Elliott?"

"I would like to be here with you, Imagany. That's why I came. But if you're going to sulk all day, maybe it is best that you take me back. Both of us can be miserable by ourselves. We don't need each other to do that."

Imagany had not turned her engine off and she contemplated whether to drive him back. She wanted him to stay now, but she admitted that she was still angry because she was jealous. She took a deep breath and said, "I'm jealous, Elliott."

"Tell me about it," Elliott said cynically. Imagany would not look at him, so he reached over and gently pulled her chin around to face him.

With his hand on the cleft of her chin, neither one of them spoke. Finally Imagany smiled but pulled away from him. She turned off the engine and got out of the car. As she closed the door, she saw Carl's car coming down the driveway.

"They sure didn't waste any time getting here," she said.

Elliott shook his head as he got out of the car and locked the door. With her mercurial ways, life with Imagany was going to be a full time job.

As Carl pulled along side of her car, Imagany noticed that she was unusually happy to see Caprice. Caprice must have felt the same way, too, because as soon as she got out of the car, the two of them hugged and fussed as if they hadn't seen each other in weeks. Carl and Elliott both shook their heads as they followed behind them carrying their laundry and book bags. Neither one of the guys had to say a word because they could read each other's thoughts.

They entered the apartment and Caprice smiled when she saw the phone still off the hook. Catching her look, Imagany decided to hang it up. But when she did so, she took the plug out of the wall so that if the phone rang she wouldn't have to know it. She reminded herself to do the same for the phone in the bedroom.

The football game was just starting as Caprice warmed the food and made a salad to go with it. Caprice zipped through the kitchen singing and humming to herself and Imagany smiled knowingly as she watched her. Imagany took two bottles of Heineken beer into the living room and handed them to the guys who were both engrossed in the Chicago Bears-New York Giants game.

Imagany went back into the kitchen and lifted herself up onto the kitchen counter. "Okay, people. Let's have the story." Caprice was so cool that she gave nothing away as she calmly stuck the potatoes into the oven. She turned back to Imagany and sang in a light and lilting voice, "I'm talkin' 'bout a strong black man!" She shook her head teasingly as she sang the words.

Imagany could not contain her excitement and was about to let out a scream at the top of her lungs when Caprice ran to her and clamped her hand tightly over her mouth. "Imagany, shut up girl! Don't you dare embarrass me!" Caprice's hand was still covering Imagany's mouth, gesturing for her to be quiet when Elliott walked into the kitchen.

"What are you two up to now?"

Both Imagany and Caprice jumped when Elliott spoke in an amused voice. As Caprice quickly turned around, she said, "Oh, nothing. We were just acting silly. You know us."

Elliott smiled as he asked her to hand him two glasses. Caprice got the glasses and handed them to him and he left shaking his head. Caprice turned back to Imagany, who still had a big grin on her face.

Imagany whispered, "Let's go to the basement to wash, then we can really talk." She gathered all the clothes while Caprice carried the detergent, bleach and fabric softener. They walked through the living room and Imagany said, "We'll be back, guys. See you in a little bit."

Carl and Elliott both shook their heads as they watched them leave. As soon as the door closed, Elliott said, "So, how did it go last night?"

Carl held his fist out to pound it lightly in the air. "Perfect! This is the one, El. I don't have to look any further." Carl sat on the floor with his back against the sofa, his legs stretched out and his ankles crossed. He brought his fingertips to his lips and kissed them.

Elliott laughed at him. "It was that good, huh?"

"Man, it was better than good. It was live!" Carl lifted his hands in a "what's up" gesture. "So what's the deal with you?"

"Imagany is special all right. I think she's the one too. But there's work to be done. I think we both have some growing up to do if we're going to make it work."

Carl said, "Sounds promising. So how about a toast?"

Elliott held out his glass and said, "Here's to the future." Lifting their glasses in the air, he and Carl toasted one another by.

***

They had barely reached the laundry room before Imagany was begging Caprice to tell all.

"Reese, come on now, tell me."

"Girl, all I can tell you is that the man does have it goin' on."

This was hardly what Imagany wanted to hear. She at least wanted Caprice to tell her something she did not already know. "But Reese, I want details." Imagany was pleading at this point.

There were so many feelings going on inside Caprice that she was unable to express any of her emotions. She wasn't ready to talk about her experience yet and when she did, the words would only come in bits and pieces. She held a sock in her hand as she went off into a daze. As Imagany watched her, she wanted to shake the story out of her, but she understood Caprice's inability to communicate her feelings.

They were separating clothes when Caprice paused as she held a pair of Carl's jeans to her chest. "It was so beautiful! Even more so than I expected it to be. He was so gentle and kind and patient and tender and everything else you could imagine. I'm in love, Imagany."

Imagany smiled as she hugged her. "I'm happy for you, Reese." Imagany tilted her head to the side. "You look happy too. I can see it all over your face."

Caprice smiled. "You look happy yourself, dahlin'. Could it be because of a certain gentleman upstairs?"

Imagany shrugged her shoulders as she angrily threw clothes into the machine. "He makes me sick sometimes, Reese. We were coming back from his dorm when a piece of paper fell out of his book bag. It had the names of about ten girls who called him while he was out last night. Can you believe that? Ten girls in one night?" Imagany shook her head in anger. "And that bitch of a cousin of yours had the nerve to call him too. I can't believe it! She knew I was with him!"

Caprice turned to her. "So what if Lavon called him? I mean, put yourself in her shoes. It's not like she thought the two of you were married. Admit it, Imagany. You're jealous, girl. Can't you see it? Didn't I warn you from day one that there would be competition over Elliott? I did and you told me no one was going to be a match for you, remember? So that's the attitude you've got to keep right now. And you've got to trust him too." Caprice stopped to shake her own head. "I've got to say this, because you need to hear it. Somehow I'm reminded of the countless number of men who you've gone through and cast aside. There were many of them and they all would come to cry on my shoulder because they thought I might be able to talk some sense into you on their behalf. Nice looking guys, all of them. They loved you, Imagany. Every last one of them. I felt bad for them, too, because I knew how much pain they were in. I told you what goes around comes right back to you, Imagany. So if you have to struggle to get Elliott, maybe it's worth it. Personally, I think he's good for you because he's not going to just spoil you all the time. I like Elliott and I hope the two of you can make things work. But again, I think the most important thing is that you trust him and give him the benefit of the doubt. So what if some girls called him. They're going to continue to call him. Just give him a chance, Imagany. Besides, it's obvious that he cares about you. Have you told him about Anthony yet?"

"Yeah. I told him I wasn't seeing him anymore though."

"Good."

"You know, we sound like two old women griping about their men. Come on, let's go back upstairs."

They entered the apartment with their empty laundry baskets and detergent bottles. "Who's winning?" Caprice asked.

"The champions, of course. You know who's going to win so don't even upset yourself," Carl said.

Imagany came out of the kitchen to say tauntingly, "I tell you! These people from New York sure are poor losers. Carl, you know the Bears are going to win so why are you fighting it? Just accept defeat with a smile." Carl was eating sunflower seeds and he threw a couple of the shells at Imagany.

When the food was hot, everyone wanted to continue to watch the game so they all ate in the living room. Caprice fixed Carl's plate and Imagany fixed Elliott's. She brought his plate to him and said, "Boo, do you want water or juice?"

Elliott never looked up from the game. "Water is fine."

Carl started laughing. "Boo? Did she just call you 'Boo?' "

Imagany came back from the kitchen with the water. "Of course I called him 'Boo.' Is there a problem?" Imagany came and stood next to Carl holding the glass of water over his head tilting it as if she were about to pour the entire contents of the glass onto him.

Carl's words sputtered out between his laughter, "No ma'am. There's no problem here."

Imagany tilted the glass even more. "Are you sure, sir? Do I have your permission to call my man 'Boo?' " Imagany let a drop of the water fall onto Carl's head.

Carl rolled over to avoid the water. "Okay! Yeah, yeah! You can call the man whatever you want! It's no problem." Still, he snickered as Imagany walked away from him.

Caprice said to Elliott, "They're crazy, Elliott."

"Yep. You and I are the only two sane people in this room."

"I'll drink to that." Elliott and Caprice held their glasses in the air as if to toast each other from across the room.

All during the game, the four of them kept up a lively stream of conversation as they ate and watched the Chicago Bears slaughter the New York Giants. Carl claimed that the Bears only won because the Giants' star quarterback was injured. Imagany countered that the Giants were just a lousy team who wouldn't have won even had their precious quarterback been available to play. As the two of them taunted each other good naturedly, Elliott and Caprice chose to stay out of it. After the game was over, they turned off the television to study. Elliott and Carl sat at the kitchen table while Imagany and Caprice remained in the living room on the floor. The study session went well. They all made a concerted effort to set aside those hours strictly for studying.

Around ten-thirty, Caprice got up to stretch and went inside the kitchen to get some water. She stood behind Carl and massaged his shoulders. "Done?" Carl asked her.

"Yes. I've done all I can for now. I might do some more when I get back to the room, but I'm finished here."

"We'll be wrapping up in about another ten minutes too. We'll leave shortly after that, okay?"

"Mmmhmmm." Caprice looked at the impressive maze of mathematical figures he and Elliott had on their papers as they punched numbers into their computer-like calculators. She walked back into the living room and saw that Imagany was still sprawled with her books around her. Caprice began to pack up their things, including the clothes that they had retrieved from the laundry room.

Minutes later, Carl and Caprice were putting on their rain coats to leave. Imagany and Elliott stood in the doorway watching them walk down the hall. When Elliott locked the door behind them, he leaned against the door and stared at Imagany, glad that they were finally alone. Imagany was gathering up all her papers and books when she noticed Elliott staring at her. He crooked his finger and gestured for her to come to him. When she stood in front of him, Elliott encircled her in his arms.

Imagany rested her head on Elliott's chest and said apologetically, "Boo, I'm sorry about the way I acted earlier. It's just that I was jealous."

Elliott smiled. "It's all right, baby. Come show me how sorry you really are." Elliott lifted Imagany in his arms and carried her into the bedroom, kicking the door closed behind them.

Chapter Fourteen

T he following week passed quickly for Imagany. She had loads of homework from each of her classes and it was an effort just to wade through it all. She hadn't seen Elliott since she'd driven him to class that next morning.

He, too, was swamped by his classes. Football practice was especially grueling for Elliott since Coach Hadley had been riding his back, chastising him daily. Hadley felt that Elliott's passes were not as sharp and accurate as he was capable of making them. The coach was aware of the many outside influences that vied for his players' attention and he warned Elliott that whatever or whoever was distracting him from his goals, he had better leave it or them alone and concentrate on his game. Hadley's advice was food for thought for Elliott. He had never met anyone who came close to competing with his first love, football. To him, Imagany was certainly no distraction. Rather, he saw her as an inspiration.

Though he and Imagany had not seen one another in days, they spoke on the phone nightly for hours at a time, sometimes well into the wee hours of the morning. They surprised themselves not only with the variety of topics they found to discuss, but also with how much they had in common. Elliott told her that his roommate was threatening to kick him out because he was monopolizing the phone every night. Imagany countered by telling him that she hoped Tyrone did throw him out because then he could come stay with her. The sound of each other's voice over the phone was enough to arouse them physically, heightening the anticipation of seeing one another again.

The following weekend, the TSU football team was traveling to Tallahassee, Florida to play Florida A&M University. The team was flying out Friday morning. Students who wished to attend the game could do so via a special bus that was being chartered for the occasion. Elliott tried to bribe Imagany into attending the game by offering her and Caprice front row. But because she had so much school work, she declined. She assured him that when his team played Grambling University in Louisiana, she would be there. Both Elliott's parents had graduated from Grambling, and they always made a point of attending the games. Elliott wanted Imagany to meet his family, so he had no intentions of allowing her to miss that particular game.

When Saturday morning arrived, Imagany slept late. The apartment seemed so quiet without Elliott's presence and she realized it was because she missed him. Hungry, she got up to fix herself an omelet. She was standing at the kitchen counter dicing her ingredients with a knife which had a large sharp blade on it when the doorbell rang. Imagany nearly cut herself as she jumped at the sudden sound of the bell. Laying the knife on the counter, she went to answer the door.

"Who is it?" Irritation was apparent in Imagany's voice.

"Anthony. Buzz me in."

Imagany panicked at the sound of Anthony's voice and her heart started pounding rapidly in her chest. She found herself quickly debating whether she should let him in. The fact that she even had to think twice about letting him in made her wonder about her hesitancy. She realized she'd been avoiding Anthony because she was not ready for the confrontation she knew would ensue. Imagany stood at the door for a full minute before pressing the buzzer, trying to think of what she would say to him. Telling herself that she had nothing to worry about, she waited for him to ring the bell on her front door. Though outwardly composed, when the bell rang she opened the door with trembling fingers.

Anthony stepped into the apartment and Imagany avoided making any contact with him as she locked the door behind him. She leaned against it with her hands behind her hips and willed herself to act natural.

Anthony casually removed his coat and laid it on the sofa. He sat down and crossed his leg over his knee and stared at Imagany from across the room without speaking. It had taken him the entire week to wrap things up in Atlanta. Upon his return to Nashville, not only had he received disturbing news about Imagany's so-called faithfulness, but he had also been given some hard evidence that had knocked the breath from his body.

As soon as Anthony took off his coat, Imagany was disappointed. She didn't want him to get the impression that he was welcome or that he would be staying long. It was unusual for neither of them to greet one another. As she returned his unblinking gaze, she slowly became aware of the coiled anger that emanated from him.

Imagany's antennas raised and she stepped further inside the room to speak defensively.

"Why didn't you call before you came here, Anthony?"

Anthony was immediately on the attack. "Since I pay the rent here, it's not required." Anger threaded its way into his voice. "But that's not how you're supposed to greet me, Imagany." He leaned forward with his elbows on his knees and stared at her unnervingly.

Small shivers coursed through Imagany as she sensed the intensity of Anthony's anger. She crossed her arms over her chest to stop herself from shivering. She was about to step further into the room, but not knowing what caused his anger, she stopped in her tracks. "If I don't know that you're coming here, Anthony, you can hardly expect me to have the welcome wagon waiting for you."

Anthony took in her reply with no reaction. He leaned back against the sofa to stare at her emotionlessly. When he spoke, he completely changed the subject.

"How have you been entertaining yourself in my absence?"

Imagany decided to ignore his question and not answer him at all. She picked up the negative vibes that flowed from him and she became irritated with the cat and mouse game he was playing. She walked toward the kitchen and spoke over her shoulder, ignoring his question. "I was just about to fix myself an omelet. Would you like something to eat?"

"Come here, Imagany."

At the uncontrolled anger in his voice, Imagany spun around to look at him through narrowed eyes. Her heart pounded heavily in her chest at his threatening tone. When she made no move to approach him, Anthony got up and walked over to her.

He stood in front of her looking down at her menacingly with his hands behind his back. In an ominous tone, he said, "I asked you what you've been doing since I've been away." A tight ball of anger existed within him. It was an effort for him to restrain himself from just beating the day lights out of her. He sensed the uncertainty within her and knew that fear was the cause of it. His eyes traveled down the length of her body only to return to stare at her hardened nipples which protruded through the thinness of her silk teddy. Through the haze of his anger, he could feel himself becoming excited, and he knew he still wanted her. His hand reached out to touch the side of her face.

As soon as Anthony raised his hand to touch her, Imagany automatically stepped away from him. She was in no way lulled by the deceptive softness of his voice. She was familiar with his tone, having heard it many times before in her life. She knew from experience that his tone and mannerism was merely the quiet before the storm. And that storm usually precipitated violence. She felt the hair on her arms rise as warning signals shot through her. Sensing the threat of danger, instinct made her back away from him.

Her sudden movement away from him angered Anthony and his hand fell to his side.

Imagany tightened her arms around her chest and said, "I don't know what your problem is, Anthony, but I want you to leave now."

As his anger rose to the boiling point, Anthony said quietly, "I'll bet you do." His hands balled into fists. "Go sit down." When she made no move in the direction of the sofa, Anthony said very soft and slowly, "You're trying my patience right now, Imagany. If I have to repeat myself, I promise you'll regret it."

Imagany realized that he was on the threshold of imminent violence. She knew it wouldn't take much to trigger him. She didn't know what he was enraged about and because she had never seen him like this before, fear got the better of her. With her heart pounding in her chest, she stepped around him and moved reluctantly to the sofa to sit down. When he loomed over her, Imagany immediately felt at a disadvantage and knew that by sitting down she had made a huge mistake.

"Since you seem to be at such a loss for words, maybe you'll have an easier time explaining this." Anthony removed an envelope from his pocket and tossed it forcefully into her lap.

Imagany's eyes fell on it and her heart dropped. Even without opening it, she knew what it contained. She reached into the unsealed envelope and took out the sheath of papers that she had signed in front of Leslie. Imagany shook her head at her own stupidity. She should have known Leslie would do this. In her haste to get her out of her apartment that day, she had even forgotten to ask for a copy for her own records. It was all there in black and white and, of course, there was no telling what else Leslie might have added to it by now.

"Why, Imagany?" Hurt, disappointment, and anger was in Anthony's voice as he stood over her waiting for an answer. His feelings showed clearly on his face. "Because of greed you settled for a lousy sixty thousand dollars? No, I know you better than that." Anthony snatched the envelope and shook out the remaining contents. The colorful used condom fell to the floor. He bent down in her face. "Whose is this, Imagany? You're seeing someone else, aren't you?" As soon as the words were out of his mouth, Anthony's pain visibly turned into rage.

Imagany was frightened of him and could no longer remain seated. When she moved to get away from him, her movement served only to push him over the brink. Anthony viciously slapped the papers from her hand, causing them to spill onto the floor. In a burst of sudden violence, he savagely grabbed her by the shoulders and pushed her down onto the sofa. She banged her head hard against the back of it as he held her in place by clamping his hands deep into the flesh of her shoulders. No longer was she the woman Anthony loved. Instead, she had become an insurgent adversary who must be taught a hard lesson. "I asked you a question! Are you seeing someone else? Answer me, damn you!" Anthony shouted at the top of his lungs.

Suddenly, Anthony began to shake Imagany furiously back and forth in his grip, as if she were but a rag doll. His hands dug deep into the flesh of her arms. As his fury rose to a heightened pitch, he screamed at her. "You are, aren't you? You bitch! You fucked someone else after all I've done for you? Don't you know I made you into what you are? Don't you? Who is he? Tell me, goddammit, or I'll kill you! Tell me who the bastard is, damn it!" With each word, Anthony frenziedly shook her body back and forth. His eyes were narrowed slits in his face and saliva spat from his mouth as he ranted at her.

Tears of rage and anguish fell from Imagany's eyes at the pain Anthony was inflicting upon her. Self-preservation made her struggle to loose herself from his hurting grasp. She screamed, "Let go of me, Anthony! Let me go!" Recognizing that she would not be able to pry herself away from his powerful grip, anger and fear propelled her to lift her knees upward to use the strength in her legs to push his body off of her, causing him to stumble backwards. Imagany stumbled, too, but was able to leap to her feet and run to a safe distance. Angry words fell from her mouth.

"You stupid bastard! Don't ever touch me again! How dare you sit in judgment of me? You, who were seeing someone else all the while we were together! Who the hell do you think you are? You thought that because you spent money on me, that gave you the right to control my life? *You* were the one who was the fool, Anthony. You're damn right I took that bitch's money and found me somebody else! And you can bet he's not an asshole who uses money for his balls! Now get the hell out of my apartment, you crazy bastard!" Imagany screamed at him, wanting to inflict as much pain upon him as he had on her.

Each word was a direct slap in Anthony's face. If he had been enraged before, her words now sent him crashing tumultuously over the edge. A rage that turned into insanity coursed through him and he knew instantly what he had to do: kill her. His only intent was for her to die a slow death. In a sudden movement that surprised Imagany, Anthony strode forward and savagely back-handed her across her face with a jolting force that sent her flying across the room. When she hit the floor, her head thudded hard against the wooden edge of the leather sofa. The impact dazed her. The room began to spin and her vision became clouded.

Anthony stood over Imagany and viciously back-handed her several more times. Blood sputtered from her lips with each blow. "You were nothing but a stupid child when I met you! Do you hear me?" Anthony pointed to his chest. "I made you into what you are! If it wasn't for me, you'd be nothing!" He grabbed her by the throat and stabbed his finger against the bridge of her nose.

"Don't you realize how much I loved you? I could have given you the world and laid anything you wanted at your feet! To think that you settled for a lousy sixty thousand dollars only shows what a dumb bitch you really are! I want to know who the son of a bitch is that you're fucking and you're going to tell me! Nobody makes a fool out of me the way you have, Imagany, and you're going to pay for it." Anthony's voice quieted to a steely rage as his hands went to slowly unfasten the buckle of his belt. He unwound the leather belt from his pants and wrapped the buckle part in his hand, twirling the leather around his hand for further reinforcement. Before he killed her, he intended to give her the beating of her life. Raising the leather strap in the air, he brought it down upon Imagany's body with a force that resounded throughout the apartment. Anthony proceeded to beat her as if she were a demented animal.

Imagany flinched and cried out in agony as the sting of the belt rained itself down upon her thighs, her hips, her back, her arms, and her legs. Through the fuzz of her clouded mind, her knees curled up to her chest in an effort to protect herself from the blows. As the belt continued to lash down upon her, she found the strength to crawl toward the kitchen. All the while, she was conscious of Anthony shouting obscenities at her but the only thing she could think of was another time in her life when she had taken a similar beating.

As Anthony continued to beat her like the madman he had become, he made the mistake of stepping too close to her. Imagany found the strength to throw herself at his calf and sink her teeth into his leg with the ferociousness of a blood thirsty animal. So deep did she bite him that she tasted his blood in her mouth. As Anthony's ear piercing howl tore through the apartment, she felt as if her teeth would fall out of her mouth.

Out of desperation, Anthony reached down and frantically grabbed Imagany's hair, jerking her head with a strength that forced her to release her teeth from his leg. He stepped back and gave her a mighty kick to her chest that knocked the breath from her body. Pulling her by the hair, he twisted her around and threw her onto her back. He grabbed her silk teddy and yanked it downwards, ripping it from her body. Backing away from her, Anthony quickly unzipped his pants for his final humiliation of her.

Dazed, but knowing what he was about to do, Imagany crawled backwards on her hands, toward the kitchen, shuffling her feet in front of her. Anthony bent down to grab her legs, shoving them apart. Imagany twisted away from him and once again tried to crawl toward the kitchen. She struggled to her feet and was heading toward the kitchen counter when Anthony grabbed her hair from behind. He twisted her around and shoved her further into the kitchen and pushed her against the counter with a force that once again knocked the wind out of her. Again, he back handed her across her face, causing more blood to spurt from her lips.

Imagany knew she was fighting for her life and all she could see in front of her was her father's face. One hand gripped the counter for support while the other groped behind her for the knife that she knew would surely be there. Her fingers gripped the handle of the blade and just as Anthony raised his hand to slap her one more time, she brought the knife from behind her and plunged it deep into his right shoulder.

Anthony screamed as the knife dug its way deep into the flesh of his shoulder, tearing both cartilage and tissue as it went. Imagany held the knife in her grip and pulled it from the now bleeding gash to stab him repeatedly in his shoulder and arm.

Anthony staggered backwards in shock and when Imagany picked up a nearby vase and smashed it across his head and face, he fell hard to the floor. She knelt over him and pressed the knife to his throat. Her tears and her pain mingled with her words. "Touch me again, you bastard! Go ahead, touch me! I'll kill you! Goddamn you, I'll kill you!"

Imagany was on the brink of insanity herself. Just as she was about to thrust the knife into his throat, something clicked inside her brain. She stopped herself. She continued to kneel over him pressing the knife to his throat when the sight of all the blood spilling from his body suddenly brought her back to her senses.

Hurt, drained, and weary from the entire ordeal, Imagany mechanically fell to the floor with her knees drawn to her chest and her back against the refrigerator. She felt so empty inside as she lowered her head into the circle of her arms. Though she felt drained, no tears would come forth from the depths of her soul. Imagany lifted her head to stare vacantly at the knife in her hand, noting, with no reaction, the drying blood which stained it. She looked over at Anthony, who was lying in a pool of his own blood, unconscious.

Dried blood was all over her as she stared at Anthony for a very long time. She had no knowledge of how much time elapsed. Neither did she feel remorse for what she'd done. Imagany slowly picked herself up off the floor, ever conscious of the pain she was in. There was no spot on her body that did not ache. She threw the knife into the sink, and stepped over Anthony to call an ambulance to come get him. She answered the 911 operator's questions as best she could before walking naked inside her bedroom to put on another gown. She winced in pain as she slid the blood-stained gown over her head and turned to look at herself in the mirror.

Imagany was horrified at the sight of her own face. The swelling alone was repugnant. Her lips were enlarged several times their normal size and dried blood stained their corners. Dark bruises covered her entire face. Unable to look at herself, Imagany closed her eyes and turned away from the mirror. She hugged her arms to her chest and sat on the corner of the bed and rocked herself gently back and forth. With nothing but coldness inside her, she stared blankly at the bedroom wall, but still the tears would not come.

She didn't know how long she sat quietly on the bed rocking herself. When the bell rang, she got up to press the buzzer without even inquiring as to who it was. In less than no time the doorbell to her apartment rang and she opened her door to allow the paramedics to enter.

Imagany pointed to the kitchen area as the two men bustled into the apartment. She saw their horror at the sight of her bruises and she turned away. She didn't need their help and she certainly didn't want their pity.

As the men tended to Anthony, who lay unconscious, they fired questions at Imagany. What had happened? How long had he been laying here? Did he attack her? Did he force his way into the apartment? Imagany refused to answer any of their questions and the paramedics realized she was in shock. They patched Anthony up to stem his loss of blood and called for a stretcher.

One of the paramedics approached Imagany and said softly, "Miss, we're going to have to fill out a report and the police will come back to ask you some questions. You're in shock and we think it would be best if you came to the hospital with us to get treatment. Do you understand me?" The paramedic had seen many cases of domestic violence in his life and he assumed this was what had taken place. She was probably just another battered wife or girlfriend who had reached the end of her rope. He noted with distaste the marks and bruises on her face. What a tragedy that any woman would allow herself to be subjected to being beaten by her husband or lover. He thought it even more tragic that so many women waited until it was too late to try to get out of their situations.

Imagany continued to stare at him blankly and when the stretcher arrived, he turned away from her to help lift Anthony onto it. They rushed him out of the apartment and Imagany quickly locked the door behind them before they could again try to talk her into coming with them. In a trance-like state, she walked inside her bedroom and gingerly lay on top of the bed. Curling herself into a ball and hugging her knees to her chest, she felt as if all the loneliness in the world had lain itself upon her shoulders.

Imagany didn't need anyone to tell her that life was unfair. Because of this, she had no regrets about stabbing Anthony. What perturbed her most about the act itself was that she had actually wanted to kill him and it troubled her that she had been about to take another human being's life. She lay there, hurt and confused, trying to come to grips with this new discovery she had made about herself. As she lay deep in sorrow, a coma-like sleep overtook her drained and aching body. But before sleep could claim her, a lone tear finally escaped from the corner of Imagany's eye.

On Sunday afternoon, Caprice stood outside the library entrance waiting for Imagany to meet her as they had planned. The two of them had agreed on Friday to study together and then hang out and go get something to eat. Caprice glanced impatiently at her watch. She had been waiting for over half an hour now. Imagany was not an unpunctual person and it was not like her not to call if she'd had a change in plans. Caprice walked to a pay phone and dialed Imagany's number. The phone rang and rang. Even the answering machine refused to kick in. Caprice hung up the phone thinking that possibly Imagany was on her way to the library or that she had called the room while Caprice was on her way here. Fifteen more minutes passed and knowing that she needed to get started, Caprice entered the library and chose a seat closest to the entrance so she could see whoever came and went. She spread her books about her and became engrossed in her studies, glancing up periodically whenever someone entered.

Four hours later Caprice stretched in her seat and got up to call her room to find out if Imagany had left a message on her answering machine. No one had called so she went back to her table and started wrapping up. She was slightly irritated because Imagany could have at least called and left a message on her machine to say she wasn't coming. If Elliott was in town, she could understand that Imagany might want to spend the time with him, but he and Carl weren't expected back until late in the evening. Caprice packed up her things and returned to her room.

***

Tall decrepit projects loomed in the background. The eighteen-floor structures were linked together to form what is commonly known as the Ickeys. Broken windows, where fires had occurred in many of the apartments, showed like missing teeth from that of an old dying dinosaur. The buildings obviously hadn't been painted in many years and the decayed structures were badly in need of repair.

The neighborhood was akin to a concrete jungle, for no grass or trees aligned these mean streets. The playgrounds for the children were littered with broken glass, wine and whiskey bottles, as well as empty crack vials.

A group of males played rough-shod basketball on an area where the court had been cleared of all debris. Zabree stood hesitantly across the street from the playground where the men were playing basketball. As she shifted her book bag to her other shoulder, her hands trembled as she struggled to get up the nerve to approach them. Here on 29th and State Street, one had to walk with bravado to show one was no stranger to the neighborhood. Zabree's eyes focused on Mario as he drove to the basket with the ball. She knew the guys surrounding him were his bodyguards and that they were armed and dangerous.

Mario and his boys was where Zabree got her supply of drugs. Mario, himself, was the drug king in this particular territory and he wielded what Zabree perceived as a lot of power. She also knew that he liked her. He had told her point blank several times that if she ever ran out of money for the slice, as the drugs were called, to just ask for him personally and he would see that she was taken care of. Zabree was far from naive. She knew Mario only wanted to sleep with her and that the drugs would be her compensation. He had even told her that if she ever needed a place to stay, she had only to look him up.

Dressed in a short, black mini-skirt with a matching black jacket and black leather flats, Zabree knew she looked more than attractive. With her looks, long hair and shapely body, she came close to passing for model Beverly Johnson's twin.

She took a deep breath and crossed the street to approach the playground. She reached the chain-link fence and entered through a large torn gash in the fencing. The guys hadn't noticed her yet and they continued to play as she made her approach. She stopped short of six large hulking figures who were leaning against the fence and addressed the one whom she knew to be the head bodyguard, Andray. Zabree knew that in order to speak with Mario she had to go through his henchmen and that she would not be allowed to approach him without their permission.

All six of the guys were in their latter teens to early twenties and their guns bulged from beneath their leather jackets. They eyed her closely as she neared them, checking her out from head to toe. Zabree felt self-conscious with them looking at her as they did, but she was determined not to show it. She stepped closer and spoke directly to Andray.

"Can I speak to Mario?"

The six of them closed around her as she spoke and Zabree knew her voice trembled. Her heart was pounding hard and fast in her chest. She was frightened, too, because she didn't know what to expect of them, so she continued to stare only at Andray, ignoring the others who surrounded her.

"What chu' need to talk to Mario for?" Andray leaned back against the fence and crossed his arms over his burly chest. He stared Zabree up and down, admiring her body as he waited for her to answer him. Sensing no threat from her, he assumed she was just another ho who didn't have the dough for the slice, and had come to plead her case.

Zabree threw her head back and tucked her hair behind her ear. "Actually, it's a personal matter." Her voice was stronger now.

"Well, bitch, that's all fine, well, and good. But, you see, there *is* nothin' personal between me and the man. So if you want to speak to him, you either tell me what it's about or you take your black ass back wherever the fuck you came from." Andray pushed himself off the fence and stood in front of her looking down at her.

Zabree could not continue to look Andray in the eyes. She stared down at the ground and said quietly, "It's about a proposition he made me."

Andray glanced around at his posse and said tauntingly, "Yo homies, did I stutter or somethin'? Was I speakin' french? Didn't y'all just hear me tell the bitch to spill her guts or get the fuck down the road? Is she stupid or what?" Laughter spread around the group as Andray humiliated her in front of all of them.

Determined not to cry in front of these jerks, Zabree was about to walk away when voices spoke from behind her.

"Yo, what's goin' on?" The guys parted as Mario and three other guys stepped forward to see what was happening.

Zabree turned around and a smile of relief lit her face as she saw Mario step to the front with the basketball tucked under his arm. Sweat glistened off his bronzed muscles and he looked so handsome to Zabree as he stood there with no shirt on.

"Well, well, well. If it isn't Ms. Sunshine. What brings you to this part of the hood and how can we help you?" Mario waved his hand to indicate himself and his boys.

"Says she has a prop'sition for you." Andray spoke before Zabree could and Mario raised his hand to silence him, gesturing for Zabree to speak.

"I came to speak to you about something." Zabree looked around her at all the guys who were listening and said, "It's personal."

Mario looked her up and down as he tugged at his chin and finally said, "All right then, come with me." He tossed the basketball into Andray's chest and raised his five fingers to indicate that he would be only five minutes. He lead Zabree to where his 500 SEL white Mercedes was parked and unlocked the door for her to climb in. Shutting the door behind her, Mario went to the other side to get in. He casually rested his back against the door and said, "Okay, babe, you've got five minutes. Talk."

Zabree felt much more comfortable now that they weren't surrounded by his henchmen and she felt free to speak what was on her mind. She came right to the point. "I'm here because you once told me that if I ever needed a place to stay I could come to you." Zabree laughed ironically. "Well, I need a place now, so here I am." She shook her hair and turned to him so that he could take in the contours of her body.

Mario's eyes took in the sexy picture she presented before him and he knew that taking her in would be nothing but a word. He had noticed her months ago when he first started dealing drugs from the school that she attended. It was typical of him to wait for the women to come to him and when she had seen him sitting in his Benz outside the school one day, she had. He made his interest obvious and when she started fronting by playing hard to get, he was not interested in chasing after her. He had chosen another girl that day, someone who knew what time it was. He even remembered telling Zabree to look him up sometime. Now, here she was coming to him ready to move in. No problem. But Mario also didn't need any headaches. He ran a pretty smooth operation and she looked like she came from a pretty decent family. The last thing he needed was cops breathing down his territory looking for some runaway girl. But if he did decide to do it, he wanted to make sure she knew that he was doing her a favor. Yeah, she was fine and all, but that didn't mean shit. He had fine women demanding his time twenty-four seven. He stared at her and said, "And what do I get in return for housing and feeding you?"

Zabree knew she had him. She tilted her head to the side and as sexily as she could, "Whatever you want."

Mario smiled and reached his hand out to run it through her hair. He ran his hand down her neck and trailed his fingers across her chest, trailing them down her breasts. "Rule number one: You do whatever I tell you."

Zabree knew he was telling her that she would have to sleep with him. As handsome as he was with the slight gap in his front teeth and his curly hair, she found it an appealing idea. Anything would be better than the current situation she was in. "I will. But there's just one thing."

"What's that?" Mario asked.

"Rule number two: That I be with you and you only. No one else."

Mario smiled. He liked her already. "Deal, babe. You realize what you see behind you will be your new home?"

Zabree swallowed and slowly nodded her head.

"Cool. Now, what about your parents? Won't they be looking for you?"

"No, they won't. You don't have to worry about them. Once I'm gone, they'll rejoice. Believe me, they want me to go. So I promise you, you won't have any problems where they're concerned." Zabree was lying. She knew her folks would hit the ceiling when they discovered her missing, but she would do almost anything just to get away from her environment.

"How soon do you want to come?" Apparently Mario was satisfied with her answer.

Zabree had already thought it over. "Tomorrow after class you could meet me in front of my high school. I'll have my things with me."

"Three o'clock?"

"Yes," Zabree replied.

Mario reached over and opened the door on her side, motioning for her to get out. "I'll be there, babe. Don't be late and don't change your mind."

Zabree got out of the car and bent down to peer inside. "Thanks, Mario. You won't regret helping me." Zabree slammed the door and walked away, throwing her bookbag over her shoulder. Somehow, she felt she was doing what she had to do to save her sanity. The guilt she felt about what was happening between her and her father was becoming too much for her to bear. If she continued to stay at home, she would surely go crazy. She felt as if everyone in her family had turned their backs on her. Especially Mog. Zabree would never have gone off and left *her* had their situations been reversed. But she could forget Mog now. She would do what she had to do to survive with Mario until she could get on her feet and support herself. No more would she have to deal with her father's constant advances or her mother's constant looks of denial. Well, after tomorrow, she wouldn't have to look upon any of their faces ever again. She couldn't wait. Zabree thought to herself, *sometimes strangers treat you far better than your own family.*

***

Sunday evening around eleven-thirty, Caprice decided to try Imagany's number one more time before she went to bed. The phone rang continuously with no answer and finally Caprice replaced the receiver in its cradle. All day long Imagany had not called to tell her why she hadn't made it to the library and now Caprice was starting to worry. It just wasn't like Imagany. Even when she went into isolation, she left her answering machine on. Caprice got up from the bed and gathered the things she needed to go take a shower. She wasn't gone from the room more than fifteen minutes and when she got back, the phone was ringing. She dashed inside the room and snatched up the receiver.

"Hi."

"We won!" Carl's voice yelled into the phone and Caprice smiled at his naked enthusiasm.

"Wonderful! Is Elliott back, too?" Maybe Imagany was with Elliott.

"No. The team is supposed to be back in a half-hour though. Did you miss me?"

"Of course, dahlin'. How could I not?" At least Caprice knew Imagany was not with Elliott. "So how was it in Tallahassee?"

Carl talked and talked and Caprice could tell he was still excited from the trip. She listened, content to let him share his thoughts and feelings. In the back of her mind though, were worries about Imagany. She was sure Imagany was okay, but until she spoke to her, Caprice would continue to worry. She and Carl talked for over an hour and when they hung up, she dialed Imagany's number again to no avail. She fell asleep with the thought that, come tomorrow, she would wait for Imagany outside of her statistics class.

The next morning, Caprice woke with bags under her eyes. She had slept fitfully, tossing and turning all night long. She'd had a nightmare in which she and Imagany were trapped inside someone's house and they couldn't find their way out. A man's voice kept saying over and over that they should look for the thirteenth door and not stop running until they found it and that whatever they did, they must not open the seventh door. Somehow they had lost count of the doors and Imagany had opened the wrong door. When a large hand snaked out and pulled Imagany down into the depths of nowhere, Caprice woke up shaking.

She shook her head as she stood up to stretch. Her roommate, Myra, was still sleeping soundly. It was only six-thirty in the morning. Caprice walked to the phone and dialed Imagany's number. The phone rang and rang and after a while, she hung up and got ready for class.

At eleven-thirty, Caprice was sitting anxiously through her biology class, chomping on the eraser of her pencil. She realized the instructor's words were going right over her head because thoughts of Imagany kept running through her mind. She glanced at her watch and noted that Imagany would soon be getting out of her statistics class. Suddenly, Caprice gathered her things and hurriedly left the classroom. The instructor looked at Caprice curiously because it was unlike her to leave class early.

Meharry was only a swift fifteen minute walk from Fisk, and Caprice walked briskly. She knew Imagany would not miss any of her classes and she rushed to get to the building where her class was being held. Caprice reached the building and climbed to the third floor. Just as she reached the class room, some of the students were departing. Caprice peered inside the room and her heart dropped when she saw no sign of Imagany. She noticed one of the sorority girls that Imagany had once introduced her to and she caught her as she was about to leave the class room.

"Excuse me."

Dena Hipskind turned to face Caprice when she realized she was speaking to her. Dena remembered her from the time Imagany had introduced them. "Hi."

Caprice spoke breathlessly, "Hi. Do you know if Imagany was in class today?"

"No, she wasn't. She wasn't in our earlier class either. We were supposed to get together after this class to study for a test tomorrow, but she didn't show up." Dena shrugged her shoulder. "I've got to go. But if you see her, tell her to give me a call, will you? The name's Dena Hipskind."

Caprice watched Dena walk away and she followed her toward the exit on wooden legs. Somehow, she had the gut feeling that something was terribly wrong. Imagany never missed any of her classes. And it was unlike her not to call. Her sixth sense kept telling her over and over that something had happened to Imagany. Caprice quickened her step and walked out of the building. She fumbled through her purse and found her last bit of money and went to hail a cab.

Her heart pounded in her chest as the cab pulled into the parking lot of Imagany's complex. She spotted Imagany's car and a small feeling of relief passed through her. Maybe she was inside. Caprice paid the driver and stuffed her change back into her purse. She hopped out of the cab and dashed inside the building just as a couple was exiting. She caught the door to the entrance before it had a chance to lock and ran up the three flights of stairs. Caprice was zapped of all energy when she reached Imagany's level. She walked to her door and rang the doorbell several times. Her keys to Imagany's place were back in her dorm room, but since Imagany's car was outside she knew that she was probably inside the apartment. When no one answered, she banged on the door with her hand.

Imagany lay in the same spot where she had fallen asleep more than twenty-four hours ago. Through the thickness of her sleep, she heard the doorbell and someone banging on her door. She thought someone was coming to attack her and her hands flailed against the bed. Imagany was fighting in her sleep when suddenly she was wrenched awake.

Her body tensed as she struggled to recognize her surroundings. As her head cleared, she slowly noticed that she was in her own bedroom. She heard a voice at the door. Whoever it was continued to press the door bell and bang on the door. As if she were in a stupor,

Imagany sluggishly got up from the bed and stepped cautiously out of the room. Her mind was still befuddled with sleep and she had to hold onto the wall for support. She entered the living room and thought she heard Caprice's voice through the door. Still feeling a great deal of pain throughout her body, Imagany approached the door hesitantly and pressed her ear against the door. She listened to be certain it was Caprice.

Imagany called haltingly, "Reese?"

Caprice heard Imagany through the wood of the door and spoke anxiously, "Imagany, it's me. Open the door."

Imagany stared at the door as if she were confused. It was Caprice, wasn't it?

"Mog, please, open the door. It's me."

There! It had to be Caprice. No one other than her sister Zabree called her by that name. Imagany listlessly fumbled with the lock on the door and released the latch. She finally unlocked it and Caprice entered the apartment.

Caprice stepped inside and a gasp of horror escaped from her mouth at the sight of the swelling and bruises on Imagany's face. As she dropped her book bag to the floor, she shook her head and said, "no" over and over. Caprice shut the door behind her and took Imagany into her arms. Like a lost child, Imagany nestled her head in the crook of Caprice's arm and the two of them sank to the floor.

Caprice hugged Imagany tightly to her chest and tears fell from her eyes when she saw how frightened and confused Imagany appeared. She rocked her back and forth in her arms as if she were cradling a child. As tears poured from her eyes, a burning anger akin to hatred consumed Caprice's heart. There was no doubt in her mind that Anthony was the one who'd done this to Imagany.

Caprice lifted her hand to wipe the tears from her face. She spoke softly to Imagany, who was clutching her tightly as if she feared letting her go.

"Imagany, let's get up so we can put something on your face."

When Caprice moved to help lift Imagany up, Imagany held her tightly and whispered imploringly, "Don't leave me, Reese."

"No dahlin', I won't." Caprice reassured her as she helped her back into the bedroom and tucked her into the bed. Caprice went inside the bathroom and took out two aspirin and got some water and brought it back into the bedroom to give it to Imagany.

Imagany sat up at Caprice's request and swallowed the aspirin and water. Within minutes she was fast asleep.

Caprice got up and went back inside the bathroom. She took from the medicine cabinet bandages, cotton balls and some hydrogen peroxide to salve onto Imagany's face. She knew the peroxide wouldn't burn or sting and, therefore, would not wake Imagany from her sleep. She soaked the cotton balls with the peroxide and lightly touched them to the bruises on Imagany's face. Caprice pulled the thin sheet off of Imagany and lifted her gown. At the sight of the belt welts and marks on Imagany's skin, an intense anger shot through Caprice. She swabbed more of the peroxide onto Imagany's legs and thighs. Afterwards, Caprice sat on the bed with her hands between her thighs, her head thrown back as she looked up at the ceiling to say a silent prayer. With a deep sigh, she got up from the bed and left the bedroom, closing the door behind her. She walked up front and stared at the disarray of the living room.

Caprice picked up vases and lamps that had been knocked to the floor. She assumed there had been a struggle. She went into the kitchen to get a dusting rag and stopped short when she noticed the dried blood stains on the floor. Caprice hadn't noticed it before but a trail of blood lined the floor all the way to the kitchen sink. Her mouth opened in a silent gasp as she walked toward the cabinets. She looked down into the sink and saw the blood-stained knife. Revulsion shot through her and Caprice quickly filled the sink with water and poured a heaping amount of dish washing liquid into it.

She nervously cleared away the rotting green peppers, tomatoes and cheese that had been left sitting out on the counter. Caprice went into the closet and got a bucket and some Pine Sol and proceeded to thoroughly scrub the place down. She washed up what few dishes there were and gathered all the garbage, throwing the blood-stained knife into the bag along with the rest of the trash. Caprice grabbed Imagany's keys and took everything down the hall and threw it down the incinerator.

She re-entered the apartment and put on a pot of peach potpourri to simmer so that its smell would fill the apartment. Taking out Imagany's tea kettle, she boiled water for some tea. Caprice came back into the living room and sat on the sofa and stared around her. Yes, this was a beautiful apartment and yes, all the furnishings in it were beautiful too. But to Caprice it could never be worth what Imagany had to go through to get it. She turned over and over in her mind what could have taken place in the apartment that had led to the blood on the knife. She'd seen only bruises on Imagany's body so she could only assume that she had stabbed Anthony. *Stabbed him!* Damn! A shudder went through Caprice's body. It all seemed so terrifying to her. She remembered thinking that had she owned a gun she would have shot Anthony. But those thoughts had crossed her mind in the heat of anger, and Caprice knew that she would never have been able to do it.

The tea kettle started whistling and Caprice got up to turn off the fire underneath it. She lowered the fire under the pot of potpourri and returned to the sofa. She curled up and, minutes later, was fast asleep.

Caprice awoke several hours later hungry enough to eat anything that was put in front of her. She boiled water again and looked inside the refrigerator to see what she could find. Imagany had some chicken breasts inside the refrigerator already thawed so she took them out to make chicken salad. She cleaned and seasoned the chicken and set it on to boil. Deciding to check on Imagany, she quietly stepped inside the bedroom.

Imagany's head rested against the pillow and she opened her eyes and tried to smile when Caprice entered the room. Pain shot through her face and lips when she tried to smile and it ended up turning into a grimace.

Caprice sat at the foot of the bed and smiled at Imagany. "How are you feeling, kiddo?"

Imagany shook her head as she sat up. She pulled the sheet over her legs, self-conscious because of the marks on her body. "I've seen better days, girlfriend." Imagany's words were slurred from the swollenness of her lips and jaw.

Caprice laid down on the bed and cradled her head in her hand. She stared at Imagany and asked, "Hungry?"

"A little. Maybe just toast and some tea." Imagany's voice croaked as she spoke.

"Come on, I'll make it for you." Caprice got up and led the way into the kitchen. She noticed that Imagany avoided looking into the mirror.

They entered the kitchen and Imagany sat down at the table. She appeared kind of shy and Caprice realized she was self-conscious about her bruises.

"Reese, can I ask you something stupid?" Imagany was drawing imaginary circles on the table.

"Yep." Caprice realized Imagany would feel more comfortable if she didn't stare at her so she continued to make the toast and the tea without looking at her.

"What day is it?"

Caprice stopped and she turned to look at Imagany. "It's Monday, dahlin'."

Imagany leaned back in her chair and closed her eyes. If today was Monday, she had no idea of what had happened to the rest of Saturday and Sunday. She opened her eyes and saw Caprice staring at her. Imagany shook her head and said, "I guess I slept through Saturday and Sunday. Two days of my life gone by without notice." Imagany stared down at the table.

Caprice buttered the toast and spooned sugar into the tea. She brought everything to the table and set it down in front of Imagany. Then she fixed herself a cup of tea and sat down.

Imagany picked up a slice of the toast and broke it in half before gingerly biting into it. Her jaw was so sore she could only take little bites of the toast at a time. She slowly ate a slice of the toast and pushed the other two slices toward Caprice. She was really in no mood to eat anything, but she felt the need for something hot. She took a sip of her tea and set the cup down on the table. Leaning back in the chair, Imagany lifted her hand to lightly trace the bruises on her face. She knew how bad she looked and she had no desire to see herself in any mirror. She caught Caprice staring at her and said softly, "I guess it looks pretty bad for the home team, huh?"

Caprice smiled and said, "Like you said, kiddo, you've seen better days. But don't worry, the marks will go away. It's nothing that a little fade cream won't fix." Though Caprice was full of questions, she was willing to let Imagany tell her story at her own pace.

Imagany pushed the saucer of tea to the center of the table and lowered her head into her arms. "Reese, Reese, Reese," she mumbled over and over.

Caprice looked on in sympathy. Maybe if she attempted to find some humor in the situation, it would make Imagany feel better. But somehow she couldn't find much to laugh about. After awhile, Caprice finally asked, "What happened, Imagany?" She hadn't meant to pry, but curiosity just got the better of her.

Imagany lifted her head and spoke softly. "It was a nightmare, Caprice. I felt like I was having a bad dream. I pray to God it'll never happen again. No." Imagany spoke firmly. "It *will* never happen again." Imagany proceeded to explain to Caprice all that had happened. She started from the beginning when Leslie Lowe had first come to the apartment. She told Caprice everything, even about the money. She described Anthony's anger and portrayed how he had beat her with his belt. Imagany told her that it reminded her of the time when her own father had beat her that way once before. Only then, she had taken it lying down. But Saturday morning, something had snapped inside her, because before she knew it she had stabbed Anthony and in her mind she had been stabbing not just him, but her father as well. When she finished speaking, she stared up at the ceiling.

Caprice was spellbound by Imagany's story. She told Imagany about how she had waited for her outside the library and when she didn't show up, how she had called numerous times, and about how worried she had been.

Imagany listened intently and when Caprice was finished, she said, "You know, Reese, what's happened is done and over with. The only thing I want to do now is forget it by putting the entire incident behind me. I'm not bitter because Anthony got his, just as I got mine. I guarantee you he'll think twice before he hits another woman in his lifetime. And I'll think twice before I let someone's money entice me. I'll grow from this. The one thing I do know is that any bastard who raises his hand to harm me again, will surely die."

Imagany leaned her head back against the chair. Moments passed and she lifted her head to stare around the apartment. "I'm going to move, Reese. I don't want to spend any more time than I have to in this apartment. It holds too many bad memories for me now. I think I'll start looking in the paper for a place tomorrow."

"What about your furniture?"

"It's mine, so I'm taking it with me. Everything that's in this place, I've earned one way or another. Including the car."

"What about Elliott?"

Imagany's lips curved in an attempt to smile. "I feel like he's the one bright spot in my life." Imagany shook her head. "I can't let him see me like this, Reese. Not just him, I don't want anyone to see me. It'll probably take about two or three weeks for my face to clear up. I think what I'll do is just stay inside for about a week and after that I'll just pile on my makeup."

"You're going to miss a week's worth of classes?"

"I'm going to have to."

"But what about Elliott?"

"Yeah, I know. The question becomes, how do I keep him away for a week? I've got to think of something." The two of them thought about what she could say to him and finally Imagany said, "I know. You call him for me and tell him that I had to go home to Chicago for an emergency and that I'll be back," Imagany waved her hand in the air, "oh, let's be on the safe side and say next Tuesday. How does that sound?"

Caprice nodded her head. "It could work. After all you're not going to be anywhere where Elliott or Carl will run into you and your car is going to be parked in the same spot. I don't see why it wouldn't work. But of course you couldn't answer your phone."

Imagany spread both her hands. "No problem."

"Naturally, I'll have to come and stay here with you. I mean, you couldn't possibly take care of yourself."

Imagany knew Caprice was asking to stay with her and she inclined her head humorously because she had taken it for granted that Caprice would stay with her. "Agreed."

"It'll be just like old times when we used to have our slumber parties, remember?"

"Yeah, they were fun, weren't they?"

"Imagany?"

"Hmmm?"

"What are you going to do with all that money?" Caprice had to know.

This was something Imagany had thought about countless times. "I could use it to start my own business when I graduate. But I think I'm going to use the money to start over, Reese. Me and Zabree. I've been thinking about her and I want to bring her down here with me so that we can be a real family."

Caprice shook her head as she thought about what she would do if she had that kind of money at her disposal.

Imagany interrupted Caprice's thoughts. "So here's the plan, kiddo. We'll make out a grocery list and get everything we need for the week. You get all your clothes and books and bring everything back over here. And after that, you can take a cab to class every morning." At Caprice's raised eyebrow, Imagany said, "It's only four dollars each way. I think I can swing that. What else is left?"

"Well, I'm going to have to think of something to tell Carl, too. Because when he finds out that I'm over here, and especially if he thinks I'm by myself, he's definitely going to want to come over and spend some time."

"I'll bet Mr. Beasley *will* want to come over. Maybe you could tell him that some other girls are over here too, and that no men are allowed."

Caprice shrugged her shoulders reflectively. "Maybe. What a tangled web we weave, when we set out to deceive."

"Tell me about it," Imagany said, speaking from the heart.

Caprice got up to take the chicken out of the pot to dice it up. She looked over her shoulder and said, "I think the plan will work."

"I hope so," was Imagany's only reply.

Chapter Fifteen

aprice retrieved the things she needed from her room and did all the grocery shopping for the rest of the week. Later that evening, she called Elliott to inform him that Imagany had been called home because of an emergency. Elliott told her that he had been trying to reach Imagany all weekend long. He asked her if everything was all right. Caprice said she didn't know what the emergency was but that if she heard from Imagany before he did, she would surely let him know. She ended the call by asking him to get in touch with her should Imagany call him first.

Imagany was sitting near her as she made the call. When Caprice hung up, Imagany asked, "So, how did it go?"

Caprice put together her fore finger and thumb to form a small circle. "Piece of cake. I could tell he was very worried, though. He kept wanting to know if I knew what was wrong." Caprice sighed and said, "I hate deceiving him."

"I know, kiddo, me too, but it has to be done." Imagany had a mud pack on her face to help reduce the swelling. She got up to rub fade cream over her sore body. When she finished, she asked Caprice to rub some onto her back. As Caprice soothed the cream over her skin, Imagany sighed and said, "I'm going to miss not talking to Elliott for a whole week."

"Maybe you can call him and pretend you're calling from Chicago."

"I may just do that. I wonder how the game went for him. I didn't even get the chance to speak with him about it."

"Well, Carl said the team won so I guess the two of them must be pretty ecstatic. Speaking of Carl, I'll have to call him to let him know I'm going to be staying here." Caprice closed the jar and put it on top of the dresser. "I noticed you looking in the apartment rental section of the paper. Did you find anything?"

"Yep. There are some apartments for rent right off of White Bridge Road that I want to take a look at. I'll go have a look at them sometime next week."

"You'll find something." Caprice got up from the bed. "I'm going to go call Carl. Aren't you hungry yet?"

"As a matter of fact, I am. I guess that's a good sign, huh?"

Caprice inclined her head.

As Caprice talked to Carl, Imagany went to fix herself something to eat. She wanted something soft because her jaw still ached whenever she chewed. She spooned some of the chicken salad that Caprice had made onto a platter and placed some crackers beside it. She took her plate back into the bedroom and turned on the TV. She put it on mute and flipped through all the channels. Monday Night Football seemed to be the best thing on as the Washington Redskins battled the Green Bay Packers.

Imagany sat back and ate a small spoonful of the chicken salad. She wasn't interested in the football game so she gazed at the ceiling and thought about what she wanted out of life. Most important for her was that she finish college and go back to Chicago to begin her career there. She wanted to own her own business. But in addition to that, she wanted to be a journalist. To become an anchorwoman was her ultimate goal. She wanted to one day do documentaries on child abuse, to help make people aware of what was going on in the lives of abused children. When speaking to people about it, Imagany found that the topic of child abuse was one that made many people uncomfortable. They assumed that it could never happen to their child or that they had never known anybody to whom it had happened. Sadly enough, Imagany also knew that a lot of people assumed it was something that just didn't happen to little black children. What a fallacy! She shook her head, knowing she was living proof that such things did occur.

Imagany made a mental note to call Zabree when Caprice got off the phone. Before she could help anybody else, she would have to start by helping Zabree. She tossed several ideas around in her head. The more she thought about it, the more logical it seemed for Zabree to come live with her in Nashville. She could afford it now. She could get a two-bedroom apartment and she could even get a job. So could Zabree if it came down to it. It would be hard, but together, the two of them could make it.

Imagany was deep in thought when Caprice walked into the bedroom. Caprice laid at the foot of the bed and had that far away look in her eyes. Imagany knew she must have had a good conversation with Carl.

"And how is Mr. Beasley?"

"He's doing quite well. Didn't I tell you he would want to come over when I told you you weren't here? Do you know he was all set to be on his way as soon as I got the words out of my mouth? I had to quickly tell him that though you weren't here, three other girls were. I told him we had planned to have a slumber party and when you couldn't make it, we decided to have it any way." Caprice turned on her back and raised her knees on the bed.

Imagany heard the rapture in Caprice's voice so she asked her, "Do you love him, Reese?"

Caprice answered matter-of-factly. "Yes. I think he's a godsend. You hear all these terrible stories about the men from New York and here he is the perfect gentleman." Caprice stared in Imagany's direction. "Dr. Caprice Beasley. How does that sound to you?"

Imagany laughed as Caprice savored the sound of her would-be name. "Sounds like a plan."

"Does to me, too, honey. Wouldn't it be wonderful if it actually happened?"

"Let's think positively. It *will* happen. Hey, check this out." Imagany grabbed her fork from her plate and rose to her knees on the bed. Using her fork as if it were a microphone, she pretended to be a newscaster. "This is Imagany Renfroe coming to you live from NBC Towers. We're here in Chicago to interview the famous, successful newlywed couple Drs. Carl and Caprice Beasley. As you all know, the Beasleys have just been nominated as Nobel Prize candidates. Do the two of you have a few words to say to your adoring public?" Imagany playfully stuck the fork in Caprice's face.

Caprice grabbed the fork and said, "Yes. I would like to say a few words of encouragement to all the single ladies out there. Don't give up ladies! Your Prince Charming awaits you!" She laughingly handed the fork back to Imagany.

Imagany took the fork and whispered in a deep voice, "And there they go, folks. They're off to honeymoon in Rio de Janeiro, Brazil. I know all of us wish the happy couple continued bliss and success. Once again, this is Imagany Renfroe live from WLAB. Back to you, Bob." Imagany started bending at the waist as if she were taking bows.

"So in other words, what you're really trying to say is that you'll be married before I will, huh?" Caprice waved her hand in the air.

Imagany laughed. "Of course not." Before she could explain further, the telephone rang. The two of them looked at each other and Imagany motioned for Caprice to answer it.

"Hello."

"Hi, Reese. Where's Imagany?"

Caprice thought she recognized the voice. "Zabree?"

"Yeah. Who else did you expect, knuckle head?" Zabree answered saucily.

"Hey, watch yourself, kid. Hold on for Imagany." Caprice handed the phone to Imagany and left the room to give them some privacy.

Imagany took the phone and said, "Hey, kiddo. I was just about to call you."

"Yeah, right," Zabree said sarcastically.

Imagany laughed. "No really, I was. I came up with what I thought was a fantastic suggestion and I wanted to throw it at you."

"I'm listening."

"I'm getting ready to move and I wondered how you would feel about coming down here to live with me. Just you and me, kid. Just like old times." Imagany changed the sound of her voice to imitate Bugs Bunny. "So, whaddaya say?"

On the other end of the phone, Zabree didn't want Mog to know she was crying. She wiped tears from her face and smiled. How often in the past had she longed for Imagany to say these very words? But now, it was too late. She had someone else who was going to care for her. Slowly, Zabree said, "Mog, that's what I called to talk to you about." Before Imagany could interrupt her, she continued. "No. Not about coming to live with you, but about living elsewhere. Remember when I told you I was thinking about leaving home? Well, I just did. As a matter of fact I did it today. I wanted to surprise you." Zabree really had no intention of telling Imagany anything. It was just that here in this decrepit building, she had been overcome by loneliness and had needed to hear the sound of Mog's voice.

Imagany clutched the phone to her ear. Zabree had taken her by surprise. "Where did you go? Who are you staying with? Do I know them?" Imagany had a multitude of questions.

Zabree decided to stretch the truth. "I'm staying with a friend and her parents. Their place is on State Street."

"State Street! Not the projects, I hope?" Imagany was worried now.

Zabree laughed bitterly, Imagany had hit the nail right on the head. "No. Not in the projects, silly. They live out further south. Much further."

Imagany breathed a sigh of relief. "Do I know them?"

"No. She's a friend from my high school. Her parents are really cool, too. I had to explain to them what my situation was, though. But at any rate, I'm going to get a job so that I can help pay my share of the bills. Mom and Dad don't know where I'm staying, and I'd like to keep it that way."

Imagany thought it over. "You're sure you'd rather stay with them than come here with me?"

"Yeah, I'm sure. When I get my new phone number, I'll call and give it to you. In the mean time, don't call Mom or Dad, okay?"

"Sure kiddo. Are you happy, Bree?"

"Yep."

"I guess that's all that matters then, kid." Disappointment showed in Imagany's voice.

Zabree heard it and knew that if she didn't get off the line, she would burst into tears. "Well, anyway, I'm running up their bill so I'll have to go. I'll call you soon, okay?"

"Yes. Try to make it very soon. I love you, Bree."

Zabree heard her but instead of saying it back to her, she hung up the phone. Tears coursed down her cheeks as she gathered her knees to her chest. Her heart ached and she felt so all alone. As hard pressed as she was to admit it, she missed her family. She really had had no intentions of calling Mog, but somehow she couldn't stop herself from picking up the phone. If only Mog had asked her sooner. Zabree would have welcomed the opportunity to go live with her. Zabree didn't know what she had expected when she'd agreed to come here with Mario. But it certainly wasn't this. Not this dump. Somehow, she had thought that because Mario drove a nice car, he would at least have a nice home. Boy, was she ever wrong. When Zabree came into the building earlier, her first thought was that even animals lived better than this. The stench of urine and garbage was everywhere you turned. And the apartment itself wasn't much better. If she was going to stay here, this entire apartment would have to be thoroughly cleansed and remodeled. She would talk to Mario as soon as he came back.

The apartment that Mario and his boys operated out of was connected to the one she was in. Zabree knew they made and sold drugs out of the apartment next door because Mario had his boys securing it twenty-four hours a day. Just seeing the crack heads lined up outside waiting for the drugs was enough to make Zabree swear to never touch the stuff again. Mario had told her earlier that as his woman, she would be expected to dress the part. Also, whatever she wanted was hers for the asking. The only trouble with that was that Zabree didn't really know what she wanted.

***

Imagany got up and took her plate into the kitchen, where Caprice was making herself a cup of tea.

"Is that all you're going to eat?" Caprice noticed that Imagany had barely touched her food.

Imagany set the plate on the table and sat down. "I guess I should eat the rest of it."

"Yeah, you should. You haven't eaten anything other than two slices of toast in the last couple of days. Your body needs the nourishment, dahlin'."

"I know." Imagany took another bite of the food and said, "I invited Zabree down here to come live with me."

Caprice came to the table and sat down. "Really? What did she say?" Caprice knew that Imagany had serious personal problems in her family. She also knew what they consisted of, but since Imagany didn't like to talk about it, Caprice never pressed the issue.

"Seems like I asked too late. She's already moved in with another family. My Mom and Dad don't know where she's staying and I think it's for the best. Zabree says she's happy, though, so I guess I can console myself with that."

"That's deep," was all Caprice could manage to say. She thought about her own childhood growing up as an only child. Sure, there had been times when she had given her parents hell, but for the most part, Caprice had had a wonderful childhood and she considered herself lucky to have her parents. The thought of running away from home had never occurred to her.

"For some strange reason, Reese, the thought of your mother just crossed my mind. Remember when we were little, how we used to tell everybody that we were sisters? And even when they knew we weren't, I still used to insist that your mother was mine. I envied you because of your parents, Reese. I can't even count the number of times I used to wish we could trade places. It never fails to amaze me when I hear people say they would give anything to repeat their childhood years. Me? I wouldn't do it for all the money in the world." Imagany pushed the plate of chicken salad to the middle of the table and motioned for Caprice to help her eat it. Though it was delicious, Imagany just didn't have the appetite for it.

Caprice took a cracker and slid some of the meat onto it. "I guess I know what you mean because I'm one who would love to repeat my childhood. But I believe the things that happened to us then helped shape us into who we are now." Caprice leaned back in her chair and said, "Look at you. I mean, you're the strongest person I know."

Imagany looked at Caprice in surprise.

"No, it's true. You're the most positive and the most determined person I've ever met in my life. You've always been a go-getter. You see something you want, boom! The next thing I know, you've got it. And I always get a kick out of watching people who have misjudged you. They see your looks and they automatically think you're an air head. Boy, don't they get shocked every time! I remember in high school, I could never understand how you could party just about every night of the week and still manage to get straight A's. You were valedictorian and they even voted you most likely to succeed. You have more strength within you than you give yourself credit for. I don't know anybody who could have gone through what you've gone through and remain as positive as you are."

Imagany looked at Caprice and said simply, "Thank you. I don't know what else to say. I guess we tend to view ourselves much more differently than others do. God knows there are times when I don't even see the strength, Reese. But I can always see yours. Yours is a quiet inner strength. Sometimes you have a shy quality about you, but your strength is always there. Right along with your other characteristics, like your ability to give of yourself so unselfishly. I've never met anybody who's as unselfish as you are, and I probably never will. You're caring. Look at the way you came in here and helped me today. Anybody else would have come in looking stupid and asking a million and one questions." Imagany shook her head. "And boy, when you love someone, Reese, that person has never been loved like it before. You talk about me? You were the one whom I followed around in high school. When it came to hitting the books, you were the one I competed with. I guess we're just two birds of a feather."

"I guess you're right." Caprice picked up the now empty plate and tea cups and took them to the sink to wash them.

"Enough of the heart-to-heart talk. If we keep at it, we'll both end up crying. Besides, there's studying to be done." Imagany stood up from the table.

Caprice dried off her hands and said, "Let's go hit the books, kid."

The next morning Imagany woke Caprice up early and even fixed breakfast for her. She called a cab and saw Caprice off to school, feeling a bit sad that she was not going herself. She locked the door behind Caprice and went to take a bath. After applying a mud pack to her face and putting some medicated Vaseline on her lips, Imagany consoled herself with the fact that the swelling on her face was slowly going down. Her only hope was that all the swelling would be gone by the end of the week. Somehow, though, Imagany doubted she would be that lucky.

Chapter Sixteen

The days dragged by for Imagany. She missed Elliott sorely and found herself eagerly looking forward to the time when Caprice would arrive at the apartment from school. It seemed that in the period of a week, their relationship had grown even stronger. Imagany found herself wanting to talk more about her childhood experiences, a topic she had always managed to avoid.

She had called all of her instructors to let them know that she'd be missing a week of classes due to an emergency at home. They had each given her assignments to do in her absence from class and Imagany welcomed the opportunity to keep herself busy. But even her school work was not enough to keep her thoroughly occupied, so she spent a good deal of each morning meditating.

She was only partially satisfied with the healing of her face. A lot of the swelling had gone down but in its place, more bruises had formed. Imagany could deal with the bruises more readily because she knew makeup would hide them.

She called the building management to inquire about breaking the lease on her apartment. Since her rent was paid up for the next several months, Imagany wanted to have that money refunded to herself. The management people explained that if she broke her lease she would forfeit her two month's security. This she found agreeable, as long as she was refunded the seven months' rent that she had coming to her. She finalized her decision to move by informing them that she would be out of the apartment by the end of the month.

Imagany had Caprice go to the Farmer's Market to ask for all the newspaper and boxes they could give her so she could begin packing her things. By the end of the week, boxes were strewn everywhere but at least the majority of her small items such as her dishes, knick knacks, sheets, towels and many of her clothes were packed.

By the time Friday arrived, Imagany felt a deep sense of gratitude toward Caprice and she wanted the two of them to have a candle-lit dinner as a token of her appreciation.

Knowing how much Caprice craved Mama Leone's beef spare ribs, Imagany called for home delivery. To go with it, she ordered the black-eye peas with rice and gravy, corn bread and candied yams. She made corn-on-the-cob and creamed spinach herself.

By the time Caprice arrived at the apartment, Imagany had everything set up. Caprice walked through the door exclaiming, "My goodness, what is that delicious smell? Please tell me my nose is not deceiving me." She dropped her book bag to the floor and skipped into the kitchen. Caprice stared at the fine cutlery and dishes and said, "Oh, I get it. You're kicking me out and inviting Elliott over to eat, right?"

Imagany laughed. "No, dahlin'. All that you see is from me to you. With love, I might add. So go wash up and come have a seat." When Caprice went into the bathroom, Imagany removed all the food from the oven and stood back to admire her handiwork. There was so much food on the table that it looked as if the two of them were about to engage in a food extravaganza. And the roses that Imagany had ordered were simply beautiful.

Caprice came out of the bathroom and took in the scene before her. "I'm impressed, dahlin'. What's the occasion?"

Imagany put her hands on her hips. "Why does there have to be an occasion? Can't I simply order dinner for me and my best friend? Is there a problem here?"

Caprice inclined her head as she threw her hands into the air.

"All right, then. Have a seat, please." Imagany gestured for Caprice to sit and started fixing their plates.

"Um, excuse me, but may I ask the chef a question?" Caprice had her elbows on the table and she pressed her fingertips together.

"But of course. Your wish is my command. How may I help you?"

Caprice said jokingly as she pressed one hand to her chest and waved her other one in the air. "Well, I don't want to cause any problems here. I just want to get the facts. Can you simply explain to a slow person like myself why you are about to sit down to such a nicely set dinner table with all that sickening mud spread over your face?" Holding both her hands steady in the air, she said, "I mean, like I said, I don't want to cause any problems. It's just a question."

Imagany laughed as she touched her hands to her face. She had forgotten to remove her mud pack. No wonder the delivery people had stared at her as they had. She had assumed they were staring at her bruises. Imagany crossed her arms over her chest and tilted her head to the side as if she had developed an attitude. "Oh, so what you're really trying to say is that I look like a monster and that I shouldn't be allowed to eat until I make myself presentable, right? In other words, because I'm black I've got to go eat in the back, right?" Imagany started gesturing with her hands as if she were a home-girl. "Here I am bussin' my black behind in the kitchen all day to feed your ungrateful butt and the only words of thanks that I get is 'why come you look like you do!' Well, hey," Imagany started jerking her neck in circles. "I ain't got to take this."

Caprice was so busy laughing at Imagany that she couldn't speak. Finally Caprice said, "Look, girlfriend. Either you go wash your face or you sit down and eat. Whichever one you prefer is fine with me. I just thought, and maybe I was wrong, that because we're eating ribs, and you know how we eat ribs, I just figured that maybe you would want to have a clean face. I mean, we all know that whenever you eat ribs, you end up getting the sauce all over your face and all in your hair. So if there's no problem, just sit down and let's eat. I mean, maybe it's just me."

Imagany cleared her throat, her tone suddenly humble. "Well, um, now that you put it like that, I think I will go wash my face. So hold that thought, my sister. I'll be right back."

They stuffed their faces in contented silence as they put away as much of the food as their stomachs would allow. When they finished eating, they sprawled out on the living room floor, too full to do anything else.

As they lay on the floor rubbing their stomachs, Caprice said, "Thanks for the dinner. You know you didn't have to do it."

"Yes I did. You didn't have to spend the whole week over here with me either, but you did. Anybody else in their right mind would have spent the time cuddled up with their man."

"Maybe, maybe not. You would have done the same for me, too, so it doesn't matter." Caprice changed the subject. "Tell me about how much you miss Elliott."

A gigantic smile lit Imagany's face. Though she still experienced some discomfort when she smiled, the thought of him was worth it. In a husky voice, she whispered, "Reese, only me and the good Lord will ever know how much I've missed that man. At night, I dream about his arms around me, his lips touching mine, tasting me, teasing me, holding me."

Caprice took a swig of her wine cooler and said, "Hey, kiddo, watch yourself now." Caprice could feel the room temperature rising.

"Child, that's how much I miss my man!"

"Well, when are you going to call him then?"

"Just as soon as I get the strength to get off this floor. Right now, Imagany was too stuffed to even think about moving."

"Well, I'm down with that. How 'bout a toast?" Caprice suggested.

"Girlfriend, yes. Let's drink to our men."

"Yeah. Let's pour a few drops for the folks who couldn't be here." Caprice poured her drops right into her mouth.

"There you go," Imagany replied.

The two of them lay on the floor making plans to call Elliott and Carl. Before they knew it, they were both out like a light.

Eight-thirty that evening, the phone rang, startling both of them out of their sleep. Caprice picked up the phone and from the expression on her face, Imagany could tell it was Carl on the other end of the line. Imagany pulled herself to her knees and crawled into the bedroom.

She lay on the bed and shortly afterwards, Caprice came into the room. She sat at the foot of the bed with a forlorn expression on her face. Imagany asked her, "What's wrong?"

"Carl asked me if I wanted to go to the movies with him." She shrugged her shoulders. "I told him I couldn't because I had other plans."

Imagany sat up in the bed and stared at her sternly. "Caprice McKnight! If you don't call Carl Beasley back and tell him that you've changed your mind, I will do it for you."

"But Imagany, I don't mind staying here with you."

"No, Reese. Go with him. You haven't seen him all week long. The man wants to be with you, so go. I'll be all right. Besides, I can always call Elliott if I start feeling lonely." Imagany waved her hand to shoo Caprice away. "Scat now, go!"

"Okay, okay! I'm going." Caprice stood in the doorway indecisively. "Maybe I should go back to the dorm and have him pick me up from there."

"Uh, uh. Just call him and tell him that you'll come downstairs when he rings the bell. So, go on and call him before he makes other plans."

Caprice hopped off the bed and went into the living room to call Carl. She came back into the bedroom with a radiant smile on her face. "All right, my sister! The man is on his way. Come on, Imagany, make me beautiful."

Imagany got up from the bed and went to her closet to pick out something for Caprice to wear. "Black is where it's at, Reese. And with your legs, kid, this mini bad boy is the only way to go."

Caprice showered while Imagany picked out a black mini skirt and selected a matching top for her to wear. A wide belt and black suede pumps completed the outfit. Simple but elegant.

When Caprice came out of the shower, Imagany pulled Caprice's hair back into a ponytail and tied a large black scarf around it. Caprice dressed quickly and surveyed herself in the mirror.

"You know, girlfriend, I've got to hand it to you. What you can do with a person in less than fifteen minutes is truly remarkable."

"The credit belongs to you, dahlin'. You can't work with something unless you have the right material. With your looks and body, how could I go wrong?"

The door bell rang. Caprice sprayed on a touch of Halston cologne and dashed to the door. She turned back to Imagany and asked, "Mog, you're sure you're going to be okay?"

Imagany placed her hands on her hips. "Yes, I am. Now will you get out of here and leave me alone?"

Caprice unlocked the door and stepped out into the hallway.

Imagany came to the door and called to Caprice as she was going down the stairs. "Hey, Reese?"

"Yeah, honey?"

"Knock 'em dead for me, will you?"

"Gotcha!"

Imagany locked the door to the apartment and went into the kitchen to clean up the mess they had left. She didn't think Caprice would be coming back to the apartment again that night, so she put all the food away. She washed up the few dishes and went back into the bedroom to stare despondently at the telephone.

Unable to stand the solitude any longer, Imagany picked up the phone and dialed Elliott's number. The phone rang twice before the person whose voice she preferred to hear more than anyone else's in the world, answered the phone.

"Hello."

Imagany melted at the sound of his sweet voice. It had been much too long. "Hi, baby," was all that she could manage to say.

Elliott breathed deeply into the phone. In a husky voice, he whispered, "Hi, yourself. How are you?"

Imagany stretched out on the bed. "Oh, Elliott. I miss you, baby."

Elliott groaned. "Aww, sweetheart. Where have you been? Where *are* you?"

"I'm in Chicago, sweetie. I had to call you though. Elliott, all week long, I felt like I was dying. God, how I've missed you."

Elliott smiled into the phone. "Are you okay?"

"Yea, I'm fine."

"What was wrong?" Much concern was in Elliott's voice.

"One of my aunts took ill. They don't know if she's going to make it."

"I'm sorry to hear that. How long are you going to stay in Chicago?" Elliott was able to breathe a sigh of relief knowing that she was all right.

Imagany wanted to scream into the phone that she had never left and beg him to come over to her place. Instead she said, "Baby, if you want me to, I'll come back tomorrow."

Elliott laughed. "What about your sick aunt?"

"To be honest, Elliott, I never liked the woman anyway. She's a mean old bitch and I say to hell with her. After all the dirt she's done, it's time for her to go on to another place. So please, baby, say you want me to come back tomorrow." With laughter in her voice, Imagany pleaded with him.

Elliott laughed. "Imagany, that's terrible. You shouldn't speak ill of the sick like that. How soon can you get here, baby?"

Imagany smiled. "Did you miss me, Boo?"

"Does a bear shit in the woods? Hell yeah, I missed you, woman. What are you trying to do to me? Do you know I've been glued to this room all week long waiting for you to call me? I almost lost my mind."

"Elliott?" Imagany whispered to him in her most sexiest voice.

"What sweetheart? Talk to me."

"I love you, baby."

"Ummm, ummm, ummm. Imagany, don't do this to me. You know you're over six hundred miles away. Why are you teasing a brother like this?" Imagany's voice was sweet music to Elliott's ears.

"Because I want to, baby. Love me?" Imagany teased him further.

Elliott thought to himself that if Imagany had any idea of how much he loved her, she would be scared of him. "More than you know," was his only reply.

Imagany was suddenly turning herself on, so she lightened the conversation. "Boo, tell me how the game went."

"It went okay, baby. We won, what more can I tell you?" At this moment, football was the last thing on Elliott's mind.

"There's a lot more you can tell me, dahlin'. Like how have you been occupying yourself? Have you been good, Elliott?"

Elliott laughed. "Of course, I've been good. Aren't I always?"

This was not the answer Imagany wanted to hear. "Elliott, I asked you a question, baby. Have you been behaving yourself?"

Elliott chuckled. "Yes, I always behave myself. Don't I?"

"Mmmm. You tell me, Mr. Renfroe. Again I ask, have you been a good boy?"

"Yes, ma'am, I have. If I were misbehaving, I wouldn't be in this lonely room all by myself waiting for my woman to call, now would I?"

Imagany had no answer to that. "I guess not sweetie."

"Here it is, I go away to play a game, thinking that when I come home, my main woman is going to be here waiting for me."

Imagany interrupted him, "What do you mean, your *main* woman? Don't you mean your *only* woman?"

"Of course, baby, you know you're my only woman. Anyway, as I was saying before I was rudely and crudely interrupted. What do I find after returning from a hard day's work? I find that my woman has skipped off to another city without so much as even leaving me word of where she's going or how I can get in touch with her. Low down, dirty shame! Damn! Talk about treating a black man wrong. Just *kick* me to the curb! You don't love me, Imagany." Elliott pretended to be deeply wounded.

"Boo, that's not true and you know it. Of course I love you. If it wasn't for my sick old aunt, I'd be in your arms as we speak. How're you gonna play me?" Imagany was having no part of the guilt trip Elliott was trying to teasingly lay on her.

Elliott was not finished yet. "I tell you, the things we black men have to put up with. When a man loves a woman, his work is never done."

"Elliott Renfroe, cut it out. What am I going to do with you?"

Elliott laughed. They were both quiet for a moment and then he said, "You know Imagany, sometimes you don't realize how much a person means to you until they're not around anymore. In this past week I've come to realize how much I really care for you. We've only known each other for several months and already you've made an indelible imprint on my life. I never thought I'd see the day when I'd be so hooked into a woman that I'd be afraid to go take a leak because I'm scared she might call while I'm away. It's overwhelming to know that a person can have that kind of effect on you."

Imagany's heart softened. "It's really very simple, Elliott. We spend our whole lives trying to attain the goals which we've set. All the while, in the back of our minds, we have an idea of the kind of person we would like to spend the rest of our life with. We go through a series of relationships that either bring us closer to our model or take us further away from what we're really seeking. Whether they work out for us or not, it doesn't matter because in the end each relationship affords us an opportunity to grow. Ultimately, relationships give us an idea of either what we do want or what we don't want. Am I making sense to you?"

"Yeah, I'm following you. Go on."

"Well, sooner or later, if we're lucky, we meet the person who encompasses all the things we tell ourselves we want in a mate. We say to ourselves, 'okay, this is it.' This is the one I can spend the rest of my life with. This is the person whose children I want to bear or this is the person I want to bear my children. But to confront the person with that knowledge is absolutely terrifying. There are no guarantees that the person will feel the same way. It's all about risking rejection. No one likes to be rejected, Elliott. It's a fear that we never overcome. But it's also a chance we must take if we're to find true happiness. I guess what I'm trying to tell you is that you took a chance just now by telling me how you really feel. I'd be honored to be your wife and to bear your children because I love you and I feel you're that special person for me. But unless we take a chance on each other, we'll never really know if we're meant for one another. So I thank you for sharing what you just did. I'm willing to take the chance, Mr. Renfroe. Are you?"

Elliott had lain on his bed to take in everything Imagany had said. Instead of answering her question directly, Elliott said, "So in addition to everything else, my baby is a philosopher. Your talents never cease to amaze me." Elliott paused before saying, "I agree with everything you've just said. I hadn't thought to look at it like that. To be honest with you, Imagany, you scare me. I think it's because you seem so mature for your age. I don't know if I'm ready for you yet. One part of my mind tells me to snatch you up before someone else has the opportunity. And the other part tells me to run as far away as I can get. You're like a magnet that keeps drawing me back. A puzzle that I've got to piece together. I tell myself it's too soon for me to be feeling the way I feel about you. But whenever I think of my future, I see you in it. So to answer your question, yes, I am willing to take a chance on love. It's not even a question of what do I have to lose but more along the lines of what all do I stand to gain."

Imagany suddenly felt proud of Elliott. She knew so many men who never allowed themselves to express what they felt and who kept things hidden inside. She wanted Elliott to know that he could always feel free to express his emotions to her. "Elliott, I'm not asking you for anything that you don't have to give. Everything will come in due time. Understand me, Mr. Man? Let's be frightened in this thing together so that we can learn from one another." Imagany did not want him to think that she was begging him to ask her to marry him.

Elliott got her message loud and clear. At this moment, his only wish was that he could see her face to face. "Now, tell me again what time you expect to make it back home."

"Baby, I promise you that as soon as I hit the ground tomorrow, I'll be running in your direction."

Elliott sighed into the phone. "Now, baby, that's what I needed to hear."

Imagany awoke the next morning with mixed feelings about having to leave the apartment to search for another one. She had made appointments to see several other apartments and now that the time had come for her to keep them, she found herself reluctant to go outside.

Imagany stood in front of the mirror and stared at herself. The swelling was gone but the bruises on her face and body were obvious. She peered closer at her face and thought that if she became creative with her makeup and applied a good amount of foundation, she could pass presentably. But her arms, legs, thighs and hips that told the true story.

Making up her mind to go, she began putting on her makeup. She went through the whole nine yards applying concealer, foundation, eyeliner, eye shadow, blush and lip gloss. She stepped closer for a final analysis and decided that if she were on her way to a party or a lavish engagement, she would fit right in. But for a mere sweater and blue jeans, she definitely had on too much makeup. Too bad, she thought to herself as she pulled her hair into a ponytail and dug out a Chicago Bears cap to put on her head. She pulled the brim of the cap down low on her face hoping this might make her look less made up. She put on a pair of white sneakers and was all set to go.

She stood in front of the door jumbling the keys in her hand trying to decide if she was forgetting something. She checked to make certain the gas was not on and that she had turned off the lights in the bed and bath rooms. Standing in front of the door once more, Imagany fumbled through her purse to make sure she had money just in case she needed to stop and buy something. She counted forty-eight dollars and found herself neatly arranging it in her wallet when, suddenly, she stopped and looked at the door.

Imagany realized that she was stalling for time. It dawned on her that she was afraid to leave the apartment. She stepped closer to the door and put her hand on the knob, but was unable to turn it. She turned around, determined to open the door, when Anthony's image came to her mind. What if he were standing outside her door waiting for her? Her heart began to pound in her chest. Willing herself to open the door, she unlocked the door and peered outside into the hallway. No one was there. The place was quiet. She stepped outside and hurriedly went her way.

Chapter Seventeen

hen Imagany returned to her apartment, the first thing she did was turn on her air conditioner and run bath water. Tossing in some of her scented bath beads, she removed her clothing and stepped eagerly into the tub.

She wanted to hurry up and call Elliott to let him know she was back, so she didn't linger inside the bathroom. She dried herself off and smoothed Ralph Lauren lotion onto her arms and chest. It was when she started rubbing the lotion onto her hips, thighs and legs that she began to have second thoughts about seeing Elliott. Though the marks and bruises on her face were starting to fade, there were so many of them remaining on her body that Imagany knew she wasn't ready for Elliott to see her looking this way. She went inside the bedroom and dialed his number.

When Elliott's roommate, Tyrone, answered the phone, Imagany said, "Hi, Tyrone. It's Imagany. Is Elliott there?"

"No, you just missed him. He told me that if you called, to tell you he'd be back shortly."

"Okay. When he gets in, can you just tell him I'm back and ask him to give me a buzz?"

"Yeah, I can do that. Hey, Imagany?"

"Yes?" Her tone was friendly.

"You got any friends you can introduce me to?"

Imagany was completely taken aback. "I don't know, Tyrone. What kind of person are you interested in meeting?" Imagany had only met him once and she simply didn't have the heart to tell him that she didn't know a damn soul who would be interested in meeting him.

"Anybody with big titties and a big ass will do me just right. It don't even matter what she looks like as long as she can walk and talk. Okay?"

Imagany's mouth dropped open. She couldn't believe what Tyrone had just said. Surely the brother was joking. But Imagany could tell from the tone of his voice that he was dead serious. She remembered what Elliott had told her about Tyrone and shook her head. "Uh, I don't know, Tyrone. Let me see what I can come up with. I'll get back to you."

Imagany hung up the phone feeling relieved that Elliott wasn't there. She snuggled into her pillow and curled up to take a light nap.

She had only been dozing for a little while when the phone woke her. "Hello?"

"It's me, baby. Were you sleeping?" Elliott asked.

"I must have dozed off for a minute. I called you earlier."

"Yeah, I just got in and saw your message. Imagany, I'm coming over, so I'll talk to you when I get there. Go back to sleep."

Imagany woke fully from her sleep. "Elliott, Boo, I . . ." She couldn't think of a thing to say to him that would prevent him from coming.

"What is it?" He heard the indecision in her voice.

"I just . . . Boo, you can't come yet."

"Why?" Elliott wasn't following her

"Well, Imagany couldn't think of anything to say. "Because I look awful, that's why."

"Imagany, what are you talking about? I could care less what you looked like. Enough of this madness. I'm on my way."

"Elliott, wait . . ." Imagany spoke into the phone but the line was dead.

She quickly got up from the bed and, like it or not, began to hurriedly apply makeup to her face. She had just finished putting lip gloss on her lips when the door bell rang. She went to the intercom and buzzed Elliott in. He dashed up the stairs and was at her door in less than no time. Imagany unlocked the door and let him in.

Elliott stepped into the apartment and pushed the door closed behind him. He noticed all the boxes piled up against the wall and a look of surprise appeared on his face. "Are you moving?"

Imagany could only stare at him. It was as if she were seeing him for the first time. "Yes," she said quietly. He wore a thin black turtleneck shirt and black dockers. The man had never looked so good to her before.

Elliott finally brought his gaze to her face. Without warning, he wrapped her in a tight bear hug and swung her around. He set her down and wound his fingers into the thickness of her hair and was about to kiss her when he noticed the amount of makeup she was wearing.

Elliott lifted her face and asked, "Are we going somewhere?"

Imagany suddenly felt shy. She pulled her chin from his grasp and pressed her face against his chest. "Nope." Her reply was muffled into his chest.

Elliott lifted her face away from him and once more raised her chin. He examined her face closely with a curious expression on his own. He couldn't detect the bruises underneath all the makeup but still he knew something was not right. "Then why are you wearing so much makeup?"

Imagany tried to pull away from him. She was beginning to feel very self-conscious and she felt like she would cry if he pressed the issue.

Elliott sensed her vulnerability. He held her to him tightly. His kiss on her forehead helped ease the tension which was starting to develop. Before Imagany could protest, he pulled her into the bathroom.

Elliott closed the bathroom door and turned Imagany toward the mirror. As Elliott stood behind her, Imagany had no idea of what he was up to. She soon found out. He bent his head and pressed his lips tenderly to the side of her neck. As tiny shivers of pleasure coursed through her, she tilted her head to the side.

Elliott lifted his head and reached into her medicine cabinet and took out her cold cream. He pressed the cream into her hands and said softly, "Take off the makeup, baby. I want to see what you look like beneath all the cosmetics." Elliott's tone was gentle but firm.

Imagany closed her eyes. She should have known this was what he wanted. "I can't, Boo." Her voice indicated how defenseless she felt.

Elliott stretched out his hand and lowered the cover on the toilet seat and sat down. He reached over and steered her between his legs. With his hands on her arms, he pulled her down to the floor. Positioning her on her knees between his legs, Elliott told her, "Yes, you can. It's no big deal. It's simply something I want you to do for me. What are you hiding from?" Elliott lightly grasped her chin. He pulled her head forward and kissed the corner of her mouth. With his lips to her ear, he whispered, "Imagany, you should know me better than to think I would ask you to do something that was harmful. If you don't want to take your makeup off, you don't have to. But I want you to."

Imagany had closed her eyes when Elliott started whispering into her ear. She heard the caring note in his voice and tears began to course down her cheeks. She hadn't intended to cry. She just felt so open and vulnerable. With her eyes closed, she felt Elliott wipe the tears from her face.

"Look at me, Imagany."

Imagany laughed softly. Now she was even more self-conscious. She lowered her head to stare at the floor. She couldn't bring herself to look at him.

Elliott stood up and pulled her up with him. Imagany's eyes remained on his chest as Elliott told her, "I'm going to go into the bedroom and get undressed. When you come inside, whether you have on makeup or not won't matter to me. So do what you have to do, baby, but don't take too long. Capeesh?"

Imagany smiled as Elliott walked out of the bathroom. She stepped in front of the basin. She stared at her face before picking up the cold cream to spread it evenly onto her face. She slowly removed her makeup. She washed off all traces of the cosmetics and went to meet Elliott inside the bedroom.

When she stepped into the room, Elliott had dimmed the lights. He lay on his side, stripped of all his clothing, watching her as she entered the room. Imagany walked to the head of the bed and untied her gown, letting it fall to the floor. Naked, she crawled onto the bed and kneeled in front of him, her hair spilling flatteringly upon her shoulders.

Elliott's eyes greedily took in the beautiful vision that knelt before him. The heavy firmness of her thrusting breasts, the narrowness of her waist and the sensual flaring of her hips greeted him and caused his stomach muscles to contract. His maleness had hardened the moment she had stepped into the room, but now as he watched her, it pulsed with a throbbing stiffness. He lifted himself up on his own knees and pulled her closer to him. With Imagany still kneeling on her knees in front of him, his senses were alive with pleasure. He sensed her vulnerability and his arms enfolded her in his grasp. He rubbed his nose in her hair, across her forehead, over her neck before finally touching his lips softly to hers.

Imagany was lost amidst the tidal waves of his gentle assault. She heard him whisper her name hungrily and her arms wrapped themselves around his neck. His hunger fed her own and the only thing that she wanted was to belong to him fully. As he pulled her down to the bed beneath him, with a whimpering sigh, she yielded to him her body, her mind and her soul.

Elliott covered her body with his and buried his head against her neck. He positioned himself between her thighs, planted her legs against his sides and kneaded her buttocks firmly with his hands. As his lips drank thirstily from hers, he played havoc with her emotions. When he felt her toes curl against him, he knew her surrender was complete. But again it was not enough. Elliott wanted to feel her body thrash against his. He wanted to hear her demanding sweet whispered sighs of pleasure and he wanted to feel that sweet music that only her body could make for him. When her legs parted into a wider "V" and when she dug her nails viciously into his back, he knew she was completely ready for him. And only then did he begin to satisfy her hunger, in turn slating, slaking and quenching his own. They made love with a zesty passion, hungrily devouring each other as they rode the waves of passion and pleasure, clinging to one another with a certainty that they each were where they rightfully belonged.

Afterwards, Imagany clung to Elliott, unwilling to release her grip on him. Elliott rolled to his side, holding her body against him. He breathed heavily into her neck. When he regained part of his strength, Elliott lifted his head and pulled a pillow underneath both of their heads. The two of them shared the same pillow as they nuzzled their noses together.

"How do you feel?" Elliott's voice was tender as he spoke to her.

Imagany's laugh was in her throat. "Exhausted, baby."

"Good. Maybe now you'll let me get some rest."

Imagany tightened her grip around Elliott's neck. "That doesn't mean I'm about to let go of you though."

"I don't want you to let me go. Just hold me as tight as you want." Elliott felt her nestle closer to him and the two of them fell asleep curled up to one another.

Some hours later, Elliott felt Imagany tug her arms from around his neck and it aroused him from his sleep. He opened his eyes to find her sitting on the edge of the bed. Propping his head on his hand, he admired her backside. He was staring at her curves when he noticed the first of the marks on her lower back. Unsure of what he was seeing, Elliott reached over and turned on the bedside lamp.

When he turned on the lamp, Imagany realized he was awake and she turned around toward him. "Hi, sleepyhead."

Elliott pulled her on top of him and kissed her. He flipped Imagany onto her back and sat up on his knees. Because she thought he was about to tickle her, she laughed and rolled away from him onto her stomach. With much more light available, Elliott stared in astonished horror at the bruises and marks on her hips, thighs and legs.

Imagany's face was pressed into the bed. When Elliott didn't move to touch her, she noted his silence and turned around to look at him curiously. She saw the expression on his face and a sinking feeling gathered in the pit of her stomach. Knowing that there was nothing she could do about it now, Imagany sat up and curled her legs underneath her.

Elliott quietly got off the bed to switch on the overhead light. He walked back to the bed and sat down with a serious expression on his face.

One look at his face and Imagany knew what he was about to ask her. She decided to beat him to the punch. "It's okay, Boo."

Staring at the bruises which were apparent even on her upper thighs, he asked her, "What happened?"

Still sitting on her knees, Imagany threw her neck back and stared up at the ceiling. Tears softly rolled from the corners of her eyes. Elliott was quiet as he waited for her to answer him. Imagany lowered her head to gaze at him and said, "Please, Elliott. I'm not ready to talk about it yet."

Elliott could respect her desire not to want to talk about whatever had happened. But still, he needed to know something for his own peace of mind. He stood up and reached for Imagany's hand. She extended her own to him and felt him pull her toward the edge of the bed.

"Come here." Elliott spoke in a no-nonsense tone.

Imagany sighed. She knew he only wanted to examine the marks on her body. She knew, too, that his curiosity would not be satisfied until he saw the marks fully, and so even though she dreaded it, Imagany got off the bed and stood in front of him to get it over with.

For the first time, Elliott noticed the bruises on her face. He stared at all the marks on her body. When he finished looking her over, Elliott sat Imagany on top of his knees and wrapped one of her arms around his neck. He was full of questions. There were so many thoughts running through his brain. He sensed from her quietness that she still was not ready to talk about it yet. But he had to know how and why.

Imagany pressed her face into his chest. She knew he wanted answers, but unfortunately she couldn't give them. She didn't feel like lying to Elliott anymore, nor did she want to go into a full-fledged description of what had happened and who had done it to her.

"Imagany, I can tell these marks were made from a belt. Whoever put them there used a great deal of force in order for the bruises to turn so dark. Just tell me what happened, baby. Don't shut me out. Talk to me, please."

Imagany raised her head and stared Elliott in the eyes. Her guards were down, causing her to feel even more defenseless. She debated with herself whether or not to come clean with him. She shook her head and suddenly the phrase "you can run but you can't hide" ran through her mind. She felt vulnerable but found herself saying, "Elliott, it's a long story. It's not a pretty one, nor is it one that I'm proud of telling. In the back of my mind I have the feeling that if I tell you what you want to know, you'll think less of me, and I couldn't bear that."

Elliott knew Imagany was trying to tell him something she wasn't sure how he would take. "Imagany, baby, you don't have to worry about me passing judgment on you. Who am I? I'm nobody's judge or executioner. We've all done things we're not proud of. But you must separate those things from who you really are and know that if you wouldn't do them again, they don't matter. It's not about what you did in the past, it's not even about what you did yesterday. It's the present that counts most. Yesterday is gone and cannot be changed." He wanted her to know she could trust him. He pushed her off his knees and pulled her down onto the bed with him. When they were comfortable, he said encouragingly, "Go ahead, trust me, baby. You can talk to me." They laid against each other and as Imagany nestled closer to him, she sighed and began to tell her story.

"The first time I came to Nashville, I came to visit the campus at Fisk University. Fisk was paying for me to come so I had nothing to lose. I flew down by myself for the weekend and toured the campus and liked what I saw. I knew that because of its strong black heritage, Fisk was the school for me. Anyway, that same weekend I made up my mind to come here. After I'd toured the campus, I got myself a map and took a look around the city. I went to the art museum to see what they had on display and noticed they were holding some type of fundraiser. I circulated throughout the place and was standing in front of a Van Gogh painting when a man came up and stood beside me. We admired it and started discussing what we liked and didn't like about it. Pretty soon we were walking around looking at all the pictures, discussing each one. He was such a distinguished looking man that I felt important just walking along beside him. I could tell by the way he was dressed and from the way he carried himself that he was someone accustomed to wealth. It seemed as though every other painting we came to someone would come up to him to shake his hand and greet him. I knew then that he was someone of influence."

"I remember being dressed in a cream skirt suit. But still, I felt out of place standing next to him. He was so much older than I was and so much more mature! I guess with the way people kept coming up to him, I felt like I was keeping him from something. So when the next person walked up to him, I thanked him for the conversation and was about to leave when he held my arm and detained me. When the person left, he apologized for not introducing himself and told me his name was Anthony Barrington of Barrington Industries. It didn't mean anything to me so I just gave him my name and shook his hand. He asked me if I was from Nashville and I said no and told him why I was there. After that, he invited me out to dinner and because he seemed like such a gentleman, I accepted. We had dinner that night and I explained to him that I was only a senior in high school and that I wouldn't be starting college until several months later. We had a nice time that night and because I was leaving the next day, I told him I couldn't stay long. He gave me his private telephone number and told me to be sure to look him up when I started college in the fall."

Imagany unwrapped herself from Elliott and sat up to tell the rest of her story. "When I came to Fisk in the fall, sure enough, I looked him up and he remembered me. He invited me out to dinner again and from that time on, he continued to wine and dine me. While other students were eating dinner in the school cafeteria, I was dining in the most luxurious restaurants that Nashville has to offer. A couple of weeks after the school term had started, I was sleeping with him and after that I began to spend a lot of time at his home out in Antioch."

"By that time, Caprice had come down to enroll in Meharry Medical College. She wanted to know why I never seemed to have much time to spend with her. I told her I was dating someone but left out the fact that he was so much older than I was. She kept wanting to know who the mystery person was because she claimed that I was being secretive about the entire affair. Maybe I was. Anyway, he started buying me lavish gifts and they were expensive things, too. If I saw something I wanted, it was mine for the asking. His thing was clothes. He loved buying them for me. He would buy me something new to wear and then take me out as if to show me off to all of his friends. I didn't mind being his show piece because I enjoyed all the attention."

"But I began to get spoiled, Elliott. By the end of the first year I had asked him to buy me a car and when my birthday came, he picked me up from my dorm room in a shiny red convertible BMW. I knew it wasn't his car because he drove a Rolls Royce. I got inside the car and he kept asking me whether I liked the car. I thought the car was beautiful. It was brand new, how could I not like it? He took me to see a play that evening and when we went to his house he told me that he had bought the car for me and that it was mine. Well, the next morning I couldn't wait to show Caprice, so I hightailed it to her dorm to take her for a spin." Imagany laughed at her remembrances.

"Well, you know Caprice. Her initial reaction, of course, was wariness. She wanted to meet the person who could afford to buy me all of the nice things that she was suddenly seeing me with. The car was the last straw. Can you believe she refused to ride in it until I introduced her to Anthony? Elliott, I dreaded introducing the two of them! It was okay for me to meet all of his friends, but I was too self-conscious to want any of my friends to meet him. It wasn't that I cared about what anyone else thought, it was Caprice's opinion and approval that I wanted. Anyway, I let the two of them meet and it was a disaster from the very start. They didn't like each other and neither one of them made any attempt to hide their dislike. I knew I could never let them interact with each other again."

"When Anthony told me I could have my own apartment, I was ecstatic and simply knew that I would just have to keep them from bumping heads with each other." Imagany paused to look at Elliott who now had his hands behind his head as he listened to her story. The expression on his face was unreadable.

"Well, to make a long story short, he gave me money to furnish this apartment and all that you see in here is my choice or creation. I never dated any of the guys on campus because Anthony monopolized so much of my time. He was jealous, too, so I had to be very careful not to give him anything to be jealous about." Imagany laughed bitterly. "I quickly became used to this lifestyle. But once the excitement faded, I began to feel empty inside. Like I was nothing more than a mindless possession. It wasn't that I was seeing someone else, I just needed to have some space and time for myself to think and re-evaluate how my life was going."

"Not too long ago, he started pressuring me to marry him. The first time he asked me, I thought he was joking. I guess I took it for granted that he felt like I did. That what we had was nice, but that come graduation I would be like, 'see ya!' Turned out that I was wrong because he really did want something more. He wanted something that I didn't have within me to give him. When he told me that he loved me, I panicked. It was all becoming too much. Sure, I liked him. I was even grateful for everything he had done for me. But I started feeling pressured and confused. Not long after that, I wanted out of the relationship. Whenever he bought me something new, I began to see it for what it really was. A means to further entrap me. I began to see how my own greed had blinded and locked me into something that I didn't know how to get out of." Imagany covered her face with her hands. She took a deep breath and began to speak again.

"About a week after I met you at Meharry for the first time, a woman came to pay me a visit. She told me her name was Leslie Lowe and that she, too, was dating Anthony. She said she had known him since childhood. Apparently Anthony told her he wanted to marry me and she must have freaked out. She told me how for years she had been after him to marry her and now all of a sudden here I was just out of the blue about to be married to her man. Elliott, I thought to myself that God must have heard my prayers. I told her up front that I didn't have the slightest intention of marrying Anthony and that for all I cared, she could have him. That, in fact, by taking him off my hands, she would be doing me a favor. I didn't see him for a couple of weeks after that. I guess he was away on business. But it was fine with me because I was avoiding him anyway. I was trying to find a way out of the relationship and didn't quite know how I was going to do it."

"By this time, I had met you for the second time in TSU's gym and I debated whether or not to get involved with you. That first night in the car when you touched my chin, I knew I was going to see you again. It was just a matter of time. Suddenly, things began to happen too fast for me. I knew I wanted to be with you because I was beginning to fall in love so I knew I had to tell Anthony it was over. Maybe he knew I was seeing someone else because he could tell I didn't want to see him anymore. I just couldn't find it within me to sleep with him again. After you and I got together, as far as I was concerned, Anthony was a figment of my imagination." Imagany craned her head back and closed her eyes. She shook her head and told the final part of the story.

"Last Saturday you were away playing in the game. Someone rang my bell and when I answered the door it was Anthony. I panicked because I wasn't ready to see him yet. I couldn't ignore the door because he had already heard my voice and he knew I was home. I buzzed him up and when I let him in, he had an attitude. Leslie told him what I had said to her and he was convinced that I was seeing someone else. He confronted me with it and when I didn't deny it, we said some angry words to each other. He told me that after all he had done for me, I should be thanking my lucky stars. I told him that everything he had done for me didn't matter anymore because I had made it up in my mind that the entire affair was over. Somehow, we started arguing and before I knew it we were actually fighting. He was enraged, Elliott. I never saw him like that before and I was frightened. I fought back as hard as I could but he's a man who's much stronger than I am. He slapped me around some and when I fell, I hit my head against the sofa. I was dazed. And while I was laying there, he took off his belt and started beating me. I must have blacked out because when I woke up he was gone." Imagany chose not to tell Elliott about her stabbing Anthony. Somehow, she didn't think he was ready for that.

"For the next week I didn't go outside because the bruises were so bad. The swelling was so hideous that I couldn't bear to have anyone see me. Not even Caprice and especially not you. I wasn't answering the phone and Caprice got worried about me so she came over and I had to let her in. She was horrified when I told her what had happened. I told her that the only thing I wanted to do was forget the whole incident and go on with my life. I wanted to take the entire experience, put it in my pocket and just move on. In a way, I guess I feel like I deserved what happened to me, as if I just paid my dues for forgetting where I came from. But since my face was so messed up, I wondered how I could avoid seeing you. Though Caprice didn't want any part of it, I made her call you and tell you that I had to go away. It was the only thing I could think of that would keep you away until my swelling went down. By the time Saturday rolled around, I was so lonely because I missed not talking to you and seeing you. I couldn't take it anymore, I had to call you. And so I lied. I just told one big lie right after another. I'm sorry now, but I felt I was doing the best thing at the time. If I had to do it all over again, Elliott, I can't even honestly tell you that I wouldn't do it the same way. So today I went and found another apartment and started packing because I've decided to move. I don't even want to be here anymore. Too many bad memories. I'm ready to start afresh. And there you have it, Boo. That's my story." Despite her attempts to display a nonchalant demeanor, tears trickled down Imagany's face and she could not bring herself to look at Elliott.

Elliott took a deep breath before expelling it. At a loss for words, he could only shake his head. "Right now, I'm just really angry. I feel like I could go find this Anthony Barrington and just beat the living shit out of him. This guy sounds like a real asshole. I don't know what more to say." With feelings of anger and jealousy inside him, Elliott tried to imagine how he would feel if he were cake-daddy to some woman who started fooling around on him. No matter how much he loved a woman, he could never see himself hitting her. He would much rather release the person to her own devices and say adios! Elliott pulled Imagany closer to him and hugged her to give her comfort.

She welcomed the touch of his body against hers. She needed his approval right now and she relaxed inside the gentle strength of his arms. They held each other, neither of them wanting to speak, each lost in their own thoughts.

Finally, Elliott asked her, "What are you thinking about?"

"How relieved I feel now that I've told you the truth. I feel like I've just had a heavy burden lifted from my shoulders."

Elliott took a moment to consider what she had just said. "Remember last night when I told you about how I missed you?" He felt her head nod against his chest. "You thanked me for sharing what I had said. At the time I didn't feel like I had shared anything of significance. I simply spoke what was on my mind. Anyway, I feel that I should be thanking you now for sharing what you just did. It took a lot of courage to tell me what really happened. I understand why you didn't want to see me and I don't blame you at all. I'm glad that you've decided to move, too. I couldn't let you be here alone. I think it's best to just start over. I think also that you're being too hard on yourself. You didn't do anything wrong by being impressed with the things this man's money could buy you. Any person would probably have done exactly what you did. I don't think I know anybody who could say no to a man or woman who's offering them a brand new BMW. You did what you had to do. But it's over now so you can forget him. Besides, you've got me to help you put the past behind you." Elliott's hands caressed her back as he spoke. He sighed and shook his head.

"Remember when you found out about all the women I had dated? You were angry with me, but you didn't judge me. That's how I feel right now. I love you, Imagany. And my love for you is not based on your actions. What happened doesn't change that. You wanna know something? I called my dad to ask him how he knew my mom was the one for him. He said it wasn't even something he knew how to explain. He said he had a feeling in his spirit. He just knew it. That's how I feel about you, Imagany. I can't explain it. I just know it. Forget about this Anthony character, baby. He's history."

Imagany felt a deepening sense of gratitude toward Elliott. She found it hard to believe that she had just bared her soul to him as she had. She found it even harder to believe that he hadn't passed judgment on her with all that she had told him. She was the lucky one in this relationship. Lucky to be here and lucky to have him. That Elliott truly loved her unconditionally would take some time to get used to.

They got up together to fix something to eat. Imagany reheated the food that she had gotten from Mama Leone's. It tasted just as good as it had the day before. They ate in the kitchen since it was the only place in the apartment other than the bedroom that did not look barren. While they ate, Imagany told Elliott about the new apartment she had found. She described how big it was and told him that it was her intention to be out of her present apartment no later than Friday.

Elliott could tell by her enthusiasm and excitement how much she was looking forward to the move. He took it for granted that she would need his help and was surprised when she told him that she was going to have a moving company do everything for her. When they finished eating and washing the dishes, they went back into the bedroom.

"Imagany, the Alphas are giving a party tonight at the Que Club for the football players. Would you like to go?"

"Sure. I don't mind. Besides, I can't even remember the last time I went to a party." Suddenly a thought occurred to her. "Wait a minute, hold up. Are you trying to tell me that Elliott Renfroe knows how to dance?"

At the laughter in her voice, Elliott twisted around to stare at her. "Are you kidding, woman? You think I do my only dancing on the football field? I consider that a challenge. Woman, you haven't seen anybody dance until you've seen me on the floor."

Imagany laughed at his bragging. "I accept the challenge. We'll see tonight who can dance and who can't."

"Since it's an Alpha party, Carl will have to be there, which means that Caprice will probably be there, too."

"Oh, good! What time is it going to be?"

"It starts at ten, but we'll get there around eleven."

"Let me call Caprice to see if she's going to be there." Imagany dialed Caprice's number and her roommate, Myra, answered the phone. Imagany was shocked when she recognized Myra's voice. "Myra? Get the hell out of here! Girl, what are you doing there?" Dismay was apparent in Imagany's voice. Myra was hardly ever in the room on a weekend night. Something had to be going on.

"Um, excuse me, darling, I beg your pardon. But I do live here. Need I remind you?" Myra jokingly shot Imagany down with her sharp words.

Imagany was not having it. "No, sweetheart. Allow me to make the minor correction. Your name may appear on the mail slot, girlfriend, but you don't live there. Let's get that fact straight. You may sleep there periodically, such as every blue moon, but we all know yo' black butt don't live there. So don't even try to get me to start lying on this phone, Myra. Now that I've set you straight and put you in your place, is my partner there?" Myra was laughing on the other end of the line.

Elliott shook his head as he listened to her on the phone with her girlfriends. He simply thought they all were crazy.

Caprice came to the phone and Imagany asked, "Whaz up, girlfriend?"

When Elliott realized she was talking to Caprice, he motioned for Imagany to give him the phone. Imagany slapped his hand away.

Caprice said, "Nothing much, sweetie. It's your world and I'm just living in it. How you be?" Caprice had to have been in a good mood to be talking like she was.

"Hangin', my sistah. Just hangin'. What can I tell ya? Listen, I've got someone here who's about to lose his beeswax if I don't hand him the phone. The man must be dying to talk to you. Hold on." Imagany finally passed the phone to Elliott.

Elliott took the phone and said, "Am I speaking to Mrs. Carl Beasley?"

These words were sweet music to Caprice's ears. When she yelled loudly into the phone, even Imagany could hear her. "Speaking! This is she! How may I be of service to you?" Caprice was glad Elliott was there with Imagany.

"Yeah. I'm about to tell you. I want to know why you lied and told me my woman was in Chicago when she was right here all the time. I thought you and me were tight, Reese. I thought you had my back. But I see now you were pulling my leg all the while. I'm going to have to start calling you the Chi-town shyster." While Elliott was trying to make Caprice feel guilty, Imagany was trying to grab the phone from him to explain to Caprice, but Elliott used his arm to hold her away from him.

When Caprice realized he was only teasing her, she started laughing. "Hey, blood. What can I tell you? We sisters have to stick together like you brothers do. Is there a problem?"

"No, there's no problem. I'm just going to have to tell 'the man' how you played both *him and me* so he can straighten you out."

Suddenly, Caprice was apologetic. "Elliott, you had better not tell Carl what I did! How can I redeem myself?"

Elliott laughed when Caprice started begging. "Hmmmm. Let me think about it. Since I can't come up with anything right now, you're going to have to be in my dog house until I can come up with something. In the mean time, just hang loose. I'll get back with you soon enough." Elliott smiled as he handed Imagany the phone.

Imagany took the phone and said to Caprice, "Girl, these men are too much, aren't they? What is a woman to do?"

"Hell, yeah, girl. When he first started talking, my mouth hit the floor. You told him the truth?"

"Yep." Imagany wasn't going to go into further detail than that. Not with Elliott sitting right in front of her, staring at her.

"The whole truth?" Caprice was pleasantly surprised.

"Sure did, girlfriend."

"How did he take it?"

"You know, I haven't seen Ambi in a long time! How is she?"

Caprice took the hint and started laughing. "Girl, I'm sorry, I don't even know what I was thinking about. He's probably sitting right there staring you dead in the mouth. Am I right or what?" Imagany's laughter confirmed Caprice's statement.

Imagany said, "Elliott tells me that the Alphas up at Tennessee State are throwing a party at the Que Club tonight. Are you going?"

"Oh, yeah. I'll be there. I didn't ask you to go because I didn't think you were ready to go out yet. But I guess I was wrong about that, too. Tell me what some good lovin' won't do for a woman! Revamp a woman's entire constitution! All I know is just this morning, the girl told me she wasn't leaving her house for at least a month. Now all a sudden, since her man has paid her a visit, not only is she talking about leaving the house, the girl is planning on painting the town red! I'm talkin' 'bout a strong black man!"

Caprice had Imagany laughing. She knew, too, that Imagany couldn't come back on her with Elliott sitting right there beside her.

Imagany said, "Reese, girl, stop it. Stop being bad."

"Hey, can I help it if the man put a whammie on you? Be grateful, my sister. I've even got ol' Myra laughing over here. And we all know her black behind is never here. Why do you think we nicknamed her 'Casper-the-friendly-ghost?' Maybe I should go touch her to make sure she's real and not a figment of my imagination." Caprice was on a roll.

Through her laughter, Imagany said, "Reese, hold up. What's got you going? Are you sure you're not the one with a story to tell?" Imagany wondered what had Caprice on the war path. It seemed to her that Caprice was the one who had just gotten ahold of some really good lovin'.

Caprice was just happy to be going out for a change. "What can I tell you? So you'll really be there tonight?"

"You bet. Mr. Renfroe here claims he can dance. I want to be there to witness it." Imagany raised her foot to trail her toes along Elliott's back.

"What time are you two getting there? Maybe we can meet up."

"Elliott says about eleven o'clock. So I guess we'll leave a little before then." Imagany's line beeped to let her know someone else was calling her. "Hold on a minute, Reese. Let me see who this is." Imagany clicked over and Carl was on the other end. "Hi, Carl. How are you?"

"Hey, Imagany. Is Elliott there?"

"Yeah, but you two can't talk long because I've got Reese on the other end. Hold on." She passed the phone to Elliott and he and Carl talked, making arrangements about who was going to ride with whom and what time they all were going to get there. Elliott handed the phone back to Imagany.

Elliott said, "Carl wants Caprice to ride with us because he's got to be there early. He's going to pick her up and drop her off here so that the three of us can leave together."

Imagany relayed what Elliott had just told her to Caprice. "Good," Caprice said. "I can return the clothes of yours that I have and borrow something else at the same time. Did he say what time he was coming?"

"I'm not sure. Want me to ask Elliott?"

"No. That's okay, let me just get off the phone. He may be trying to call me. I'll see you in a little bit."

When they hung up the phone, Imagany said, "It's nine o'clock, Boo. Shouldn't you be leaving to go get dressed?"

Elliott was engrossed in some news program that was on TV. "No, baby. I'm going to wait until Caprice gets here, then I'll leave." Elliott just didn't want to leave Imagany in her apartment by herself.

The reason for his wanting to stay never occurred to Imagany. She rose from the bed to plug in her hot curlers to start curling her hair. She decided to put some waves in her hair so instead she used her crimping comb. She was just about finished with her hair when the door bell rang.

Elliott sprang up from the bed. "I'll get it."

Imagany looked up in surprise at Elliott. When he left the room, Imagany suddenly realized that he was feeling protective of her.

Elliott opened the door for Caprice. The two of them hugged each other before Elliott came back into the bedroom. "I'm going to go back to the room now to get dressed. I'll see you two around ten-thirty. Don't keep me waiting, ladies."

Caprice locked the front door behind Elliott and returned to the bedroom. She plugged in Imagany's curlers and started curling her own hair. "So tell me, how did he take it?"

Imagany knew what Caprice was talking about. "Girlfriend, that man is all right. I opened myself up to him like I've never done with anyone else and I must say he took it okay."

"Isn't it nice to have someone you can tell your feelings to without that person misjudging you or holding it against you?"

"It certainly is, Caprice. I feel truly blessed."

They picked out the clothes they wanted to wear and started getting dressed. Caprice wanted to wear a classy lavender pantsuit while Imagany chose a black velvet mini dress. The dress was off the shoulders leaving her shoulders bare. It clung to her chest, accentuated the narrowness of her waist and molded her curvaceous hips.

Imagany admired her hour-glass figure in the mirror. "Hey. If I must admit it myself, my sister, I do have it going on!"

"Damn, Imagany. What are you trying to do? You planning on stealing the show or what? Elliott is going to flip for sure when he sees you. I'll bet you the brother is gonna be like 'you're not going out in that dress!' But hey, if you got it, I say flaunt it."

They put on their makeup and Imagany decided she would wear only enough to hide the marks on her face. She wore a pair of gold hoop earrings and pinned a pendant to her dress. Choosing to wear no necklace, she wore a single bracelet on each wrist and was set to go.

The two of them stood back and admired themselves, knowing that they both looked dynamite. Minutes later Elliott arrived and Caprice buzzed him up. He came through the door dressed in a navy blue suit and tie. Imagany heard Caprice exclaiming about how good Elliott looked, and she came out of the bedroom to see for herself. She stood staring at him with her hands on her hips because even God knew the man looked good enough to eat.

Elliott stared back at Imagany with his own mouth open. He cleared his throat loudly and said to Caprice who was standing by with a knowing grin on her face, "Excuse us for a second, Reese. I need to speak with someone whom I think just lost her mind."

"Sure." Caprice glanced at her watch. "Just make it quick because I've got a party to go to and a man to meet. So don't hold up the program, folks."

Elliott walked over to Imagany and turned her around, pushing her along in front of him into the bedroom, and closing the door behind him. Imagany figured Elliott was probably going to read her the riot act about her dress. She thought to herself, aren't men too much? If Elliott saw another woman with the same dress on, he would probably break his neck trying to talk to her. But let his own woman wear it and he was having no part of it. Imagany was further surprised when Elliott simply buried his head between her breasts.

Elliott was unable to restrain himself. He breathed her smell in deeply. "You really look good in this dress, Imagany."

"What? You mean you didn't bring me in here to tell me to take it off?"

"Of course not, baby. I just know that I'm not going to be able to leave your side tonight. There are going to be too many men there who will be salivating when they see you. Come on, let's not keep Caprice waiting."

Imagany shook her head. "Elliott Renfroe, you are too much for me."

"I fooled you, didn't I?"

"Yes, baby, you certainly did." They joined hands as Elliott led her out of the bedroom.

Chapter Eighteen

or Imagany and Elliott, the ensuing months were filled with love and shared joy. They came to better understand one another and their relationship grew. In their spare time, they went to movies, parties, plays and concerts. Imagany was even able to influence Elliott with her love of art. Their physical attraction for one another also deepened as they learned what pleased each other, and what angered or brought them down.

They made love in every part of Imagany's new apartment. There was no space too small for the two of them to become creative. And become creative, they did. They came up with new ideas and techniques for their lovemaking as if they were trying to reinvent the wheel. They could be anywhere inside the apartment when the mood hit them. In the kitchen, in the bathroom, in the living room, in the bedroom or in the closet. No area inside the apartment was off limits from their frolicking.

As the seasons changed, midterms rolled around and so did finals. When the two of them entered their senior year of college, Elliott was faced with a major decision. He had several teams in the NFL wanting to draft him prior to graduation. Imagany knew the kind of money the teams were offering him, but somehow she felt his education should come first. Her contention was that so many players left school before they graduated and once inside the league, they never went back to finish. She wanted Elliott to finish for himself as well as his family. She reasoned with him that by the time he graduated, the teams would be offering him even more money. She wanted to be able to tell their children that their father had a degree and that he was not just another athlete who never finished college.

Elliott's biggest fear was that if he stayed another year, he might get injured and lose his opportunity to play in the NFL. Imagany suggested that the two of them pay his parents a visit to discuss it further.

While Elliott's father was of the same opinion as Elliott, Mrs. Renfroe felt the same way Imagany did. She and Imagany had developed quite a bond and they shared the same opinion now. She, too, wanted to see Elliott graduate from college. After all, how many pro football players could boast of having a degree in Electrical Engineering? Not many. This was the deciding factor which won Elliott over. He and Imagany returned to Nashville on Sunday evening and on Monday, Elliott told his coaches of his decision. The entire team was ecstatic. With Elliott on board for another year, they were guaranteed another spot at the top of their conference.

In the middle of their senior year, Carl proposed to Caprice. Caprice readily accepted. After graduation, they decided to get married in New York and go back to Chicago to live. Caprice would do her internship at the University of Chicago's Hospital while Carl would apply for a position with McDonnell Douglas. Imagany was as excited for Caprice as Caprice was for herself. Imagany would be the maid of honor and Elliott the groom's best man. Not long after that, Imagany received another surprise. Zabree started calling her on a regular basis. She still did not have a number where Imagany could reach her, but she never let on to Imagany that her problems were as severe as they were. For Zabree's problems were many . . . .

***

The months until graduation were approaching so fast that it frightened Imagany. As the time drew nearer, she found herself plagued with depression. Whenever Elliott was around her, she tried as best as she could to lift her spirits, if only for his sake. Imagany knew that her depression stemmed from the thought of having to participate in the graduation ceremony.

One evening, the two of them were sitting at the dinner table when Imagany said, "Elliott, I've been considering just picking up my diploma and skipping the graduation ceremony."

Elliott looked up, surprised. "Why, baby?"

"Because I think the ceremony is an occasion to be shared with family members, that's why. And since none of mine are coming . . ." Imagany shrugged her shoulders. "Besides, the whole affair is no big deal anyway. It'll all be over in less than two hours."

Elliott put down his knife and fork. "Imagany, that's not the point. You've spent four years at Fisk. Four hard years. That in itself is worth celebrating. You've worked damned hard for your degree and you should be telling yourself that the ceremony is something you deserve. And even if it is something for families to share, how do you know your people won't come? Have you asked them?" Elliott knew she had problems within her family but he could never get her to talk about them. Whenever he did try, she would get defensive.

"Elliott, even if I did ask them, I'm not sure they'd come. As much as I hate to admit it, I'm afraid to ask them. It's been so long since I've spoken to them, what would I even say? 'Hi, it's me! How about coming to my graduation?' Knowing my father, he would probably laugh and slam the phone down. No thanks, Elliott. I guess it's just you and me, kid."

"Is that why you've been moping around like someone who's lost her best friend?"

Imagany laughed self-consciously. "I have not."

"If you say so. But consider this: even if your parents don't come, I want to see you walk across that stage. You'll be there for my graduation and I'm going to be there for yours. Does that make you feel better?" When she nodded, he said, "Now can I at least finish the rest of my food?" Elliott spread his hands. "Are you sure there's no other earth shattering crisis for me to solve?"

Though she made light of it, it bothered Imagany that she wouldn't have any family present at her graduation. She would just have to be satisfied with having Elliott there.

The graduation ceremonies for Imagany and Caprice were two days apart. Fisk was holding theirs on a Tuesday and Meharry's was the following Thursday. Elliott, Caprice and Carl attended Imagany's graduation and the trio also went to Caprice's. Caprice's family flew down from Chicago to attend her ceremony. Her parents had met Carl previously and had already given them their blessings to be married.

TSU's graduation turned out to be the one not to miss. Oprah Winfrey and Les Brown were the guest speakers and the two of them had the crowd fired up. Afterwards, both families got together and they all went out to eat.

The following weekend was the NFL draft. Imagany and Mr. and Mrs. Renfroe all flew to New York to be there with Elliott. Since Carl was already in New York with his family, he came, too. The four of them quaked with excitement as Elliott was drafted third by none other than the Chicago Bears. Imagany screamed so loud that Mrs. Renfroe thought her eardrums would burst.

The weeks after graduation were spent by each of them settling last minute details before they departed from Nashville. While Elliott, Carl and Caprice had only their clothes and small personal items, Imagany was not so fortunate. She had to arrange for all of her things to be put in storage. While she settled things for herself in Nashville, she had Caprice scout out an apartment for her in Chicago's Hyde Park area.

Since Carl was not arriving in Chicago until later in the month, Caprice invited Imagany to stay with her and her family until she could move into her own apartment.

The McKnight family lived in the Pill Hill section on Chicago's south side. By the time she parked her car and rang the doorbell, Caprice's parents had already left for church. Caprice answered the door and the two of them hugged each other frantically. Imagany dragged herself inside and flopped down on the living room sofa.

"Boy, am I tired," Imagany said with a sigh.

"You should be. You've been driving all night." Caprice sat on the couch next to Imagany. "Guess who called this morning?"

Imagany looked at the excited smile on Caprice's face and said knowingly, "Carl."

Caprice shook her head. "Uh, uh. I meant Mr. Renfroe."

"Elliott called? When?" Imagany had a sudden burst of new found energy.

"He called around eight-thirty this morning. I told him that you hadn't made it into town yet so he left the number to the hotel where he's staying."

"I haven't spoken to Elliott in about a week. But I need to take a shower first and then I'll call him. I'm starving, too."

"I knew you'd be hungry so I saved you something to eat. I'll warm it for you while you're in the shower."

"Thanks, kid."

When Imagany got out of the shower, she tried reaching Elliott but he was not in his room. As she hung up, Caprice walked in with a tray of breakfast food. While Imagany ate, they rehashed graduation tidbits and talked about the upcoming wedding. Caprice also spoke eagerly about her internship at the University of Chicago's Hospital. When she tried to get Imagany to tell her about the job that she would be interviewing for, she saw that Imagany had fallen fast asleep. With a smile on her face, Caprice got up from the bed and turned off the light. She left the room wondering if Imagany had even told her parents she was back in town.

Hours later, Imagany awoke feeling relaxed and refreshed. She went downstairs and found Caprice's parents sitting in the living room. They were making preparations for the wedding. They glanced up and saw Imagany watching them with a smile on her face and they jumped up to hug her.

Caprice was in the kitchen preparing dinner when she heard all the exclamations. She poked her head around the corner and saw Imagany sitting on the floor, holding court. She shook her head as she went back into the kitchen. Imagany always had been able to wrap her parents around her fingers. There were times when Imagany had gotten her out of all kinds of scrapes and jams. It was as if Imagany was the second child that her parents had never been able to conceive. Caprice remembered once asking her mother when she was about seven or eight years old what the word "incest" meant. She would never forget how wide her mother's eyes had gotten. Her mother had never explained to her what the word meant but instead had grilled her about where she had learned it. Innocently, Caprice had told her that Imagany used the word often and that she simply wanted to know what it meant. It had sounded like such a grown-up word, Caprice wanted to be able to use it, too. Her mother had warned her never to use the word because it was not a nice one and thereafter, Mrs. McKnight began to watch Imagany closely. Maybe that was when the closeness between Imagany and Mrs. McKnight developed. Caprice believed that her mother probably knew more about that aspect of Imagany's life than she did herself. It was certainly something that Caprice and Mrs. McKnight rarely discussed.

Caprice had prepared meatloaf, corn bread, string beans and mashed potatoes. When everything was done, she set the table and went into the living room with everyone else to lie on the floor. She rested her head on Imagany's outstretched legs and with a smile on her face, listened to her spin her tales.

After dinner, Imagany decided to go back up to the bedroom and was climbing the stairs when Mrs. McKnight called to tell her the phone was for her.

Knowing it could only be Elliott, Imagany rushed inside the bedroom and snatched up the phone.

"Hello?" Imagany spoke breathlessly into the receiver and heard someone replace the other end downstairs.

"This is the IRS trying to locate Imagany Jenkins. May I speak with her please?"

"Elliott!" Her heart melted at the sound of his voice.

"Hi, baby. It's been a long time, hasn't it?"

"It's been too long, Boo. How are you?"

"Oh, baby. It's been a madhouse on this end. I thought I had a lot of paperwork when I was in school, but that was nothing compared to this. There were so many papers to be signed that I had to hire lawyers just to help me sort through the legalese. My dad's been a big help, too. Since he's a lawyer, he knew the right sports lawyers to hook me up with. You know, now I see why lots of players get ripped off all the time. You've got to have someone by your side whom you can trust. But don't let me go off on a tangent. How are you feeling? Did you settle everything in Nashville?"

"Yeah, pretty much so. I miss you, Boo."

"I know, baby. I miss you, too. That's why I've been calling. Oh, and because of one other reason, too. I've been advised by my lawyers that for tax purposes, I need to buy some property. So I wanted you to come with me to pick out a house for us. How does that sound?"

"Us? Did I hear you right, Elliott Renfroe? Did you just say 'us' as in me and you?"

"I sure did. Did I stutter when I spoke? If I'm going to live here in Chicago, it's only natural for you to be right beside me."

"Wow, Elliott. This is deep, man."

Elliott laughed at Imagany's choice of words. "So what do you say, kid? Will you live with me or what?"

Imagany said jokingly, "Hey, since I don't have anywhere else to live right now, it sounds like a good idea to me. Just make sure you don't have me living somewhere down in the Ickeys."

"What are the Ickeys?"

"Private joke, baby. Never mind. When can we go looking for a house?"

"Your job interview is tomorrow morning, right?" Elliott was thinking quickly.

"You got it."

"Okay. So why don't we go after that? The lawyer told me about a house in Sherwood Hills."

"Wewww! Sherwood Hills? That's where Michael Jordan lives! Now I'm really impressed."

"Hey, only the best for my baby and me. So I'll be waiting for you after the interview, okay?"

"You bet. I love you, Boo."

"I love you, too, baby. See you tomorrow."

They hung up and Imagany turned on her back to lie on the bed with her hands behind her head. She had the biggest grin on her face when Caprice walked into the bedroom.

"What's up? I heard you flew up the stairs when you got this important phone call. Elliott, right?"

Imagany nodded her head. "Reese, he asked me to go look for a house with him tomorrow."

Caprice, who had sat on the bed, jumped up and said, "Get the heck outta here! He proposed?"

Imagany laughed and sat up. "No, knuckle head. Calm down. We're just going to live together, that's all."

Caprice's disappointment was obvious. "But Imagany, don't you want to get married? I think I would have kicked Carl between the legs if he had asked me to live with him."

"And there's nothing wrong with feeling that way. Sure, I would love to marry Elliott. But not right now. He's just come into all this money and he needs time to settle himself. Time to be sure that I'm the person he wants. After awhile, we may very well get married. But now is not the right time for either of us. I want to discover what I can do as Ms. Imagany Jenkins, not Mrs. Elliott Renfroe."

"Imagany, that's crazy. What are you and Elliott going to be doing while you're living together that you won't be doing if the two of you got married? And besides, how can you risk the chance of some other woman coming in and erasing all the ground work which has taken you years to lay?" Caprice threw her hands up in the air. "I don't understand you, Imagany."

"Reese, some things you and I have never seen eye to eye on, and this is just one of them. If what Elliott and I have is strong enough, if it's meant to be, God will provide. I'm not saying that I don't want to marry Elliott, all I'm saying is that we should wait. If the man finds someone else in the interim while I'm living with him, then so be it. But I refuse to spend the rest of my life mapping out ways to get Elliott Renfroe to ask me to marry him. I love Elliott, but I've got my own life to live. One that does not revolve around him."

Imagany saw the look on Caprice's face and tried to explain further. "Look at it this way, Reese. Elliott is on the brink of major success. His star is about to rise. You and I have both seen him play so there can be no doubt about that. As he progresses, people and things will gravitate to him. Don't get me wrong, I want to be right there with him every step of the way. But I need him to know that I'm a separate entity from him. He must understand that I'm with him because I love him, not because I want whatever he can offer me. If I marry him now, I don't know that he will realize that. I want Elliott to know that Imagany Jenkins has something to bring to this relationship, too, and that I'm going to be a successful woman in my own right. I don't ever want him thinking that I got what I'm going to attain by following the tail end of his star. He's going to have to look at me and acknowledge that I'm someone who can stand on my own merit."

"How many times in my life have I heard men tell women, 'you ain't nothin'! You'd be nowhere without me!' As long as God sees fit to let me breathe upon this earth, not another soul will ever say those words to me. I'm not trying to imply that Elliott is like that, but I grew up hearing my father say it to my mother. And as hard as I fought to break the cycle, I went and chose a man like Anthony who said the same words to me, too. I can't allow that to happen again. The bottom line, Reese, is that I want Elliott to love me for me. Not because of anything that he's done for me."

Caprice listened intently and when Imagany finished, she said, "When I said what I did about kicking Carl, I only said that because I wouldn't want my folks to ever know I was living with a man. You're different, Imagany. I don't agree with you but I can understand how you feel. It's just that sometimes I need to stop and realize that it's okay for us to agree to disagree. If you're happy with it, then that's all that really matters." Caprice wanted to say more but she decided to drop the subject.

***

Imagany's interview with NBC for the position of Newsroom Assistant was being held downtown on Michigan Avenue. She interviewed with three people around a large conference table. They fired questions at her, one right after the other. Imagany was sure their intent was to see if she would lose her composure or become rattled and be thrown off guard. She did neither, answering their questions confidently, eloquently and articulately. When the interview was over, she was asked to wait outside while the three of them held a conference of their own. About a half an hour later they invited her back inside the room and told her the job was hers.

Imagany left the building filled with excitement. She walked the two blocks to her car and drove to the Marriott Hotel to meet Elliott. She turned her car over to the parking valet and went inside to the front desk. Imagany wore a dark blue two-piece suit. The skirt was short, showing off her legs to perfection, while the jacket was double-breasted and waist-length. Her only jewelry was the gold necklace around her neck along with her watch and bracelet. She had wet set her hair the night before and it hung to her shoulders in a wave of tiny curls. In her three inch pumps, she was aware of the admiring glances that were thrown her way as soon as she walked through the doors.

Imagany approached the desk and told the receptionist she was looking for Elliott Renfroe. As she was led to the table where Elliott was sitting, Imagany noted that the room was full of businessmen but few women. Nearly all of them glanced at her as she walked by. Three men sat at the table with Elliott. They glanced at her admiringly as Elliott stood up to peck her on the cheek. When Elliott introduced Imagany as his fiancé, she paid it no mind. She sat down and listened with rapt attention as the lawyers went over in detail the fine points of Elliott's football contract.

When the men departed, Elliott and Imagany dined alone. She sat back in her chair and studied Elliott with a smile on her face. Dressed in his Brooks Brothers suit and tie, he even looked like someone important.

Elliott reached across the table and took Imagany's hands in his. He raised them to his lips, kissed them and asked, "So how did the interview go?"

Imagany threw him a luminous smile and said, "I got the job."

"That's great! I'm proud of you, Imagany." Elliott thought the two of them made a fine team.

"Thanks, Boo. Oh, but forgive me! Do I still have your permission to call you 'Boo?' Or am I now required to join the ranks of your adoring fans?"

Elliott laughed at her as he released her hands. "I will always be Elliott 'Boo' Renfroe. That much will never change. And I thought you already were my adoring fan. Have you had a sudden change of heart?"

Imagany blew him a kiss from her side of the table and said, "Never."

"You know, we should have gone upstairs and called for room service. Whose idea was it to eat lunch in this stuffy place anyway?"

Imagany smiled at him. "I think it was your idea, sweetie."

"Hmmm." Elliott pulled at his chin. "Why don't we flag the waiter and just tell him to have our meal brought to our room?"

Elliott called the waiter over and told him what they wanted. He stood and pulled Imagany's chair out for her and led her upstairs.

Later in the day, they met with their real estate agent, who had several homes in Sherwood Hills that he wanted them to look at. He was humorous and made sure they were comfortable as they went from home to home. Imagany appreciated the simple fact that he was a brother who was out there doing it for himself. When they pulled into the driveway of the third home, Imagany knew it was the one for them. The house looked like something right out of Architectural Digest. If there was such a thing as a house with refined dignity, Imagany felt this house would be the one. Inside, the rooms were very spacious. As she eagerly explored each room, a wealth of ideas sprang to her mind about how she would decorate the place. She flew up the winding staircase and yelled down from the top, "This is it, Elliott!" Like an excited child, Imagany ran from room to room with her arms outstretched.

Elliott finally caught up with her inside one of the bedrooms and said to the real estate agent, "Excuse us for a second," before closing the bedroom door.

Imagany was staring out the window when Elliott walked up behind her and wrapped his arms around her. He kissed her lightly on the ear and said, "Right now, I feel like the luckiest man on earth. I feel as if

God has smiled on me by blessing me in so many ways. But most important of all, I'm grateful that He's given me you to share all of this with. Without you, Imagany, I don't know if any of this would mean the same to me." When Imagany twisted around in his arms to look at him, Elliott said, "It's just that I wouldn't have anyone other than my family to share it all with."

"Thanks for letting me be the one who you've chosen to share it with. I know you and I are going to be happy together, Elliott. I want us to be just the way your parents are with one another. And I want our children to be blessed the same way we are." Imagany kissed Elliott on the chin. "Do you like the house?"

"Sure, I like it, but it's rather intimidating."

"That's because there's no furniture in it. Wait until I fix this bad boy up. It's going to be so warm and homey that you won't be able to wait to get home from a hard day's work."

Elliott laughed. "I can hardly wait for that now. Shall we tell the agent that we'll take it?"

"You bet, baby."

Taking her hand, he led her out of the room to go in search of the real estate agent. They found him inside the kitchen making notes on a pad.

"So what have you two decided?"

"We've decided to take it."

"That's great. For both me and you." They laughed because they knew he was referring to his forthcoming commission. The house was costing Elliott three million dollars, so the agent's commission would be a good one.

Later that evening, Imagany took Elliott to Caprice's house and the five of them had dinner there. Imagany told them all about the house they had found and about her plans to fix it up. Mrs. McKnight got up to bring more coffee to the table and said, "So when are you two getting married?"

Elliott, who was sitting beside Imagany, took her hand in his and said, "That's what Imagany and I are trying to decide now. As soon as we set the date, everyone will know."

The moment passed as Imagany got Caprice to tell Elliott about her internship at the University of Chicago's Hospital. Hours later, Imagany packed some things to spend the night with Elliott at his hotel and the two of them left. He was flying back home the next evening to spend a couple of weeks with his family before returning to Chicago.

On their way back to the hotel, Elliott asked, "Did it bother you when Mrs. McKnight asked us if we were going to get married?"

"No, Boo, it didn't. All things happen in their own time and this is one of them. When the time is right for us to get married, we'll know it."

Somehow, this was not what Elliott had expected to hear from her. "Well, what's wrong with now?"

"I think we both need time to grow, that's all. We need time to decide if this is what we really want. It doesn't make sense to rush into something only to find out later that we've made the wrong decision."

Imagany was driving and Elliott turned to her. "Wait a minute. Are you saying that we still need to make up our minds about each other? I thought that had been settled long ago."

"Not necessarily about each other, but about the things we want out of life."

"I don't know that I'm following you, Imagany. Are you saying that you need time to find out whether there's someone out there that might be better for you than me and that I should be looking for someone better than you?"

"No, baby, I'm not saying that. Calm down. All I'm saying is that the two of us need to develop further before we make such a tough decision. Both of us are young and we've got our whole lives ahead of us. Let's just take things one day at a time. I'm sure that one day, you and I will be married. I can hardly wait for the time when folks will be calling me Mrs. Elliott Renfroe. But I'm not rushing you. When you put that ring on my finger, I want you to know in your heart of hearts that you've selected the right person. Capeesh?"

Personally, Elliott did not understand. But if that was the way she felt about it, then he would wait before asking her to marry him. He thought about the diamond ring that he had purchased from Cartier Jewelers earlier that morning. All day he had been waiting to ask her "the question," as he chose to call it. He had almost asked her while they were standing inside the bedroom at the house. But he couldn't get up the nerve. Elliott knew one thing. When he came back to Chicago in time for Carl and Caprice's wedding, Imagany had better be ready. By then he wouldn't want to hear any more of this talk about them both needing time to grow.

Chapter Nineteen

aprice's wedding was a week away and Imagany spent much time helping Mrs. McKnight with all the preparations.

She had been working at NBC for nearly two weeks. The work was tiring and demanding, but it was also fulfilling. She found everything involved in putting together a news piece exciting. Though her job and Caprice's wedding preparations took up a great deal of her time, she still missed Elliott sorely.

Imagany was driving to Caprice's house after work one day when she suddenly found herself driving in the direction of her parent's home. She was on Ninety-Fifth Street near Wabash before she was even aware of where she was heading. Since she was so close, she told herself she would just drive by, look at the house, and keep on going.

Imagany drove slowly down the street. When she came to her parent's home, she parked on the opposite side of the street. The house looked the same, freshly painted, lawn hedges neatly trimmed. To the outside world, it appeared the perfect little home. As she continued to stare, the years seemed to fall away.

She remembered the harsh words she and her father, Robert, had said to one another the day before she left for college. She remembered, too, her mother standing in the background, pacing back and forth as she and her father shouted at each other. They had argued because her father hadn't wanted her to go away to school. He'd believed right up until the day she left that she was only bluffing. He had warned Imagany that she'd better not call home and ask him for a dime. She screamed back that she wouldn't take a dime from him even if he offered it because it was sure to be tainted and warped, the same way he was. After she yelled at him, he hauled off and slapped her. But he turned away from her, thinking that had settled it.

Imagany was fed up with all of his tyranny. She picked up a heavy crystal goblet and smashed it upside his head. With blood spilling down the side of his face, Robert had tried to kill Imagany that day. He slammed his fist into her forehead, knocking her out. When she came to, he beat her savagely with his belt. Bruised and sore, Imagany left the next morning. She hadn't seen or spoken to either of her parents since. That had been four years ago.

She lifted her head and took a deep breath to throw off the bad memories. She had no desire to see her father again. She had too much unresolved anger. She knew she should be getting on to Caprice's house. But the chance to see her mother, a chance to look upon her mother's face one more time and ask her the questions that she had been wanting an answer to for all these years was too much for her to resist. Imagany stopped herself short. Hadn't she promised herself that she'd never set foot inside that house again? Just one look at her mother's face, she reasoned. Once more would be enough.

Imagany opened the car door and got out before she talked herself out of it. She walked up to the door and pressed the bell. She was about to walk away when the door opened behind her. She spun around and stared into her mother's eyes. Somehow she looked different. And yet she looked the same. Imagany stared at her and realized her mother had aged.

Geneva stared at her daughter, whom she hadn't seen or spoken to in over four years, in surprised shock. When she stepped forward to embrace Imagany, her heart wrenched and tears fell from her eyes. She pulled her inside the house.

Imagany stepped inside and leaned against the closed door. She watched Geneva turn away to wipe tears from her eyes. Expecting her to follow, Geneva stepped further into the room.

Imagany followed her into the living room and sat on the edge of the sofa. They stared into each other's eyes with many unspoken words between them, so many questions left unanswered and so much lost time.

Geneva leaned forward and finally asked, "How have you been?"

Imagany stared at all the gray in her mother's hair and shook her head. She said quietly, "I'm making it, Mother."

"You look so pretty. I always knew you would make it, Imagany. Even as a child you had an inner strength."

Imagany looked away. She hadn't come here for compliments. She had too many questions which she needed answers to. She changed the subject. "So how are you?"

Geneva dabbed at her eyes. "I'm doing okay. Everything's still the same."

Imagany could imagine they were. With her father still using her mother as a springboard for his anger. "I don't remember all the gray in your hair. It becomes you, though."

Geneva touched her hand to her hair and laughed self-consciously. "I guess we all must age sometime." They sat in silence for a while before Geneva said, "I called your school and they told me that you graduated." Now why had she admitted that?

Imagany's head snapped back in surprise. She didn't think her mother cared as much. "I almost called to invite you to the graduation ceremony, but I didn't think you'd be interested in coming."

"I would have been honored to come. I've missed you, Imagany. I know you probably don't believe that. But it's true. Ever since you walked out that door, I've missed you. There hasn't been one single day when I didn't think about you or wonder how you were doing."

Imagany stood up. If she didn't leave now, she would start to cry. She hadn't come here to do that. She could cry anywhere, but not here. She was walking toward the door when her mother's words stopped her.

"Imagany, wait. I just want you to know that I love you. I know I never said it to you when you were a child, but it's true. I've always loved you. I just didn't know how to show it. But I look at you today and I see a grown woman who's come into her own. And you didn't need me or your father to do that. I even wanted to call you while you were away at school. But every time I picked up the phone, I put it down because I realized I had almost nothing to say to you. And what I did have to say, you wouldn't believe me because I've never said it before. I'm sorry about that now. I know it doesn't change the past. It could never right the wrongs that were done to you or to your sister. I guess that's why she left me too. I only hope God is looking over her wherever she is." Tears trickled down Geneva's face as she spoke.

Imagany had intended to be strong. She wanted to look upon her mother's face and be able to just walk away. But she couldn't. She walked back to the chair and sat. Suddenly, her body began to rack with sobs. Imagany buried her head in her hands as all the years of hurt and pent up frustration came rushing back. How often in the past had she longed for her mother to even acknowledge that she loved her?

As her tears poured forth, Imagany felt as if a part of herself was dying. She cried all the tears that for years were trapped inside her. When her tears finally subsided, Imagany found the courage to say to her mother all the things she had dreamed of saying. She stared at Geneva through the midst of her tears. Her voice was full of sorrow and sadness. "For years I did everything to gain your approval. But somehow, nothing I ever did was good enough for you. So I thought it was me. I grew up feeling like I was dirty and that I wasn't good enough for anybody decent to love."

"Everything that happened to us, I thought it was all my fault. Whenever he hit you, I thought it was my fault, and whenever he abused me, I still thought it was my fault. The first time he raped me, you let me believe that was my fault, too, and the same was true whenever he raped you. I grew up tired of everything always being my fault. And now, after everything is said and done, you sit there and tell me you love me and expect me to believe you? What gives you the preconceived notion that those three words will erase all the hurt inside me and wipe the slate clean? What makes you think that I should just forget and start anew? It doesn't work that way, Mother. What about what I feel? Don't my feelings count? How long was I supposed to keep overlooking the things that were done to me? What did I ever do to you but love you more than you've probably ever loved yourself? How was I supposed to know that you were jealous of me? I was only a child, for God's sake." Imagany stopped to shake her head and wipe her eyes.

"I don't understand a mother's love that makes her deny what's happening right beneath her nose. You knew he was molesting me. I told you. But you refused to see it or believe me. You knew when he started with Zabree. He's sick, Mother. And in my eyes he deserves to die for what he did. But you allowed it to happen and for that I can never forgive you. You're the one who's got to live with that burden and then you've got to try to live with yourself. I'm sorry. I don't want to hear that you love me. It's too late. The only thing I want to do is find Zabree and help her heal like I'm trying to heal. I tell myself every day that I'm bigger than this shame that I carry around with me like some beast of burden. I can overcome this. Regardless of the things Robert did to me when I was a child, he wasn't able to touch what I have on the inside. And that's what gets me through each day." Imagany stopped. She suddenly had a hollow feeling within her. She stood up to leave. "I'd better go now. I don't want to be here when he gets here."

As Imagany walked to the door and turned the knob, her mother quickly came behind her.

"Imagany, I know why you feel the way you do. But I need to tell you about Zabree. She's in trouble. I know it because I dream about her at night. If you never come to see me again, just promise me you'll find her."

Imagany turned around to face her mother. "No, Mother. Zabree is fine. I know she is because I've spoken to her. You're just worried because she doesn't call you."

"If I believed she was all right, I would be happy for her. But I checked all the high schools in Chicago. She's not enrolled anywhere. She must have dropped out. And something else. When she left, she didn't take a thing with her, not so much as a stitch of clothing. Nothing, Imagany. Even when you left, you took things with you. If she were staying with another family or even if she were working somewhere, we could track her down. Your father has written her off, but I can't. She's my blood. She came from me. I know I can't ask you to love me. But if you only do one thing, find your sister for me, and if she's all right, then drop me a note and I'll be content with that. Just find her, Imagany."

Imagany turned away from her mother and walked out the door.

***

Carl and Caprice got married on one of the most beautiful days anyone could ask for. The skies were clear, and the sun was shining. They were married at the Apostolic Church of God on 63rd and Dorchester, the same church that Caprice had attended all her life. She wore a gorgeous gown of white lace with a long train. She had never looked more stunning. All the bridesmaids wore pink to match the pink and white decorations and flowers. The cake was five layers tall and had a gazebo on top of it with a black couple standing underneath it.

When the time came for Caprice to throw her bridal bouquet, she threw it in Imagany's direction so she would be forced to catch it. Afterwards, the wedding reception was held at a large ballroom on the south side.

As their wedding gift, Elliott and Imagany gave the happy couple a brand new 500 SEL Mercedes along with the money they needed to get their own place. The huge two-bedroom apartment in Hyde Park that Caprice had found for Imagany, she and Carl could now keep for themselves. Since Caprice's parents had footed the entire bill for the wedding, Carl's parents were sending them to Aruba for three weeks as their wedding gift. After the ceremony was over, the couple headed back to her parents' house to change for the reception.

Elliott and Imagany drove to the reception in Elliott's new silver Jaguar. By the time they arrived, the ballroom was packed with people. The music was lively and there was so much food and champagne that everyone couldn't help but have a good time.

In the wee hours of the morning, on the way home from the reception, Elliott and Imagany were still excited over everything that had happened that day. They talked nonstop about how beautiful Caprice looked, how handsome Carl looked, and how happy the two of them were as a couple. Imagany snuggled up to Elliott and sighed contentedly. The way she felt right now, it might as well have been her that had gotten married.

They climbed the staircase arm in arm singing "Always And Forever," Carl and Caprice's wedding song. Later, Elliott held Imagany in his arms as they relaxed amidst a tidal wave of bubbles. "It's been a long time since we've taken a bath together, hasn't it?"

"Yep, kiddo, it surely has. Where have you been all my life?"

Elliott was trying to think of a way to ask Imagany to marry him. The truth was that he didn't want to have to wait until they were in a romantic moment. He wanted to ask her and get a simple answer in return.

Imagany was searching for the soap when Elliott asked, "Imagany, will you marry me?"

Imagany thought Elliott was only teasing her. She found the soap and said, "Sure, Boo. Just let me know when and I'll be there."

Elliott stilled Imagany's hand. "Imagany, I've never been more serious in my life. Will you marry me? Just yes or no."

Imagany heard the serious refection in Elliott's voice and she turned around in the tub to face him. She raised herself to kneel between his legs, staring him in the eyes. She tried to read the expression on his face as he returned her gaze unblinkingly. She thought of the words she had spoken to her mother about having never felt worthy and about never having felt like someone could or should love her. She hadn't lied then and she wasn't lying as she spoke now. "Elliott Renfroe, the man who has touched my heart in so many wonderful ways. You've made me open up when I didn't even think I could. You've made me feel love that I didn't even know I had inside me. Because of you, I've discovered emotions I never knew existed. And through you, I've learned to give of myself without expecting anything in return. As your wife, I'd be the happiest woman on this planet. Does that answer your question?"

Elliott felt an overwhelming sense of relief. As God was his witness, he had expected her to say no. With a half smile on his face, Elliott said, "Let's get out of this tub and go do the wild thing."

Imagany sat back on her haunches. "Elliott Renfroe, that's not romantic."

"I know, but it serves the purpose, doesn't it?"

They dried themselves off and headed toward the bedroom.

***

The following weekend, while Carl and Caprice were sunning themselves in Aruba, Imagany started furniture shopping. When Elliott asked if she wanted to hire someone to do it for her, she adamantly told him no. Everything that he was to see their home become was going to be her doing. She knew what she wanted, where she wanted to put it and most importantly, she knew where to get it. Elliott came with her the first couple of times, but after that, he knew he didn't have the patience or the will to go shopping with Imagany. He handed over his credit cards and bid her goodbye.

While Elliott was away at the Bears' training camp, Imagany busied herself with her job and decorating the house. He was going to be away for three weeks and she wanted to get as much accomplished in his absence as she possibly could. Everyday after work, she went shopping for the house. She purchased huge abstract paintings, chandeliers, light fixtures, plants, carpeting, vases, living room furniture, bedroom furniture, dining room furniture and all types of gadgets for the kitchen.

Two weeks after Carl and Caprice's wedding, Imagany was walking downtown on her lunch break when she passed a news stand. She spotted a Jet Magazine with Denzel Washington on the cover so she stopped to buy it. She only had fifteen minutes left on her lunch hour so she stuck it in her purse to read when she got home. When she arrived home later that evening, she walked through every room of the house admiring the beauty of the place. With its bright interior and beautiful large plants, the place was warm and welcoming. She wasn't used to luxury on this scale, so everything was still fresh and new to her. Every day when she got home, Imagany walked through the entire house, still trying to adjust to the fact that the house was her's and Elliott's.

She took a shower and went in search of something to eat. While eating, she flipped through the pages of the Jet. Suddenly a gasp of excitement burst from her lips. Pictures of recent newlywed couples appeared on the page and right in front of her eyes was a stunning picture of Carl and Caprice. They were poised a little to the side of their wedding cake. Caprice was holding the knife in her hand while Carl stood behind her with one arm wrapped around her waist and the other hand covering the one which Caprice was using to hold the knife. The caption read, 'Truly Blessed. Newlywed couple Mr. & Mrs. Carl Beasley were recently united in bliss at St. Alban's Chapel. Carl Beasley is a graduate of Tennessee State University and is employed at McDonnell Douglas as an Electrical Engineer. Caprice Beasley is a graduate of Meharry Medical College and is currently interning at the University of Chicago's Hospital.'

Imagany grabbed the phone to call Mrs. McKnight. When no one answered, she hung up and sat back down and shook her head. She happily turned the page and received her next shock. With a smile on her face that showed all five hundred of her teeth stood a glowing Leslie Lowe with Anthony Barrington. Without reading the caption, Imagany stared at the photograph of the couple. Too many unwanted memories came rushing back. So Leslie's wish had finally come true. In disgust, Imagany tossed the magazine aside and rose from the table.

When Imagany arrived at work the following day, the station was a madhouse. Every Tuesday and Thursday, she went into the field with the NBC television crews. She loved being on the scene when the crew filmed something live. On this Thursday, as they cruised the streets of Chicago in search of something newsworthy, Imagany was preoccupied with thoughts of Zabree. Although she hadn't given her mother's words about Zabree much thought, for some reason she was thinking about them in detail today. Key phrases her mother had used kept coming back to her. "Even you took things with you" and "she must have dropped out" were constantly floating through Imagany's mind. By the end of the work day, Imagany was trying desperately to recall the last time she had spoken to Zabree. Before she left work, she called the phone company in Nashville to ask if there was any way she could find out the phone numbers that were placed to her apartment. She hung up disappointed.

On her way home that evening, Imagany stopped at a downtown pet shop to purchase supplies and accessories for her fish tank. She browsed through the store looking at all the animals as they played feistily with each other. She was standing before a large glass window which displayed four rottweiler puppies when one of the animals caught her eye. While the other puppies were trying to sleep, one was running around. He looked so cute to Imagany as he turned in circles chasing a piece of straw that was stuck to his rear. A smile appeared on Imagany's face. She knew that when she left the pet shop, the little puppy would be going home with her. She walked up front to the counter and asked how much they were and was shocked when the attendant told her the puppies were a whopping two thousand dollars each. Imagany thought about the things she could buy for two thousand dollars but decided to get the puppy anyway. He was purebred, had all of his shots and he came with papers. She wrote out a check for everything and headed home. At least she now had something to keep her company while Elliott was away.

Once inside her house, she set up a space for the puppy in a corner of the large kitchen. She was laying down a bed of newspaper for him when an advertisement caught her eye. MISSING PERSONS FOUND, CALL PRIVATE INVESTIGATORS AT (312)388-0779. Imagany sat back reflectively before tearing off the ad and putting it to the side. When little Leo was settled, she headed upstairs to undress.

She sat on the bed and stared at the number to the private investigator's firm. Tapping her fingers against her thigh, she picked up the phone and dialed the number. A courteous female voice answered the phone.

"Epstein, Bergmann & Associates. How may we help you?"

"Good evening. I was calling to find out if I could have someone found."

In a pleasant voice, the woman said, "Okay. Is the person a relative or friend?"

"She's my sister."

"May I have your name please?"

"Ms. Jenkins." Imagany was wary.

"What we do, Ms. Jenkins, is invite you to come in for a free consultation. We try to obtain as much information as we can from you and if you have a picture of the person, we ask that you bring that along, too. Once again, the initial consultation is at no cost to you and if we think we cannot take on your case, we let you know up front. Would you be interested in setting up an appointment?"

"Yes, I would. Do you have anything available for tomorrow evening?"

"Hold please and I'll check." After a moment, she returned to the phone and said, "Is six-thirty convenient for you?"

"Six-thirty is fine. Where are you located?" She gave Imagany the address and reminded her to bring along a picture of her sister.

Imagany hung up and showered. Afterwards, she went downstairs to quiet the puppy and to find something to eat.

The next day, there was an air of expectancy about Imagany as she rushed through her day at work. Not only was she going to see the investigators about Zabree later that evening, but Elliott would be arriving home early the next morning.

Imagany left her job and found the address on Jackson and Wacker with no problem. The receptionist led her inside an office where a tall, handsome black man rose to greet her. The man extended his hand and said, "Hello, Ms. Jenkins. I'm Teferro McClodden." He took note of the ring on her finger.

When the receptionist closed the door behind her, Imagany said to Teferro, "I must say that this is a very welcome surprise, Mr. McClodden."

Teferro smiled at her as he leaned back in his chair and pressed his fingertips together. "Why? Because I'm black?"

Imagany returned his smile. "Yes. With a name like Epstein & Bergmann, how could I be anything but surprised? But I'm happy to make your acquaintance."

"Thank you, and please, call me Teferro. What brings you here today?"

Imagany leaned forward and told Teferro all about Zabree. How old Zabree was, the high school she attended before she was thought to be missing, the names of friends that Imagany knew Zabree associated with. Imagany told him how Zabree had even called her from time to time while she was living in Nashville. When she finished, Teferro asked her if she had a picture of Zabree.

Imagany removed the five by ten photograph of Zabree from her purse. She handed the photo over to him and he studied it for a while. Placing the photograph upon the desk, he said, "She's a very beautiful girl."

Imagany smiled. "Yes she is. Both on the inside and out. I've got to find her, Teferro. She's all the family I have left in this world. I can't stress how important this is to me."

Teferro folded his hands and leaned forward on the desk. "Ms. Jenkins, I don't mean to sound disheartening or discouraging, but I must be honest with you. Sometimes it can be very difficult to locate a person, especially if that person doesn't want to be found. And it's expensive. I would suggest you file a missing person's report with the police department."

Imagany interrupted him. "If I thought something could be accomplished that way, I'd be more than willing to go that route. You know as well as I do how backlogged the police department is. And I've already considered the fact that this might be expensive. It's something I've got to do."

Teferro stared at her reflectively. He rose from behind the desk and came around to sit on top of it. "If your sister is anywhere in the Chicagoland area, it won't be so bad. But if she's gone to another state, that's where the expense comes in. There's air fare involved plus money for man hours spent. I'm not turning you away. I just want you to know what you're up against. There are many unscrupulous people out there who would take your money and run. I'm not one of them. I'd be more than willing to take on the case."

Imagany's smile was full of relief. "I appreciate everything you've just said and I thank you for your honesty. But this is something I have to go ahead with. My life will be incomplete until I find my sister. So talk to me about your fees."

Teferro told Imagany his fee before giving her a detailed plan of action.

Chapter Twenty

lliott returned from training camp physically drained but mentally filled with zest and vitality. Football season started soon and he was full of hopes and aspirations for the upcoming season. When Imagany flooded him with questions about the Bears' training camp, Elliott answered them with the attentive patience that was his by nature. He described how he had spent a lot of his free time talking with old timers such as Walter Payton, Willie Gault, Mike Singletary and Richard Dent.

He was also amazed at the transformation which the house had undergone in his absence. True to her word, Imagany had made the entire place look lavish, warm and inviting. Elliott knew his favorite room in the house would be the recreation room because of all the electronic gadgets Imagany had purchased for him. Moving from room to room with Imagany following closely behind him, Elliott felt like a little kid in a candy store who had just been told that everything in it belonged to him.

The final addition which Imagany made to the household took Elliott totally by surprise. With one arm wrapped around his waist, Imagany used her other hand to cover his eyes and led him through the house toward the kitchen area. Sitting him down in one of the kitchen chairs, she told him to keep his eyes closed until she returned. Imagany quickly came back with a small bundle in her arms and told Elliott to hold out his hands. He did so and into his outstretched arms, Imagany placed the tiny Rottweiler pup.

Elliott laughed as Leo licked the palms of his hands. He lifted the little puppy to his chest and stroked him tenderly.

"He's beautiful. Where did you get him?"

"From a pet store downtown," Imagany told him as he held Leo in the air examining him. "You like him, Boo?"

"Of course, baby. How could I not? Just look at the size of his paws!"

"Yes, he's going to be huge. I'm just glad you like him. Since I named him, I can cheerfully leave everything else up to you."

Elliott loudly cleared his throat and placed little Leo on the floor. "Now that's something we need to talk about. Whose idea was it to get a dog anyway?"

Imagany sat on Elliott's lap and wound her arms around his neck. "I think it was yours. I vaguely recall you saying something about a house full of children and animals. Well, there's your first wish, baby, so now we'll have to work on the second one."

Elliott felt himself become aroused at the tone of her voice in his ear. He stood up with his hands on her hips. "I think we should try to work on that right this minute. What do you think?"

"I say, let's go do the wild thing." Imagany had a sexy smile on her face.

As Elliott led her out of the kitchen and up the stairs, he said, "Those aren't romantic words, you know."

"I know, but they serve the purpose, right?"

The two of them reached the top landing when Leo, who had followed them, started yelping at the bottom of the stairs. They both turned and stared down at the puppy. Elliott nudged Imagany and said, "Don't just stand there, go get your baby."

Imagany laughed as Leo sat helplessly at the bottom of the steps. He was too small to climb the stairs by himself so Imagany ran down and carried him up in her arms. Inside the bedroom, Imagany set Leo down on the floor. He wiggled playfully between her legs. When Imagany kicked off her slippers, he jumped on one of them, growling and shaking it between his teeth.

Recapturing Elliott's attention, Imagany climbed on the bed on her knees and in striptease fashion, slowly pulled her nightshirt over her head. She teasingly removed her underwear, aware that Elliott's gaze was riveted to her every move.

Elliott could literally feel his mouth salivate. Without uttering a word, he quickly removed his clothing and joined her on the bed. He pulled Imagany on top of him and showed her a little magic of his own.

***

Carl and Caprice came over later that evening. They both were so darkened from their time spent in Aruba that they were barely recognizable. They came into the house, amazed at the beauty around them as both Imagany and Elliott took pride in showing them the place.

They were all seated at the dinner table when Elliott stood up to propose a toast. "Here's to prosperity, longevity, happiness and to the best two married couples that ever became friends."

Carl said to Caprice, "Correct me if I'm wrong, but aren't we the only married couple in this room?"

"Yes, baby. We are. Unless they know something we don't."

Imagany stood up to touch her glass to Elliott's. "I agree with Elliott, here's to the second happiest couple in the world. Thank you, baby, for asking me to be your wife."

Carl and Caprice were ecstatic. "So when are you guys jumping the broom?"

Imagany blew Elliott a kiss from across the table before sitting down. "We haven't set a date yet. But it'll be sometime soon. Elliott doesn't want me to be an unwed mother." When Imagany finished her statement, all eyes were focused on her. Especially Elliott's.

Carl caught the surprised expression on Elliott's face and laughed. "Are you trying to tell us that you two are getting married and are about to become parents?"

"No, Carl. We're going to get married first and then we'll become parents at a later date." Imagany noticed the way everyone was staring at her so she said, "Calm down, people. I'm not pregnant. One step at a time, please. Marriage first, and then about. . ." Imagany paused, "Well, we'll just see about kids later."

After they finished eating, they curled up in the living room to watch a movie on cable TV. Before the movie ended, one by one, they started yawning. A short while later, the television was watching them.

***

Football season, started off with a bang. Elliott was fortunate to have been chosen by the Bears. Had he gone to any other football team in the league, they would have benched him for at least a year or two. When the Bears' star quarterback was injured, they needed someone who was able to play at a moment's notice. Elliott begged the coach to just give him a chance. Against his better judgment, and to the dismay of many others, the coach granted Elliott permission to play.

Elliott had studied the players intently during his time spent in training camp. He knew the weaknesses and strengths of the players as a team and he realized that he had something valuable to offer them.

The first time he was sent onto the field, the sportscasters all made wisecracks, denigrating the coach for sending in a player who was still so wet behind the ears. Thinking that Elliott was about to make a fool of himself, everyone knew they were at the very least about to see some footage for a football bloopers tape. No one took him seriously. Not even his own teammates. Elliott's first series of passes were caught by the receivers with ease. And his next pass was caught in the end zone for a touchdown.

People skeptically attributed Elliott's first touchdown pass to beginners' luck. But after he successfully completed his next five passes, even the crowd started to sit up and take notice. The Bears had some of the best linemen in the league so the pocket surrounding Elliott was a good one, affording him plenty of protection. The few times when it did collapse around him, Elliott scrambled all over the field, jumping over and dodging both opponents and teammates alike. So adept was he at eluding attempts to sack him that he soon earned the nickname "Scrambler."

In the second half of the game, the Bears trailed the Green Bay Packers twenty-eight to seven. With Elliott as quarterback, each time the Bears came into possession of the ball, they scored a touchdown. Before the fans knew it, the score was tied at thirty-five with less than two minutes left on the game clock. The Bears were in possession of the ball when Elliott's next pass was caught at the twenty-yard line and was run in for the touchdown. When they made the extra point, the score was forty-two to thirty-five. Everybody, including the doubters, knew that the offensive unit had done their job. All that was needed now was for the defense to prevent the opponents from scoring. As the next series of plays were put into action, the Bears' defensive unit held strong and the clock ran out for the Packers. After the game, the entire team streamed onto the field, lifting Elliott onto their shoulders and carrying him off to the sidelines amidst the screams and chants of the fans.

On Monday morning, every newspaper in Chicago was full of details about the young, black, upstart quarterback from Tennessee State University who had taken over the game and won it for the Bears. Many of the sports reporters touted Elliott as the newest wonder boy on the block, while a few conservatives claimed it was much too soon to judge him because in all likelihood, Elliott had only had beginners' luck.

As the season progressed, so did Elliott's performance. He slowly but surely began to disprove all the naysayers who were chanting that his luck would soon wear off. Through much practice and careful preparation on his part, plus the support of his coaches and teammates, Elliott's performance began to get even better as he honed his quarterback skills to a fine point. He quickly came to know which receivers were his go-to men. He learned which men to throw his short passes and which ones would better receive the longer ones. As Elliott made even further progress, so did the entire team. Already known as a team not to be taken lightly, with the Scrambler at the helm, the teams around the league were starting to sit up and pay close attention to the Chicago Bears.

Soon, playoff season rolled around and the Bears were still in good shape. No one on the team thought they would make it this far. Certainly not without a well-known quarterback. No one could have guessed that come playoff time, the Bears would still be alive.

As the Bears continued to eliminate other teams from the playoffs, they began to believe they could make it to the Super Bowl. They started believing not just in themselves, but in Elliott, too. When just four teams were left with playoff berths, the Bears knew they had a chance to win it all. They were playing the New York Giants for the conference championship. A win against the Giants would send them to Super Bowl XXX.

The game between the Giants and the Bears was a rough and dirty one. In one of the most fierce and bitter rivalries since the Hatfields and the McCoys, both teams fought and played tenaciously. But in the end, the Bears were victorious. Now that the Bears were in the Super Bowl against the Denver Broncos, Elliott's playoff performance was lauded on all levels. The media was constantly comparing his style of play to that of Denver quarterback, John Elway's. His picture was plastered on posters everywhere. The captions read, "Elliott Renfroe for President!" Magazines vied to get his picture on their covers and all the talk show hosts were competing to interview him.

The amount of fan mail that arrived at their home each day amazed Imagany. She knew that Elliott was under a great deal of pressure and stress and she tried everything within her means to keep him calm and soothed. With all the pandemonium surrounding him, Elliott was in constant contact with his old coach at TSU, Coach Hadley, who advised him to hire a public relations agent. Elliott's father was able to help him out in that area, too. He simply contacted one of his partners from Grambling who was able to handle all of Elliott's PR.

After a barrage of prank phone calls were made to their home, Imagany had the phone number changed to an unlisted number and she became very protective of their privacy. The one thing that didn't fail to amaze her was the amount of women who suddenly were after Elliott. As a mere fiancé, she definitely commanded no respect from other women. One evening when Imagany came home, several women were hanging around trying to catch a glimpse of Elliott. The very next morning, Imagany called to have a wrought iron security gate installed around their entire property. She also had an alarm system installed inside their home. Anyone wanting to gain access to their property would either have to have to know the security code or be buzzed in.

All during the week of Super Bowl madness, the two teams were constantly being pitted against one another in the press. The Denver Broncos vs. the Chicago Bears. The odds were three-to-one in favor of the Broncos because of their star running back, Terrell Davis and their flamboyant quarterback, Elway. Because the Broncos were the defending Super Bowl champs, most fans were betting against the Bears.

The night before the Super Bowl, Elliott was quieter and more contemplative than Imagany had ever seen him. The two of them were snuggled in their hotel room talking and holding one another as they had done so often in the past. Imagany unwound herself from Elliott and went to her luggage to dig out her Keri lotion. She came back into the room and crawled onto the bed to straddle Elliott's back. She uncapped the lotion and massaged a portion of it onto his naked body.

As she massaged his shoulders, she asked him, "What's on your mind, baby?"

Elliott was quiet for a long time. Then he began to speak softly. "I'm thinking about how in all the time I've been playing this sport, I've seen people drop like flies. And I can't help but feel that what I saw in those days will be nothing compared to what I'm likely to see while I'm in the NFL. Every time I play this game and am able to walk off the field after it's over, I give thanks to God. Seeing all the people hurt around me makes me realize that no man is invincible and that life offers none of us any guarantees."

Imagany listened intently as she slipped off of Elliott and gestured for him to turn over. When he lay on his back, she climbed back on top of him and massaged more lotion into his chest.

Elliott clasped his hands behind his head and continued. "When I was in high school, all I knew was that when I had that football in my hands, I felt like I was the captain of a ship. When I told people I wanted to be a quarterback, they'd smile this funny smile. I knew that they were thinking it was great for me to have such a far-fetched dream. But no one really believed it could be accomplished. When I continued to pursue my dream, people would say to me, 'El, man, just give it up! You know there are hardly any black quarterbacks in the league. You can't be one because they won't allow it. Don't you know that no matter how good you are, they only want a white boy to lead the team?' But I had this dream, Imagany, this vision that I could accomplish all the things that God put me here to do. When I look at myself today, it's hard to even believe that I'm following my dream."

"Growing up in the South like I did, I've seen racism in some of its ugliest forms. I've seen people go out of their way to try to make others feel like they're less than nothing. Racism is a bitch. If you're not a secure person, it makes you doubt who you are. And even more frustrating is the fact that it can make you doubt the things you have within you. Every time I play a game, I look into the stadium and see that there are more white faces there than there are black ones. That's when the realization hits me that white people love us! They're drawn to us, too, but they would do anything to never have to admit it. They imitate our ways and copy everything about us. Yet, they'll never admit that either. Do you realize that blacks have managed to excel in every field in which we've ever chosen or been allowed to enter? I don't think we realize how much we have to celebrate and be proud of."

"All I know is that when I'm out there on the football field, I do my damnedest to play the best I can. When it's all said and done, I want to be remembered not as a black NFL quarterback, but instead for being the best person that God gave me the presence of mind to be. Right now, I'm just nervous about tomorrow's game. I feel as if I'm carrying the weight of this entire team. It's a lot of pressure. I'm nobody's hero. I'm just someone who strives to be the best at whatever I do. That's all. I want to go out there tomorrow, and whether we win or lose, still be able to feel good about me, Elliott Renfroe, not the myth or the legend that the magazines and newspapers are trying to make me out to be."

Imagany looked down at Elliott, her gaze full of love and respect. "You're blessed, Elliott Renfroe. Do you realize that some people go through their entire lives not knowing what it is they want out of life or even what it is they want to be or love to do? Can you even imagine how many people go to their graves with their God-given talents lying dormant within them? But not you, Elliott. When I watch you out there on the field, I see a man who's in control. A man who has the people around him guessing and on edge because they never know what his next move is going to be. You're good at what you do, baby, because no one can do it quite the way you do. I know you're facing a tremendous amount of pressure. But the one thing I've come to know is that the Man upstairs never puts more on us than we're able to handle. Whether the Bears win that game tomorrow or not, it doesn't matter. It's not the be all or end all for me or for you. When we leave here tomorrow night, baby, I'm still going to love you and be there for you. Regardless of how the outside world perceives you, Elliott, to me, you're still the man I love. The man I've chosen to spend the rest of my life with. You got that?" When Elliott's lips twitched into a smile, Imagany knew that he did.

***

The crowd was beset with Super Bowl mania. Even the sports announcers were having trouble being heard over the loudness that pervaded Sun Devil stadium. As the two teams were introduced, a frenzied excitement laced the air. Amid the wild and furious screams of the crowd, Super Bowl XXX was underway.

Chapter Twenty-One

While Imagany was enjoying herself in the warm climate of Phoenix, Arizona, Teferro McClodden was busy plodding the pavements of Chicago's lower South Side. The temperature was freezing cold and the harsh wind nipped him with biting fierceness. Chicago's "Hawk" was flying high. Dressed in worn sneakers, faded jeans and a thickly insulated Chicago Bears jacket, Teferro McClodden had come to scout the most infamous projects on the south side, known as the Ickeys.

Teferro had done his homework. He had gone to Lindbloom High School, where Zabree was last seen, to pass around her picture to some of the students at the school. At first no one had wanted to give him the time of day, but when he mentioned that a sizable reward was involved, many of the students were suddenly eager to talk. He was told that if anyone could give him information about Zabree Jenkins, that person would be Jamarra Sanders. Zabree and Jamarra were known around the school as best friends. When Zabree dropped out, everyone naturally assumed Jamarra knew the reason why. Many had approached Jamarra to find out the dirt, but the unfortunate reality was that people's memories were short. Curious one day, forgetting the next.

Teferro stood waiting for Jamarra Sanders outside her fourth-period study class. He had paid another student to point her out to him and just as she was about to enter the study room, Teferro approached her.

"Excuse me, Ms. Sanders, my name is Teferro McClodden. May I have a word with you?" Teferro conspicuously flashed his badge at Jamarra as he led her inside the room.

Jamarra's eyes widened at the sight of his badge and she searched her mind for an inkling of what he wanted. They walked to an unoccupied section of the room and took a seat at an empty table. Jamarra laid her books on the study table and demurely took a seat. Folding her hands together, she sat in curious silence as she waited for him to explain what this was all about.

Teferro began by trying gain her trust. "I didn't mean to frighten you, but I'm trying to find a friend of yours and I need to ask you some questions."

Jamarra relaxed, she knew what this was going to be about even though she pretended not to. "Who?"

"Zabree Jenkins. I take it you knew her?"

Jamarra inclined her head slightly.

"Her sister is very worried about her. She's hired me to find her. It appears that Zabree just disappeared about a year ago. Her sister has been trying to find her ever since. I asked around the school and everyone I talked to says you were closest to her. I'm here to ask for your help. If you know anything, I'd like you to tell me. If Zabree is in trouble, her sister would like to find her before someone else does."

Jamarra stared at Teferro, trying to decide if she could trust him. "Why don't you ask Zabree's parents? It seems to me like they would know where she is before I would."

Teferro sensed Jamarra's indecision. "Her sister doesn't want her parents involved in this matter. Unfortunately, I'm not at leisure to explain why."

Jamarra wanted to believe him. She had her own thoughts about why Zabree's sister wouldn't want Mr. and Mrs. Jenkins to know Zabree's whereabouts. She believed, too, that if anyone could help Zabree, it would be Zabree's sister. Staring past Teferro, Jamarra hesitated and then began to speak slowly.

"Up until about a year ago, Zabree and I were the best of friends. I've known her since we were in grammar school together. Zabree has got to be the most trusting and naive person that I have ever known. Not a dim wit, mind you. She was a straight-A student. She was simply too trusting. She was the type who assumed that everyone had good intentions because she was like that herself. Sometimes I would tell Zabree point blank that she had book sense but no common sense. Most people were attracted to her because of her beauty. But I believe her looks were something she was never quite comfortable with. It was also hard to get her to open up to you. But if she did open up, there was nothing she wouldn't do for you. She would give you her last dime if you asked for it."

"When we decided to come to Lindbloom together, I asked her why she never invited me to her home. She never gave me a straight answer and I didn't question it. I think that was one of the reasons we were such good friends: I never pried into her personal business. She knew my family well, but if you asked me about hers, I wouldn't have been able to tell you diddly squat. I did meet her mother, though, because she would come to all the plays when we were in grammar school." Jamarra shook her head.

"Mrs. Jenkins is one beautiful woman. You look at her and you know where Zabree got her looks from. The only person Zabree would talk about was her sister. She wouldn't even mention her mother unless I asked her about her. She never volunteered information. It was so weird to me because I thought everybody talked about their parents, if they had them. Not once did Zabree ever mention to me that she had a father, so I just assumed she didn't have one. I remember once telling her that she and her sister should try to pursue careers as models. I told her that with their looks, I was sure they could make it. Zabree told me modeling was something she had always wanted to do, but that her father would never hear of it. She mumbled something about how her father would kill her if she ever left home. I was shocked because that was the first time in my life that I had ever heard her mention her father." Jamarra spoke in disbelief.

"Can you believe that? I've known Zabree like the back of my hand for practically all my life and I don't find out until the two of us are in high school that she has a father who actually lives with her. When I think about it now, it still blows my mind. The entire situation was so deep to me. But I guess it goes to show that I didn't know her as well as I thought I did." She gave an ironic laugh.

"Like I said, when we first came to Lindbloom, all the guys were after Zabree like white on rice. She couldn't handle all the attention, so she shied away from just about everybody except me. Guys would come up to me all the time to try to get me to hook them up with her. It was funny to me because people acted like I was either her mother or her pimp. One day, I convinced Zabree to go out on a double date with me, my boyfriend and this guy who was a friend of my boyfriend's. He was a nice guy. He was a little on the quiet side so I thought he would be okay for Zabree. In order for her to go, we had to tell her mother that we were going to be studying late at my house. Fine."

"We went to the movies and had a great time. On the way home, my boyfriend had a blow out in one of his tires. He didn't have a spare one in the trunk either, so it took us about three hours to find another tire. There we were, stuck all the way out in Lyons, Illinois. So it wasn't like we could catch a bus back or anything. When it started getting late, Zabree got more nervous by the minute. And then it was like all of a sudden she just panicked. She started crying and carrying on. My boyfriend got mad and started yelling at her to shut up. That's when I lit into him, snapping at him and telling him to shut the hell up. I was so pissed off that I made the other guy get in the front seat while I sat in the back holding Zabree's hand. I had never seen Zabree scared like that in all the time I had known her, and for some reason, I was scared for her, too. I held her hand all during the way back and by the time we reached her home, her teeth were chattering. She was holding my hand so tight that it hurt. And then I realized she was afraid to get out of the car. I opened the door and said 'fuck it.' I was going to go in there and just tell her folks the truth."

"By this time, I regretted asking her to go to the movies in the first place. We rang the door bell and all of a sudden somebody yanked the door open. When I looked at the man who stood inside the doorway, I swear to you, I was never so afraid in my life! I stepped inside only because Zabree was still clutching my hand. That's when he slammed the door behind us. I tried to find the courage to speak but I couldn't get a word out of my mouth. I couldn't look at him either so I stared around the house. With God as my witness, I tell you, I felt such a sense of evilness coming from that place that my flesh started to crawl. All I knew was that I had to get the hell out of there."

"Before I could turn around and leave, her father whacked Zabree across the face. I was stunned! I mean, he hit her so hard that she fell to the floor. Because she was still holding my hand, when she fell, I almost stumbled to the floor with her. In a blink of an eye, the man took off his belt and started beating the shit out of Zabree right before my eyes. I mean, the man never even let me explain that it was all my fault! I remember standing with my back against the front door just crying while he beat her. And when he finished, he yelled at her to go upstairs and get undressed!" Jamarra's eyes flooded with tears. She pulled some tissue from her purse to wipe her eyes and she blew her nose angrily. "To this day, I still remember how her mother was just pacing in the background while that man beat Zabree like he did. The woman never even lifted a finger to help her own daughter!"

Jamarra slumped dejectedly as if the wind had been knocked from her body. "But then, who am I to talk? I didn't lift a finger to help her, either. I was too scared. When I got home that night, I was ashamed of myself because I knew in my heart that I was the cause of everything. Zabree hadn't wanted to go to the movies. She only went because I kept pressuring her to come. That night, I couldn't sleep. I cried all night long. I couldn't wait to see her to tell her how sorry I was. I wanted to erase the wrong that had been done to her because of my own guilt."

"This all happened on a Friday night. That following Monday, Zabree didn't show up for school. She stayed out the entire week and I wondered if it was because of all the marks and bruises which she probably had on her body. Every night I called her home, but her mother would answer the phone and tell me that she was sleeping or that she couldn't come to the phone." Tears continued to fall from Jamarra's eyes. "Her mother tried to play me like I was stupid. Anyway, the next week when Zabree did come back to school, she couldn't even face me. Every time she would see me coming her way, she would go in the other direction. I knew it was because she felt embarrassed. To be honest, I was too. But, still, I felt I owed her an apology. After all, we were still best friends, right?" Jamarra looked at Teferro as if she expected him to answer her question.

"I didn't catch up with her until about a week later. When I did finally catch her, I cornered her in the hallway. When I turned her around to face me, her eyes were so glassy that I knew she didn't even know who I was. She had to have been on some kind of drug. I felt like the bond which we had shared for so many years was suddenly gone. Just like that." Jamarra snapped her fingers. "For the rest of the day, the whole incident bothered me. I waited for her after school to try to talk to her again. She recognized me by then. Maybe the drugs had worn off or something, I don't know. She told me not to worry about her. She said she was going to be just fine because someone else was going to protect her. Someone who would never desert her like her sister did. When I saw the spaced out look in her eyes, Mr. McClodden, it frightened me to death. There was nothing in her eyes but a blank, empty stare. So I backed off and just left."

"A few days after that, I saw her riding away in a Mercedes Benz with some cat they call Mario. I know for a fact he's into dealing drugs. And that's where Zabree must have gotten her drugs from. I never saw

Zabree again after that day. But guess what? Sometime later, maybe about two weeks or so, Zabree's father showed up at my doorstep with two policemen. The bastard had the nerve to accuse me of talking his daughter into running away. Can you believe that bullshit? I played the dumb role so well that night, that by the time those policemen left my parent's house, *he* was the one looking like an asshole!"

"My parents knew I was putting on a show. They just didn't understand why. After the police left, they asked me to come clean with them and I did. My parents knew Zabree, so I told them the truth. Afterwards, I looked my mother dead in the eye and told her that I didn't know where the hell Zabree Jenkins was. I told her that wherever Zabree went, I would bet my life that she was better off there instead of being with her own mother and father." She shook her head. "I was supposed to be her best friend. I was supposed to have done something more to help her. But I didn't. I just didn't know." Jamarra wiped her face a final time before staring past Teferro with a blank look in her eyes.

Teferro watched Jamarra in silence. He saw before him a young girl filled with guilt at her own inability to help or save her best friend. He hadn't had to pump her for information. It was all too obvious that this girl had needed to talk to someone. He also knew that he had gotten all the information she had to offer him and he could tell that she still grieved for Zabree. Teferro had no answers for Jamarra. He took her hands in his and said to her, "Thank you. You've been a tremendous help. If her sister, Imagany, were here with me, I know she would thank you." Unable to offer her any more comfort than that, Teferro stood and walked away, leaving Jamarra to stare sadly into space.

Teferro cased Lindbloom High School for the next few days. The temperature was still freezing as he sat inside an old battered Chevy pick up. The vehicle wasn't much to look at, but since he didn't want to draw attention to himself, it served the purpose. He had been parking in different spots near the school all week long and on Friday, his dogged efforts paid off. Around two o'clock in the afternoon, a white Mercedes Benz pulled up and parked a little ways down from the school. Soon, he noticed several students approach the car one after another. Teferro jotted down the license plate number of the car and when it pulled off around four-thirty, he followed it.

He tailed the car to State Street and watched it pull in front of some projects on the Twenty-Ninth block. Teferro knew the name of the projects and he also knew its reputation. He parked his truck on a side street and watched the occupants of the white Mercedes make several cash transactions with passersby before getting out and entering one of the buildings.

Teferro got out of his truck and locked the doors. Though if someone really wanted to steal it in his absence, even with the doors locked there would be nothing he could do.

He saw a group of boys playing full-court basketball down the street from where he stood. Even on such a cold day as this one, he noted that the kids still had to find a way to release their energy. Dressed as he was in his torn up jeans and sneakers, Teferro fit right in. He took a seat on a nearby bench that was off to the side and watched as the boys shot hoops with hungry looks in their eyes. He knew every one of them was aiming to be the next Michael Jordan.

"Hey, bro', can you spare a butt?" Sitting on the bench, further down from Teferro, was a young man who might have been anything he had chosen to be in life, except that Teferro could look at him and tell he had chosen a life of drugs. So much wasted potential! Teferro reached into his pocket and removed a pack of cigarettes. The guy couldn't have been any more than twenty or twenty-one, but already he was aged far beyond his years.

Marshon's eyes fell on the cigarettes in Teferro's hand as if they were gold. Edging down the bench in Teferro's direction, Marshon reached out and took the cigarette Teferro offered. He searched inside his dirty army coat and said, "Can't find my lighter, bro'. Got a light?"

Teferro smiled to himself. He knew the guy probably had never owned a lighter in his life. Teferro reached inside his jacket and found a book of matches. Without looking at Marshon, he passed him the matches.

"Priddy fuckin' gen'rus of you, man. Thanks."

Teferro turned to face Marshon and said, "I've got more than just cigarettes for you, if you can give me some information."

Marshon instantly grew wary. Though he certainly needed the cash, the last thing he needed in this hood was for anybody to see him giving someone information. Something so simple was enough to get him killed. But damn! He sure could use some dough for some slice.

Teferro looked away from him and said, "All I need you to do is look at a picture. If you don't know the girl, there's still ten bucks for you. If you do know her, there's even more in it for you."

Ten bucks was more money than Marshon had had in awhile. "Yo, man, just don't let nobody see you slip me the dough."

Teferro removed the pack of cigarettes from his jacket pocket. Holding a wallet-sized picture of Zabree in his hand, he put a folded ten dollar bill against the pack and passed it all to Marshon.

Marshon took it and cupped his hand as if to light his cigarette and stared at the picture of Zabree. Yeah, he knew her all right. He passed the pack back to Teferro and stared ahead of him.

Teferro had caught the look of recognition in Marshon's glance. Marshon might not know where Zabree was, but at least Teferro knew the guy had recognized her picture. Teferro continued to watch the figures on the court. "Twenty dollars for any information you can give me."

"Shit, man, twinny dollars can't even buy me a hit off the pipe. Fiddy dollars 'll get you her name. Gimme a hunnerd and I'll take you to her."

Teferro felt excitement course through him. But he knew from experience that he had to be careful. In this neighborhood, people were known for getting ambushed all day long. He bargained with Marshon. "Fifty dollars for the information you provide. If I see you're on the up front, then we'll talk about more."

Marshon lit his cigarette and spilled his guts. "About a year ago, the bitch in the picture came here to live with a dude they call Mario. She was the baddest ho I've seen since I been livin' here. And I been livin' in the Ickeys all my life. You could tell she didn't belong here, man. She just never fit in. She was even goin' to school, too. Before we knew it, she had Mario's pad fixed up real tough. Bought all this boss new shit and had the crib lookin' righteous. After 'while, she had Mario stop everybody from comin' over. Mario's boys all started sayin' that because of her, he was gettin' soft and that if he didn't watch hisself, somebody was gon' pop him off. I guess that scared ol' boy, cause next thing we knew, he wouldn't let ol' girl go to school no mo'. Prolly got scared someone was gon' snatch her. I didn't see her again 'til about seven months later. But when I did see her, man, I didn't even know the bitch. She must've started usin' the slice, man. She was so skinny she looked like a skel'ton. Her hair what used to be long and priddy, was gone, man. I ain't lyin' neither. The bitch was damned near bald headed. Hair was that long." Marshon snapped his fingers. "Not long after that, Mario put her out, man. Just kicked the bitch out! And you know where all the ho's go when they ain't got no mo' money for the slice. They be over there in what they call the outhouse, man, sellin' they bodies cheap. And that's where the bitch is now."

"Where's the outhouse?"

"It's right here in the Ickeys, man. Two apartments where the walls been knocked down. That's where folks do their drugs. If the ho's gotta give it up, they go in the next room. Want me to take you?"

"No, just tell me which apartments they are."

"One-E and One-F. Can I have the dough now, man?" Marshon's eyes were already full of anticipation for his next hit off the pipe.

Teferro believed Marshon, and he could tell Marshon was already dreaming about the drugs he was about to purchase. He reached into his jacket and took out a fifty dollar bill and slid it to Marshon along with the pack of cigarettes. He stood up from the bench and walked away.

Marshon sat staring at the fifty dollar bill in his hand as if it represented all the money in the world. All he knew was that he could now afford several hits of the potent drug called slice. He even had enough dough to get himself some happy sticks. Suddenly, Marshon needed a hit real bad. He jumped up from the bench like a madman and ran as fast as he could to go buy the drugs. His conversation about Zabree Jenkins was long since forgotten.

Chapter Twenty-Two

With a nostalgic smile on her face, Imagany looked up from the newspaper. All morning, she had been going through every paper she could get her hands on looking for articles about Elliott's grand Super Bowl performance. Ever since the two of them returned from Arizona, the phone rang nonstop. Now that the Chicago Bears were Super Bowl champs, everybody and their grandmothers wanted a piece of Elliott Renfroe.

When Elliott woke from his sleep, Imagany was lying on top of him. Feeling his body stir underneath her, she lifted her head and asked sleepily, "Mr. Scrambler? What are you going to do now that you've just won the Super Bowl?"

Instead of giving the appropriate answer, Elliott said with grogginess in his voice, "I'm going to take a leak and then I'm going to get my wife to fix me something to eat."

Imagany laughed. "Elliott, you're supposed to say, 'I'm going to Disney World.' "

Elliott looked and sounded as if he were still half asleep. "I've already been to Disney World. Come on, kid, let's go scramble up some food."

While Elliott dragged himself to the bathroom, Imagany ran down the stairs to set up the breakfast she had already cooked. She had bacon, sausages, eggs, biscuits and hash browns all warming inside the oven. She quickly put everything onto the table and took a seat as she waited for him to come downstairs.

Elliott smelled the food long before he even reached the kitchen area. He came inside and smiled at Imagany from the doorway. She stood up, gesturing for him to sit before she mockingly spread his napkin in his lap.

Elliott looked at all the food on the table and said, "You mean to tell me you dragged poor Caprice out of her bed just so she could come here and cook all this food?"

Imagany laughed as she shook her finger at him. "You see, you thought all the time I spent around Caprice was in vain. Didn't you ever wonder why I watched her like a hawk whenever she was in the kitchen?"

"Now that you mention it, I did always wonder why you ran in the opposite direction whenever she pulled out a pot or a pan. I guess you were taking pretty good notes. I'm proud of you, kid."

Imagany flipped Elliott the bird sign from across the table. She filled her plate with sausages and hash browns and ate as much as she could. She finished her food and watched contentedly as Elliott went back for seconds and then thirds.

While Imagany washed the dishes, Elliott took Leo into the living room with him to play back the many messages on the machine.

After drying her hands on a clean dish towel, Imagany went up front with Elliott. Just as she was walking into the living room, she heard Teferro McClodden's voice on the answering machine.

"Imagany, this is Teferro McClodden. I have some information which I think will be helpful to you. Please give me a call at your earliest convenience."

Imagany's heart leapt in her chest.

Elliott was lying on the floor listening to the messages when he caught the passing expression on Imagany's face. "Who's Teferro McClodden?"

Imagany came and stood over Elliott. She knelt down on the floor and sat cross-legged in front of him. Leo crawled onto her lap. As she enfolded the puppy in her arms, she knew it was time to talk about the things she had kept secret nearly all her life. "Elliott, it's time for me to tell you the truth about my life."

***

Two days after she returned from Phoenix, Imagany sat in the offices of Epstein & Bergmann, listening to what Teferro McClodden had to say.

Imagany had driven straight to Teferro's office right after Elliott left for an early morning interview with NBC's Bryant Gumbel. He also had appointments later in the week to have his picture taken for the covers of Sports Illustrated, Newsweek, Ebony, Jet, Emerge, GQ and People Magazines.

As Imagany listened to the grave and sobering words of Teferro McClodden, she sat in stony silence while he recounted the unmitigating facts surrounding her sister's circumstances. Imagany's heart was heavy with grief. She felt largely to blame for what happened to Zabree. While she had been so caught up in her own life with Anthony and Elliott, she hadn't even been concerned about the person who should have meant the most to her.

Teferro looked at Imagany with sympathy in his eyes. He knew how hard she was taking everything he had just told her. But he was, after all, being paid to give her the bare facts. He got up from behind his desk, pulled his chair closer to hers and clasped her hands in his. "You've got all the facts now, Imagany. You know where your sister is. You can go to the police and get them to get her out of that place." Teferro saw the look of dejection on her face. "Imagany, you must go to the police for help. It's insane to even think about going there by yourself. The Ickeys is a very dangerous place. Take the information which I've given you and go to the police."

Imagany pulled her hands from Teferro's grasp. She needed time to think and time to formulate a plan of action. "Thank you, Teferro. You've been of tremendous help. I can't thank you enough for what you've done." Imagany pulled her checkbook from her purse and wrote out a check for five thousand dollars. She handed it to Teferro and stood up to leave.

Teferro glanced at the amount of the check which Imagany had just handed him. It was triple what his fee would have been. "Imagany, you don't owe me this much."

Imagany had reached the door. She turned around and said, "But I do, Teferro. Without your help, I wouldn't even know where to begin to look for Zabree." Though her heart was heavy, she tried unsuccessfully to smile at him. "See ya."

"Imagany, wait." Teferro stood up and came to the door. He stood looking down at her as if he wanted to say something but wasn't quite sure how to say it. He hesitated and then seemed to change his mind. "Your fiancé played one hell of a game."

Imagany knew this was not what Teferro had intended to say to her. He had probably seen her picture somewhere with Elliott's. Imagany managed to smile at him before closing the door behind her.

Outside the wind blew unceasingly as she walked hurriedly to her car. Despite Teferro's advice, she couldn't go to the police for help.

She had her own reasons. Imagany knew this was a time when she would simply have to help herself.

It was noon time when Imagany pulled up and parked her car in front of her parent's home. She got out and went to ring the door bell. Her mother answered the door, surprised to see her.

Imagany stepped inside the house and shut the door behind her. Before Geneva could say a word, Imagany said, "I know where Zabree is, Mother. But I need help getting her out of the place where she is. Even though she's under age, the police won't help me and you know why. So that leaves Robert. He's got to help me get her out."

Geneva looked confused. "Robert's upstairs. But where is Zabree? What's all this talk about the police?"

"Please, just go wake him up. There's not enough time for me to explain." Imagany stared at her mother with a serious expression on her face. Geneva turned and climbed the stairs to go wake her husband.

Imagany sat on the edge of the chair as she waited impatiently for her father. She was tapping her fingertips on her knees when she heard his footsteps come down the stairs. Imagany stood as Robert walked into the room.

She automatically stood straighter as she stared at her father whom she hadn't seen in years. He looked the same. He certainly hadn't aged like her mother had. Robert was tall, had broad shoulders, thick muscles and was a very physically attractive man. When Imagany had been a very young child, she had thought the world of him. But as she'd grown older, she had learned to look beyond his surface good looks to the base person existing within.

Neither one of them spoke as they stared at each other. Imagany wanted him to know that she was a different person from the one who had stood before him five years earlier. She had matured since that time and more importantly, she wanted him to realize that she no longer feared him.

Her voice was quiet and convincing when she spoke. "I know where Zabree is and I came here to ask you to help me get her."

Robert stared at his daughter unblinkingly thinking only that she was the very essence of her mother. "Where is she?"

"She's in a project on 29th and State Street called the Ickeys." When he said nothing, Imagany prompted him. "Will you help me or not?"

Robert sat down in a nearby chair and continued to stare at Imagany. For a while he said nothing and then he finally spoke. "When Zabree left my home, she made her own bed. Wherever she is now, she has to lie in it."

Imagany shook her head as she stared at him contemptuously, unable to believe that he would deny his own flesh and blood. She really shouldn't have expected otherwise. When she spoke, her voice was full of seething scorn. "When I came here to ask for your help, I considered the fact that you might say no. Still, I had to ask. Why I expected you to help in the first place is now beyond me. If it wasn't for you, Zabree wouldn't even be where she is right now." She folded her arms across her chest. "I just want to tell you this one thing before I leave here today, Robert, because I never intend to lay eyes on you again. For years, I've hated your guts. I had so much hatred inside me that I used to lay awake at night and dream about your death. But now I realize that death would be too good a thing for you. All the hate I've carried around with me for years is suddenly gone. I realize that you're not a man, Robert. You're nothing but a sick, demented, twisted, and pathetic excuse for a human being. Someone whom I can no longer afford to let live rent free in my head. So when you do die, Robert, I hope it's a horrible death. And after that, my only wish is that you rot and burn in hell." Imagany stared at him with venom. She dared him to touch her. With all the emotions raging within her, Imagany knew with a surety that if he laid a finger on her, she would take him out, or either be killed in the process.

Not trusting him for one moment, Imagany backed toward the door with her hands in her coat pocket. Her eyes never left Robert's face. She twisted the door knob and slammed the front door behind her to go in search of Zabree.

Geneva sat at the bottom of the staircase. She had heard every word Imagany said to her husband. A proud smile came to her face at the knowledge that this beautiful, strong-willed girl was her daughter. She heard Robert leave the living room and come into the hallway. Her smile quickly faded as she hurriedly stood up with her hands clasped to her elbows. She watched as Robert pulled on his coat and removed two of the many forty-five caliber hand guns which he kept locked inside his gun case. Geneva knew better than to ask him where he was going. So she said nothing as he buttoned his coat and slammed the door behind him.

It was a little past one in the afternoon when Imagany pulled up to 29th and State Street. In this desolate neighborhood, there was no such thing as safe parking. But because of her desperation, she knew she had no choice except to park her BMW on a nearby side street. She knew also that the likelihood of it being there when she returned was nil. Securing her purse, she got out of her car to search for the address Teferro had given her. Imagany found the place and stared at the building in amazed horror. She considered it a travesty of justice that people could be allowed to live in such a decrepit structure. Shuddering, Imagany stepped carefully on the crumbling concrete that led to the entrance of the building.

Robert pulled up just in time to see Imagany walking up the court way of the project known as the Ickeys. He double parked his car and quickly hurried after her.

When Imagany entered the darkened hallway, the putrid odor of urine and human feces assaulted her nose. There was another scent that was mixed with it which was equally as strong. Imagany knew it was the stench of some kind of drug. She walked further down the hall stepping over humans in her path who laid drunkenly on the hallway floor. She passed two kids who were kissing in the darkened corridor and stopped to ask them for the information she needed.

"Where's the outhouse?"

The boy turned and looked Imagany up and down before pointing down the hall. He wondered how much she was selling her body for.

Imagany continued down the hall until she came to the last door. She paused before twisting the knob to enter. As soon as she walked through the door, her lungs were immediately filled with the thick smoke from the room. Crack, cocaine, heroine, marijuana, the room reeked of all these drugs and more. Imagany coughed and nearly gagged as she covered her nose with her arm. She walked in and stepped over more sprawling bodies that lay on the concrete floor. She saw spaced out people talking to themselves and huddling against walls. Some were curled up by themselves in corners while many others were clutching pipes to their chests, holding them as if they were their only possessions. Imagany walked slowly through the maze of degenerate and lost souls peering closely at each one. She had to consciously remind herself that the person she would find would look nothing like the girl she once knew.

Imagany came to the second room and saw a girl huddled in the corner with her arms wrapped around her knees staring off into another world. She knew instinctively that it was Zabree. As she approached her and knelt down in front of her, tears of anguish sprang to Imagany's eyes. She felt her heart break into tiny pieces when she saw how decimated and thin Zabree had become. She looked so sick and unhealthy that Imagany recoiled from the sight of her. Surely this thin and tiny girl with hardly any hair on her head could not be the vibrant person whom she knew as her sister. She wore nothing but a filthy, thin torn Tee-shirt and dirty torn up jeans. Imagany lifted Zabree's head and spittle dribbled from the corners of her mouth. Her eyes were glazed and there was no look of recognition or comprehension inside them.

Imagany quickly removed her own coat and lifted Zabree to put the coat on her body. She hoisted Zabree against the wall and was about to take her from the room when voices behind her stopped her in her tracks.

"Yo! Where the fuck you think you going wit' her?"

Imagany turned to see three thuggish looking boys approaching her menacingly from the adjoining room. Although Zabree was light, her weight was still too much for Imagany to run with. Before she knew it, they were standing in front of her.

"What chu doin', bitch? You caint take nobody outta hea'. Don't chu know da house rules?"

"Naw, man. Look atta, she don't know shit. She stealin' one o' our ho's! We gotta teach this bitch a lesson." The three thugs surrounded Imagany and Zabree threateningly.

Imagany was rooted to the spot, paralyzed with fear. Her body shook with tremors. As adrenaline shot through her veins, she had the strong urge to urinate. She knew she had no chance of fighting the three of them off. Still, she held on tightly to Zabree. Just when they were about to attack her, a voice from behind rang out boomingly.

"Everybody freeze!" With her heart pounding heavily in her chest, Imagany recognized her father's voice.

The hoodlums panicked and dashed in the direction from which they came. They screamed, "It's a cop! Everybody get the fuck out! Mario!"

Pandemonium reigned as those who were able to run ran past Imagany and Zabree. Amid the pushing and shoving of all the people, Imagany dragged Zabree along with her to the entrance of the doors. She heard a door burst open in the room behind her. After that, all hell seemed to break loose. Imagany heard gun shots ring out from one of the rooms which she had just exited. She got Zabree safely out of the apartment and dragged her out of the building down the street to her car. When Imagany got to the area where she had parked her car, it was too late, someone had already stolen it.

Through her tears, Imagany saw a pay phone at the end of the street. Praying that it worked, she lugged Zabree with her to the phone. She snatched up the receiver and clutched the phone to her ear. With trembling fingers, Imagany dialed 911 and when the operator answered, she shouted quickly into the phone. "Operator, I think a policeman's been shot and wounded. I'm standing here on 29th and State Street and I need an ambulance for my sister." Hysteria laced Imagany's voice.

The operator tried to get Imagany to calm down as she attempted to get more information from her.

Imagany screamed into the phone, "Didn't you hear me, goddammit! I'm in danger out here! What the fuck difference does it matter what my name is?" Even as Imagany screamed, people continued to run wildly from the building. Her greatest fear was that someone would recognize Zabree and try to prevent her from taking her with her.

The operator connected Imagany to the police station at the 22nd Precinct. "Officer Greeley. Twenty-second Precinct."

"Officer Greeley, my name is Imagany Jenkins. My father is police officer Robert Jenkins with the Twenty-first Precinct."

The officer interrupted her, "I know Officer Jenkins."

"I believe he's been hit, sir. There were gunshots fired inside the building. I'm down here on 29th and State Street. My sister is badly hurt and someone just stole my car. I'm scared that they're after me. Please, I need help." Imagany spoke quickly, her sentences barely coherent and jumbled together. Even to herself she was hardly making sense.

"Hang up the phone and stay where you are, Ms. Jenkins. I'll send some squad cars immediately."

Relief washed over Imagany as she disconnected the line. She had one more call to make. She dialed the newsroom at NBC. When someone picked up the line, Imagany spoke quickly but more calmly. Less than a minute later, Robin Frazier, her supervisor was on the line. Imagany told her what she needed.

Imagany hung up and looked around her in desperation. People shouted as crowds gathered in front of the building. As she wrapped her arms tighter around Zabree, a chill began to seep into her bones. She was freezing with no coat on but she knew Zabree had to be even colder with no shoes or socks on her feet. Imagany dragged Zabree to a nearby abandoned car and sat her upon its hood in an attempt to keep her bare feet off the ground.

The Twenty-Second Precinct was less than five blocks from 29th and State Street and yet, police cars never patrolled this area. Snipers were known to wait atop the tall project buildings for stray police cars which might unwittingly drive by. Less than five minutes later, the first police car pulled up. Imagany ran out into the street waving her arms wildly to flag down the police car.

The police car came to a screeching halt and Imagany ran to the driver's side and quickly explained what had happened. After calling for backup, the officer got out and put Zabree into the back seat of his car until an ambulance came. He wanted Imagany to get in too, but she refused. She wanted to be seen by the news crew when the news van arrived. When five other squad cars drove up, the policemen got out and entered the project building with their guns drawn.

More gunshots were heard from inside the building just as the NBC television crew pulled up. Some of the shots were so loud it sounded as if cannons were being fired. As more people streamed out of the building, the news crew quickly set up and started recording everything live.

Imagany watched in dismay as a full scale riot broke out in front of her eyes. More police cars arrived on the scene as the police tried to disperse the crowds. By the time the ambulance finally came, Imagany had seen enough. She gratefully rode to the hospital with Zabree.

Imagany sat in the hospital's waiting room for the next six hours, waiting to hear some word about Zabree. She awoke from a restless sleep and approached the desk to inquire for the fifth time about her sister. All they could tell her was that as soon as they were told something, they would let her know.

The hospital's waiting area was full of other people who were also waiting to see a doctor or were waiting to receive word from one. At ten o'clock that evening, someone turned the overhead TV to a news channel. The story which all the news stations were covering was the one about the largest drug bust in the history of Chicago which had occurred earlier that afternoon at 29th & State Street. One police officer had been killed and five others were wounded in the line of duty. A picture of her father was flashed on the screen as the officer who was killed. The anchorman reported that after receiving a tip from an informant, police officers had tried to enter the building with a search warrant. A riot had broken out between police and several reputed drug dealers and six gang members were slain in the ensuing gunfire. Pictures of the slain gunmen were also flashed on the screen. Apparently, drugs were being manufactured on the premises and over seven million dollars in cash was found inside one of the apartments along with a hundred kilos of cocaine. So far, fifteen people had been arrested in connection with the drug bust.

Imagany watched emotionlessly from her seat in the corner. She couldn't worry about her father. Her only concern was for Zabree. At ten-thirty, her name was finally called. She walked listlessly to the front desk and listened to what the doctor had to say. He told her that Zabree had overdosed on heroine. Though she was alive right now, because she was also suffering from pneumonia, it was doubtful that Zabree would make it through the night.

Imagany stared at the doctor, shaking her head in denial. "She'll make it, Doctor. She's a survivor like me."

The doctor stared at Imagany through tired eyes. He had seen countless numbers of people who never wanted to accept the fact that their loved ones were not going to make it. His job was only to present them with the facts, not to change anyone's mind.

"When can I see her?"

"You can go in now." The doctor gave Imagany directions and she quickly walked away.

Zabree lay unconscious in the bed with all kinds of tubes hooked up to her body. Imagany pulled up a chair and sat close to the bed. Zabree had tubes inserted in the back of her hands and Imagany lightly held onto her fingers. Even though she knew Zabree probably couldn't hear a word of what she was saying to her, Imagany poured her heart out anyway.

With tears coursing down her cheeks, Imagany spoke passionately. "Bree, the doctors are all saying that you won't last through the night, but I know it's not true. They simply don't know you like I do. They don't know how strong you are on the inside. But, see, I know all these things because I know you're a survivor. And you know something else, Bree, I found out that what happened to us in the past doesn't even matter anymore. It's only the here and now that counts. That's what I wanted to tell you. Remember how we used to think that all men were dogs? It's not true either, Bree. I know now that there are good, strong, loving black men out there. And it is possible for us to break the cycle we grew up in. All men aren't like Robert. He was sick, Bree. That's all. Sick. But he's dead now and we can go on with our lives. I know you're going to get well because there are so many things left for us to do. So many things we still have to accomplish. I realize there are a lot of things that we never did together, but it doesn't matter, because as soon as you get better, we're going to start doing them. You'll see. And Bree, I never deserted you. I just couldn't take Robert any more. So I had to get away. I made a mistake by not taking you with me and I know that now. But I'll make it up to you, I promise. You've got to promise me something too. Just promise me you'll get well, Bree. Just promise me that." Imagany stared at Zabree with tears of love in her eyes before resting her head upon the bed.

Hours later, a nurse came into the room to check on the patient. When she saw Imagany asleep in the chair, she stepped to her and shook her lightly. "Miss, miss?" When Imagany raised her head, the nurse said, "Visiting hours were over a long time ago, miss. You have to leave now."

Imagany got up sluggishly from the chair. She turned and asked the nurse, "What time can I come back tomorrow?"

"Visiting hours are from ten in the morning to ten at night."

"Thank you." With one last look at Zabree, Imagany turned away to go call a taxi.

It was three o'clock in the morning when Imagany turned the key in the lock. As soon as she closed the door behind her, she heard Elliott quickly coming toward her from the living room area.

Elliott approached Imagany and said, "Where the hell have you been?" Worry, concern and anger were all in his voice.

Imagany looked at Elliott through drained and tired eyes. Both her mind and her body were exhausted and depleted of all energy. She didn't feel like explaining anything to him. Sleep was the only thing that mattered. Without uttering a word, Imagany walked past Elliott and dragged her fatigued and weary body up the stairs to the bedroom.

Elliott watched as Imagany barely made her way up the steps. Her appearance was so disheveled and unkempt that wherever she had been, Elliott was certain she had been through hell. He saw her pause at the top of the stairs as if to rest for a moment. He was angry with her but it was only because he had been so worried about her. Though he was curious about where she had been, the blank and distant look in her eyes had prevented him from saying anything further. He knew that wherever Imagany had been, it had taken something out of her. The woman whose eyes he had peered into a moment ago was not the same person whose lips he had kissed when he had left the house the day before.

Minutes later, Elliott climbed the steps and went inside the bedroom. He stared at Imagany who lay knocked out on the bed with every stitch of her clothing still on her body. He approached the bed and slowly removed all of her clothes. Covering her naked body with the sheets on the bed, Elliott turned away and left the room, closing the door behind him.

Imagany didn't wake up until sometime later that afternoon. When she came to, though she still felt drained and tired, she dragged her body out of bed and went to call the hospital to find out about Zabree.

She was told by one of the nurses that Zabree was still hanging on, though she was having difficulty breathing. Imagany hung up the phone in relief. She knew Zabree was going to make it. All Zabree needed was to know that somebody still cared about her.

Elliott came into the bedroom as Imagany was hanging up the telephone. He stood inside the doorway and stared at her with the sheet wrapped around her body and her hair standing all over her head. Elliott stepped into the room and took a seat in a nearby chair. "Don't you think you owe me an explanation about last night?"

Imagany sat back down upon the bed. "I guess I do." But somehow, she didn't feel like giving him one. Without looking at Elliott, Imagany gave him all the details about what had transpired the day before. She held nothing back. When she was done, she didn't want to talk anymore. She got up to take a shower to get dressed to go to the hospital.

Elliott listened to Imagany's story, touched by the courage and strength she had shown. Suddenly, Elliott said, "I'd like to go to the hospital with you."

Imagany continued on her way to the bathroom. "No, Elliott. You have your appointments to keep and I don't think you should miss them." Besides, she wanted to be alone with Zabree. She stepped into the shower and hurriedly cleansed herself off. After wrapping a large bath towel around herself, she came back into the bedroom to tug a comb through her hair and pulled it into a ponytail.

Elliott hadn't budged from the chair. "Why are you shutting me out, Imagany?" Her entire attitude was one of cool detachment.

As Imagany hurriedly pulled on a sweater and some jeans, she said to him, "I'm not shutting you out, Elliott. It's just that right now, my only concern is for my sister. It has to be. Because while I was in Nashville having the time of my life, thinking only of myself, living under Anthony and then chasing after you, my own flesh and blood was living in that hellhole of a project. If anything happens to her now, I'll never forgive myself for that. And I will never, ever, be that selfish again, Elliott. Instead of thinking of myself, it's time for me to think about my sister for a change and time for me to concentrate on the people I love." Imagany turned away from him to find a pair of shoes to put on.

Elliott got up and came over to the bed. "I thought I *was* one of the people who you loved, Imagany. Are you telling me something different now? And since we're on the subject about us, you seem to have it all figured out. Let me know what the deal is so that I, too, can have a clear understanding of what's going on."

Imagany threw her hands into the air. "I don't know what more to tell you, Elliott. All this you, me, relationship stuff is just not what's important to me right now. My sister is what matters most. I don't have any other answer for you. All I know is that I need time to be alone and time to get myself together."

"And in the mean time, what am I supposed to do, Imagany? Put my life on hold because you can't seem to make up your mind about what you want out of life? You expect to just waltz out of here and keep me waiting in limbo for the rest of my life? Take your ego out of it, Imagany. Stop thinking that the world revolves around you."

Imagany stared at Elliott as she put on her coat to leave. She had no intentions of arguing with him. "I'm not asking you to put your life on hold for me, Elliott. Every person's got their own life to live and you've got to do what's best for you. I can't ask you to wait for me. The only thing I know is that I've got someone who needs me more than anything else in this world. And if you can't deal with that, then maybe you should be looking for someone else." Imagany removed her engagement ring from her finger and tossed it upon the bed. She walked out of the bedroom without looking back.

Elliott turned to stare down at the diamond ring left lying on the bed. He picked it up and held it in the palm of his hand. With a wealth of mixed emotions in his heart, Elliott cupped the ring in his hand and angrily threw it across the room.

Chapter Twenty-Three

 magany sat in a corner of the hospital room. Thoughts of Elliott, Zabree, her mother and even her father filtered through her mind. She moved her chair closer to Zabree and bowed her head upon the bed. With her hands folded together, she prayed like she had never prayed before in her entire life. She prayed only for God to spare her sister's life.

When visiting hours were over, Imagany had no desire to return to her home. She hailed a taxi and gave the driver the address to her mother's house.

Geneva came to the door dressed in her house coat and slippers. Imagany walked inside and closed the door behind her. She removed her coat and hung it on a nearby coat rack before following Geneva to the back of the house. Her mother sat watching a re-run of the Arsenio Hall show almost as if she were in a daze.

Imagany took a seat at the table and watched Geneva rock quietly back and forth with her arms folded across her chest. Her mother always rocked in this manner when something was troubling her. Unfortunately for Geneva, this seemed to be most of the time. This rocking back and forth was a trait which Imagany had inherited from her mother. Without even thinking about her actions, Imagany pulled her chair as close to Geneva's as she could and wrapped her arms around her, pressing her mother's head into her chest. Suddenly Geneva's body began to rack with sobs. She reminded Imagany of a small, hurt child who had been deserted by both her parents. As she smoothed the hair on her mother's head, Imagany thought about how their lives had come full circle. Had anyone told her that she would one day hold her mother in her arms, comforting her and offering her solace, she would never have believed them.

Imagany realized that although her father had abused her mother, Geneva had depended on him for just about everything as surely as a child depends upon its mother. Imagany could no longer despise Geneva for that. Obviously, her mother had been raised and taught to believe that she needed a man to take care of her and that once she got married, no matter what happened afterwards, she had to stay with her husband. Now that Robert was dead, Imagany knew Geneva was probably wondering how in the world she would make it without him. Imagany thought of all the life insurance policies that her father had kept on himself, not to mention the insurance policies which his job also provided. She realized that right now her mother was probably a very wealthy woman. She knew, too, that if her mother could trade all of that just to have her husband back, she would do so in a moment's notice. How frightening it must be for her mother to suddenly have him snatched away.

Geneva's tears quieted and Imagany reached up and tore a paper towel off the rack. She smiled sympathetically as her mother wiped away her tears. But Imagany was unable to grieve with her. There were no feelings of remorse within Imagany. She knew she would never mourn her father's death.

Her mother blew her nose and asked her, "You've heard about your father?"

Imagany lifted her hand to her mother's face and smoothed her hair away from her eyes. "Yes, Mother. I was there when it happened." At her mother's surprised look, Imagany told her what had transpired when she arrived at the project buildings on 29th and State. She told her about Zabree and how she spent the last couple of days in the hospital with her. When she finished, Imagany realized that she hadn't even called to report her car as stolen.

"Will she make it?" Geneva appeared to be preparing herself for additional heartache.

"Yes, Mother, she'll make it." Imagany spoke with confidence and assuredness in her voice.

Geneva stared off into the distance. "The police want me to come downtown to identify your father's body." Her shoulder's slumped. "I don't know if I can do it."

Imagany pressed her mother's hand. It was time she started learning to stand on her own two feet. "Yes you can. I'll go with you and we'll do it together, okay?"

Geneva nodded her head slowly.

Imagany stood up. "Come on, let's get some rest. We've got a lot to do tomorrow." Imagany turned off the TV and followed her mother upstairs. The next day, Imagany and Geneva went downtown to identify Robert's body.

Later, they drove to the Twenty-First Precinct to claim her father's things from his office. They packed up two boxes full of her father's belongings and two police officers kindly carried them out to her father's car. Without telling her where she was taking her, Imagany drove to the hospital to take her mother to see Zabree.

When they pulled up in front of the hospital, Imagany could feel Geneva's excitement. They went inside and were told that they could go right in to see her. As the two of them sat on either side of Zabree, Imagany carefully watched her mother's face. Tears came to Geneva's eyes as she pressed her face to Zabree's hand. Imagany could almost read her mother's thoughts. Geneva was thinking that Zabree was just a shell of her former self, but at least she was alive. They sat with her for four hours and just before they left, they checked with Zabree's doctor for an update on her condition. They were told that she was hanging on and only time would tell if her condition would improve or worsen.

They drove home from the hospital and her mother made dinner for the two of them. Over dinner, Imagany brought up the subject of her father's burial.

"Mother, I think we should have Robert's body cremated."

At the mention of Robert, Geneva got that far away look in her eyes as she slowly stirred the food on her plate. Staring ahead of her, she said, "Whatever you think is best is fine with me."

Imagany put down her knife and fork. She wanted Geneva to realize that she was here for moral support, not to take over and make important decisions for her. "No, Mother. That was only a suggestion. You tell me what *you* think is best."

Geneva stared at her daughter. Imagany had so much of her husband's strength and determination within her, that she didn't even realize it. "I think that would be the best thing. It's not like he had other family here in Chicago. Aside from you, Zabree, and me, he had no one else. It's less painful this way, too." Geneva seemed to drift once more, lost in her own thoughts.

Imagany picked up her knife and fork and continued eating. She knew her mother had a long way to go before it could be said that she had achieved a measure of independence. It might take months or it might take years but she knew the day was coming. Geneva was going to be surprised at the things she could accomplish without the aid or help of her husband. Imagany couldn't wait until that day arrived.

***

Caprice heard the news about Imagany's father's death from her own mother. She had worked late the night he was shot so she didn't hear about it until the next day. She called Elliott and Imagany's house but the phone went unanswered. Thinking that Imagany might be at work, she called NBC and was told that Imagany was on leave of absence. Three days later, after dropping Carl off at work, a concerned Caprice drove out to their home in Sherwood Hills. She spotted Elliott's Jaguar through the wrought iron gates and pressed the intercom on the gate.

"Who is it?" His voice was laced with irritation.

"It's Reese, Elliott."

The wrought iron gates opened and Caprice drove through. She parked and walked to the door.

Elliott opened the door for Caprice and she stepped in saying, "I've been trying to reach you two for the last several days. I heard about Imagany's father so I came by to see how she's doing." Caprice stared at Elliott's unshaven, unkempt appearance. With no tact at all, Caprice said, "God, Elliott, you look awful. Where's Imagany?" She stepped further inside the foyer, staring around the house. When Elliott stood holding the door open behind her, Caprice turned around.

She saw the weird expression on Elliott's face and asked, "What's wrong?"

He sighed and slammed the door. Without saying a word, he walked toward the kitchen leaving her to follow.

Caprice walked behind him and heard him say, "She left."

When they entered the kitchen, Caprice stared at the mess the place was in and didn't even have to ask what he meant. "Where did she go, Elliott?"

Elliott went to one of the kitchen counters and poured coffee into a cup. "Have no idea."

Caprice took off her coat and laid it on the back of one of the kitchen chairs. Rolling up her sleeves, she went to the sink and ran water to clean up the mess that Elliott had created.

She let the dishes soak and came back to the table to sit down. Caprice stared at Elliott who looked as if he hadn't slept or shaved in days. "What happened?"

Elliott came to the table and sat down across from Caprice. He took a sip of the hot coffee before giving Caprice the facts as he knew them.

By the time Elliott finished, she had refilled his cup and gotten a cup of coffee for herself. Caprice reached over and squeezed Elliott's hand reassuringly. "Elliott, you have no idea how much Imagany loves you."

Elliott grunted disbelievingly.

"No, Elliott, I'm not feeding your ego. I mean it. She really does love you. I think in her own way, she even felt unworthy of you."

Sucking his teeth, Elliott said, "Come off it, Reese."

"You just don't get it, do you, Elliott? Even after everything she's told you about herself, you still don't understand. Sometimes you men can be so blind it angers me. Don't you know that whenever Imagany looks at you, she sees somebody who's wholesome and good? Somebody who's kind, caring and considerate? But most of all, she sees you as someone who's never judged her for any of the things she's done, whether they were right or wrong. That's not to say you're perfect, Elliott; Imagany realizes that. But you accepted her unconditionally and that's what mattered most. If you let her walk away now without putting up a fight, it'll be easy for her to tell herself she never deserved you in the first place. She can always say to herself that she can't miss something she's never really had. Have you for one moment since Imagany's told you what her life was like, stopped to consider the consequences of her story? Have you thought about the odds she's had to overcome to be the person she is today? How many women, or men for that matter, do you know who would be able to go through what she has and still be as strong and positive as she is? Have you ever listened to her dreams the way she's listened to yours? Were she sitting here right now, Elliott, Imagany could tell me what your goals are for the next five years. Can you name for me five of hers?" Caprice could tell by the look on his face that he couldn't. She shook her head.

"I think you should be proud of the fact that Imagany doesn't want to hang onto your coat strings, but instead has dreams and visions of her own. It's not about what you can give her or do for her, Elliott. She's capable of doing for herself." Caprice shrugged her shoulders. "I don't know what you expect out of a relationship, but I do know that it takes two to make one work. The bottom line, Elliott, is how would you feel if your only sister had become hooked on drugs while you were off pursuing your goals? How would you feel knowing that you could have helped your sister all while she was going through what she was? That's an unbearable amount of guilt to have to shoulder. Who wouldn't want to atone for something like that? Wouldn't you need time to get yourself together?"

As Elliott sat reflecting on Caprice's words, she stood up from the table. Trying to keep her irritation out of her voice, Caprice said, "Anyway, I didn't come here to lecture you. So let me just straighten up this mess and be on my way." Caprice stared at all that had to be done. "Jeez, Elliott. Even Imagany wouldn't let the place get like this." Caprice walked to the sink and began to wash the dishes.

***

While Geneva was in the kitchen preparing coffee, Imagany sat at the dining room table with two insurance adjusters. It was two weeks after the cremation of Robert's body and the adjusters had come to go over the final details of his insurance policies. Geneva poured coffee for the four of them as they scrutinized all of the paperwork, making sure all signatures had been obtained.

With all the insurance policies that Robert had carried on himself, Geneva was about to come into over 2.8 million dollars. As soon as Imagany discovered the amount of money involved, she called Elliott's father, who was able to refer her to an estate lawyer. After all the documents were signed, the two of them saw the adjusters out of the house. The only thing that remained to be done was for Geneva to decide how she wanted to spend the money.

Imagany had long since returned to work. Everyone had patted her on the back for being the one to break the story about the largest drug bust in the history of Chicago. NBC news station wanted to play up the fact that the slain police officer had been Imagany's father. But Imagany adamantly fought against the idea and her employers agreed to honor her wishes. Imagany realized that by breaking the story she was in good auspices with some important people and she decided to take advantage of the situation. She submitted a request to produce a mini documentary on sexually abused children. Though interested, the "higher-ups" believed that her subject was such a touchy one that they refused to make her any guarantees. Imagany got them to agree to at least let her work on it. She was told to submit her ideas on paper and if the producers were interested, then they would do a special feature on it.

Imagany left work that Friday evening with a feeling of euphoria. Doing a series on child abuse was in part what she had always dreamed of accomplishing. She knew the subject well and she knew how she wanted to present it.

As she did everyday when she got off work, Imagany went straight to the hospital to visit Zabree. Zabree's condition had not improved, but at least it had not worsened. She had so much heroine in her system that the doctors were still doubtful about her recovery. But Imagany knew there was room for hope.

She was listening to the radio station on her way home when the station announced they were about to play the first release from Phyllis Hyman's newest album, Prime Of My Life. Imagany felt an electric current shoot through her as the DJ gave the name of the record. "Meet Me On The Moon." As the song played, Imagany listened to Phyllis croon to her lover as she invited him to meet her on the galaxy so that their hearts could be as one.

Throughout the song, thoughts of Elliott floated through Imagany's mind. She shook her head as tears fell from her eyes. She couldn't hold back the pain, nor could she deny her feelings for him. She wondered if Elliott knew Phyllis had a new album out. She wondered how he was doing, whether he was feeding Leo properly or even if he were taking care of himself. But she couldn't allow herself to dwell upon her memories of Elliott. There was still too much pain associated with remembering. Imagany wiped away her tears. She parked her car in front of the house and went inside.

As she came through the door, Geneva was getting ready to leave for an exercise class which she had recently enrolled in. Imagany took Geneva's initiative as a positive sign that she was finally beginning to have a renewed interest in herself.

The house was quiet after Geneva left. Imagany was in the kitchen pouring herself a glass of orange juice when the doorbell rang. She went to the door and opened it to find Caprice standing on the doorstep.

Imagany smiled at Caprice, suddenly realizing how much she had missed her. "So are you coming in or are you going to stand out there and look stupid?"

Caprice laughed. "Hey, watch yourself, kid. If I've learned how to look stupid, just know that I copied the look from you." As she stepped inside, Caprice realized this was only the second time she had ever been inside Imagany's house.

Imagany led the way upstairs to her bedroom. She closed the bedroom door behind them and Caprice took a seat in one of Imagany's papasan chairs.

They stared at each other before Caprice said, "I'm sorry to hear about your father."

Imagany shrugged her shoulders as she took a swig of her orange juice. She set the glass on the bedside table and pulled her knees to her chest. "You know me, Reese. There's no need for me to pretend with you. Anytime someone takes pleasure in making other people's lives miserable, it's bound to come back to them. He merely got what he deserved." Imagany changed the subject. She had no desire to talk about her father. He was history now. "So how've you and Carl been?"

"Just hangin', girlfriend. You know how it is." Caprice stood up and removed her coat. She was dressed as if she were going out for the evening in a very sexy black mini dress. When she sat back down, she watched Imagany closely as she said softly, "I saw Elliott about a week ago."

Imagany had been about to comment on Caprice's dress, but at the mention of Elliott's name, she clasped her arms around her knees and closed her eyes. Why did Caprice have to do this to her? Her emotional scars were still too raw to talk about Elliott.

Caprice knew she had touched a sore spot. She pressed Imagany further as she said, "He said to tell you that he loves you and that both he and Leo miss you very much."

Imagany took a deep breath, unable to stop the flow of tears from falling from her eyes.

Caprice got up from the chair and sat on the bed. "I know about Zabree, Imagany. I went to see her before I came here. Did you forget that I work at the University of Chicago's Hospital? I even saw you the day you and your mother came to visit her. I just didn't want to intrude. I wanted to wait for you to call me. But I guess a simple phone call was too much to expect from a best friend." Caprice had bitterness in her voice.

Imagany wiped the corners of her eyes. "I guess I deserve that. I'm sorry."

"Imagany, when are you going to learn to stop shutting out the people who matter most to you whenever something crucial happens to you?" Hurt and anger was in Caprice's voice.

Imagany continued to keep her eyes closed. "Why do I get the impression that that's a loaded question?"

"Because it is loaded. I can understand your shutting me out. You've done it before. But Elliott? He's hurting, Imagany. Is it right to make him suffer, too?"

Imagany finally opened her eyes to stare at Caprice. "What about Zabree? Is that fair?"

Caprice shook her head. "Nobody ever said life was fair, Imagany. We're all dealt shitty hands from time to time. We have no choice but to deal with them. Nobody is telling you not to care about what happens to Zabree. We all care about her, Imagany. But whether you accept the fact or not, life goes on. And if you're not careful it'll march on without you." Caprice folded her arms across her chest and the two of them sat in silence, neither of them looking at the other.

"Zabree is going to make it. I know she is. She's a survivor." Imagany spoke passionately.

Caprice turned to look at Imagany who still had traces of tears on her face. "Of course she'll make it. But what about Imagany? Will Imagany make it too? Or will everybody around her be forced to suffer because of *her* preconceived notions about life?"

Imagany sighed frustratedly. "What do you want from me, Reese?"

Caprice sighed too. "I guess I'm afraid of losing our friendship, Imagany. I'm afraid of waking up one day and finding out you're no longer there for me. You're an integral part of my life and I don't want anything to ever change that." Caprice got up and walked across the room to Imagany's dresser. She picked up a framed portrait of the two of them hugging one another. The photo had been taken years ago when they were still in high school. Caprice stared at the picture before turning back to Imagany. "Besides, if not you, who else will tell me that my colors aren't matching?" Caprice made a halfhearted attempt at humor.

Imagany smiled but when she spoke, her tone was serious. "It's frightening to be alone, Reese. I never thought I'd see the day when I would miss someone as much as I miss Elliott. But my mother needs me here, Reese. It's like I still have all this unresolved anger toward her and yet, I can't overlook the fact that she needs somebody, too." Imagany shook her head. "I don't know, Reese, at times she's so helpless I feel like I've got to stay here with her."

At Caprice's sudden smile, Imagany asked, "What?"

"I'm remembering how when we were younger, whenever we would stumble across a sick animal, I don't care what kind it was, you would pick it up and take it home. You always thought you could save it and make it well. Many times you did heal them, too, but there were also times when you couldn't. And when you couldn't, boy would you cry. I used to say to you 'but Imagany, you knew it wouldn't make it, so why are you crying?' and you would say, 'because I wanted to save it, that's why.' That's you. Always trying to save the world. We all have within us a need to feel needed, Imagany. But there's got to be a limit to it. You can't right all the wrongs that your father did to the three of you. Only God and time will heal those wounds. Yes, both your mother and Zabree do need you. But so does Elliott. Don't let someone as special as he is just walk away. Your mother will take care of herself. I guarantee you, if you were to leave here tonight, she'd make it."

Imagany sat for a while in silence, reflecting on Caprice's words. "You're right, Reese. What can I say? It's like you always force me to look into a mirror and then leave me to face what's standing there. Sometimes I do have a tendency to get caught up in what's happening around me. So much so that I do exclude everyone and everything else. Elliott once told me that I act as if the world revolves around me. He was right, Reese. I'm guilty of that at times, too. I'm also guilty of letting my pride get in the way. I love Elliott more than I've ever loved anything or anyone in my life. Through him I've learned the true definition of a 'strong black man.' It's not someone who has a large penis. Instead, it's a man with visions and goals for himself. One who not only knows what he wants in life, but who's not afraid to go after it. Someone who can stand firm on the things he believes in. That's what Elliott represents." Suddenly, Imagany had an overwhelming desire to hear Elliott's voice. "I'm going to call him and just tell him how much I miss him."

Caprice stood up. "Good. I'm sure that'll make his day. That also brings me to the reason why I came over here." She went to get her purse.

"What? You mean to tell me that chewing me out like you just did wasn't why you came here?"

"I won't dignify that with an answer." Caprice rambled through her purse and pulled out a pair of tickets. "Do you see these babies?" She held them up in her hand. "I am holding in my hand the last pair of tickets to see none other than the one and only Ms. Phyllis Hyman."

"You wench! No wonder you're dressed to kill!" Imagany jumped off the bed and snatched the tickets out of Caprice's hand. She gasped as she stared at Caprice. "These tickets say eight o'clock!"

"That's right dahlin'. So if we're going, we've got to get a move on."

Epilogue

*I*magany and Caprice sat at a table in the corner of the crowded room. It was a good thing the overhead lighting was low because as Phyllis Hyman finished singing "I Found Love," tears streamed down Imagany's face. Every word of the song seemed to hit home and Phyllis may as well have been singing the song for her and Elliott. Only Elliott wasn't there. With tears coursing down her cheeks, Imagany was thankful that Caprice had gotten up to go to the ladies' room. Caprice had said something about all the smoke in the room bothering her eyes. Imagany lowered her head as she hunted through her purse for some Kleenex. Her only thoughts were of Elliott. As much as she loved that man, how could she have been so stupid to tell him not to wait for her? Tears spilled onto her dress. Damn! Where the hell was her tissue?

Elliott spotted Imagany across the crowded room and walked over to her table. He quietly took a seat in the empty chair and watched as she rambled in her purse. He heard her sniffles and knew she was digging for tissue. He pulled his handkerchief out of his pocket and handed it to her.

Imagany took the handkerchief without even looking up. "Thank you," she said, wiping her running eyes.

Elliott smiled. "That's all I get? A simple thank you?"

Imagany's head jerked upwards. She would know that voice anywhere. A silly grin sprang to her face and she softly whispered his name.

"Elliott."

Elliott smiled at the obvious glee that was on her face and in her voice. With her mascara smeared around her eyes, she had never looked so beautiful to him. He stared into her lovely eyes, and was about to ask why she was crying. But before he could touch her or even get a word out of his mouth, Imagany threw her arms around his neck and hugged him.

With laughter in his voice, Elliott pulled her onto his lap. "Imagany, you're choking me!"

Imagany didn't care. She lifted her head and gazed into his eyes. "I love you, Elliott Renfroe."

"Then marry me."

"Just tell me when and where."

"How about right now?"

Without saying a word, Imagany eased herself off of Elliott's lap and took both his hands. Elliott stood and led Imagany toward the exit.

Outside, a stretch limousine awaited them and Elliott ushered Imagany into it. As soon he opened the door, Imagany saw Carl and Caprice sitting inside with gigantic grins on both their faces.

She had forgotten all about Caprice! After hopping into the limo, Imagany's surprised expression turned into one of slow enlightenment. She finally began to put the pieces of the puzzle together. No wonder Caprice had so temptingly lured her out of the house. She, Carl and Elliott must have planned this all along!

Imagany smiled as she said, "You all planned this, didn't you?" No one said a word. They simply shrugged their shoulders and lifted their hands simultaneously in the usual "beats me" gesture.

Elliott threw his arm around Imagany's shoulders. He gave the driver the signal to take them to where the minister was waiting to perform the marriage ceremony.

Carl grabbed a bottle of Dom Perignon champagne from the ice bucket and popped the top. As the cork flew from the bottle, champagne spewed over its neck and Caprice quickly held elegant crystal glasses underneath the foaming bottle.

Amid all the happiness and laughter, the four of them were together again, just like old times.

THE END

Dear Readers,

I hope you enjoyed experiencing *Preconceived Notions*. Believe it or not, Elliott is more than just a figment of my imagination. A true flesh and blood character, he represents all that black men are to me: strong, compassionate, loving, sensual, motivated, self-reliant, spiritual, and always growing in grace.

If, by chance, Elliott Renfroe possessed qualities that you found endearing, then you'll love my second novel, *A Twist of Fate*. Another true-to-life character, Sam Ross is the hero who steals Ashela Jordan's heart—but only after many precipitous struggles. Together, they find that true love carries a cost all its own.

Secondly, I want to personally thank all of you who've called, written, and kept me in your prayers in lieu of the publishing difficulties I encountered while trying to bring my work to the public fore. But God *is* faithful and He never fails to make good on a promise. For every seemingly insurmountable obstacle, our Heavenly Father has an answer! And our timing is always in His hands.

Lastly, I invite each of you to render me two small favors: First, turn the page for a sneak preview of *A Twist of Fate*. And then I'd like you to record your thoughts about *Preconceived Notions* on the following websites:

1) Amazon.com
2) Lushena.com

A Twist of Fate will be available in December 1999 wherever Lushena books are sold.

Happy reading,

Robyn Williams

Prologue

The Grammys, New York City

uccess. Ashela Jordan whispered the word, unaware that it slipped from her lips, sounding almost like a curse. She'd craved it, fought all her life for it, doing some things in the process to attain it that even now she wasn't proud of. She'd excused many of her actions by telling herself the means always justified the end. *But what did it profit her to gain the world only to lose her soul?*

The stage was set for her to silence all of her adversaries. Inside her dressing room at Radio City Music Hall, away from all the chaos that reigned just outside her door, Ashela leaned back into a soft, black, classic leather chair. In less than an hour she would be on stage performing with the legendary Grover Washington, Jr. Nearly five years had passed since the two of them appeared together in concert. Their reunion tonight at the American Music Awards was eagerly anticipated by all. Many of the gossip mongers questioned whether their duet would rekindle a long-rumored romance.

There was much at stake for her in tonight's performance. While it would feel good to see and match moves with her one-time mentor, Ashela knew it would feel even better to prove to him that he'd been wrong to write her off. But not just Grover. Everyone who'd doubted her ability to make a comeback in this tough, dog-eat-dog music industry would know they'd severely misjudged her. Tonight she would prove that she was a force to be reckoned with. For on this night, the attention was hers alone. The headlines were hers. The adoration was hers. Wasn't this what she'd always wanted? A self-satisfied glow stole over Ashela. It was a coveted honor to be a part of the American Music Awards' entertainment venue. As one of the chosen few, she knew her upcoming performance would signal to everyone that she was back on top.

All her hard efforts culminated in this moment. At thirty-four years old, Ashela had reached the pinnacle of her success as a singer, songwriter and jazz musician. She was dubbed by her critics as a musical genius, the ultimate female Grover Washington-Babyface mixture. To her credit, she'd headlined with the likes of Richard Elliott, Gerald Albright, Najee, Wynton Marsalis, Al Jarreau, David Sandborn and a host of others.

A gift inherited from her mother, lyrics came easily to Ashela. For years she'd spent much of her time writing songs for some of the most famous singers in the business: singing sensations such as Luther, Whitney, Janet, and Vanessa. Ashela's musical lyrics sometimes sold for millions and were sought after by the best of the best. Music fulfilled her and creating it was all Ashela knew. As a youngster, it helped her find her way through the oft confusing and tangled webs of life, and as an adult, her music sustained her through a rocky period when she'd lost the will to live. Music inspired her, made her heart soar, and through it she could now understand where her mother's own inspiration had come from.

Every track on Ashela's latest CD, *Giving It My All*, had been produced in London, England, where she'd lived for the past three years. The album was released in the United States some months ago and it was the hottest release of the year. Already, it had sold well over eight million copies and had reached multi-platinum status. Ashela had racked up an impressive ten nominations for her solo album including, album of the year, record of the year, and song of the year. Her ten nominations were two shy of the single year record set only by Michael Jackson and Kenny "Babyface" Edmonds. The album's title cut, a duet with Rachelle Farrell, was number one on the jazz charts, another release was number one on the R&B charts, and nearly all the other tracks were among the Hot 100s. Four of the songs had been made into videos and each was a hit with every MTV and VH-1 outlet.

It felt incredibly good knowing that many in the audience, as well as many out there in TV land, would be watching the awards ceremony because of her.

While on the one hand Ashela was exultant—she was proud of herself because of the way she'd outsmarted the competition; but on the other hand, she couldn't rid herself of the disquiet that presently engulfed her. An inner turmoil which she knew wouldn't subside until certain issues were faced and dealt with, gnawed at her. On this night, Ashela struggled with her own host of demons. As tumultuous memories of the past resurfaced, some of those demons raged full throttle.

Yes, she was back on top after being in exile for what seemed like an eternity. Now that her star had risen again, she couldn't afford to make the same mistakes. This time around, Ashela would do things differently. But unlike before, she'd do them the right way. Her time away from the U.S. had mellowed her and given her a new outlook on life. While her demeanor could still be as hard as nails, she wasn't nearly as cold hearted and calculating as she'd once been. For starters, she'd learned that she couldn't always control everything and everyone around her. She was more level-headed, less prone to fiery temper tantrums where everything in her path invariably wound up being destroyed. And despite ample opportunity to do just the opposite, she no longer thirsted for revenge.

Maybe that's what motherhood did to an individual: caused one to take into consideration other people's feelings. Such a concept had been foreign to her for many, many years.

The path Ashela had taken enroute to her success was certainly not without mishap. She'd done what she had to do to get where she was. If she'd crossed some people and burned bridges in the process, it was all a part of making it. *To the victor goes the spoils.* Like a soldier crawling through enemy territory, her personal journey was fraught with casualties of war. Memories of bitter recriminations, severed friendships, and images of broken hearts surrounded her like lifeless bodies left littering a battlefield. These talisman were her daily reminders that success came with its own price-tag. She'd found that fame and fortune could be had by anyone so long as they were willing to pay the asking price. Had she paid too much?

In her opinion, money and power, if not used wisely, did corrupt. Without proper stewardship, the more of either one attained, the more one wanted. One of the harshest lessons Ashela was forced to learn was that no amount of either could protect her from the treachery and deceptiveness that accompanies betrayal.

A restlessness stirred deep within her. She rose from the chair and walked to the sofa where her instrument lay. Ashela knew the reason behind her familiar pangs of unease. An indelible yearning infiltrated her system causing her pulse to race in a way that had nothing to do with her upcoming duet.

Sam. His name hummed through her mind much like the way his body once hovered over her own. A sudden chill swept over her and she clasped her arms around herself to keep from trembling.

Samuel Ross. Unconsciously, she shook her head. Somehow, Ashela knew deep down in her spirit the man was inside the building. Even after so many years, s*he could feel his presence.*

If time was supposed to remedy a wounded heart, why hadn't it healed hers? Truth was, there was no magic elixir to soothe the flash of pain that clutched at her heart. Anger, remorse, and, yes, even the one admission she was loathe to confess gripped her as she stood gazing down at her horn.

Sam Ross. How she'd hated and despised him these past several years because of what he'd done to her.

And yet, fool that she was, Ashela acknowledged that she still loved him. How could she not? After all they'd been through, after all they'd shared . . . Was this the way things were really meant to end between them?

As long as she was being totally honest about the past, Ashela recognized that it was in part her own stubbornness that had caused the demise of their relationship. She wondered if Sam thought about her a tenth as much as she'd thought of him. She'd be content to know that he experienced a minuscule of the heartache she'd gone through. The nights were worst for her—endless hours when she'd miss his nakedness next to hers. If she saw him tonight, would he even acknowledge her? Or would he treat her merely as a business acquaintance?

Dear Heavenly Father, if only she could turn back the hands of time! If she wasn't beset with so much damnable pride she could go to him, tell him she'd made a huge mistake, ask if they could start over. But that wasn't how she operated. A part of her wanted to come clean, but the other part would rather go to her grave than grovel for a second chance with a man who probably hadn't thought twice about her since the day he'd made it obvious that he was writing her off.

Ashela steeled herself and decided that maintaining her pride was worth more to her than trying to reconstruct a relationship that in all likelihood would only be one sided. Her only recourse was to try once more to forget about Sam Ross. Somehow, rather than risk rejection, she'd will her heart to go on. She wasn't the first person to experience such heart-wrenching pain, neither would she be the last. She recognized every person in life encountered some love and some pain at some time.

There was but one matter that she resolved within herself to disclose to him. Could she find the courage to do it?

A knock at her door startled her. It was the stage manager giving her the nod that she was up next to perform. Ashela picked up her instrument and headed for the stage.

As she and Grover walked into the spotlight from separate entrances, they met center stage. Grover was already blowing his sax, as if serenading her. Ashela stood close to him and was all smiles as she glanced out at the sea of people. She lifted her arm to her forehead as if she was about to faint from being in such close proximity to the legendary performer. She clasped her instrument to her heart adoringly. Her swooning theatrics brought forth laughter from the audience. When Grover reached a lull in his song, Ashela lifted her own sax and chimed in, beginning to serenade him. Immediately, Grover Washington dropped to one knee to indicate his love-struck capitulation and the crowd went crazy. The moment he stood, the two of them started blowing their horns in unison, creating a melody of their own, all to the wild applause of the audience.

***

The cords of his stomach muscles tightened the moment Ashela Jordan appeared on stage. He knew her better than anyone else in the building and he also knew her on-stage dramatics were just part of what was to be her crowning achievement. He was a mere spectator in her midst as she accepted the thunderous applause. It was her night to shine, Sam thought. And to spend playing to a whole new audience. However, he sensed several undercurrents behind her performance. Predominantly, a message that seemed to say, "I didn't need any of you to make it to where I am."

Sam Ross' body had tensed the moment the announcement was made that hers was the next act up—even the audience's expectation level had seemed to shoot through the roof. And now that she was on stage, Sam's hungry gaze was riveted. She was sensational to watch. Every note played reminded him of times when she had played only for him. Even though he'd not seen her in years, she looked the same as he remembered her—only more beautiful.

Skin the color of caramel. Hair cropped close around the sides and nape of her neck. Thick, asymmetrical curls topped her head. A square jawline, thick eye-brows, full pouty lips, and dimples for days. Dressed in a Valentino original, the long-sleeved gold lamé gown molded her every curve as her hips swayed invitingly.

An image of her riding him as they laid upon silken sheets flashed through his mind. Beads of sweat shown on her body as Sam reached up to grasp her full breasts. With her back arched and head tilted to the side, he remembered her in the obvious throes of passion. Lips parted in a silent gasp. Nails engraving his thighs. His hands sliding down to grip and pull her hips even closer as she twisted atop him. She was his sensual dream. The vision faded as his hands gripped the arms of his chair. He had a strong desire to possess Ashela in ways that he had on so many other occasions. The urge to reacquaint himself with her womanly ways was overpowering and he willed his emotions back under control. He couldn't afford to give in to salacious memories of her. Such remembrances were what led to his being stung by her before.

Well over six feet, Sam, himself, was a deep, dark, chocolatey, gorgeous, "make-yo'-toes-curl" type of man. Suave *and* smooth, his muscled physique was hidden beneath a dark blue, double-breasted, Gianni Versace suit. He was in his late forties and possessed an animal magnetism that could sneak up on a woman and enthrall her before she even recognized what was happening.

The fact that Sam had much money, and was rumored to be the most powerful man in the music industry, put him on a level far above the likes of a Quincy Jones. Women flocked after him by the droves.

Sam's gaze became reflective. He couldn't help but admire Ashela and he knew a part of him still craved her. Although several years had passed since he'd last seen her, memories of her were fresh in his mind. Sam still couldn't figure out what it was about her that made it impossible for him to forget her. Maybe it was her craziness and unpredictability, her "still-waters-run-deep" attitude. Or maybe it was her fieriness as a lover. Nobody came close in comparison.

To be totally honest, Sam couldn't recall all that had transpired to cause them to part as such bitter enemies. But he remembered a time when they'd been able to settle all their differences through communication and lovemaking. But then unfortunate circumstances forced him to make hard decisions and afterwards, he never had the opportunity to explain himself. They had been too angry with each other. Before he knew it, she'd packed her things and left. Sam shook his head. Now that he thought about it, even convicted felons got the chance to tell their side of the story. Ashela had left without giving him warning. No opportunity to express what he'd felt. No chance for a rebuttal. No chance to change her mind.

Like everyone else, Sam thought her duet with Grover was incredible. A kaleidoscope of musical genius. Teacher being impressed by the student. He'd sensed from the creative tension in the air that their performance would be a dynamic one. He knew also that the millions of television viewers would be eating it up as much as the people in attendance.

As he watched the two of them harmonize, many emotions welled inside Sam. He wasn't caught up in all the speculative talk about Ashela and Grover. He knew Grover Washington personally and could vouch for the man's faithfulness to his wife. He also knew Ashela. Sam's stomach muscles wrenched as a familiar sadness washed over him. It was unfortunate that the two of them had parted the way they did. His pride had been wounded when she'd left. And as much as he hated to admit it, she'd taken a piece of his heart when she disappeared.

He couldn't comprehend her ability to just walk away from something as powerful as they'd once shared. Sam guessed that was the callous side of Ashela that he hadn't wanted to see. Not that he, himself, was innocent. He'd done some things out of anger and jealousy, so he could understand her bitterness toward him. Still, regardless of the hostilities that existed between them, he felt there remained some unfinished business.

Sam realized that life's levels, from glorious comfort all the way down to anonymous misery, were unavoidable. He also knew all too well how swiftly a man or woman's fortunes could change: one could be master of the universe one second—and destitute the next. Ashela had persevered and made it back to the top, proving her tenacity. He admired her for that. After what he'd done, she had a right to hate him. But Sam knew also that she had once loved him.

Persistence was the key to unlocking any closed door. And so, too, Sam knew it could be the key with re-conquering Ashela.

Suddenly, a feeling of elation coursed through him. He didn't know how he was going to get Ashela Jordan back. But, just as with everything else in his life, the game wasn't over until he'd won. Somehow, he'd formulate a plan of action, devise a strategy that couldn't miss. Regardless of the stakes—no matter what it took—Sam wouldn't be satisfied until Ashela Jordan was his once again.

I ENJOY KNOWING YOUR THOUGHTS. WRITE TO ME AT:

P. O. Box 378377
Chicago, IL 60637